AFTERWINDS

Advanced Praise for Hal Dennis's

AFTERWINDS

"Hal Friedman has crafted a real page-turner with AFTERWINDS. Not since Stephen King's THE STAND have I been this invested in a post-apocalyptic epic. This is an intensely human story and a haunting vision of the future with a complex mythology and a large cast of vivid characters. There's much to savor here. I can't wait for the next installment."

    —Bryan Cogman
      Co-Producer /Writer, GAME OF THRONES

"An epic story about a fragile world with more consumers than there are resources. An epic story about a future that could be very real."

    —J.D. Trafford, best-selling author of "No Time To Run"

AFTERWINDS

World of the White Light
Book One

Hal Dennis

iUniverse LLC
Bloomington

AFTERWINDS

World of the White Light, Book One

iUniverse books may be ordered through booksellers or by contacting:

iUniverse
1663 Liberty Drive
Bloomington, IN 47403
www.iuniverse.com
1-800-Authors (1-800-288-4677)

ISBN: 978-1-4759-9814-6 (sc)
ISBN: 978-1-4759-9815-3 (hc)
ISBN: 978-1-4759-9816-0 (e)

Library of Congress Control Number: 2013912110

Printed in the United States of America.

iUniverse rev. date: 8/2/2013

Prologue

1

The dog ran back and forth on the lawn of the White House as the sun was rising. Its white fur glazed with a shimmer of gold made it seem almost ethereal, rather than an adopted mutt the president had taken in to show animal lovers he had a heart.

As the dog ran, slobber coated the ball in its mouth, and its breath huffed with a whistle out its nose. Suddenly it came to a stop and dropped the ball at the foot of its master. Looking up, it gave a wide grin, baring its white teeth and long pink tongue. It waited, wagging its tail, anticipating the start of the next journey of "find the ball."

Its master bent to grab the ball, despite its wet condition, and threw it again. It glided through the air, dripping rivulets of dog spit as it spun. As the dog excitedly bounded after it again, the man who threw it turned his attention to a man in a black suit with hidden eyes behind dark sunglasses who was walking up to him.

"Mr. President," the man said with a reverent tone, "the Pentagon is on the emergency line. They say they need you immediately."

"I'm sure they do," was all the president said. The dog, affectionately named Veto, returned the ball. The president grabbed the ball and threw it again, this time with all his might, infusing it with all his frustrations, sending the ball farther than it had ever gone before. For a second the president was reminded of playing college football way back in 2011. He was a fairly good quarterback, even though the NFL was not in his future.

Too bad the NFL no longer exists in 2063; it makes Sundays very boring, he thought.

"Sir, we don't have enough time for this! The Joint Chiefs have been alerted to the emergency and are being escorted to the bunker. You need to move now!" The urgency in his voice was palpable. Sweat beaded up on the man's forehead, and the president could see his hands were shaking too.

"You better run along now," the president said. "If you're aiming for a chance at survival, standing here with me won't achieve that."

"Please, sir ..." the man pleaded.

"I'm not going." The dog returned with the ball again. The president threw it. That's when he heard it—the dull hum of an engine in the distance.

Not long now, he thought.

"Better go," the president said as he threw the ball again. "By my estimates, it will take at least four minutes to get to the bunker below; I don't think you have that kind of time. Good luck though. Oh, and please don't wake up the First Lady and my girls—better they sleep through it."

"President Mitchum," the man said, a tremble now apparent in his voice, "I ... I can't leave you ..."

The president nodded. "Suit yourself. However, if you don't mind, please, no talking. I was hoping for some final moments of peace before the end."

The two men continued to stand there as the sun slowly rose in the East. The president just allowed the seconds to tick away with every throw of the ball.

Peace at last, he thought. *Thank God almighty for peace at last!*

2

The white light engulfed the Capitol at seven forty-five in the morning on November 3, 2063. Other white lights would strike every major and minor city in America within minutes of the first strike. Cities from Los Angeles to Miami were flattened to cinders. To the survivors, the cause of the massive explosions and subsequent white light was unexplained. Outlying areas of every city were destroyed, and most of the overpopulated areas were wiped clean. By the time the sun rose along the West coast, most of the country was in flames, and survivors were doing whatever they could to survive.

The following records their stories.

Part One:

Collapse

Althaus

1

"Good morn', Reverend Althaus," said the parishioner as she walked past him on the front stoop of the church.

"Good morning," the reverend replied, shaking the woman's dirty hand as she went by.

This was the way of it for the reverend. Every morning he would open the church for what he aptly named Sunrise Services, and every morning the congregation—consisting of the downtrodden and needy—would flow in. Reverend Barrett Althaus would attempt to bring hope to the hopeless with his words about the grace of God. It was a subject he wasn't sure was very helpful in times like these.

"Not many here this morn', eh, Reverend?" the dirty-handed woman asked. Althaus knew her name was Jillian Harkness, a sixty-five-year-old ex-debutante, now relegated to trying to eke out a living on the farm her husband had inherited. Like most of the country, they fell into hard times in the fall of 2035, when America's agriculture was hit with the still-uncured crop disease known as S-643; the farming community knew it as the Great Pestilence. Never having recovered, farmers had been forced to sell land to the government and live off that money as long as they could.

For Jillian Harkness, the money ran out long ago, leaving her with only a dilapidated farmhouse and welfare. Every winter she still planted crops, even though her husband had long since died. She hoped that by spring they would be in full growth, but throughout the country, America's soil proved dead year in and year out, preventing any sort of growth. Whatever S-643 was, it wasn't going anywhere, and it made farming impossible. That's why food had to be imported and why the price of it had risen so high.

"It is a small group today," Althaus replied. "Hopefully more will be coming soon."

"Mayhaps it's the rain that's keepin' 'em away," Jillian added.

"Perhaps," Althaus agreed with a nod.

Althaus looked out from the stoop of the church.

Kansas. Once a beautiful and lush state, it now was filled only with dust and rock. The breadbasket of the country was no more than another desert, though it was one with seasons. Rain and snow fell hard and often, and on a November day, it could be so cold and unpleasant even a penguin would have stayed inside. It made getting to church an extremely difficult task. Most wouldn't brave it, but Althaus came every morning no matter the weather.

The church was made of old wood and stone, a turn-of-the-century antique, barely able to fit more than a hundred in at a time (though that had hardly been a problem for Althaus). The church groaned as the wind whipped around its edifice. Althaus shook his head at the great whine it made as it fought against the wind and found himself hoping that some act of God would come and topple it over so they could rebuild and start anew. Yet it still stood.

"I saw you runnin' this morn', Rever'n," said the next parishioner, Elvin Williams, as he walked up the stone steps of the church. Elvin's face, as always, was plastered with the biggest grin Althaus had ever seen. Elvin was born with Down-Syndrome and had all the features one would associate with someone stricken with such a malady—the big forehead, the rounded frame, and the large smile that brought such happiness to everyone Elvin met. Whatever Elvin's mental acuity, he was a joy to be around. Althaus wished he could be so blissful.

"Did you?" Althaus said with a slight smile.

"Ya run ev'ry morn', in't that true?"

"Yes, I do," Althaus replied. With every word, Althaus could tell how excited this discussion made Elvin, as if sharing this story was some kind of secret between the two of them. Althaus knew, however, that everyone in town was aware that he ran. He just never let Elvin know that. "It keeps me close to God," Althaus added.

"I come 'ere ta feel dat way, cuz 'o you," Elvin said with another bright smile. Elvin was older, probably somewhere in his late thirties, though he possessed the positive outlook of a seven-year-old. His comment touched Althaus greatly. He hoped he wouldn't disappoint Elvin, but knew eventually he would.

That's the big secret, Althaus thought. *I'm a phony.*

Ostensibly though, so was the world at large. Especially the government. Elvin was a perfect example. He was one of a growing number of mentally handicapped people. Though in the 2000s there had been a steep decline in such cases due to early detection, in utero screening, national health care, and women's right to choose, by 2045 all those advances had been lost. In 2044, due to the severe overpopulation of America, the government finally repealed President Obama's Obamacare. With the decline in the country's status as a world power, it was decided that national health care was just too expensive to keep. This made it impossible for the poor to receive appropriate medical assistance, leaving pregnant woman unable to get the tests they needed. Compounding the problem was the fact that Roe v. Wade had been overturned in 2022. So even if a wealthier woman were able to get the tests that indicated she was having a baby that might have a chromosomal anomaly, she no longer had the right to abort the fetus. All this, in Althaus's eyes, meant that people like Elvin had been let down by the government they had hoped would help them.

"Ha!" Another man let out a loud laugh from behind Elvin. It was Elvin's aging father, Albert—Al to his friends, which Althaus was glad to not be one of. The only reason Albert even came to church was because his son insisted. While in Althaus's eyes, Albert wasn't the best of men, he was certainly a decent father to Elvin. "I heard what you said to my boy there about your exercising, Rev," Albert said.

"I meant it," Althaus reiterated.

"Sure, sure ..."

Althaus was taken aback by his response.

Is he doubting what I said?

"Whatever the reasnin' ya do it, ya were deep in thought when we saw you, that's fer sure. What's a man like you thinkin' about, I wonder?"

An honest question, thought Althaus. *Now, what's the answer?*

"About God," Althaus replied.

2

Every morning Althaus woke around four in the morning and did four hundred crunches and four hundred sit-ups. After his sit-ups, he began his run to the Church of the Holy Anointed, packing a small backpack filled with five bottles of water and his habit, an all-black shirt and pants, complete with white collar. Though he was not a priest (he could marry and have children if he chose to, which he did not), he did prefer to dress like one, as was the tradition for Methodist preachers. Often Althaus found running peaceful and a way to clear his mind. On the morning of the Attack of the White Light, however, his mind was filled with dread and unanswerable questions.

As he ran, Althaus realized the truth about himself. Sure, his body was strong and his looks handsome, but inside, his soul was empty—which was not a fortuitous thing for a preacher whom people looked to for guidance. The truth was, though, he simply had no guidance to give anymore.

As he ran that morning with the cold rain pelting against his face, stinging his skin like a million tiny bees, he thought about the discussion he had a day prior with Clarence Solomon, the local Baptist preacher from the far-wealthier Church of the Cross. It was a very honest and painful discussion that he wondered if he should have even brought up.

From Clarence's reaction, Althaus concluded he should have kept his mouth shut.

3

"I'm struggling with my belief in God," Althaus said simply, not wanting to make the man sitting across from him too uncomfortable. They had decided to meet in a neutral zone. Neither man wanted the other to feel uncomfortable by being in the other one's church. Instead, they met at Lucille's, a small coffee shop at the East corner of town. Clarence often came to this spot; it was the African American part of town, after all, so it was near where he lived. Though Althaus stood out like a sore thumb inside Lucille's, pale as he was, he liked the atmosphere and how they played old jazz standards from a bygone age, so he agreed to the meeting spot.

"Really?" Clarence replied. "How so?" The calm reply surprised Althaus. Clarence was known for his staunch beliefs and his short temper with those who would question God. This reaction from Clarence against type compelled Althaus to continue.

"Well, it's the day-to-day grind of it all. The way we are supposed to bring hope and the word of God to those who may be struggling in their belief. But what do you do if you, yourself, are doubting? They don't tell you how to handle this in school." Althaus could tell his words were beginning to disconcert Clarence.

"That's because you're not supposed to be feeling them," Clarence said with a firm confidence and admonishing tone.

"Oh, come on," Althaus said. "You've never felt any doubt?"

"No," Clarence said, closing the door on any further discussion of this. "In fact, Barrett, I'm going to pretend we never had this conversation. My advice to you is to find the light in your soul and find it quickly. God only helps those that help themselves. Don't wait for him to intervene in your struggles or the struggles of our country. We need to do for ourselves. Once you find the hope in yourself, you'll find it is easy to spread the word of God. Then you will feel right again."

4

With the thick raindrops falling on Althaus's body, hitting even harder as he ran faster, he noticed that his clothes were soaked. Thinking of Clarence Solomon's words, Althaus tried to imagine this as some kind of new baptism. Yet with every prayer he said to bring him back to God, he could not erase the doubts from his mind. Though he rationalized that he was different from Clarence—and from his flock, for that matter—Althaus couldn't help but be disappointed in himself much the way Clarence had been.

Althaus had always seen himself as pure of mind, body, and soul. Which was why he worked out so intensely. He wanted his visage to resemble what he presumed was God's image, even if his soul hadn't been worked out in quite the same way.

Whatever the case, his doubts were real and here to stay, a fact that brought dread to Althaus. He knew a time would come to meet his maker and he would have to answer for all this. At that moment, his Father would not see the perfection Althaus had strove for, but instead, a wounded and flawed man. One who, in his most honest moments, knew he was ready to give up a life of the cloth.

Taking a final deep, calm, and soothing breath, Althaus slowed down in front of the church. Despite the storm, he walked around the grounds trying to catch his breath and loosen his body. Coming to a complete stop, Althaus looked at the wooden front door of the church. He stood staring at the cross that hung above it. A shiver coursed its way through his body.

Tell me how to help you, Althaus thought, *and hopefully myself.*

5

The congregation was small the morning of the Attack of the White Light. Maybe twenty souls. As Althaus looked out on the familiar faces, he hoped his feigned confidence hid his true thoughts.

"Good morning," he stated to the few and hearty believers.

"Good morning," they all responded.

Althaus turned his head, looking through one of the five large and vaulted windows on the side wall of the church. The sun was rising, barely making it through the clouds. This made the morning dark, gray, and sullen. Althaus shook his head.

Another beautiful morning in Kansas, he sarcastically thought.

"Sunrise Services ... it's hard to call it that given the fact there isn't any sunshine."

The small group laughed, which in turn brought a smile to Althaus's face.

"Still the sun does rise, doesn't it? Every day we wake up early and come here to praise God, in hopes that today will be a better day than it was yesterday. Sometimes this works, and we find our daily lives improved. We can forget about the 17 percent unemployment rate, we can forget about the rampant famine in this country and overpopulation, even America's third-world status and the lack of suitable education for our youth. Perhaps we can even forget the violence that has taken over our biggest cities, making them nothing but large dens for criminals and gangs. But how long does it last? How are we able to prolong this feeling of improvement before we come crashing back down to our dreary lives, where we find ourselves cloaked in overwhelming sadness, as if this sadness was our clothes, not just a feeling."

At this, Althaus looked down at his habit, feeling its symbolic meaning pulling at his skin. It had been hard putting the uniform on that morning, and it made him sick to his stomach that he was even wearing it at all.

6

The black of the habit felt like more than just a simple color. It represented more than the staunch puritanical faith he was supposed to embody. To him, on this day, it was as black as his soul.

Wiping the rain from his body with a towel in his office, Althaus prepared himself to dress. Doing so, he knew in a way that he'd be nothing more than a wolf in sheep's clothing, a pretender trying to be something he wasn't.

How can I keep doing this, day after day?

He wasn't sure of the answer, but he knew he had to.

Althaus's office was small and dark, lit only by a lamp that stood behind his plain wooden desk. His chair was slatted wood and uncomfortable, leading Althaus to try to spend as little time as possible in it. However, given the state of the world, that had been a losing battle.

How many hours have I spent sitting at that desk, listening to the despair of those in need? A hundred? Five hundred? They are uncountable.

It used to be that the way he looked in the cloth, with his perfect body, was to him the personification of godliness. This belief empowered him, allowing Althaus to give the guidance necessary to help those who came to him. Was he always right in the life lessons he attempted to teach? As far as the reverend was concerned, of course he was. God himself had entrusted knowledge in his heart to compel people to do what he said. At times, Althaus felt so right that he was disappointed at the limited scale on which he was able to help.

If only God would intervene to help me to touch more lives, perhaps help me to save the world!

One day ...

That was often the thought Althaus used to soothe his own soul when he felt like giving up.

One day, I will find a way to reach the world and let them know to be strong; then things will turn around for the better.

He would tell them ... "Be strong of heart, be strong of body, be strong with God, and all will turn out right."

But would it really?

Even he was unsure of that conclusion, and thus Althaus began to doubt.

On the morning of the Attack of the White Light, Althaus dressed slowly. Each time he put on an article of clothing, he felt like he might as well have been putting on an outfit laced with poison. Once dressed, he stared at himself in the mirror. Upon seeing his reflection, he felt like a hypocrite. Yet, he had a job to do. The sun was rising, and a new day had dawned. People had come to the Sunrise Service to hear him speak. With any luck he might even have something good to say.

7

Althaus had long since stopped preplanning what to say in his sermons. Nowadays he simply liked to wing it. It got the adrenaline pumping, stirring him up in a way that simply reciting a written speech no longer achieved. Without this rush, it might have been impossible for him to speak at all. In the old days, when he was a younger man, he found he needed little to get his blood flowing to give a good oration. Now that he was forty-one, graying at the temples and having to wear reading glasses, it was more exciting for him to not know what he was going to say. Which made the congregation only eat it up even more.

As Althaus continued his speech, with the sun trying to break through the clouds, he was beginning to hear vocal agreements from the few on hand. Hallelujahs and mmmm-hmmm's were breaking the still air. This was how he knew he was reaching them. These calls encouraged him to push further.

"Our president—President Mitchum—is a great man! He is finally giving us what we need," Althaus continued.

"Praise God!" said a woman in the back.

"Hallelujah!" said a man to Althaus's right.

The pews of the church were wood and hard, cracking due to neglect, but by now the uncomfortable seats didn't matter anymore. Everyone was standing, raising their hands to the sky, hoping that maybe just by reaching for it they might attain some of God's glory.

Althaus continued, "He has seemingly been sent from on high to deliver this country from ourselves. Yet what has he done? What has he really done? Can we be sure this man has been sent to us by God?"

"Mmmm-hmmm!"

"Devil sent!"

"We can only hope he will continue the work he has done so far in attempting to bring us out of the wilderness. But what if it ends tomorrow? What if he accomplishes only what he has to date, and leaves us needing more? What do we do then?" Althaus looked out on the congregation; their hands were down, but their eyes were on him. They were his to command. "Should we look to some faraway God for the answers? Should we only turn our needs and failings to him? Or do we have to take control somehow? Do we need to look at ourselves and ask how we can help God?"

This final section seemed to land on the group like a blow. This was not the speech they had been expecting. It was something different. Althaus could tell as well.

Am I about to tell them my doubts?

Althaus had always possessed an amazing gift for oration. Even when he was in school, his teachers told him that his flock would live and die at his every word. So far, he had only brought joy to them with what he said.

Is this to be death?

He could feel the congregation's pulses racing and waning at his rhythm; he could feel them needing him to go one step further.

Yet can I?

Should I?

These were the thoughts that occupied his mind as he attempted to conclude a speech he would never finish. Quickly there was a flash of bright light that filled the whole church, as if the sun had not only come out from behind the clouds, but had landed right outside the window. Everyone was blinded for the brief seconds this happened— until suddenly all the light was quickly sucked up, peeling away as if the light was a spill moving in reverse.

Then came a rumbling sound.

"What is that?" Althaus said to the congregation, only to be greeted by an even-louder rumble and a crash of wind so great the wood of the church began to crack and fly everywhere.

His body fell from the pulpit; the heat in the wind was searing his skin. He could no longer see anyone in front of him; the church was consumed where he was by a storm of dust. This dust hit him like stones hitting a guilty man in Old Jerusalem facing the mob. As Althaus hit the ground hard, a second, more powerful flash of light surrounded him. Acutely aware of the power within this wave of white light, Althaus thought it could only have come from one place.

God himself.

As fear gripped him, Althaus realized he was finally seeing God's wrath. His prayers had been answered.

Annette

1

Annette Bilkins's dry, raspy guffaw filled the one room of her trailer more easily than a baby filled a diaper. The place wasn't large to begin with, and Annette could be loud even when she was trying to be quiet. Taking a puff from her smoldering cigarette, Annette continued to laugh, smoke escaping from her nose and mouth in quick spurts with the pace of her chuckling.

"You kill me, you know that, Harv?" she said in between the laughter and the smoke.

Harvey, a portly man, with a bald spot only slightly covered by the wraparound he had spent years growing, looked at her in shock.

"What?" he said. "I'm serious!"

"I know you are, honey, that's why it's so damn hilarious." Again she puffed the cigarette; this moment of pause gave her the chance to see how hurt Harvey really was. "Harvey, don't be so damn sensitive. I'm not going to marry you. I'm not going to marry anyone!"

"But why? We'd be good together! I already live next door; we don't even have to live together."

"You really know how to sweep a woman off her feet." She laughed again, this time louder than the last.

"I just want to take care of you," Harvey said, lowering his head like a lost puppy.

"I know you do," Annette said while placing a hand on his arm. "Listen, would sex be enough? I can give you that. Just don't ask me for marriage. That's not in the cards."

With that, Harvey looked up with a smile on his face, and as quick as Annette could put the cigarette out, she found herself below a sweaty janitor, who loved her like none of her four husbands ever did.

2

When Annette finally woke up again, she looked at the clock. It was 2:25 a.m. Pacific standard time, which meant it was 4:25 a.m. outside of Chicago, where her youngest son, Sean, now lived. She thought about giving him a call, but she knew he wouldn't be allowed to answer.

Jail is like that, she thought, *so many rules and restrictions.*

Quickly she looked over at Harvey. He was fast asleep, snoring up a storm, and pleased as punch that he bagged a babe for the first time in ages. Not that Annette saw herself as a babe anymore, far from it, but she was still good in the sack.

Probably rocked his world anyway, she thought, trying to hold in her laughter. The last thing she wanted to do was wake him.

He'd probably want to go again, and I'm waaaay too old for that.

Getting up from the bed, Annette pulled on a robe she kept in the tiny bathroom attached to her already-small bedroom. Pausing a moment, she looked at the dark bags under her eyes in the mirror. She studied her skin and gray hair, where her roots were showing.

Time for more dye in a box, she thought, reminding herself to buy some at the store. However she knew a quick dye job wouldn't fix the real problems. She was sixty-two now, and she felt old. Even her skin seemed more like sandpaper than something a man would want to touch. Life had been tough on her, and it only took one glance in her direction to come to that conclusion.

Sneaking past Harvey, she exited the sliding plastic partition from her room and entered the living room/kitchen of the fancy trailer she lived in. Truth be told, the place was a sty. She hated to clean, and hated to do dishes even more, which meant they piled until she absolutely had to do them. If she'd had the money, Annette would eat out just so she didn't have to do dishes, but she was poor, and the state of her furniture conveyed as much. Everything had holes in it, or piss stains from the cat she had once owned that was now long-dead. Nothing she had was new; it was all secondhand or taken with her from house to house and from marriage to marriage.

Just once it would have been fantastic to have been able to sign up for a registry, she thought as she contemplated her horrible marriages. Again she laughed, this time unable to hold it in.

After all, my marriages were to some of the worst men in the history of the planet. If that's not comedy, what is? Plus, there was no way any of them would have had the friends or family that would buy wedding gifts.

Sitting on her couch, which she realized was one good gust of wind away from disintegrating, she turned to her right to look at the small end table beside it. Covered with nicks and dings, it fit right in with the rest of the decor of the trailer—low-class chic. On top of the little faded brown table was a picture of her family. It was taken two winters earlier when they were all relatively happy. Studying it, going from face to face and running her hands over each son, her fingers came to rest on her youngest, Sean. His face held a smile from ear to ear; a glimmer of hope even seemed to shine out from behind his blue eyes. His blond hair was longer than he normally wore it, and his innocent, pure face looked as if it didn't have a care in the world.

Little did they all know then that six short months later, everything would change. The last she would see of him would be in a visiting room after a sentencing hearing.

3

"I'm so sorry, Mom," Sean said with a deep-seated anger in his voice. He was a strong boy, but he always had a soft spot where his mother was concerned, and he could never hide his feelings all that well.

"It's okay," Annette said, trying to reassure him. "You were trying to protect someone."

The two of them were in a small anteroom right next to the court. Not three minutes earlier, they had been rushed inside here after the judge had sentenced Sean to seven years in a maximum-security prison. The room around them was white brick, cold, and had the smell of bleach. The scent was so strong she could feel it singe her nose hairs.

It was the perfect setting for such a dramatic scene.

"I should have known better than to take it that far," Sean admonished himself. Obvious pain and regret made his voice crack.

He was right to a degree, Annette realized: he should have known better than to kill a man, but the act was done and now he had to pay the price.

"Hey," she said, pulling his face to hers, "it's gonna be okay."

At that moment, she let out one of her famous laughs.

"You hear me? It's going to be just fine. It's only seven years. It'll go by so fast you won't even notice you're gone."

"Mom," he said with a questioning tone.

"No," she simply stated. "You have to make the best of it, and that starts right here, right now. You need to find a way to smile. Turn this into something good."

"That's impossible."

"You keep talking like that, and you'll be dead in no time. You hear me? They'll kill you in there if they even so much as sniff that you're weak. You are not weak! I didn't raise a weakling. Did I?"

"No."

"You think I got through four husbands, two that were abusive and one that was a drug addict, because I was weak?"

Maybe I'm taking it too far, she thought. Then she remembered that Sean was the son who stood between her and husband three even though there was a belt swinging down on her at the time. He took that beating for her, knowing she could hardly stand. That was not a weak son.

"Besides," she added, "you need to come back for Michelle and Winnie. They need you."

Sean nodded in agreement. She hugged him again as two guards came up to them and began to pull him away. Watching him leave in his orange jumpsuit, her mind filled with thoughts. *How unfair the whole thing is ... the justice system in this broken country is completely out of whack ...*

Then she thought ... *What good is this? My son is in jail, and I need to be positive for him.*

"Anyone bothers you, crack them one across the jaw!" she yelled after him, producing a smile on Sean's face just as the doors closed behind him.

Then she was alone.

4

The laws concerning murder in the United States of America drastically changed in 2031. The early part of the twenty-first century saw a rise in homicide, justifiable and not, to an unprecedented degree. So much so, that a law was passed, the Wilkes Act, that made the punishment for murder extremely harsh.

The Wilkes Act was born in the mind of Senator George Wilkes, who presided over North Dakota during one of the worst crime sprees in the history of the United States. Due to the huge economic depression across the state (and the country), many of the poor were forced to live in large ghetto-like communities, sometimes eight people to a small one-bedroom apartment, where they could all share resources and depend on each other for help. These living conditions were self-imposed, but frankly, the country pushed them into the areas by building these huge tenement sky-rises, with cheap rents and free utilities. It was the return of the "projects." The buildings had been part of the 2022 City Reclamation Project, a countrywide urban repopulation, where the government moved ex-farmers or poor struggling families out of the outlying areas and into the bigger cities in hopes of revitalizing those areas. However, with no jobs being created, these huge buildings quickly descended into disrepair and chaos.

By the time everything went to hell, it was too late to have stopped it.

Murder rates across the country quickly rose in the nine years of the City Reclamation Act, but nowhere so steeply as in North Dakota. Many so-called experts tried to reason it was due to the cold and longer winters, claiming they affected the brains of the people in the tenements, but in truth, the reason for the rise in the murder rate was purely and simply greed. People needed things others had, and they were forced to kill to get it as they had no jobs or money to buy it. In addition, those who were attacked were, in turn, forced to protect themselves, often leading to more murder or even revenge killing to prove they weren't just victims. Eventually the killing was just a vicious cycle, where no one was truly innocent.

As cities like Fargo, Bismarck, Grand Forks, and Minot were thrown into warlike existences, the outlying areas, filled with the rich who could afford housing, tried to separate themselves from the chaos. They went as far as building walls around their settlements, the idea being that these places could protect themselves from the realities of the poor. Soon, all the aid these rich people had been giving to the cities was dropped, and things became even worse.

Finally, when the populace of the cities could no longer take the violence, the residents exploded. Riots destroyed much of what was left of the areas, moreover many of the rich settlements were attacked and burned to the ground. With a death toll that climbed past the hundreds into the tens of thousands, North Dakota Senator Wilkes proposed his act.

Many believed that had most of the inhabitants of the cities been put in jail after their first acts of murder, be it in self-defense or otherwise, then they would never have been around to incite the riots that killed so many innocents. Therefore, the Wilkes Act created harsher standards of punishment, stipulating that:

"Any death caused by the hands or act of another human being, be it by accident or willfully, shall result in at least a seven-year sentence or carry a maximum sentence of 50 years to death."

This was how Sean Bilkins was put away for seven years for protecting himself, a child, and the woman he loved.

5

The flash of white light was what brought Annette out of her memories. The light was so bright and so blinding, the whole trailer lit up like there were twelve spotlights on at the same time, pointing straight into her eyes. It was so bright it even woke Harvey. Sitting straight up in bed, he looked around as the light quickly went out.

"Is that aliens?" he asked with all seriousness.

"No." She laughed. "I mean, really, Harv—"

"Well, what was it?" To her, his pleas for answers sounded like the whine of a five-year-old wanting his mother.

It was highly annoying.

"Does it look like I know?" she snapped back at him. "It seemed like it came from Old Los Angeles. Perhaps those criminals that live there finally blew it up." She gave out a small laugh with this thought. Perhaps she was only trying to lighten the mood, but when the rumbling started, she realized that maybe what she had said hadn't been a joke.

The sound grumbled up from below them, surrounding the trailer on all sides. Everything in the trailer was shaking back and forth, and what few decorative doodads she had were falling off tables and shelves, breaking to pieces on the floor.

Perhaps it's the big one, she thought.

Living in a suburb of what was left of old Los Angeles, she was always primed for earthquakes. Still though, this one seemed different. The movement of her trailer wasn't the same; it was rocking back and forth instead of shaking. This being her seventh earthquake, she figured she could tell the difference. The other ones had been predictable in the way they made the earth move below her. However, the motion of this was something else altogether. It felt more like some violent storm was surrounding the trailer and engulfing the whole place, like a rogue wave preparing to flip over a boat.

As the shaking continued, Annette jerked Harvey from the bed. "Come on!" she said.

She quickly placed herself and Harvey in the flimsy doorway of her bathroom. If it was an earthquake, she would at least be prepared.

That's when the wind hit.

"What's going on?" Harvey asked as he clutched the thin metal doorway with all his might.

"If I knew, don't you think I would tell you?" she replied.

Suddenly the windows of the trailer blasted inward; glass broke apart and flew everywhere, like shrapnel from a bomb. Instinctively she ducked to protect herself; Harvey wasn't as smart. A huge chunk of glass flew across the air, and with the speed and force of a jackhammer, severed his head straight off his body. Annette watched in horror as his body slunk down pumping out its river of life onto the floor.

"Dear God!" she said aloud.

The wind didn't stop there though. With it whistling through her trailer now, everything was being tossed around, almost floating on the air; it seemed the force of energy was creating a vortex inside her home.

When will it stop? God, this quake is going on a long time ... Her thoughts raced ... *After all, how long are quakes really supposed to last? A minute? Two?*

And what is this wind?

A great creaking came from the walls of her trailer, as if the metal itself were crying out for help. This frightened her to the core. The sound only got worse as more light began to break through the cracks in the metal that had been forced open along the seams of the trailer by the wind. No sooner did this happen than her ceiling suddenly ripped away. One-second it was there, and the next it was gone. The wind now whipped down on her from above, entering her home like some swarm of unwanted locusts, blowing her hair and robe in crazy angles around her. Annette could feel static electricity rushing through the strands of the hair on her arms and legs, lifting them straight up like blades of grass. Looking up to where her roof used to be, she could see nothing but the blinding light.

Is this the white light of death described by those who crossed over and somehow came back?

The light got brighter and brighter all around her, and then it was gone again. Yet the wind stayed, continuing its damaging barrage. It seemed to be growing more powerful by the moment, finally lifting her body up off the ground. The floating might have felt pleasant if she weren't being flung so fast through the air. The jerking motion made her lose her meal from the night before. Annette hadn't thrown up since the last time she was pregnant.

Annette, now flying like some kind of crazed bird that had lost control of its natural-born talent, found herself trying to grab onto anything she could find blowing with her in the wind. It was useless, though; the debris around her could not be caught. Furthermore, she had lost all sense of direction. She could not tell where she was going or what was in her way, leaving her to hope that if she died, it would be quick and painless.

Like Harvey, she thought.

Given the events of her life, though, she doubted she was going to be that lucky.

It was then she saw it—the roof of her trailer sticking straight up from the ground, like a sail in the wind. It had somehow lodged itself into the dirt and gotten stuck there. She was about to fly by it … *If I could only grab it and somehow hang on …*

Reaching out her hands, she quickly clutched the roof, but found she couldn't stop her momentum. Her fingers dragged on the metal, squeaking like windshield wipers across a dry surface.

Come on! She pleaded with herself. *Find some grip!*

Finally she did. It was the sunroof! The windows had been blown out, leaving a ledge for her fingers to extend around. There she held on for dear life. After another minute of holding as firmly as she could, the wind suddenly stopped, and her legs, which had been whipping about, came crashing back down with the thud of gravity. Letting go of the roof, Annette slid her body down the metal, and for a second she could have sworn she was on a slide at a park.

Taking a deep breath, she realized she was alive and that the world seemed to be spinning around her. Black started to fill her vision, and just as she was about to cry out for help, everything went dark and she was aware no longer.

Nell

1

Mark and Nell had been dating for a year, and they had fooled around quite a bit. Early on in their relationship, Nell decided that if Mark broke up with her, it wouldn't be because she didn't treat him right. Right, that is, where high school boys are concerned. However, even she was surprised when they decided to go all the way.

The discussions had started about two weeks earlier, when Mark's best friend Taylor had lost his V-Card to the longtime school tramp, Lindsey King. Rumor had it she had slept with most of the high school fight team—most of them at the same party. The party had been at Mark's house because his parents were away for the weekend. Until that time, she had never attended a party, but she had heard stories. Indeed these stories were true: people were drinking, smoking, making out, and in the case of a good number of the varsity boys, lining up outside the laundry-room door awaiting their turn with Lindsey. Sexually, Nell would never be mistaken for Lindsey, but that was probably a good thing. Still, when Mark suggested they consider having sex, who was she to deny him at least a conversation?

2

"Would you want to?" Mark asked Nell, trying not to sound too pushy about it.

"Wow," was all Nell could say back. When she had gotten his note in fourth period to meet him at the ring, she had no idea it would be about this. Since Mark was the captain of the school fight team, Nell assumed he had a litany of reasons for her to meet him there, and a discussion about losing their virginities together never entered her mind as one of them.

"It's fine if you don't want to," Mark quickly added. "I mean, it's a big deal, and I understand if you're not ready. Hell, maybe I'm not ready … I don't know … It's just that … I love you … and …"

Nell's mind wandered as he continued to reason it out for her. She was in a gym; a fighting ring stood in the middle. The ring was canvas, like a boxing ring, and lifted off the ground about as high. The only difference was the ring did not have ropes surrounding it; instead, it was completely open, and part of the goal was to push the other fighter off the mat. The room itself always smelled of stale sweat and feet, and with training bags and dummies hanging down from the ceiling, this was hardly the most romantic setting for the discussion. All Nell could think about were all the bloody fights she had seen in here, most dominated by her boyfriend.

Fighting, which mixed old-style boxing and the mixed martial arts craze of the early 2000s, was the only sport allowed in the country anymore. Football, basketball, hockey, and baseball were all banned and shunned after the salaries of the players became so exorbitant the public couldn't stomach them anymore. When everyone is starving or fighting for their lives, watching rich babies try to catch a leather ball simply wasn't entertainment anymore. Most felt learning how to play these games simply wasn't a usable skill in life. However, fighting was. In these days, everyone needed to know how to protect oneself, so joining the fight team was the popular thing to do, at least in the affluent towns on the outskirts of every city in America.

The town of New Dallas wasn't any different. Situated a hundred miles outside of Dallas, Texas, New Dallas was more to the East, almost to the Arkansas border, and was still trying to pretend it was a place from some bygone age. Made up of small neighborhoods with cul-de-sacs and white, two-story houses, if one didn't know better, they might think this was a town right out of an American dream. In New Dallas, living proper and free of sin was the most important goal of all. Which is why Nell couldn't believe what she said next.

"Okay," Nell said quietly.

"What?" Mark asked in disbelief.

"Okay," she said again, this time louder and with more confidence. "I want to do it. Let's do it."

"You're sure? I'm not pushing you into it or anything?"

"Not at all," she replied. "I love you too, and I'd be lying if I said I didn't think about it."

"Really?"

"Yes, really." She paused a moment, letting it all sink in. "Let's have sex."

The ease with which she agreed to go through with having sex was surprising to her. Yet, when push came to shove, Nell loved Mark Fitzpatrick, and she figured this was the best way to show him. So, they made a plan.

"My bedroom has a trellis," Nell said. "It leads all the way down to the ground, so despite my window being on the second floor, it's an easy climb and descent to get in and out of the house. My friends and I used to sneak out all the time using this route during sleepovers. My parents never woke up."

Now though, it would be used for an even sneakier purpose, one far less innocent than just sneaking out with the girls to run wild, Nell thought.

Then she continued, "You will wait until midnight and sneak into the house by way of the trellis. Once inside ... we'll make this the most memorable night ever."

"We'll have to be quiet?" Mark asked.

"Of course," Nell said. "My parents will be home, but at least this is better than in the back of a car ... or in a laundry room at a party."

3

Mark Fitzpatrick was not only the captain of the school fight team, he was also class president and an all-around great guy. All of Nell's friends were jealous of her for landing him and told her so.

"What's your secret?" Jody Copland once asked Nell. Truthfully, she didn't know how to answer. She was perhaps the most surprised out of everyone. In her mind, she was plain, didn't really have a great personality, and was simply forgettable. While Mark was muscular, handsome, and could charm anyone he needed to. So, Nell's answer was always the same.

"I make him really good cookies," which she did. Every fight day she would make him his favorite chocolate chip cookies and have them waiting for him after. She didn't really know if this was what kept him with her—she assumed not—but to Nell, it was as good a reason as any.

In truth it didn't matter, because after they made love, Nell knew Mark would be hers forever.

4

The night that would—in her mind—make Nell a woman was long, and little did she know of the White Light that would change everything about her life.

First, she had to have dinner with her parents. Then do her homework. After that indomitable task, she would have to top it all off by acting as if nothing was out of the ordinary. Yet her mind raced with thoughts, both pleasant and scary.

Will it hurt? Her friends said it did.

Will I bleed? She knew she would.

Will it also be wonderful and something special that I can hang onto for the rest of my life? She truly hoped so.

There was also the fear that her parents might hear and walk in on them.

Oh, God, that would be mortifying!

Her father would fly off the handle. Nell's parents were so religious, always making her go to church, all the while employing strict rules on language and boys. No cursing up to and including the word "damn." No boys allowed in her room day or night. Nell's parents had hardline political views (to her at least), often remarking the reason America had become such a disgrace as a country was because God had abandoned it long ago.

"Too many homos and Jews were allowed to run the country! At least we've taken it back, though!" Her dad's often bigoted and hateful remarks scared her, but his uneducated banter was not going to stop her from becoming a better person than he was.

Nell did not necessarily know what it was she wanted to do with her life when she "grew up." She just hoped it would be something good, something that would have an impact on the world. As far as she could tell, her parents were part of the problem, not the solution. She supposed she loved her parents as much as any teenage kid loved his or her parents, but she was not naive enough to ignore their flaws or their hackneyed attempts at keeping her sheltered from the world they deemed "morally corrupt."

On the night in question, it struck Nell as ironic that given all their pushing and prodding, she was going to break every rule they had set forth for her. If caught, this would be the biggest act of rebellion conceived of, except maybe for waking up one morning and telling them she was gay. That would probably get her kicked out of the house. Which to her was not the worst thing that could happen.

As night fell on their family home, she retreated to her room to do homework. She loved her room. It was girly, though not too much so that it made people feel like she thought she was a princess. A few floral touches, yellow walls instead of pink, even a cloth overhang that enclosed her bed, made it seem grand and put together, but there were no dolls or stuffed animals. Those days were long past. She liked that her room was somewhere between that of woman and girl.

Just like me, she would think.

Still, the most important reason she loved her room was that it made her feel safe. A realization that was going to be even more important that night, when she gave herself freely to Mark.

Feeling safe will make all the difference in the world.

Her parents were busy conducting their nightly tradition of watching religious programs in the den when she shut the door of the room behind her. With any luck, they would be too consumed with Holy Rollers to pay attention to her.

Hours passed at a snail's pace. In her room, Nell could hear every movement her parents made. The TV was clear as day, and she tried to block out the preachers on TV lamenting the "devil's influence" on the youth of America. All Nell could do was swallow her opinions and keep her eyes on the prize. Soon, she heard her mother's footsteps walking up the stairs to her room, assuming—as usual—her father would soon follow. However, that was not the case. He kept watching TV. He was staying up late!

Of all the nights! She thought as she gazed at the clock, which read 10:15.

Come on, go to sleep.

Her father didn't, though. Ten thirty passed. Then ten forty-five. At eleven fifteen, she opened her bedroom door to take a look. Perhaps he had fallen asleep, needing to be awakened and pushed off to bed. As she walked out into the hallway, though, she saw movement. Her father was standing at the bottom of the stairs, gazing up at her with his dark, reproachful eyes.

"You're still up?" he asked.

"So are you." She smiled, hoping to joke with him. He did not reciprocate her mood, which was not good.

Can he possibly know?

"I'll be headed to bed soon," he said. "You should too. Nothing good happens this late at night."

He had to know, but how? Nell's mind was racing. What could she do now?

"Dad ..." she said with a kindness in her voice she hadn't spoken to him with in years.

"Yes?" He continued to stare at her, but she just could not think of anything to say. "You have something to say to me?" The tone in his voice conveyed anger.

She thought a moment. Did she have something to say?

"I love you." These words escaped her mouth faster than she even realized they were coming. To her surprise, though, they seemed to have worked. A smile swept across his face.

"I love you too, sweetheart." Then he switched off the TV. "Let's both go off to bed, shall we?" When he reached her at the top of the stairs, he put his arm around her. Feeling the need to do so, she placed her head against his chest. Her father's little girl one last time.

After tonight, she thought, *it will all be different.*

As she went back into her room, she closed her bedroom door, leaving it open a crack. Spying on her dad, she waited to hear the bedroom door click shut, signaling her father's entry to sleep land, and then she closed her door all the way. Now Nell knew she was safe. Usually once her parents were down, they were out. She peered at the clock: eleven thirty. Plenty of time for her parents to be sound asleep.

At 12:01 a.m., Mark arrived at the window. She quietly let him into the room.

"Hi," he said.

"Hi," she returned with a smile.

Then they kissed.

5

Nell's happiness was all she could think about as she waited for the sun to come up in her window. It was 4:45 central time, and she knew she had better wake Mark up; he needed to leave before her parents woke. She was rolling over to do just that when she saw a huge flash of white light spread across her room. She turned to the window to see what it was, but by the time her eyes reached it, the light was gone. Now just an orange glow peaked through the white of her drapes.

What was that? She thought. *The sun?*

Quickly she stood, all the while trying not to wake her sleeping lover. She reached the window and moved the drapes away.

Fear ran through her.

It hadn't been the sun she saw rising at all. It was a strange orange glow off in the direction of Old Dallas. It was almost the color of flames, making the sky grow from darkness to light.

Its not the sun either, Nell reasoned. *The sun rises in the East; this light is coming from the West.*

Whatever the orange glow was, it was in the distance, but with how it was spreading across the dark purple sky, Nell could tell it was getting closer—and quickly.

Suddenly, a deep, grumbling rumble grew from that far-off distance, like a tractor starting its engine. This sound was what woke Mark. He sat straight up in bed. She turned to him.

"Mark?"

"Nell?"

Just then a strong force hit her, pushing her off her feet, followed shortly by another brilliant white light. Nell tried to block out the light by guarding her eyes with her arms—she even closed them tightly—yet still she could see the light.

After what seemed like the longest moment of her life, the bright light was suddenly blotted out. Darkness swept over her again. Nell reached out, searching for Mark, but her eyes were not working at all. All she saw now was black. That's when her house shook, and her legs were swept out from under her. Nell's stomach lurched as her body became weightless, but then she hit the ground, followed by the sound of crashing timber and breaking glass.

Once everything had settled, Nell discovered she couldn't move. The house had collapsed around them, leaving her lost in total darkness.

Sean

1

Clink! went the steel doors as they automatically closed behind Sean. He hated that sound and everything it had come to represent in his life. The bad decision making, his uncontrollable emotions, even his unrequited love for a woman who couldn't have cared less that he was serving seven years for her—all of that was wrapped up in that one awful sound ... *Clink!*

It echoed back to him, bouncing off the reinforced mortar walls. Locked inside his eight-foot-by-eight-foot home, Sean was forced to face the realities of another twenty hours before he would be able to see the light again. Until then, he was supposed to think on his crimes and do nothing else. Here in Milford Penitentiary you weren't allowed to read, draw, write, or do anything except think. It was considered the toughest place in the US penal system to do one's time and was built precisely for that reason.

Milford Pen, nicknamed "the Playpen" by its inmates, was located along the Great Lakes, halfway between Chicago and Detroit. The conditions in the building were often cold, dark, and damp. Very few people served their whole sentence in Milford. Most died before they could. That's why being sentenced to Milford was like receiving a death sentence. If another inmate didn't kill you, you were almost guaranteed pneumonia would.

Developed by President Winston Milford in 2029 as part of the Milford Initiative for a Tougher Penal Code, the Playpen became synonymous with failure. Invented to reform the penitentiary system in America, all it did was create more violence and more criminal activity. Inside was one of the worst places on earth. Dirty and violent, the Playpen swallowed people up whole and single-handedly helped raise the murder rate of the country by 3 percent. However, on this night, the night of the Attack of the White Light, not even the inmates of the notorious Playpen could have predicted just how true that death sentence was.

"Roll call!" the prison guard called out to cell block G, which was situated on the eastern end of the complex.

"One," the first prisoner called out.

"Two," said the second.

Milford was shaped like a giant U. The two arms extending north held the prisoners, while the bottom part, facing south, was where the guards kept an eye on things. In between the arms was a small patch of land covered in dirt, where, during one hour of every day, the prisoners were allowed to walk in a circle for exercise. If a prisoner so much as looked at a guard sideways, the privilege would be taken away. In Sean's short time at Milford, he had his exercise time taken away ninety-seven out of 201 days.

"Twelve," said a prisoner from behind his closed door, through the airholes in the thick plexiglass that allowed him to look outside into the corridor.

"Thirteen," said another.

Sean's number was 47. It would be awhile before they got to him. So Sean lay down on his cot, staring up at the white, pockmarked ceiling, contemplating his fate.

How could I have let this happen to me? He wondered. *Why am I so stupid? No, not stupid—passionate.*

That was the way most people had described Sean in court. It was apt. When Sean believed in something, he let the world know it. He was the first to stand up for the little guy, and he never thought too far ahead about the repercussions for his actions. If he had been born in another day and time, a time when people had scruples, he would still be a free man. Still given the way America now treated its prisoners, it was like living in 1800 France.

"Twenty-five."

"Twenty-six."

It was all because of the Wilkes Law, Sean told himself. *Any murder of any kind landed a man, no matter how good, in jail. Be it manslaughter or self-defense, murder was all treated the same.*

Nonetheless Sean got through it by realizing he *was* indeed a good man. Even if the country no longer thought so ...

Or Michelle ...

He knew it.

"Twenty-nine."

"Thirty."

Yes, Sean thought, *I'm passionate ... But so what?*

Sean didn't like to make excuses. True, the reason for the murder he committed was the defense of another person; true, Sean did not maliciously or cold-bloodedly set out to commit this crime, but he was going to pay the price anyway. In Sean's ideal world, his life should be just as forfeit as that of the man he killed. Since that man would never have a child, never see the world improve, or even see another sunset, Sean couldn't help but believe he should be condemned to suffer the same, good man or not. That's why to his relief, there was no outside window in his room and he was not allowed visitors for the first year of his incarceration. As for letters, he assumed he wasn't allowed to receive them, because for all his time in the pen, he'd never gotten one.

"Times have certainly changed," Sean heard his mother, Annette Bilkins, say, when the rules of his jail sentence were explained to her. According to his mother, in her youth, jail sentences were less harsh, often referred to as "easy time." What he was about to face was anything but! Too bad this was all due to being in love with a girl he could never have.

"You are a dumbass!" his mother said to him the day he was arrested. "I thought I had raised you better than this."

Sean thought she had as well, but his actions proved differently.

Still, he had to remind himself, *love makes people do stupid things, things that are out of their control ... things that they regret.*

Which was exactly what happened to him.

2

"Thank you for taking her again," Michelle said to him as she handed Winnie over. Winnie was four and still in diapers, probably because Michelle was too lazy to try to potty train her. From the smell wafting off Winnie, Sean was positive she was dirty, and almost as certain it had been hours since the last changing.

"No problem, Michelle," Sean said with a smile. "You know I'm glad to help whenever you need me."

"Thanks."

Sean stared at her as she started grabbing Winnie's few possessions from her purse. A bottle, a stuffed giraffe, and a binky for her to suck on, even though Winnie was way past the age that pacifiers were advised. Despite Michelle's complete incompetence as a mother and her horribly haggard appearance, Sean still couldn't help but see her as that vibrant and beautiful sixteen-year-old he first fell in love with. This made him blind to the fact Michelle herself had given up on her life.

"I'll be back from the gas station around four in the morning," she said. "I'll pick up Winnie then. Come here, baby—give Momma a kiss."

Michelle bent over to kiss her daughter, and as Winnie arrived to do so, Michelle for the first time got a whiff of the stench off her daughter.

"Woof," she said, pulling back. "You'll need to change her. She stinks!" This order rankled Sean a bit, though he'd never let it show.

"Will do," was all he said.

That's when Michelle pulled out her hand mirror from her purse and checked her reflection.

"How do I look?" she asked Sean.

"Great, as usual." Though he wasn't sure why she needed to know that just to go to work.

"You suck-up!" she said, slapping him on the upper arm. "See you in the morning. God, I hate graveyard shifts!"

With that, she walked off, leaving Winnie and Sean alone. Just the way they liked it.

3

"Forty-seven."

Sean snapped out of it suddenly as he heard the pause after the called number.

"Forty-seven!" the guard repeated again, this time with pure spit and fire.

Shit! I didn't answer fast enough ... This is bad.

Jumping off his bed, Sean ran over to the door.

"Forty-seven!" he called out, only it was too late; a guard was already at his door. With his baton, the officer smacked the plexiglass window, sending Sean back defensively.

"Why did you take so long to answer?" the bastard asked as if Sean had taken hours to say his number.

"I ... I ... fell asleep, sir. I'm sorry."

"Fell asleep, huh?" A smile crept across the guard's face. "Hey, open up cell 47," the guard said into his earpiece.

Oh shit! Oh shit! Oh shit! was all Sean could think.

Clink! went the door, but this time it swung open. Slowly the guard, a man of considerable size and tension, entered the room. Sean tried not to take a protective posture, which would just irritate the guard into hurting him even more, so instead, Sean tried to relax and show no fear.

"Do you need more sleep, 47?"

"No ... Not at all ... I'm fine."

"I don't believe you."

"Please," Sean began to plead, but he knew his cries were falling on deaf ears.

"Back up against the wall, arms up and legs out."

Sean didn't move at first.

"Do it!" the guard screamed. "Or I'll stick this rod so far up your ass you'll be shitting splinters."

Sean did as he was told and went to the wall. Spreading his arms and legs out, he waited for what would come next. To his surprise, it wasn't a beating; instead, the guard pulled his arms up to the metal spikes in the wall used for hosing down inmates, and with his titanium cuffs, he attached Sean to them.

"Enjoy sleeping now, 47." With that, the guard let out a huge laugh and exited the room.

Clink! went the door again, and Sean let his weight drop as much as he dared. An excruciating amount of pain went through his shoulder sockets, making him feel like they might burst from the skin if he put his weight down on them.

That's when he understood: he was going to have to stay up all night.

4

Sean delved into his memory.

He searched for somewhere to hide.

He looked for a world to lose himself in, so that he no longer had to feel the pain of the jail cell and his arms being torn from their proper place.

Finally, after a long amount of thought, Sean came to rest on a memory he felt safe in, one with just Winnie and him ... one from that last night of freedom long ago ...

5

Sitting on the floor of his apartment—a cold, hard linoleum that was a staple of the government-built tenements of Old Los Angeles—Sean and Winnie played with some Barbies that he had bought at a pawnshop in Chinatown. He had bought them knowing that Winnie often visited and needed things to play with, and given the fact that Barbies were no longer manufactured, he thought they would be a fun treat for her the next time she was there. He was right.

As they dressed and undressed them, Winnie smiled. She smelled infinitely better since he changed her diaper, and he could tell she was much more comfortable too. He was happy about the times they got to spend together. At least he saw her happy in these moments. He shuddered to think about what her daily life was like when it was just her and her mother.

"Tanks for dees, Unckey Shun."

"You're welcome, sweetie," he said. He didn't know why she didn't talk better for a four-year-old, but he assumed it was because all she had for day care was her mother, which, given the circumstances he knew they lived in, wasn't much.

"Wha her nem agin?" she asked while studying the plastic blonde's perfectly angled face.

"Barbie," he said.

"Ber-bee … Ber-bee …" she said repeatedly, and in many different ways, as if she was trying the name out on her tongue like she was trying the clothes on the doll. She was attempting to find the perfect fit.

"Unckey Shun?" she suddenly asked in a serious tone, which implied a serious question.

"Yep?" he replied.

"Er you mah dud-dy?"

The question hit Sean like a ton of bricks.

Oh, how I wish I were, he often thought. Regardless, he wasn't.

"No, baby, I wish, but I'm not."

Unfortunately, that unique honor was accredited to Michelle's stoner high-school ex-boyfriend, who managed to get himself killed by a group of gangbangers only a year after they had all graduated. With him out of the picture, Sean had visited Michelle a lot, checking up on her, hoping that one day she would see him as more than just a friend. Having grown up only three trailers from each other, Sean knew this was an impossibility. They were more like brother and sister than boyfriend and girlfriend; hence the name "Uncle Sean." It had been that way for so long it was unlikely to change.

These depressing facts never stopped Sean from helping her, though. This help was just an ill-conceived attempt to win her heart, but he did it anyway. Whether it was picking Winnie up from their apartment, or taking her to his apartment and watching her for the night, just as he was now, he tried to always be there for Michelle's call. Sometimes he watched Winnie because Michelle was working, or on a date, or sometimes because she was binging on drugs, which Sean didn't approve of ... However, what could he do? He wasn't in a position to say anything to her. After all, he was only a friend.

Odd, then, that Winnie asked her next question:

"Kin I cull yuh Dud-dy?"

Sean wasn't sure of what to say. He looked deep into her eyes. He could tell all she wanted was someone to love her with all his heart. How could he say no?

"Of course, you can," he replied. "But it has to be our little secret."

They sat there the rest of night playing with those Barbies, reading books, and playing pretend Daddy and daughter. It broke his heart to put her to sleep, as he hoped the night would never end, but he did. He wrapped her up in a sheet and a blanket on his couch, tucked a comfy pillow under her head, and sang her off to dreamland.

Only a few minutes afterward, Sean dozed off himself, while sitting in an uncomfortable wooden chair he had pulled up next to her makeshift bed.

6

The pain was intense, and it slapped him right out of his memory. While he reimagined that night, he had let his body sag a bit, pulling his right arm so tight that he could see the bulge of his shoulder through his shirt. If he had come to any later, his arm would have popped right out and torn who knows how many ligaments.

With a great growl, Sean pushed the pain away and refocused his energy. He straightened his legs and tried to find some determination to go on.

How much time had passed? Sean had no idea, but he knew he needed to switch tactics. Pleasant memories were too comforting; they were lulling him to sleep. He needed painful ones.

Ones with the hurt of the deepest kind.

7

Sean awoke with a start, but he was no longer in the jail cell. This was his memory again ... from years ago. It was the morning he ended up killing a man, the day after Winnie had asked if she could call him Daddy.

Wiping the sleep from his eyes, he looked around his small apartment. All was as it should have been: the room was dark, the front door was locked, and Winnie still slept on the couch where he had put her the night before. As far as he could tell, everything was okay.

So what woke me up?

He sat a moment in the morning darkness, listening to the rhythm of Winnie's breathing, trying to figure out what was nagging at his gut. That's when he looked at the clock on the microwave in his small kitchen.

6:45 a.m.

Michelle was late ... which was not so odd ... Still, three hours late? That was really odd. The most Sean had ever experienced Michelle being late was a half hour; now she was late almost three. In this town, that could only mean one thing, and Sean was hoping for once Old Los Angeles would surprise him.

It didn't.

8

He remembered every detail of that morning, which was the worst of his life up to that point. The morning was cool and damp, eerily calm and quiet. Bundling Winnie up, he placed her into the car, buckled her in the car seat, and drove her the fifteen miles to the gas station. Winnie had fallen back to sleep during the ride, so she was blissfully unaware of the goings-on at the station. Not Sean though; he could see it all.

Three gang members were harassing Michelle. They had set the whole building on fire and were now tossing Michelle from punk to punk, pulling at her, slowly and torturously stripping off her clothes. These kinds of events were on the rise everywhere across America, especially in the old cities, which time had cast off into practical lawlessness.

Sean could feel his anger building inside.

If anything ever happens to my two girls, I'll go insane, he thought, but secretly he knew he was already there.

Wasting no more time, he grabbed the tire iron always kept in the backseat for protection. The gang members had Michelle pushed to the ground, and she screamed for help. No one else was coming to the rescue as far as Sean could tell. It was up to him alone to save her from the impending rape or murder. With the cold metal in his hands, he felt the strength of conviction solidify inside of him. He loved Michelle, and no one was going to hurt her ever again.

The leader of the three men was on top of her. It was going to be his turn first. He clearly was the one that needed to be taken out. With a quickening step, Sean descended upon him. One swing down on his head with the tire iron, then another, and another! The leader fell sideways off Michelle. Blood squirted in sprays all over the surrounding area. The pavement was covered with blood spatter; Sean could feel the heat of the blood against his skin, but he did not stop. He kept hitting the leader over and over until the man's face was a mass of pulp. Hit after hit, he could feel bones crushing below him, but Sean would not stop until he knew the man could never harm another soul.

"Get that slag, Bruiser!" the littlest of the gangbangers yelled.

That's when Sean turned and saw a man bearing down on him, who grabbed his arms from behind. From the gangbanger's grip alone, he could tell why they called him Bruiser. Though Sean was outmuscled, his adrenaline would not let him be overtaken. Without losing a step, he turned sideways and swung the tire iron down again, right into the nose of the man called Bruiser.

"Ahhhhhh!" Bruiser shrieked out in pain. Blood poured from his nose like it were a stuck pig. "Willy!" the big brute cried out, and that's when the little man stepped forward.

He was short, with long hair and a spike collar. His face was painted a pale sheen, and his lips were adorned with purple-glitter lipstick. The look of this man's face alone made Sean sick. He wanted to kill him. Willy had other plans.

Slowly the gangbanger unsheathed a long knife and twirled it in his hand. From his movements, Sean could tell this Willy knew how to use the blade.

"Well, come on then!" Sean exclaimed.

"You know what I call this thing, Slag?" Willy asked in a snarky tone.

"Do I care?" Sean replied, hoping to set the gangbanger's emotions loose so he could take him down.

"Impaler. And it's earned its name, I can tell you that."

"Show me," Sean said, gripping the tire iron even tighter.

That's when a cry from the car broke his glare. When he heard it, he turned to see what Winnie was crying about. The bigger gangbanger, Bruiser, was reaching into the car, trying to grab the girl.

No! thought Sean. *Not Winnie!*

He began to run toward the car. Bruiser had Winnie in his hands and tossed her to the hard pavement.

"Come on, Willy!" Bruiser screamed. "Let's get the hell outta here!"

Willy let out a laugh and ran toward the car, which screeched over to meet him halfway. Before Sean even knew what was happening, the two punks were off, driving into the sunrise. By now, though, all he could hear was Winnie's cries. Slowly walking toward her, he was cut off by Michelle, who clutched her daughter tight.

"Stop!" screamed Michelle. "Don't come any closer."

"Are you okay?" Sean asked.

"You killed him."

"He was attacking you."

"I provoked him, Sean. He was my new dealer. I couldn't pay up, and I promised to let him take it out of me another way. But then I scratched him, you see ..."

"I don't care what the reasons were," Sean stated. "I did this for you."

"I wanted him to kill me!" she cried. "I'm tired of this life. I wanted to die!"

"I'm glad he didn't."

"Winnie would have been yours," she said under tiny sobs.

"I'm sorry."

"You have blood all over you."

"It was all for you," Sean reiterated.

"Leave us alone, Sean. Just stay away!"

It was at that moment Sean heard the sirens in the distance. Despite the chaos surrounding him, he looked at himself in the glass of the gas-station doorway. He looked like a monster. Covered in blood from head to toe. Never in his life had he been afraid of his own reflection ... until now.

Michelle had every right to be scared.

The rest was history.

9

So here it was, 201 days into his seven-year sentence, and it was the night of the White Light.

As the late-night and early morning hours ticked away, it was all Sean could do to keep himself from falling asleep and popping his arms out of their sockets. Sean kept replaying these painful memories over and over, in hopes that the hurt would keep him awake long enough to prevent any serious damage to his arms—or perhaps the guard might return and free him.

Fat chance in hell of that, thought Sean.

All he needed was the sun to rise, so there would be a shift change and the roll call would be taken again. Then he would be freed. However he wasn't sure he could make it that long.

What time is it? Sean tried to figure it out, but he couldn't be sure. Time went slowly in Milford Penitentiary on a good day; hanging on a wall like he was only made the time stand completely still.

It's too bad, Sean thought, *that Milford Pen doesn't have clocks.*

As Sean hung there, his legs beginning to wobble, he could suddenly sense that something was happening outside the walls of Milford. An uncharacteristic silence descended on Milford as Sean lifted his tired head and strained neck to see what was happening. All he could see was a strange flash of white light quickly illuminate the hallway, casting shadows across the walkways of the bars from the windows. Just as quickly as he saw the light, the white flash was gone, and everything went dark again.

Though not quiet.

Milford was abuzz with noise from the inmates, all asking each other what they had just seen.

"Hey." Sean strained to call out to the man in the next cell. "What's going on?" It took all the energy he had left to say even that.

There was no immediate answer, though, and Sean didn't need one. The door of his cell started to shake violently, suddenly cracking and bending in jagged directions. Sean was shocked when the door broke completely in half, revealing the metal bars that reinforced the door. Even the ceiling, which was eight-inch-thick rows of cinder block, began to crumble. Screams started to come from the other inmates as chunks of ceiling fell in the common hallway between the cells.

"Help!" Sean yelled as he saw some of the inmates free of their cells running in all directions. One would think they would simply run for their lives or help others still trapped in their cells, but not in Milford. Instead, many took the opportunity to get even with others that they felt had done them wrong.

With another violent shake, the Milford Pen further fell to pieces. Sean could feel the fear inside now. The building was going to collapse, and he realized he had to get out or he was dead. Summoning all his strength, he started to pull with his arms at the cuffs holding him to the wall.

Everything's falling apart, he thought. *If I can just shake these cuffs free* … As he pulled, he could feel his shoulders tearing, the muscles inside popping with every move.

"Uhnnnnn!" he screamed out in pain.

All the same he couldn't stop; he had to fight through the pain.

After a few more minutes, much shaking, and even more pain, Sean had somehow pried himself free of the wall. His arms fell to his sides like the trunks of dead elephants. Thankfully, the door to his cell was wide-open now, and he could easily squeeze through; if he had had to use his arms to pry them open, he would have just let himself be trapped. Squeezing through (thankfully he was skinny), he found himself out in the hallway of the jail among the crazy jungle of people that comprised the Milford inmates. Dodging fighting men and collapsing infrastructure, Sean ran for what he assumed might be an exit. It was a large crack in the main wall of the building. As he arrived at the large chasm, he could see other inmates escaping out of it. He climbed over the wall, grimacing in pain with every pull of his arms. He had no choice but to use them.

Finally exiting into the morning sky, Sean could see the sun just peeking over the horizon, and in the distance he could have sworn he saw the burning horizon of Old Chicago. Suddenly, though, he was blinded. Another burst of bright white light encompassed the grounds around him.

"Oh, my God!" was the last remark Sean remembered making before he was blown back into the ruins of the jail. The wind that pushed him was the strongest Sean had ever felt.

Aiden

1

Aiden awoke to find himself in the basement of the clinic. It was dark, and only the pallid yellow of the emergency lighting helped him make out his surroundings. The doctor was there, as well as some nurses and other patients. Trying to fight the fog from his mind, Aiden shook his head, but this only introduced throbbing pain into his scenario as the cuts on his face all began to ache.

"Shhhh," he heard a woman's voice say. "Don't move too much; your stitches could come undone."

"Who are you?" Aiden struggled to ask through the gauze he realized was wrapped all around his face.

"I'm Nurse Ellen. You met me yesterday morning. Before your surgery. But shhhh," she insisted again. "Let me get the doctor, and he'll explain everything."

Quickly Nurse Ellen walked away. Aiden thought she seemed worried. Like something was wrong.

Oh, god, he thought. *They botched the surgery!* Aiden knew he shouldn't have gone to some seedy clinic to do this.

But it's something else, he reasoned. *Why are we in such a dark, dank room?*

As he finished these thoughts, Nurse Ellen returned, followed by a man he recognized immediately. It was his doctor. The man who performed his surgery. To Aiden, he looked grim.

Oh no, Aiden thought, *here comes the boom.*

Stepping into the yellow light, the doctor leaned down to him and smiled.

"How are we then?" he said in a tone that, despite the fact the doctor appeared to not have shaved or showered in several days, seemed altruistic and calm.

"Uhm," Aiden said as he tried to think how he was, "pain ..." was really all he could say.

"Mmmmm," the doctor added. "I'm sure. You've been in a medically induced coma for several days now, and you're probably feeling the swelling. Due to our situation, I'm afraid we haven't been able to ice down the wounds."

What is going on? Aiden thought and wanted to ask, but he didn't have to wait long for an answer.

"Aiden," the doctor said, "I'm afraid I've got some bad news. America has seemingly been attacked. To escape harm, we all retreated down to the basement, which is lined with lead walls. This is the only thing that saved us from certain death in the blast."

"Oh," was all Aiden could say in return.

2

The first time Aiden had met the doctor, they were in a bar hidden in one of San Francisco's seedier districts. The old cities were all split into districts that surrounded the government-built tenements. Aiden lived outside of town; he had some wealth, and he preferred to avoid coming into the city. Many outsiders lost their lives making a visit through the overrun cities, but Aiden's good friend, Witton Zaitchik, insisted they come.

"Wait until you meet the doctor!" Zaitchik said with his strong Brooklyn accent. Aiden could never understand why he still had it. The man, like Aiden, was in his fifties and had lived in California for almost thirty years, but for some reason he never lost that accent.

"He'll change your life," Zaitchik continued, "just as he's changed mine."

A few months earlier, Zaitchik had "work" done. In the old days, this would have been considered normal, but in 2063 plastic surgery was illegal. A law had been passed in 2052 that said no unnecessary surgeries were allowed; it was too taxing on the overflowing and broken hospital system. Even if a surgeon had his or her own clinic, most were drafted and sent overseas to help the war effort, so surgeons either liked to be a part of a hospital to avoid having to go to the front lines or they were shipped off as punishment for trying to go into business for themselves. As it turned out, the doctor had an underground clinic hidden somewhere outside of San Francisco. However, to keep it hidden, he never met anyone at the clinic directly, and he never had a real meeting discussing the surgeries. Hence, the black-market meeting in the bar.

"I mean, look at me!" Zaitchik added. "He took at least ten years off."

Aiden realized Witton had a point. The last time he had seen Zaitchik, he had been thirty pounds overweight, with deep lines on his brow and around his mouth as well as his eyes, and had a double chin working on a triple. Now he looked as thin as a man half his age who worked out regularly, and his skin was smooth and tight again. The only thing Aiden could say was still wrong with Zaitchik was the fact he couldn't talk quietly. As they sat in the bar, Aiden couldn't help but worry others could hear their conversation. Witton was practically yelling at the top of his lungs. Aiden knew his friend liked to speak in exclamation points, but this was over the top even for him. All they needed was one person to turn them into the police about a black-market surgical deal, and they would be put in jail for a long time.

"I understand," Aiden reassured his friend. "I'm here, aren't I? Just do me a favor and keep the discussion down a bit."

Zaitchik suddenly realized how loud he was talking. His eyes opened wide as he gave a sheepish smile. "Sorry ... I'm just excited for you. It's gonna change your life."

Furthermore Zaitchik would know. Friends and coworkers since the old days, Witton had been Aiden's agent when he was a movie star. Across the world, people had seen his face plastered across huge cinema screens, and his celebrity was used to sell all sorts of products—cologne, cars, even watches—but that was years ago, when Aiden was both young and an Adonis. Unlike many men, he hadn't aged gracefully. His looks had faded into crusty, middle-aged-man allure, where people now came up to him and asked, "Hey, weren't you ...?" or said, "I know you!"

Aiden couldn't even remember the last time he was bombarded by a group of women wanting his autograph or his body. No longer was he the "Sexiest Man Alive," as magazines once proclaimed. That was before, when Hollywood was still the most powerful American industry. Since then, Hollywood had been banished from the country for its lewd and lascivious behavior—not to mention its political beliefs—leaving anyone who didn't want to leave the country to reinvent themselves.

Which was exactly what Aiden did.

Despite winning an Oscar for best actor, making millions in endorsement deals, and enjoying his status as America's leading man, Aiden decided to give up "the life." Moving to Australia and reestablishing Hollywood just didn't appeal to him. In addition, between all the backstabbing, drugs, and odd religions associated with the moviemaking community, he found he had little desire to continue.

Now, though, Aiden supposed it had been the wrong decision.

I'd still be a star if I'd have gone!

Still his fate was what it was, and Aiden was always good at adapting. When he first came to Hollywood and met a young and energetic Witton Zaitchik, who told him to change his name from Melvin O'Rourke, he did it. When the producers of his first film told him to dye his hair from red to blond, he did that as well. Even after Hollywood fell and he needed to find a new life, he adapted to the Hollywood hate by becoming a government spokesperson against the arts. This allowed him to avoid being investigated for un-American activities.

When at long last his time as a representative ended, he moved to the mountains outside of San Francisco, to a town filled with rich Los Angelenos and San Franciscans. They were refugees, trying to continue their affluent lifestyles in a country that was slowly pushing the rich out. The town was called New Los Cisco, and to see it, one would have never guessed it was part of the third-world country called the United States. There, Aiden became a preservationist for the forests around the town, something he could never have seen himself doing before. Which was the whole point to adaptation: change.

At fifty-four, even his body adapted. Due to his outdoorsy lifestyle, he looked rough around the edges, as if tree branches and sandpaper were what he used to buff and exfoliate himself. This was why Witton suggested he meet with the doctor. It was a final effort to return Aiden to his former glory.

3

The day after the Attack of the White Light, the doctor ordered Nurse Ellen to try to take Aiden on a walk around the basement. The best part of this was the fact that they removed the catheter. Aiden finally felt free again. As they shuffled, Aiden took in the sight of their new home.

Buried belowground, the room had no windows; it had lead walls faced with sheet metal, and metal shelves and gurneys. A few other patients slept on these, recovering just as he was.

What a messed-up situation, Aiden thought. *What the hell are we going to do?*

As they walked, Aiden reached his hand up to his bandages. His face itched, and he wanted nothing more than to remove the gauze so he could have at it. Just as his fingers began to tug at the wounds, Nurse Ellen's gentle touch pushed his hands back down to his side.

"No touching," she said. "It won't heal right if you don't let it be. We accept nothing less than perfection."

How can they even care? Aiden wondered. *The world is destroyed.*

However, they did care, and between the doctor, Nurse Ellen, and the other nurse—Cindy—the three did all they could to keep the patients and themselves alive. Every hour everyone was forced to stay hydrated by drinking half a bottle of water. These bottles were plentiful, as the doctor had stocked up his clinic for the patients. They also had small snack foods and protein drinks, so for at least the immediate future, they could sustain themselves.

"When those run out," the doctor said, "we have saline drips we can use."

"How long do you think we will need to stay down here?" Aiden asked.

"Not sure. But we need to be prepared for a long time."

Aiden began to think about this. Somewhere he had once read that radiation from a nuclear missile attack could remain dangerous in an affected area for more than fifty years. As far as Aiden could tell, they would run out of food and water long before that. Unless they were able to leave this basement-turned-bunker, they would quickly dehydrate or starve to death.

What are we going to do? Aiden wondered, but didn't ask anyone.

"At least we are safe from the radiation down here," the doctor told them all. "These walls are strong, and hopefully soon someone will be along to rescue us."

Aiden seriously doubted a rescue was in the offing. At any rate he was relieved they were protected from the fallout.

What he didn't realize, nor did anyone else for that matter, during the Attack of the White Light, a small crack, about three inches in length and half a centimeter wide, had been blown open along the right seam of the square basement. Very slowly, each person hiding in that basement was being poisoned by radiation.

4

"I can't believe it's you!" the doctor stated as he came to sit with Aiden and Witton Zaitchick at the small table in the corner of the bar.

Aiden was taken aback by this. He hadn't expected the doctor to be so starstruck nor young. The doctor was a perfect specimen. His jaw was strong and square, his features perfectly angled and sharp. He had long dark hair pulled back into a ponytail, which extended down his back between his shoulder blades, ending where they crested. His physique was what every man wanted and what Aiden used to have. If Aiden could look half as good as this man did after the surgery, he figured he'd be getting a good deal.

"Uhm," Aiden began, "it is."

They shook hands. The doctor had a strong handshake that conveyed complete confidence in his skills. Aiden could also tell his hands were steady and therefore good at the job they needed to perform.

"I'm a huge fan!" the doctor continued. "I loved watching your movies."

"No," Aiden said, "you're far too young for that."

"Am I?" the doctor tossed in.

What does he mean by that? Aiden wondered.

After a few drinks and some old Hollywood stories that made the doctor yearn for the old days of tabloid magazines and free Internet, Aiden decided to learn more about this mysterious surgeon.

"So, you know all about me," Aiden said. "How about telling us something about you? How did you become a surgeon?"

"You don't beat around the bush, do you?" The doctor laughed and took a drink of his beer.

"Well, if you're going to be operating on me, I think I deserve to know your experience."

"Don't be insulted by him," Witton broke in, trying to save Aiden from an awkward situation. "He's not trying to be mean."

Aiden was annoyed at this. He didn't need a rescue from his old agent. This wasn't an audition!

Was it?

"No, it's perfectly fine," the doctor replied. "I'd be asking the same thing. Especially these days. You hear all these horror stories about black-market surgeries."

"You mean butcherings," Aiden added.

"Touché." The doctor gave him a sly smile back. "Originally, I went to school and became a geneticist. When testing on genes was banned during the Religious Purge, I had to change my focus."

How could this man have been a surgeon during the purge? Aiden questioned. *He would have been, like, four years old!*

"So, I signed up to go to the front."

Impossible!

"Once there, my scientific skills and medical degree were called on for combat surgery." The doctor paused to take another drink. "There's no better way to perfect your surgical skills than in the middle of a battlefield or only miles away from falling bombs. If you can keep your hand steady under threat of death, you can keep your hand steady for anything."

"Excuse me," Aiden broke in. "I hate to be this way ... but how can this be? You've got to be like thirty-four. You're not old enough to have fought in the war."

The doctor smiled wide.

"I have a secret," he said. "I'm older than you."

5

Born in 1993 to Bridgette and Torrence Savage, Gregory Savage was raised like American royalty. Torrence Savage was the wealthy son of an oil tycoon and spent most of his life helping to run his family oil company, SAVCO, out of Bakersfield, California.

There, Gregory was given every opportunity. From kindergarten on, he went to an exclusive Catholic private school. After graduation, he was sent to Stanford, where he graduated top of his class, with a major in genetics and medical ethics. Then he went to med school at UCLA, where he spent years doing research. By 2033, he was off to war.

Doctor Gregory Savage told the two men that by the time he returned from overseas, America had completely changed. Hollywood was gone, and the medical industry was bastardized into what it was now. Learning from his father, he realized that being an entrepreneur was his best option. So, he formed his underground clinic. By day it posed as an aboveboard veteran recovery facility, and indeed he did have a few veterans among the patients to lend credence to that claim; however, by night it was a different story. Most of the business that frequented his establishment were people just like Aiden, looking to feel and look better than their ages.

Just for good measure, the doctor added that even some high-ranking government officials came to him for a secret nip or tuck.

For all that it was the next revelation that amazed Aiden completely.

6

"You want to know how much I trust myself in the work I do?" Dr. Savage asked. "You obviously see all the work I've had done on myself?"

"Of course," Aiden agreed.

And amazing work it was, he thought.

"I did it all myself," Savage added matter-of-factly.

"What?" Aiden couldn't believe his ears.

How could that be? That's insane!

"I don't trust anyone like I trust myself. It sounds gruesome, I'm sure, but I promise you it's not as bad as you think. All it requires of me is some local anesthetic, my full undistracted wits, and my highly qualified nurses. I only tell you this because I want you to know, with me, you get the best."

Aiden needed nothing else to persuade him to get the work done. A week later, he checked into the clinic, where he was greeted by Nurse Ellen and registered under an assumed name, which had the backstory of a vet recovering from facial wounds in battle. On November 2 at one thirty in the morning, he was put under for the facelift, hair transplant, and youthful reconstruction.

By the time he woke up on the third, the world had changed forever.

7

A week had passed since the attacks, and it was time to take off Aiden's bandages. He was scared, of course, but in truth, he was mostly relieved. He couldn't wait to be able to scratch his healing skin and have the full use of his facial features.

As they undid the bandages, he could feel the anticipation rising. With each unwrap of the gauze, he could feel his stomach lurch up and down, as if he were on a roller coaster.

What do I look like underneath it all? Aiden wondered. *Will I be a young man again?*

As the last bandage fell away, Nurses Ellen and Cindy smiled down at him.

"Oh my!" said Cindy, with a smile creeping along her face.

"One of your best, Dr. Savage," added Ellen.

The doctor slowly came into Aiden's focus. He smiled widely as well.

"It is. If I do say so myself."

With that, the doctor lifted a small hand mirror. The reflective side was turned away still, which was torture for Aiden. He couldn't take it anymore—he needed to see himself!

"Are you ready?" Dr. Savage asked.

"Yes ... please!" Aiden begged.

Slowly and steadily Savage turned the mirror toward Aiden. As his face began to reflect back at him, Aiden smiled. Despite the bruising and some minor swelling, Aiden couldn't have been happier with the results.

"So?" the doctor asked. "What do you think?"

Aiden thought a moment. What could he say?

Looking at his reflection, he was amazed at how youthful he looked, how smooth his skin, how full his hair ... it was all he could do not to shed a tear. Even with the world having blown itself up outside their four walls, there was only one word he knew to describe what he saw in the mirror: "Perfection."

Mark

1

Mark Fitzpatrick woke quietly, despite the acute electric pain shooting through his left side. Everything was dark, and the only sound he could make out was the dripping from some water—at least he hoped it was water. Trying to get his bearings, he turned on his side, but as he did this, he screamed out in even more pain. Whatever had him pinned down was also causing his whole left side to feel as if it were being ripped apart from the rest of his body.

"I'm trapped," he said out loud, while quickly turning his head from side to side, hoping someone was around to hear him. Was there even another person around when he had gotten trapped? He couldn't remember.

Suddenly a rush of memory hit his brain. He had been with Nell, his girlfriend, in her room. They had—but where was she?

"Nell?"

No answer. Just the creaking around him, like the house settling into its new collapsed position or preparing for one more death rattle. Mark hoped the house would put off its final collapse into pancake form long enough for him to escape.

"Nell?" His voice was more panicked now. She had to be alive. She had to be close.

"Mark?" He suddenly heard a weakened female voice. He could not tell where it came from, but he knew it well.

"Mark, it's Nell!"

"Where are you?"

"I can't tell. I can move a bit, but I'm surrounded by wall—"

Thank God, she's alive, he thought. However it seemed she was no better off than he was.

"Where are you?" she asked back.

With no better answer, he simply stated, "I'm stuck."

He shifted again to double-check his theory.

Pain!

It again zapped through his body, but this time he could tell it was his foot stuck under some kind of weight. With all his strength, he tried to tug his leg out, which only intensified the feeling of being ripped apart. Once more he screamed out in agony.

"Mark! Stop it, whatever you're doing. It's scaring me."

"It's scaring you?" he replied, but the comment was more to himself than to her. Taking deep breaths and trying to focus his mind, Mark could feel beads of sweat dripping down his face. With each tickle from each line of sweat, Mark began envisioning the ways in which he and Nell could die.

The house could explode from a gas-main break.

Infection could set in—dehydration—starvation.

Or something unimaginable he couldn't even think of. All he knew for sure was he needed to find help or they would die here.

"Nell?"

"Yeah?" He could tell she was frightened, but he knew Nell was strong. That was one of the reasons he loved her as much as he did. She was so different from the other girls at school. She did not need him; instead, it was he that needed her. Now, more than ever before.

"Listen. There is no way I can shake free. You have to help me!"

"But I don't know where I am!"

"We'll figure it out. Do it together. Are your parents around? Have you heard from them?"

"No. I'd been calling them awhile before you woke up, but they haven't said a word. Mark … I think they're dead."

"Nell, you need to stay focused. We will find your parents once we get free. They're probably looking for you as it is. Right now, though, I need you to try to find a way out."

"Okay." Her voice trembled.

"Okay," he repeated back to her. After a moment, he closed his eyes and prayed for the first time in his life.

Please, let there be a way out.

Nell

1

It was so dark Nell could barely make out the shape of things. As she concentrated hard on the area around her, she started to recognize aspects of her home among the destruction. There were the metal posts of her bed sticking up from broken slats of wooden floor, which were cracked and jutting out in angles that a floor should never go: up. She could also make out what was left of her back wall. The flower wallpaper was now torn away from it, leaving only bare stucco broken beneath. Pictures and clothes were also strewn around—some frayed, torn, or eviscerated, while some looked as clean as they had before the collapse.

What Nell was not seeing, however, was a way out. She started crawling forward toward what was left of her window, the same one that had just that night led to the trellis. Ducking down to avoid the collapsed ceiling—or was it wall? It was hard to tell at this point—she got below the area where the window now hung. Broken glass was everywhere. Small shards, as well as big stalagmite-shaped pieces, blocked her every move. Just avoiding the glass was going to make getting out through the window impossible. However, once she was able to see out of it, she saw the real problem. She could see no light through the window.

Nell assumed it was day beyond the rubble, unless they had been unconscious a lot longer than she thought. It could be night, she guessed, but that would mean they were unconscious more than twelve hours, and her body certainly wasn't hungry or thirsty. Of course, she realized she was probably in shock, so who knew how her body was reacting to that? Hunger and thirst might just not be important issues for her body at the moment. More likely, though, the window was buried under rubble as well—leaving no possible exit.

"See any way out?" Mark called from some distant point that could have been to her left or right. In this chaotic environment, direction was completely lost. This ruin was her house, but at the same time, was some new form that was completely unfamiliar to her. It made figuring out her bearings almost impossible.

"Not yet!" she yelled back to Mark.

"Keep looking."

She nodded, knowing he couldn't see her, but she had to respond in some way, even if it were only for her own benefit. Nell took a deep breath, surveying what was around her. She coughed out the dusty air from her lungs. Breathing was getting tougher, which could only mean one thing: oxygen was beginning to run out.

Great, she thought. *One more problem to add to the pile.*

That's when she noticed it.

Dust.

Floating in small streams of light through the air. The streams of light were tiny, and rounded as they came through circular holes in the collapsed stucco wall. Still, light from the outside it was. Which meant beyond that wall was a way out. She crawled to it, carefully maneuvering around whatever wreckage stood in her way—broken furniture, wood, pipes, all of it made for a formidable obstacle course.

Sticking her hand into the stream of light, she could feel the warmth of the sun. It was almost burning into her skin, as if this ray of light were from a giant magnifying glass. She remembered doing that trick as a child. Burning holes in leaves, watching as they charred up and disintegrated into nothing. For a brief moment, Nell wanted to burn up into nothing. However, she knew she had a task to complete, and feeling sorry for herself would only complicate the issue. Besides, she wasn't that kind of girl.

In the next moment, with all the might she could muster, she pushed her body up against the upside-down wall. Cracks started spreading out all over its face, and increasingly light quickly came streaming in.

Escape was in her grasp.

Mark

1

It's taking too long, Mark thought.

Nell wasn't answering his cries, which worried him. He had heard a loud cracking sound not too long before, and since then, Nell was nowhere to be found.

How long has it been—ten, fifteen minutes?

He was losing track of time, dipping in and out of consciousness; the pain was just too great for him to stay awake. His body was going into shock. Through Mark's days as a scout, he knew he had to stay awake to survive. Cold, however, was coursing through his body, signaling it might be only a matter of minutes before he fell into an even deeper, more permanent kind of sleep. Mark figured this had to be because he was losing blood somewhere. There was no other explanation, which in turn made him wonder just how badly his leg was injured.

Well, at least I won't die a virgin, he chuckled to himself, while feeling a twinge of guilt and anger for even thinking such a thought. *Hopefully Nell wasn't killed trying to save me.*

Another loud cracking sound was heard, from above this time.

"Hello?" he called out, hoping to hear Nell answer back.

Another cracking sound rang out. Even louder! Dust fell upon his face; he dodged and spat it away from his mouth. The whole room was shaking around him as countless clangs and bangs sounded out around him. The sound was deafening as the cavernous area he was caught in made everything echo and increase in volume.

"This is it," he said out loud, expecting the whole structure to fall and squish him like a grape. Instead, light broke in from above.

To Mark's eyes, the light was shocking. He squinted as silhouetted forms looked down at him from above. At once he was both relieved and scared. Was this real, or some kind of pain-induced mirage? His delirium made it impossible to discern a difference. Either way, though, he was happy they were there. Several of the darkened forms came down into his cavernous space; one was the most pleasant of sights he could ever imagine seeing.

"I did it," Nell said, kissing him.

"I knew you could." He smiled weakly.

With his eyes adjusting to the light, he could see two older men, haggard and bloody but seemingly no worse for wear. They were now staring down at his foot. Both men's eyes conveyed to Mark all he needed to know.

Don't look! Don't look! Don't look! he repeated over and over in his head, but he couldn't help it. He had to see.

Mark's foot was crushed between a large chunk of ceiling and wall; he could see his anklebone, white as snow, peeking out of pale, brown, torn flesh. His foot was turned in a direction completely opposite from his leg, which was no longer attached to his foot at all. He hadn't been trapped, unable to move; it was quite the contrary. He was unable to move because his foot had been severed, and he was losing blood quicker than water ran from a faucet.

Mark should have screamed out in pain, or at least thrown up from the sight of his now-deformed leg, yet all he could say was …

"That's not good."

Annette

1

Annette could tell she was one of the lucky ones.

In her three days of wandering since the trailer was destroyed, she had seen so many disturbing things they were seared in her memory for life. Whole towns wiped out, dead bodies strewn all around, some not even in one piece anymore, while others just seemed to have disintegrated, leaving only shadows behind where they stood. Furthermore, it seemed only handfuls of survivors were to be found, most barely living themselves.

Annette had taken to calling them *the living ghosts.*

These living ghosts were mostly wandering around the ruins of their lives, practically catatonic, unable to so much as help themselves. Annette's first encounter with one came only hours after she had awakened post-destruction. Gathering herself, she had decided to walk east. Looking back toward the West revealed a view of the coastal Pacific that did not look particularly inviting. Orange plumes of smoke were spreading across the horizon, while sandstorms seemed to swirl all around, making the sky a pale brown gray. As far as she could see, Old Los Angeles was lost in a haze of smoke and fire, while the northern and southern directions didn't appear much better.

I guess beachfront property won't be a sought-after commodity for a while. She laughed to herself.

So, to her, the areas east seemed far more hospitable. Wasting no more time, she moved in that direction.

Going as fast as she could, which wasn't that fast, she managed to walk about twenty miles the first day. Despite her aching head, bruised body, and shaken emotional state, Annette found she was able to push herself forward. Something deep inside her said, "Just keep moving." Even with thoughts about her children and grandchildren swirling around her head, it was clear she had no way of trying to locate them. If they survived, she would have to hope fate might bring them together at some point in the future. Until then, Annette realized, she had to take care of herself. Which was how she came upon her first meeting with a living ghost.

Needing to find shelter for the night and hopefully some water and food, Annette stopped at the first town that wasn't flattened like a pizza. It was a town behind a mountain ridge just on the outskirts of the Mojave. Due to its positioning, it had sustained what seemed like only superficial damage. Some houses were indeed broken apart, but other than that, it seemed people might have survived. So, with the sun setting and a fear of wild animals that might be scavenging due to the blood on the air, Annette entered the town.

It was eerily quiet and dark. Electricity was clearly down, and if there were other survivors, they weren't rolling out the welcome mat for her arrival. Trying not to trip on any fallen debris, Annette kept her head up, trying to stay aware of her surroundings. That's when she spotted it.

A bonfire!

Its orange flames reached high into the sky. Smoke was filling the air and giving off a foul stench she couldn't place, but it was choking the back of her throat. She walked toward it.

"Hello!" Annette called, scared someone might answer.

Who knows what they will do? she thought.

However there was no answer back, just the sound of the wind and the crackling fire. Despite this and her growing sense of dread, she cautiously moved forward. Turning the corner, she came upon the bonfire, and to her complete horror, she saw what was being used for kindling ...

Corpses!

About to scream, she stopped herself when she noticed a couple people standing by and watching the bodies burn.

"Hey!" she called out. Still they didn't answer. She could make out that the people watching were a woman in her thirties and a man in his sixties. Annette wondered if they just couldn't hear her over the sound of the roaring fire. She approached them cautiously.

When she was only feet away, the two survivors still didn't look in her direction.

"My name's Annette," she offered. "I need a place to stay. Can you help me?"

Neither person said anything or even so much as gave Annette an acknowledgment of her presence.

"Please, I'm a survivor, just like you!" she pleaded, but all they did was stare at the burning bodies. Taking a few awkward steps backward, Annette tried to figure out what was going on.

If they can't talk to me, or even function, who collected all these bodies and set the blaze?

Just then a hand grabbed her shoulder from behind. She let out a scream and turned to face the attacker. A group of three other survivors stood there, soot covering their faces and hands, as well as blood and who knew what else.

"Stay back," she said.

"You've come to join us," one of the men said in a tone that was at once tired and sad, but also as if he were in some kind of trance.

"I'm a survivor," Annette added. "I was lookin' for a place to stay."

"You can stay with us," the man offered. "We're all going to be together again."

"All?" Annette squeaked out over the sinking feeling in her gut.

"Why, yes," the man answered calmly. "We are joining our friends and loved ones—won't you jump in with us?"

With that the man jumped into the bonfire, screaming in agony as he burned.

"Oh, my God!" was all she could say as the other two men grabbed her arms. "Let me go!" she exclaimed as she kicked and flailed to get loose.

Gotta get free, she told herself, *and help these other people. They can't* want *to do this.*

With all her might, she shook the two men off her arms. They clumsily fell to the ground, almost pulling her down with them. Not waiting another second, she ran to the woman who was staring at her fate in the fire.

"Come on!" Annette yelled at her. "You can't possibly do this! This can't be what you think is the answer."

Still the woman didn't stir. Turning back, Annette saw the two men who grabbed her. They were up on their feet now, only inches away from their fiery deaths.

"It's okay," one said to her. "Let them do it. Let us all do it! We have nothing more to live for. We're all that's left." With that he jumped in, as if he were sacrificing himself to some ancient god. Quickly he was followed by the other. Now all that remained were the woman and the older man. Annette turned her attention on him.

"Come with me," she begged, and suddenly his eyes moved in her direction.

"I ... I can't ..." he said. "They're ... all ... dead!" Tears burst from his eyes as his body convulsed in agony. "My whole family is gone—my children, my grandchildren ... I have to go!"

"I have children and grandchildren too!" she said to the man. "I'm hurting too. But this ... this is insane!"

He smiled at her. It was a sad smile, the smile of a man who had lost everything and now wanted nothing but to lose himself as well.

"I'm sorry," was all he said before joining the others.

With the man screaming in pain, Annette closed her eyes. She couldn't believe what was happening. Still, Annette had a chance to help.

She had to get the woman to respond!

Turning back to the lost soul, Annette grabbed hold of her shoulders.

"Listen!" Annette screamed. "This is not worth it! You can have another life! We all can! There has to be another way!"

In the woman's eyes, Annette could see tears welling up. They fell out the corners, leaving clean, wet trails on her face, where ash had been. Annette realized she was beginning to reach her.

"What's wrong with you? Pull yourself together!" and with that, Annette slapped her. Finally, a response! The woman blinked, and then her eyes went wide. With a glass-shattering, high-pitched scream, the woman finally let out a reaction. Holding tightly, Annette let her fall to the ground and cry out her agonies.

This was the first survivor Annette collected.

2

That night, the two slept in what used to be the woman's home. Annette came to find out that her name was Marcy, and her husband and two children had died during the White Light.

"Most of the town did," Marcy explained. "We were hit by winds that toppled our homes and brought gaseous poison on the air. Right after the attack, most of the town came together at the square, where you found us. This was a town ordinance in case of an earthquake. That way, all could be accounted for. It was one of the perks of living in a small town. Apparently the violence of the wind and the rumbling of the ground had opened up a crack below them all. It contained methane. They all died before they even knew what hit them."

"How were the five of you saved?" Annette pried, though she didn't want to push it.

"We were too slow arriving. That was it. We were just late."

For another hour, Marcy cried until she fell asleep in Annette's strong arms.

It was this night that Annette realized she was stronger than most. Which to her meant she would have to do whatever was necessary to ensure her survival and that of anyone else she came across.

3

Despite Annette's newfound determination to stay alive, it was sobering to see just how few people were left in California. California had been a state overrun with people. Between those who had fled the big cities and the many, many refugees from Mexico and other South American countries, it had been a long time since California had vast areas of low population.

Now, though, after the White Light, it was practically empty.

This shocked Annette from the start. When she awoke after being flung from her trailer three football fields into the distance, she saw a vision of flattened landscape. Where once there stood rows of portable homes, there now stood only destruction. Where once there were droves of people, three or four families stacked together, now there were only three or four people per forty square miles.

As Marcy and Annette fled the ruins of California, they picked up stragglers, each with a different story to tell but all with one special thing in common: they survived.

There was April from Gorman, who survived because her boyfriend was a firefighter and he owned a gas mask that he chose to put on her. Then Caleb from Needles, who swore up and down an angel came to deliver him from harm. Also, Ted, Milton, and Alice, all from Barstow, who survived by virtue of being in homes that were part of a new settlement and weren't surrounded by anything that could crush them. None of them were necessarily special, but none were ordinary either. Each person's life was a capsule of a time now gone, never to be seen again. Oddly enough, though, for some, that didn't seem a problem.

Out in the desert of California, in the vast and desolate Mojave, they came upon a man named Willy. He was odd, to be sure: his clothing was a hodgepodge of things he obviously collected on his journey, and his hair was shorn short as if he had just been in the military. His complexion was pale, and his neck had a line about an inch thick that was even paler, as if he'd been wearing some kind of collar around it. Completing the mystery was the fact that he didn't seem all that upset or disturbed by the world around him. Genuinely, he seemed full of energy and almost giddy about it.

At first, Annette and the group didn't know what to make of him. Which is why a debate whether he was to join them ensued.

"We don't know anything about him!" Milton said. He was older and a worrywart, so it was no surprise to Annette he took that position.

"So what?" Annette said back. "I don't know any of you, but that didn't stop me from saving your asses."

"Annette has a point," April added.

"What if he's dangerous?" asked Caleb.

"Then your God will protect you, won't he?" Annette struck back. She couldn't help but be annoyed at self-righteous Holy Rollers.

"I say we hear about how he survived," Marcy said. "Then decide if he should come with us."

"Oh, hell, no!" Annette erupted. "Do I have to be the only one here who can make a decision worth a spit? He's a survivor, just like us. My guess is he's a little off due to shock, just like we all were when we found each other … Marcy, must I remind you what you were going to do if I hadn't come along?"

"But—" Marcy tried to add, but Annette cut her off.

"He comes, and that's final," Annette proclaimed.

No one argued further.

With that she turned to Willy, who had been standing off a bit, next to a broken cactus, and simply said, "Welcome aboard."

4

At night everyone kept to themselves, not wanting to be too close to another human being. They were too scared they could be taken away at a moment's notice. Still, as the days went on, that changed. It could have been the realization that the few survivors around were all anyone had. Perhaps the sheer gruesomeness of each leveled town brought them closer together. Either way, this band of shell-shocked individuals became a small family. In a mutual, yet wordless, agreement, it was seemingly decided that none of them would speak of what their lives were before the disaster; it was simply too painful for them. Instead, they just found solace in each other's company.

For Annette, forgetting meant walking.

Day after day, from town to ruined town, she kept them on the move. As they went, they collected water from grocery stores and whatever canned foods they found. When they couldn't find any prepackaged foods in the towns, they took to learning how to hunt. As it turned out, Willy was a great hunter and knew how to use a knife.

"I named it Impaler," he told everyone in the group, which was disconcerting to say the least.

"Why?" asked Alice, who was as skittish as they came due to spending her adulthood alone with her cats, was frightened just by seeing it. Knowing it had a name seemed to be knowledge that might send her off the rails.

"Because I killed so many …" Willy paused, stopping himself from completing the remark.

Annette thought that weird … *killed so many what?* she questioned, but then let it go when he said,

"Animals. I love to hunt animals. So I named my knife to celebrate the way I kill them."

"You impale the animals?" Milton said with clear animosity.

"Yeah," Willy returned.

"Sounds good to me," Annette broke in, hoping to ease the tension. "How about you just hunt us down something so we can cook up some grub?"

He did just that. Somehow Willy would always find some kind of animal, be it rabbit, fox, or even snake. While the pickings were slim, as most of the animals were seemingly dead or hiding, it was enough to keep them going. Which was all Annette could ask for. Each day they rose with the light and wandered. Each night, they hunkered down as best they could, trying to stay warm despite the elements. Annette wasn't sure where they were going or what they would find, but as the gray skies began to spread, she realized they had to get as far away from the coast as possible.

The worst moment for them all came as they approached Edwards Air Force Base. Secret hope for them all had built inside as they knew they were getting close to it. That hope, though, was shattered when they saw that it had been obliterated by the attacks. Unable to get close enough due to the dust, wind, and radiation in the air, the search for clues as to what happened when the White Light attacked would have to wait. They moved around it, adding at least fifty miles to their trip. This revelation about the base set each survivor's mind ablaze. It didn't take long for rumors among the group to start about what exactly happened to America. As nights went on, it became a tradition around the campfire every night to discuss these theories.

"I swear I saw a nuclear missile fly right over my house!" said Ted, who had fought in France during the Fifty-year War against the Muslim extremists. From what Annette could tell, he was always seeing and hearing missiles or bombs. It could have been from some kind of post-traumatic stress, but she didn't ask.

"I think it was China," Milton added. "They could easily have called in our debt to them, and when we couldn't pay up, decided to nuke us!" This was plausible, Annette figured, but she wasn't one for being up on political maneuvering and therefore had no idea if that was what really happened.

"Or aliens!" said Alice. "I was abducted once, and they said it was only a matter of time before they attacked earth and took it over."

Most of the survivors just let that one go, for like her namesake, Alice was quite often off in Wonderland.

"Whatever it was, President Mitchum probably has counterattacked by now," Marcy added. "He is one of the best presidents this country has ever seen. He was putting us back on top, and there is no way he would have allowed us to be attacked and not respond."

At this, Willy just laughed. Annette could tell he wasn't one for authority. So far, he hadn't been a problem within the group, but she knew it might only be a matter of time. She hoped she was wrong.

"My bet is it was a computer," Willy opined one night. "Some defense computer that malfunctioned and decided to destroy humanity."

"Oh, like in that movie!" Milton agreed.

"What movie?" Willy said obstinately.

"Never mind."

Could a computer come to life and decide to destroy humanity? Annette wasn't sure. What she was sure of, however, was that the world would never be the same.

5

During their third week of walking, they arrived at a sign that read, "Welcome to Nevada." It hung down to one side, torn off from its post. It only remained upward because of one bolt loosely holding it on. In the distance, they could see the gray and orange remnants of a smoke cloud still spreading across the state.

"Was that Vegas?" Ted asked.

"I think so," Annette replied. "Best to avoid big cities. Let's move south. Hopefully there's less desert that way."

"That's a bad move!" a man said as he suddenly popped out from behind a boulder along the side of the road. Willy quickly had Impaler out, and everyone in the group was in full protective mode. "Sorry," he said. "I didn't mean to scare you."

The man, who had his hands up to signal he was unarmed, stepped forward. He was tall, around six foot one, African-American, and from his style of dress, a well-manicured man. Even if by now those fancy clothes were dirty.

"Who are you?" Annette asked.

"The name is Frank. I'm from southern Nevada. I've been making my way north; everything below here is wasted. Too many secret military installations, I guess. They were all destroyed in whatever mess did this as well."

"I should kill you for surprising us like that!" Willy yelled at the man, but Frank barely blinked.

"Shut up, Willy," Annette admonished. She could see out of the corner of his eye he wasn't happy about her remark, but he listened anyway. "So, Frank, how can we help you?"

Frank smiled. "Well, your group is one of the first I have come along, believe it or not. I'd be lying if I said I haven't been lonely. I got here maybe thirty minutes before you did, and when I saw you coming up the road, I hid. Not sure what kind of people you were ... But now that I see you're pretty decent, I'd like to ask if I can join you."

Willy lashed out. "Hell no! We got enough as it is."

"Willy, please," Annette added. "Just put the knife away."

Willy looked at her questioningly. "But ..."

"We let you in, didn't we?" Annette pointed out, and then turned back to Frank. "You stick with us as long as you can. If you fall behind, we leave you there. Got it?"

"Got it."

Frank turned and grabbed a small bag of things he had with him. Joining the group, he walked right past Willy.

"Nice meeting you," Frank joked with him.

"Fuck you," Willy responded.

6

Snow began falling on day twenty of their trek across Nevada. Snow was usual in northern Nevada this time of year; however, Annette wasn't sure if it was from winter or the nuclear fallout that was spreading across the country. No matter what the cause, their pack of now twenty survivors had fallen on hard times. Food had become impossible to find, shelter just as obscure, and many were falling ill due to the cold. To Annette, it was clear they needed to find some sort of shelter for the rest of winter, or the idea of survival would become a pipe dream.

"Maybe we should stop," Marcy pointed out.

"And do what? Wait to die? We're sleeping under rocks and cactus. We stop here, we have no hope," responded Ted.

"Well, I don't know," Marcy said, defending her statement. "We just keep walking. Every day we see nothing. Why are we even still trying?"

"We keep walking because it's the best choice we have," Annette explained. "It's our best hope. Sitting still means we are giving in to death. The farther we walk, the better chance we have of survival. Look behind us!"

Everyone turned to take a look. Gray skies and darkness greeted them. That might have been expected in the winter, but it clearly wasn't normal—it was something else, like gathering death on the wind.

"That's the fallout, folks," Annette began again. "Right now, it's west of us, and the wind seems to be keeping it there. As long as the winds don't change, east is the best direction to go."

"But why can't we just build a life here?" Alice wondered. "Can't we just settle?"

Annette looked exasperated; she would have thought the reasons were obvious. For the first time since taking on this group of survivors, she found she had nothing more to say.

"Because," Frank chimed in, "there are no resources here. No animals to kill or water source. When was the last time you heard of people trying to make a go of it in a desert? History has shown us the best place we can hope for is a place with fresh water and abundant food."

"What if that place doesn't exist anymore?" Milton blurted out.

"Then we die trying to find it," Frank said emphatically. "It's better than sitting here waiting."

Everyone was quiet now.

Thank God for Frank, Annette thought, *a man with a mind.*

"I say we keep walking," Willy finally spoke up.

"I agree," said Frank.

"Let's walk then," Annette said, and then led on.

As they walked, Frank fell in line with Annette. She turned to him and smiled.

"Thank you," she said.

"No," Frank said, smiling back. "Thank you."

7

One late afternoon, some thirty-five days after the group first crossed the Nevada border, two months since the day that changed their lives, the survivors came through a mountain pass. Exhausted and starving, they looked down into a valley that concealed the greatest sight Annette had ever seen.

A town.

The town seemed lost in time; it was so peaceful, and untouched by world events. Annette smiled at her luck.

A sign down at the bottom of the ravine read: *Welcome to the Town of Bastion.*

How appropriate, thought Annette. *Just what we were looking for.*

This would be a perfect place to call home.

Mankins

1

The roar from the panicked 1,500 people was becoming deafening.

"Everyone, just calm down!" Chief Mankins screamed over the ruckus. "Just calm the hell down!"

When no one responded, he unholstered his gun, aimed it at the ceiling, and fired. Dust fell from the hole the gunshot produced. Mankins swung his hand over his shoulder, brushing it off. Quiet befell the crowd as the shock from the noise got their attention. Chief Mankins, a man small in stature, yet big in presence, stared out from the podium. Everyone was packed into the school gymnasium, sitting like sardines on the wooden bleachers. All their eyes were now transfixed on him. Which, in truth, was just the way he liked it.

"Now, if everyone will just shut up, maybe we can address some of these concerns," said Mankins.

It didn't work.

"What are we going to do about food?" one of the people from the crowd yelled out. It was Wilma Garrett, the loudmouthed librarian. Mankins always joked that she was as old as the town of Bastion itself and just as huge a landmass.

"Or electricity!" yelled another. This time it was William Cole, who owned the grocery store. "All the fresh food we do have is rotting in my store!" Overall, Mankins thought William was a good guy, but he couldn't help but notice that when the crap hit the fan, he became a pot stirrer.

Need to remember he's weak in a crisis, Mankins notated in his mind.

"And water?" said another one. This time it was that hippie chick, Louise, the on and off girlfriend of the Kershaw boy.

Is there a couple that poses more of a threat than the two of them?

Mayor Harlen Kreuk, a round, bulbous man with a greasy

complexion, stepped forward. He had been watching the scene unfold next to Chief Mankins and was still visibly nervous about the gunfire. With his hands shaking, he lifted them into the air, trying to assuage the crowd.

"If you'll all just listen for a moment and give the chief your attention, I am sure he will answer most, if not all, your concerns."

"Why did we vote *you* in then!" said a voice from the back of the bleachers. The smart-ass comment elicited a huge laugh from the crowd. Mankins was relativley sure it came from one of those troublemakers, Winston Deerdorff, Brooks Nolan, or Clifford Montgomery. While Mankins liked them well enough and certainly saw them as a help from time to time, right now was not one of those times. Mankins glared at the back of the crowd, hoping to spot them but was unable to.

Note to self, Mankins thought, *find those three dingleberries after the meeting and scare the shit out of 'em.*

"All right, everyone," Mankins broke in. "Get your laughs out, but I'm sure we are all here because we don't think this situation is really that funny."

People seemed to agree with this comment, and they began to settle down.

"Thank you," he added once the noise had dropped to a level he could deal with. "To answer some of the questions that have already been posed, we are setting up several generators at key sites around town, such as at your grocery store, William, and Dr. Sherriden's office ... and here at the high school. As for more supplies, we have two plans we will be enacting. First, we are looking for volunteers to go over the ridge and see if there are any stalled delivery trucks that were headed our way and to try to see what can be salvaged from around us. We are hoping some of the other towns that lay beyond the valley are still intact and able to open up supply lines. The second plan is to cultivate our local resources. We have animals in our woods, such as elk and deer, plus we have land that seems like it is rich in soil enough to grow food."

A hand rose in the crowd.

"Yes, Mitch?" The chief pointed at Mitch Mularky, one of the town assembly members. He always made Mankins uncomfortable, though Mankins could never figure why. Mularky was just too erudite for his liking.

"What about the Great Pestilence?"

"As far as we can tell, it has never been an issue on our land," answered Mankins. "My feeling is we should at least be able to grow some basics. How many people here have home gardens?"

Slowly about a quarter of the room raised their hands.

"Good," Mankins responded. "This leads me to believe that if we can all grow some food, we can feed ourselves."

Some of the townsfolk began to discuss this idea among themselves. From Mankins's point of view, it seemed that perhaps they were starting to see that things would be okay. Slowly another hand rose from the crowd. It was the one person Chief Mankins had hoped would keep his mouth shut.

Quentin Kershaw.

"Yes, Mr. Kershaw," Mankins said as he pointed to him, swallowing a deep-seated hatred as far down as he could.

"Do we actually know what happened?" Kershaw asked. Quentin had an intensity about him that Mankins abhorred. He was always pushing the envelope. To Mankins, this question was a perfect example.

How the hell would I know? was how the chief wanted to answer back. Instead he said, "We have tried to achieve radio contact with others around the country. Unfortunately all our electronics seem to be dead. We are not sure why—"

"Electromagnetic pulse," Quentin interrupted.

"Is that so?" Mankins stated back.

"It's in line with the evidence we have on hand," Quentin continued. "We were trained in the Army to know the signs of a nuclear explosion. That is one of them. I think it's time we all face the facts: America's been nuked."

The whole room erupted again.

That damn Kershaw, Mankins thought, *just like his father, spouting off his damn mouth without any knowledge of the truth!*

"Now just hold on there. Everyone, calm down!" Mankins could tell he was losing the room, and he didn't like it at all. "We don't know anything of the sort. If—and I mean *if* the country has been 'nuked,' as Mr. Kershaw has theorized, then we can assume the Army will have mobilized and will be sending help to communities just like our own. That is another reason we need to send a party down the mountain.

"It is true something happened. Obviously in the last twenty-four hours our electricity has died, our phones and computers have stopped working, even our normal services like mail have stopped. But we don't have any knowledge as to why. I didn't see any mushroom clouds, did you? Anything we say now would only be guesswork. We are so far removed from the rest of the country, so secluded, we need to wait this out and gather as much information as possible. Until then, you all need to put your faith and trust in me."

Nods of agreement spread around the room.

"Trust me," Mankins continued, "I won't let any harm come to Bastion. This is my town, and I mean to protect it—by whatever means necessary."

2

The town of Bastion is located in the Wind River Range of the US State of Wyoming. Surrounded by peaks of mountains on all sides, the highest of which is the tenth highest in Wyoming, Bastion is protected from the outside world. These peaks are part of the Rocky Mountains and run northwest to southeast, and Bastion lays claim to the southmost area of the mountain range.

Since the 1500s, Native Americans roamed this region, and some settled into the valley where Bastion now lies. It was a settlement site for them, and they would often summer by the lake. During one such period in the 1700s, the Shoshones planted a tree to memorialize the significance of the area to them. By the time the Lewis and Clark expedition found the valley in 1807, the tree had grown into a massive sight. The expedition was also struck by the habitability of the area, and they set up camp immediately. Gaining strength by the cool shores of the valley's lake, the Lewis and Clark expedition was able to rebuild strength for the rest of their voyage and continued to use the area as a base camp. In fact, Bastion's town founder, John Shields, left the expedition and settled the area, so that when Lewis and Clark needed it, they'd have a place to call home. He named the town Bastion, referring to the use of the valley for the expedition.

As exploration of the mountain ranges in the area continued through the 1800s, Bastion became a staging ground for many parties that were either climbing for recreation or studying the geology and ecology of the region. After Wyoming became a state on July 10, 1890, Bastion, which had a population of twenty-five people, became the key landmark in the Wyoming coal rush. As coal mines spread across the mountains, the population of Bastion rose to two hundred. This boom in Bastion's history lasted all the way through the Great Depression, as the natural resource of coal never waned.

The skiing industry also took notice of Bastion, and by the 1950s, the town had become a top destination for those who enjoyed great glades of downhill terrain. By 1960, the town's population rose to over a thousand. From there, it saw steady growth to fifteen hundred. Mostly the population grew from natural reproduction. During the twenty-first century, while the rest of America was descending into a new economic depression, overpopulation, and chaos, Bastion and most of Wyoming were spared these troubles as the state continued to be the least-populated in the union and therefore sustainable. Bastion and Wyoming survived on their abundance of natural resources like crude oil, the aforementioned coal, and even natural gas. Which is why when the Attack of the White Light occurred, Bastion was still an untouched relic of the American dream.

Built outward from the tree planted by the Shoshones all those years ago, Bastion extended in a circular fashion. Surrounding the tree, located in a courtyard, was Main Street. Splitting off from there, four streets separated the town into sections: north, east, south, and west. Each area became a neighborhood. The North side of the town became filled with businesses, the eastern one had homes for the working class, while the western area was filled with the high-class homes of the rich. The South became a main drag and was where the town met the lake.

Like most in Bastion, Chief Mankins was a tenth-generation Bastionite, meaning his sense of duty to the place was strong. It was also misguided, which was why the chief often did whatever he could to hold as much power as possible.

3

Mankins was unstable, which most of Bastion knew. Too often when a simple crime occurred, like shoplifting or jaywalking, Mankins would have the perpetrator arrested, stuck in jail for several days, and not allow them to have their one phone call. Mankins controlled everything about the release process. If bail were going to be set, it would be set at the price Mankins wanted, so he could grease his pocket. No one challenged his authority because, as rumor had it, he knew compromising information on almost everyone in the town. The mayor of the town, Harlen Kreuk, was widely known to hold no power in any major decision. All the decisions concerning law, order, justice, and liberty fell to one man: Chief Mankins.

Which is why when volunteers to go over the mountain weren't lining up, he was forced to use other tactics in securing a healthy number of citizens to conduct the search.

"Listen," Mankins said to Taylor Middlebrooks, the chief of the fire department, "we can't send people off by themselves. A town official must be with them."

"Why don't you go?" Middlebrooks offered up as a perfectly rational option. Middlebrooks was a strong man, physically fit, and the exact opposite of Mankins himself. Because of this, he made Mankins uncomfortable. He reminded Mankins of all his flaws.

They were sitting in the fire chief's office. Made of brick, the whole fire station was a classic red building, with two levels and a garage that held the one fire engine. It even had a pole that was in use, and not just for decoration. As Middlebrooks sat behind his desk, Mankins considered his options to force his hand.

"You know, Taylor, I considered it, I really did. However, I can't just abandon the town in its time of need."

"But I can?" Middlebrooks remarked sarcastically.

"Well, you have the search-and-rescue experience, you know the region, and as a civil servent, you owe it to the town to help in any way you can."

"Is that so?"

"You know it is."

"Well, I say no. I'm not going out there. It's suicide. We have no idea what is happening out there beyond the ridge." Middlebrooks stood and walked over to the window. He looked out and saw Main Street. People milled around, going from place to place, talking to neighbors as if nothing was wrong in the world. Unfortunately, it was the exact opposite.

"Taylor," Mankins said as he walked over to him, "I'm afraid you don't have a choice. You think I'm not prepared for this? You think I don't know about your little secret?"

"Who would care anymore?" Middlebrooks said. "The world is over."

"Not my world," Mankins said back. "Bastion will survive, even if I have to use every bit of information I have to ensure it. I can bring you down—you know that—and I won't hesitate to if you cross me."

Middlebrooks's secret wasn't that damaging as far as Mankins was concerned—he knew of worse, much worse in fact—but stealing money from the county to line one's own pockets instead of improving the Bastion fire department plagued Middlebrooks's mind, and he therefore allowed the chief to pull his strings.

"All right," Middlebrooks said. "I'll lead them over the mountain."

Chief Mankins never felt guilty about using his information. He saw his power grabs as nothing more than a way to ensure the safety of the people in Bastion. As a fan of history, Mankins often read up on the great law enforcers of the past. In his mind, he saw himself as a modern-day Jay Edgar Hoover, a man of lose morals but for noble reasons.

Once Taylor Middlebrooks agreed to lead the expedition, volunteers stepped up, so Mankins saw it as the ends justifying the means. Only two days after the meeting in the gym, the group of ten men went over the southern mountain pass.

4

The night of the expedition's departure, Mankins returned home, the stresses of the day casting a shadow upon his mood.

Just need to take my pills, Mankins thought. *They'll put me right.*

Mankins lived alone now that his wife had divorced him and taken their thirteen-year-old son with her. They had moved to a town outside of Massachusetts. It was where his wife was from. They had been gone since last summer, when the big drama went down, and he hadn't heard from them since. Mostly he couldn't have cared less about his ex-wife—she was a bitch, and they hadn't been close in years—but his son was a different story. Considering what seemed to have happened to the world, Mankins was sure he'd never see him again. This fact actually made him sad.

Entering his bathroom, Mankins opened the medicine cabinet. He grabbed the bottle of antidepressants. Pushing down the childproof top and twisting, he opened them. Pouring out four of the 100-milligram pills, he turned on the faucet and drank them down with the water.

I wonder how long this water will be pure enough to drink. Thank God for the lake, he thought.

Before putting the bottle back into the medicine cabinet, he took stock of the contents inside. There was maybe a day or two worth of pills left. Then he'd be out.

Are there even enough in town to get more? He wasn't sure. But whatever was left, he needed them.

For many years, Mankins wouldn't even consider taking pills. To him, those who took pills to ease their "emotional traumas" were wimps. As he saw it, life sucked, and there was no cure for it. One could turn to drink or drugs to help cope, but eventually, that would either further ruin one's life or kill a person.

No, Mankins decided, *no man-made vices for me!*

However, he knew plenty of other cops that drank or did drugs. It was only after the big drama, when he was put on administrative leave, that things began to change.

Which was all that bastard lawyer, Floyd Kershaw's, fault!

Kershaw, along with the state DA, had him investigated for police brutality. After he severely beat a transient to within half an inch of his life, the court gave him a simple order: take pills to help control his rage or leave office. He did as he was told. After all, if Mankins was honest, he did have one vice—*an overwhelming desire for power.*

Which to him was more intoxicating than any woman, drink, or drug. The idea of relinquishing it was the most repugnant thing Mankins could envision.

Pure hell on earth.

So, despite his misgivings, he followed through with the court order. In truth, once he was on the drugs, they made all the difference in the world. They calmed him ... took the edge off. Sure, they made his mind a little less focused, but even so, they made Mankins realize someone wasn't an enemy simply because he or she disagreed. True, it was all too late to save his marriage, but the stress from the job, the hours Mankins had to spend to keep his town peaceful, were somehow bearable on the pills. Which made the end of the world a problem for his continued sanity.

5

Ed Pryor met Mankins outside his pharmacy. It was almost midnight, and Ed didn't look happy to be there.

"Next time you want me," Ed said, "don't send one of your monkeys to do your dirty work."

"Well, with the phones down, I didn't have much choice," Mankins said with a smile. "We have to go back to the days of messengers, if you can believe that."

"What do you want?" Ed stated with very little patience.

"I need you to let me into the little back room in there and let me refill." Mankins lifted his prescription bottle.

"You could have just come in tomorrow; I'd have given you whatever I could spare."

"You see, that's just it. I need more than what you can spare. I need it all."

"What makes you think I'd let you have them? Others need those ... it's not just you," Ed said back.

"Oh, I know, there's Kelly Wilson, John Boley, Robert Frazer, Francis Labiche, not to mention little Howard Tunn ..."

Ed cut him off. "How do you know all that? That is private information!"

"Please," Mankins said, "there is no such thing as private information. Not for me. Take, for instance, your situation."

"I ... I don't know what you mean," Ed began to deny, but Mankins knew he had him. Ed's wandering eyes betrayed him.

"How many fake prescriptions have you filled?"

"I didn't—"

"Don't lie to me. I know exactly how you have paid for your vacations and classic cars and boats ... and whatever else. You're a drug dealer, my friend. Which I believe breaks the law. And since as far as we know, the US judicial system is no more, I guess I'll just have to render out the justice I see fit. Too bad we don't have a larger jail; I guess I'll have to mete out punishments that don't clog the cells." With that, Mankins could see Ed Pryor begin to sweat. "Look, I need what I need. So, either help me get the pills, or I will arrest you and get them anyway. It's your choice."

With that, Ed Pryor removed his keys from his pocket and unlocked the door.

6

Two weeks after the expedition had gone over the pass and the explorers hadn't returned, people began to worry. When two weeks with no word became four, most in town began to conclude they were either dead or had found a better place and were not returning. With rumors spreading fast, Mankins decided it was time to mount a rescue party, and he knew just the right man to lead it.

Much to his chagrin, Mankins went to the Kershaw home on the East side of town. Though he was loath to ask this family for anything, he knew that Quentin was the most qualified person to lead the rescue. The question was whether he could convince him or not.

It was no secret that the chief and Quentin's father, Floyd, had bad blood between them and that when Floyd and his wife were suddenly killed in a car wreck, all fingers pointed Mankins's way. All the chief could hope for in the conversation he was about to have was that cooler heads would prevail.

As he arrived at the Kershaw home, Quentin was outside with his younger brother, Colin. Quentin was teaching his brother, who was a mere fourteen years old, some self-defense moves. Quentin had been some kind of war hero, and to Mankins, that meant nothing. To the rest of the town, however, Quentin was a revered soldier, making it very difficult for Mankins to do anything about him. Another problem was, as far as Mankins knew, Quentin was as clean as a whistle. So blackmail in this case was out.

"Don't teach him too much," said Mankins. "We wouldn't want Colin to start beating up the kids at school."

"These are defensive moves only, chief," Quentin said, barely acknowledging Mankins's presence. "Is there something I can help you with?"

"Actually there is. Why else would I be here?"

Quentin said nothing in return. The silence irked the chief.

Who does this punk think he is?

"We need to send out a rescue party."

Still Quentin said nothing. He and his brother just kept practicing.

"I thought of you to lead the group. We need to find out what happened to the others, and since you were an Army Ranger, I thought it would be the type of thing you could do in your sleep."

Still, Quentin was quiet.

What does he want me to do, Mankins thought, *beg?*

"Is there any chance you will do this?"

Finally Quentin stopped what he was doing. He turned and faced Mankins. Their eyes met, and the chief could swear he felt those two brown circles sizing him up for the kill.

"No," was all Quentin said.

"The town needs you—" but the words were ignored. Quentin and Colin were headed back into the house.

"Get off my property, chief," Quentin added. "Before I shoot you."

With that, Quentin shut the door, and Mankins was left in the driveway, powerless.

7

Eventually, Mankins was able to put a group of five more townspeople together to go on a search-and-rescue mission. This included Dr. Sherriden, who, despite Mankins's arguments to the contrary, wanted to come along in case there was a need of medical assistance. Also, Deputies Burt Harrell and Pete Charmicheal were going, as well as townies Mitch and Stella Morrison. The last two were hunters and knew the surrounding areas well. As for the deputies, Mankins hated to lose them, but there needed to be some people involved in an official capacity, which meant sacrifices needed to be made. Concerning Sherriden, the doctor insisted that his nurse, Bertha Williams, knew enough about medicine that she could hold the fort until he returned.

It was too bad, then, that two more weeks went by after the party's departure, and neither hide nor hair was seen of this group either. Faced with a questioning town looking for answers, Mankins realized he had two choices: send out another party, with the chief himself along for the ride, or put everything on lockdown and not let anyone in or out of Bastion. Out of fear for himself, he chose the latter. Mankins realized that leaving the safe confines of his snug little town meant he might never return.

Who knows what's out there beyond the valley? The world is insane, turned into something unsafe ... unrecognizable.

Mankins was scared, and as he saw it, he was the town's only hope for survival.

No more risks, he reasoned, *not for me.*

As for food, he hoped they could hold on as long as necessary by rationing out what was in the grocery store and whatever they could hunt or grow. For water, they had the lake, which got its spring from the glaciers on the peaks. Time would tell if either food or water proved to be issues.

So, while Mankins realized things in Bastion wouldn't be easy, there wasn't a better man for the job. It was at that moment he stopped taking the pills completely. Having always felt a tad fuzzy on them, he decided it was best that he remove the toxin from his system and clear his mind.

Any sacrifice for Bastion.

Althaus

1

When Barrett Althaus woke hours after the light had surrounded the church and violently destroyed it, he was shocked by the destruction that greeted him. At first, he was thankful he had survived, even said a small prayer to God thanking him, but as the day went on, he wished he had held that prayer inside.

Through the ruins of the church, Althaus helped everyone he could. Unfortunately there were few people around to receive help. The only members of the congregation who survived the destruction were Elvin Williams and Jillian Harkness. For others lost in the rubble, the most he could do was pray for their peaceful entrance into God's kingdom, hoping that the God he now felt overwhelming anger toward would greet these poor souls with open arms.

But will he, if he allowed such destruction?

"Whut da we duw nuw?" asked Elvin. His head had taken a board across it and was still bleeding, though hours had passed. Althaus wondered if he was a hemophiliac. Thankfully, Jillian and her kind heart were there to care for Elvin. Althaus wasn't sure he could have done it on his own.

"I wish I knew, Elvin," Althaus said.

"Should we try for Wichita or even Fort Hayes?" offered Jillian.

"I don't see why," Althaus remarked. "They weren't much before this happened, and I think those huge plumes of fire off in the distance represent what's left of them."

Indeed, there were several mushroom-shaped clouds off in the distance. They were far away but visible, and they were dissipating by spreading toxins across the sky.

"So it was a nuke, huh?" Jillian asked.

"It seems so," Althaus replied.

"Whut's dat?" Elvin asked with a shake in his voice.

"Don't you worry your sweet heart on that," Jillian answered back while trying to calm Elvin by patting down his hair. "You just try to be still. Everythin' will be okay."

Althaus wasn't as sure, but he couldn't let that be known.

"We should probably check our homes, see if anything is left of them," Althaus suggested.

"Good idea," Jillian seconded. "Plus there might be more survivors."

Althaus hoped she was right.

The walk from the church grounds to where they all lived wasn't far, and with every step their hearts sank deeper in their chests. The homes, the school, even the hospital—all were gone.

As it was, these buildings barely passed for what they were, Althaus thought, *but to see them destroyed like this is simply shocking.*

Arriving at Althaus's home first, it was quickly clear that there would be nothing to recover. Everything was toppled over and in flames; Althaus guessed the gas main broke when the house collapsed. As someone who never had family and didn't have fond memories of the one he came from, Althaus wasn't concerned about any memorabilia lost. The only feeling he had was ambivalence. In a way, Althaus found it freeing that his past had gone up in flames. Now Althaus could let go of the old. However, as far as he could see, the future didn't look so bright either.

"I'm so sorry about yer home," Jillian said with pity in her voice.

"The Lord giveth," he said in response, "and he taketh away."

In the back of his mind, he chuckled at the absurdity of that phrase, but thought saying it would be appropriately soothing to Jillian and Elvin—if also cliché.

"Let's move on to your house, Jillian."

Moving south, they headed toward the Harkness farm. As they went, the shock of the day's events began to catch up with them.

"Wher's mah duddy?" Elvin began to question. Althaus had wondered how long it would take him to realize he was without him.

"He's ... uh ... he's ..." Jillian was at a loss for what to say.

"I need mah dud." Elvin began to lose his composure. "Wher's mah Duddy?" He began to pull away from Jillian, flailing his thick arms, one of which accidentally hit Jillian, knocking her over. She let out a cry as she met the ground. Wasting no more time, Althaus grabbed Elvin around the torso in a bear hug. The man-boy continued to kick and scream, trying to break free.

"Wher's mah duddy?" He screamed over and over. "I wunt mah duddy!"

As Althaus continued to hold him, he found he was thankful for his great physical strength. Working out all the time gave him the endurance needed to outlast Elvin's outburst. It took ten minutes for him to calm down, but slowly, as he realized he couldn't escape Althaus's grasp, he came under control. Once he was calm, Althaus let him sit on the side of the road crying.

"I'm suh-rey," he said through the tears. "I'm suh suh-rey."

Collecting themselves, they continued on. After only a few minutes' walk on the now-broken pavement of the street, they arrived at the Harkness farm. Or rather, what was left of it. The dry soil and parched high grass were in flames, and the old farmhouse itself was leaning sideways, like the Leaning Tower of Pisa, only moments from a strong wind blowing it over completely.

Althaus looked toward Jillian. Tears ran down her cheeks.

"So many memories," she said. From the look on her face, she was feeling the exact opposite that Althaus had. "Not all of dem good, but some were da best I had."

Althaus didn't know what to say to her and knew that sometimes words weren't enough. This was one of those moments. So Althaus simply placed a hand on her shoulder, giving her physical support instead.

"The year the crops all died," she began while holding back more tears, "we din't have any money to our name. Food was scarce for us, and we ate whut we could. Both mah husband and I, we lost so much weight ... and we looked so sick ... but we did da best we knew 'ow. 'Just have faith,' my husband would tell me ... 'the Lord is testing us' ... But I coun't understan'. Why would he test us like dis? Whut did he want from us? But I did as he said. I put my faith in God and ask 'im to help us. As da days and mont's of the pestilence went on, my husband become more and more depressed. With no hope of fixing thins, he was inconsolable. One night, he started to lash out. He walk aroun' the house grabbin' pictures and plates and throwin' dem against the walls. Yellin' about how unfair it all wuz. I asked 'im ta stop, ta not destroy da house, dat it was all we had … But he didn't stop. He was actually punchin' holes in da walls, and it was like he wanta tear the place down wit' his rage. I grab him and held him, and I says ta him whut he tol' me … I tol' him to 'have faith.'"

"Right, faith," Althaus agreed, though deep down, he wasn't sure why he said anything.

Is faith even important in times like these?

"Once I said dat, he calm hiself," Jillian continued. "We made love dat night fur the first time in mont's. Dat was a good mem'ry."

As she finished the story, the house finally caught fire. The three turned away from the sight and walked on.

"Do we go ta his house next?" Jillian asked.

Althaus looked at Elvin. He was shaking and obviously scared.

"No, I think we should skip that," Althaus said. "I'm not sure Elvin can take any more."

"Whut den?" Jillian asked.

"I wish I knew," Althaus said. "Keep walking, I guess. Get as far out of the area as possible."

Jillian looked around them. The flames seemed to be gathering with the wind.

"'Spose yer right," she agreed.

2

After walking for a half hour they came to the remains of the other church in town. It too had been blown to pieces and set ablaze. On his knees in front of the church, with his head down and arms limply by his side, Clarence Solomon sat almost as if he had given up, simply waiting to be collected by the Lord.

Slowly Althaus approached him.

"Clarence?" he said.

"He's punishing us," Clarence stated calmly, as if it were just a normal statement. "We've broken God's commandment, and this is his punishment."

"I don't think this has anything to do with that," Althaus responded.

"Of course you don't," Clarence blurted out. "You don't even know if you have faith anymore. It's hard to believe he'd let you live and so many others die."

Althaus agreed. *It is hard to believe. It is odd. Which is the point, isn't it? God likes to act in mysterious ways.*

"Come with us, Clarence," Althaus implored him. "We are going as far as we can, to find help, other survivors. With any luck, we can find the army."

"Come with you?" Clarence asked not to anyone in particular.

"You're a man of God," Althaus said. "Obviously God has a plan for you. And me ... if we're both still alive. It may be God wants us together to allow that plan to come to fruition."

Suddenly Clarence's hand grabbed Althaus's.

"Yes," the man said. "You're right. He wants me to help you ... and the world. I'm his vessel."

"The world does need you," Althaus added for effect.

What an egotist, Althaus thought. Though he knew God did not like vain men, Althaus realized he needed to feed Clarence's ego to get him to go.

It worked. With Clarence up on his feet, he looked strong, and didn't wait a moment to step in front of their small group.

"I will lead," Clarence stated. "As the one of us who is closest to God, he will give me the power to guide us."

Whatever, Althaus thought as he rolled his eyes. Part of him wanted to just leave the self-righteous bastard behind, but he knew he couldn't do that. Life was too precious.

Any survivor, no matter how infuriating, is worth saving, he decided.

As Clarence began to lead them away, Jillian turned to Althaus.

"Is he serious?" she asked Althaus.

"He's a good man," Althaus stated.

"I hope so, since you want us ta follow 'im. I knew I hated Baptists fur a reason."

"Trust me," was all he could say in response.

3

As the days went on, Althaus and the others followed Clarence's lead. They moved south toward the border, hoping to find more people. Mostly they saw burned fields and the utter destruction of whole towns. Althaus couldn't believe just how destroyed the state of Kansas was; it was as if God himself had landed in the state, and then continued to impose his wrath. In the end, it seemed to Althaus that Kansas was nothing more than a smoldering fire-pit of ash. It wasn't until they reached the town of Independence that they met with more survivors—and almost lost their lives.

Situated about two hundred miles north of Oklahoma City, Independence had been a poor but surviving town. Much like Atchison, where Althaus and his group's journey began, this was a town of God-fearing farmers that had to turn to other forms of survival when the crops failed. None of these choices had been good, so most in the town were lower-class laborers who spent their days doing whatever they could to survive. Which was probably why the residents of Independence, when faced with the end of the world, immediately thought, "Every man for himself."

As they entered the town, Althaus and the rest were shocked by the form of destruction they were seeing. Standing in the street that led straight into the center of town, they had a great view of Independence's remains. Unlike other towns they had walked through, most of this one still stood. Other than broken store windows, overturned cars, and trash, there didn't appear to be much damage at all. From what Althaus could conclude, Independence, Kansas, hadn't been affected as badly as the rest of the state by the White Light. Clearly though, the town had seen better days.

"Whut happened here?" Jillian questioned.

"It's obvious, isn't it?" Althaus replied. "Whatever survivors there are here, they destroyed all of this themselves."

"But why?" Jillian continued.

"No faith in God," Clarence condemned.

"Well," Althaus broke in, "I'm not sure that can be assumed, but I'd say they panicked. And in that panic, they didn't stop and show kindness toward their fellow man."

"Should we get outta here?" Jillian wondered.

"Might not be a bad idea," Althaus agreed.

"I dun't like dis pla-ace," even Elvin added.

"We stay," Clarence commanded. "We will bring God back to these heathens."

"We're not here to proselytize," Althaus argued. "We're trying to survive."

"But don't you see?" Clarence struck back. "This is why God saved us. To return the world to his glory. If we abandon his will, God will abandon us and leave us to die."

"God isn't involved in this!" Althaus remarked. "This is just what happens when the world is left to fend for itself. This is what people do! They panic, they lash out, and they kill. Now I suggest that before we are caught up in all this, we get the hell out of here."

Unfortunately though, it was too late.

"Don't move!" A yell exploded from somewhere above them. They all looked in different directions but couldn't place where the voice was coming from. "Drop any weapons you may have and raise your arms to the sky."

"We don't have any weapons!" Althaus exclaimed.

"Do it or we kill you where you stand!" the voice yelled back. Althaus could tell from the tambour of the voice, it was a man's, but he still couldn't tell where it was coming from. The way the buildings lined the main street on each side, the voice seemed to simply echo off the brick and mortar. The same happened when the click of an automatic rifle sounded. It bounced off the walls and circled down to Althaus and his group.

He's going to shoot us, Althaus realized. *I have to do something.* But he was cut off from doing that when Clarence Solomon stepped forward.

"If you shoot us," Clarence stated, "God will smote you and drag your soul to the devil. We are people of God, and as such, we are chosen to spread his word."

A laugh sounded from that same nondirectional place. Now though it was joined by more. It wasn't just one man laughing at them; it seemed like the whole town thought they were a troupe of clowns.

"As far as we're concerned," the voice said back, "God has already sent his wrath and spared us. We don't fear him anymore."

"You should!" Clarence yelled back.

That's when a hail of gunfire bounded down in front of them. It hit the street, sending rock and dust into the air. All in the group recoiled and covered their heads, but the bullets didn't come near. It had only been a warning.

"Please," Althaus pleaded, "we just need food, water, and shelter for the night. Tomorrow we will leave immediately."

"Oh," said the voice, "is that *all* you want? I'm afraid we can't spare it. If you want it, you'll have to take it."

"You know we can't fight you," Althaus said back, realizing how pointless this all was.

"No, you can't," said the man. As he finished, more guns cocked in preparation to shoot.

This is it, Althaus realized. *We came all this way just to die.*

He had one last chance …

"I can't believe that even among such tragic events as these, men like you would resort to murder if it means you might get a leg up on your own survival."

"What can I say?" the man said, but this time, the voice wasn't echoing; it was right by them. Turning to his right, Althaus saw the man coming out from one of the destroyed storefront windows. "I'm all heart."

"Don't do this," Althaus pleaded again.

"God will not have pity on your soul," Clarence interrupted.

"Shut up!" Both Althaus and the man yelled at Clarence after his last remark. Sheepishly Clarence relented.

"You see all this destruction?" the man asked. "A few days after the … whatever they were … explosions, we were raided by the next town over. We knew them. They had been our friends. But they came in and took everything we had. To protect ourselves, we were forced to fight back. We killed them all, losing many of our own in the process. This was only six days after ... What do you think it will be like months and years from now? We have no choice but to do what is best for us."

"Even if that means killing?" Althaus challenged.

"We've already done that," were the final chilling words from the man. Finally he raised his gun and pointed it at them. Clarence began to chant a prayer to the sky. Elvin and Jillian were in tears. Althaus just stood there, his eyes latched onto the man's. If he was going to die, he wouldn't make it easy by looking away.

Phoom! went the gun, and although Jillian let out a little scream, neither Althaus nor any of his companions fell to the ground. Quickly Althaus looked around. He was shocked at what he saw.

The man had a red dot on his forehead. His face was blank, though his eyes were wide, caught in total terror. Trickling down from the red dot was a line of blood, which was starting to inch its way down the man's nose. The man made a gurgling noise and began to take a few steps forward. Althaus pushed his group back, away from the man as he lunged crazily for help.

Phoom! Phoom!

Two more sounds went, and twice more the man reacted. His shoulder went back, and then his chest exploded. Blood blasted everywhere as the man finally fell to the ground.

What the hell? Althaus thought as he looked around.

He was expecting to see a gun in a window, thinking that perhaps one of the others in the group had assassinated the man, but that wasn't it. He could see people scrambling around in the buildings, looking for places to hide. They were panicked about something.

Which was when he heard it—a distant rumbling. But not like the rumble from the White Lights; this was the rumbling of an engine.

No, Althaus thought, *not an engine ... engines!*

"Whut is that?" Jillian asked. "What is goin' on?"

"I think we were just saved," Althaus stated calmly, hoping their luck wasn't about to change. However, in many ways, everything was about to change. As they turned their attention from the buildings surrounding them, they were greeted by an amazing sight. Black tank-like vehicles surrounded by soldiers clad all in black were entering the city limits. Flying above each tank was a flag they all recognized; it was the American stars and stripes.

"Hallelujah! God heard my prayer and saved us," said Clarence.

"Or something," added Althaus.

4

Althaus had been against every military action taken by the American government over the last twenty years. He was a pacifist to be sure, but now, even Althaus was thankful for such military standards as order and martial law, given what the country had become. The surprise attacks of that November morning had left much confusion, and Althaus realized that America was going to need a lot more than small factions of people clawing for survival in order to rebuild. So, when the tanks stopped their movement and a man wearing a camouflage combat uniform with a block of stars and medals above the left breast pocket the size of an adult hand, came out, Althaus felt a strong sense of relief.

"I'm General Black," the man shouted to no one in particular. "Who's in charge of this group?"

Althaus was about to step forward, but Clarence moved first.

"That would be me, General." Clarence offered the soldier his hand, but he didn't take it. The general was older, probably mid sixties. He was white, and his hair had gone all gray. He had a toughness about him, and his body matched that. To Althaus, he looked like a man who took shit from no one.

Which is exactly what this country needs, Althaus thought.

"So, what's your name?" the general asked Clarence.

"Solomon, Clarence Solomon."

"And the rest of you?"

"I am Barrett Althaus," he said, finally getting to speak. "This is Jillian Harkness and Elvin Williams."

"Nice to meet you all." General Black nodded at them. "So, who can tell me why I just had my sniper shoot this man? I sure hope we killed the right person. It's hard to tell from a distance."

Althaus explained the whole story, by the end of which, Black was smiling.

"Good, we did kill the right man! Sometimes as a general, you have to go with your gut. From my vantage point, you all outnumbered him, but he held the gun, so it seemed reasonable to assume you were about to die. Therefore, I saved who I thought needed it."

The general's explanation seemed reasonable to Althaus, if a little too simplistic.

Why didn't he just shoot the man in the leg? Althaus questioned, *but maybe the general couldn't be sure he'd stop him if that was all he did.*

"Are there any others around?" Black asked.

"Yes," Althaus replied. "There are more in these buildings. They scattered once you showed up. But they all had guns."

"Great," the general said sarcastically. "I'd hate to kill any civilians we don't need to. Here's what I want you all to do: board the A.P.C.- sorry, the Armored Personnel Carrier, just for protection, while I send out a recon team to sweep the buildings. Once everything is clear, we will let you all go free. Okay?"

Althaus didn't even know how to respond; tears just welled up in his eyes.

"That's the best offer I've heard in weeks," was all he could say.

5

Inside the A.P.C., they were cramped. There was a driver dressed in one of the soldiers' all-black armored uniforms, and there was a munitions man who sat at a computer toward the back. The general sat in a chair toward the middle of the area, while Althaus and all his people stood around trying not to be in the way.

When the general was settled, he turned to the driver.

"Give me the com and send it out over the loudspeaker."

The driver pressed a few buttons and handed General Black a small device. Black began to speak into it.

"Citizens of Independence," Black said. Althaus could hear his words echoing out of the tank and into the town. "This is General Black, commanding officer of the United States Army Specialized Armed Combat Command. SACCOM for short! We are declaring this area under martial law. You have one minute to surrender your arms and come out with your hands up so that we can properly process you as American citizens. We will not harm you. We are here to help. If we are fired upon, we will have no other choice than to respond with lethal force. That is all."

Black handed the driver back the device and said to him, "Let's see how long this takes."

Within thirty-seconds, he got his response. The munitions officer, looking at his infrared scanner, spoke up.

"We have twenty-five noncombatants converging on this location, sir. All are unarmed."

"Good," Black said. "Now, wasn't that easy?"

Yes, it was, Althaus agreed.

6

In the following hours, General Black had his men round up the whole town and registered them. Three hundred and fifty people in all. Once that had been completed, Black instilled the rules of martial law, putting in place guards, curfews, and overall structure. There were no incidents, as everyone seemed to cooperate. It seemed to Althaus that perhaps having rules to follow was some kind of relief to them. For those who did not have homes to return to, Black handed out service tents. These were lodgings used in the battlefield that were made of metal and canvas and folded down into a small backpack-sized cylinder. When one opened the cylinder, the tent would pop out and take shape. Each tent had enough room to fit two people for sleep and nothing more.

Black offered some to Althaus and his people.

"No, we'll be fine," Althaus said. "I'm sure we can find our own shelter."

"Oh, please!" Black said, dismissing his protests. "We have thousands of them in our supply trucks. I insist."

After that, Althaus and his group had roofs over their heads.

In the days that followed, feeding stations were set up, and rations were given out three times a day. The medic from the general's battalion also set up a station for people to receive medical assistance. By the end of the week, the town functioned like a fully operating base. Although, just when everyone became comfortable, the general sprang the bad news.

Gathering everyone from the new base camp, General Black came to the front. He looked awkward standing there, clearly not used to having to talk to a civilian populace. Althaus watched him as he wiped sweat from his brow.

Black cleared his throat and began to speak.

"Good morning," he nervously said to everyone. "Over the last week, you have all seen what we can do for you. Though our rules are strict, I hope you can see that it has been for your own benefit and to establish some kind of normalcy to your lives again. As time goes on and our country settles back into its ways, we will loosen our grip. That is my goal."

Black paused a moment and nervously took a drink of water from his canteen. Althaus shook his head.

The general is doing it all wrong, he thought. *In front of a group like this, he needs to seem sympathetic and reassuring. He looks the exact opposite. As a battle commander he may have been great, but as a public speaker with compassion he disappoints.*

Black began again. "One of the major reasons I have brought you all together is to answer some questions you may have. First, the attacks … It is still unclear who or what attacked us. We do know that the weapons used were nuclear missiles, as well as bombs dropped by drone fighters. Several countries have this capability other than the United States. China, Russia, Iran, and Great Britain, just to name a few. As for communication with the government … Unfortunately we have been unable to get in contact with anyone from the White House or the Pentagon."

With this, the crowd began to murmur. Concern was buzzing all about them.

No! Althaus thought. *When delivering news like this, you need to do it in a way where it sounds less ominous; the general needs to be giving out good news and adding in the bad as a simple matter of fact.*

"Now before you all get your panties in a bunch, let me explain. This does not mean anything. Our communications have been sporadic since the attack. Just because we haven't heard from anyone doesn't mean they aren't there. I am sure our great leader, President Mitchum, has already counterattacked the enemy. But we do not know for a fact what the condition of Washington is, or how our government may be proceeding as far as emergency operations go. I can theorize about what protocol states, but that isn't going to make you all feel any better. Besides trying to reach Washington, I have sent out a message to all active troops in the country. I have told them where we are and asked them to respond and meet us. At this juncture, we haven't heard from anyone."

Another grumble rose from the now-panicked audience.

"As a general I have to assume the worst at this point. It is strategic for any invading force to attack military installations as well as large targets of infrastructure. From what we can gather, all major cities have been attacked, and many of our military bases as well. We have already gone to a few of the bases and found them destroyed. For right now, we are the last United States Combat Arms Unit."

Screams now came up from a few in the audience, and the sounds of tears as well. Althaus just stared on, astounded at the lack of tact flowing from their new commander.

Morale will be low if he keeps on like this!

"Finally, in the coming days, we will have to move on from here. According to our fallout projections, we are in the path of some serious winds and storms that carry with them radiation. Staying here is no longer a viable option. We will be moving south, headed into Oklahoma. We hope to arrive at a military base there and find it still intact. If you wish to follow, we will provide protection. As I see it, coming with us is your best chance for survival. You have twenty-four hours to decide, as we will be evacuating this site as of 0500."

Black paused a moment. He looked out on the crowd and seemed to link eyes with as many as possible. Even Althaus felt his stare.

What does he want? Althaus wondered.

"Duty and honor," Black then said. "It's all a man has to guide him to do what is right. Follow that, and we will all be okay. That is all." Black finished and walked away from the assembled survivors.

Clarence, who had been standing next to him turned to Althaus and said, "Well, that was cheery."

"Yeah," Althaus replied.

"So I guess we go with them."

"What other choice do we have?" Althaus remarked.

"I'm going to go see the general," Clarence stated. "See if I can be of any assistance as a man of God."

You do that, Althaus thought. *I'm staying out of it.*

7

As night fell, it became clear to Althaus that the survivors needed something more than just protection. They were walking around the complex of tents, tanks, and guns with heads down, shoulders hunched, and the look of defeat. Althaus himself felt much the way most of the others did. Certainly there seemed to be a sense of loss inside of him. The world was destroyed as far as he could tell.

Which left them to what? Wait? Survive just long enough until they died from radiation poisoning?

Althaus knew he could help these people, maybe even help himself, with the skills he had as a man of the cloth; the problem was he didn't want to. He was anonymous now, just one of the many faceless, nameless survivors in the crowd, and he was finding he preferred it that way.

Let Clarence have the glory and ear of God, Althaus thought. *I just want to be protected ... not be the protector.*

Which he was well on his way to accomplishing.

The soldiers, the ones clad all in black, wearing some special kind of armor Althaus had never seen before, were amazing. From talking to some of them, Althaus found out that General Black and his men had been stationed in Ohio at a secret base used to test new munitions. Due to the secrecy of their mission, even those who launched the missiles targeted to attack America's infrastructure, would not have known about their existence. There, they were testing top-secret and experimental new suits to prepare for an invasion of China. It turned out America was ready to ignite the first strike when intelligence suggested that China was about to call in their debts, wiping out the United States. Althaus found it odd how quickly the stories of these suits came out now that the world was destroyed.

I guess top-secret only applies if there is a government to keep it secret for. Althaus laughed to himself.

Truly though, nothing felt safer to Reverend Althaus than being around these men. They were strong, attentive, and able to create order from chaos, just as they had done with this town. A week in, and it was unrecognizable as the place where Althaus and his group had almost lost their lives. This attachment of Soldiers to Black's Tanker Battalion (the Eighth Special Forces Group) and its new infantry suits were apparently now America's last hope. These combined units, consisting of 250 men, were entrusted now with protecting America's future.

No pressure!

Before going to sleep, Althaus sat with Elvin. The poor man had been having nightmares every night, and Althaus found it soothed him to hear verses of scripture. Althaus remembered most of them by memory, and he told Elvin the ones he felt were the most calming. Just as Elvin was about to drift to sleep, a knock was heard on the metal of the tent.

"Whu is dat?" Elvin said with a jump.

"Not sure, but just lie there; I'll check."

They were sleeping on mats that came with the tent. The mats were one-inch-thick foam that only padded the ground, as opposed to making it comfortable. Althaus figured that was better than the actual ground itself. As Althaus went toward the flap that served as an entranceway, Elvin curled up and put the hard, scratchy, wool blanket over himself. To Althaus's welcome surprise, he looked comfortable, which warmed his heart.

At least he can still find some peace.

Exiting the flap, Althaus was shocked to find General Black standing there with two soldiers, one on each side of him.

"You're Barrett Althaus, right?" Black asked bluntly.

"Yes, I am," Althaus replied.

"I remember you," Black continued. "Saved your life that first day."

"That's right."

"Well, your friend, Preacher Solomon, came to me today."

Oh no, Clarence, what did you do?

"He told me you two are men of God," Black added.

God dammit, Clarence! Althaus thought, taking the Lord's name in vain.

"I was. But not anymore," Althaus said, hoping that would squash the conversation. But it didn't.

"Walk with me, Barrett, I want to show you some things."

They began to walk, followed by the two guards.

"For a preacher, you've been awful quiet about God in the face of such difficult times," Black began again.

"I guess I've just been waiting for a sign."

"A sign?" Black looked at Althaus through suspicious eyes. "Your friend was very boisterous, telling me he is on a mission from on high and that he can help me to make the right decisions—blah, blah, blah. It was very, I hate to use the word preachy, but ... aw, hell ... preachy!" Black let out a laugh.

"He can be that way," Althaus added.

"Can he? But not you?"

"I try to use a more subtle approach."

"Hmmm. I see," Black stated. "I can tell that about you. You're quiet, not out for the attention. I like that."

Walking down the main street of the town, which was now filled with tents, Althaus couldn't help but feel trapped. He was well aware of the two guards that walked behind them, clad in all black, not reflecting any light, and faceless. Althaus realized that if he tried to run, he could not escape. Not that there was a reason to run …

Was there?

"Hope," Black continued. "It's an important human need. Like food, water, even love. We need it. We crave it. Without it, we might as well just shrivel up and die. Which is exactly what is happening in this camp."

Coming to the hospital tent, Althaus saw that it was overflowing, even at this time of night. General Black ushered Althaus inside the hospital tent.

"Look at these people, Reverend. They're scared. Sick from malnutrition, infection, or worse." Althaus knew the 'or worse' was the slow-killing radiation poison. "Many are going to die without having a chance to get right with their maker. It has been selfish of you to withhold your talents from the rest of the camp."

"Talents? I'm just a person who can quote scripture."

"You're a purveyor of hope, Reverend. These people are dying and need to feel like there is something better beyond this life."

"Why not use Preacher Solomon?" Althaus asked, trying to get the attention away from him.

"I will, but not for this. To be honest, he gives me the creeps. But not you. You're just a regular man. One of us."

"I can't do it," Althaus began to plead with the general. "I would just be lying to them."

"Really?" Black's face was angry now. A lump came to Reverend Althaus's throat. Althaus could easily see why the men in Black's command never questioned his authority.

"I think you're full of excuses, Reverend. I think you're scared that if you give hope to these men, you will have to answer for your own sins … sins like giving up on God. I was taught to embrace what made me strong. I was taught never to give up. What would you think of me if I just decided it wasn't worth it to keep this camp going and I left you all behind? Would you understand why? Or would you judge me, just as God judges all of us for our actions? Or inactions?"

Black's stare was as powerful as a jackhammer. Althaus could feel holes being bored into his heart.

"Do what you wish, Reverend, but remember, it is not in this world that you will be judged."

Althaus took a long deep breath. He looked around at the dying and felt compelled to do something. Whether that feeling had come from God or from fear of General Black, he wasn't sure, but he knew what was right.

"I'll help."

"Good!" Black said with a wide smile. "When we arrive at our next campsite, I will be setting up a church for you. That Sunday you will give a sermon. The whole camp will attend. Everyone needs hope."

Althaus watched as Black left him alone in the hospital.

What have I just gotten into?

Aiden

1

It wasn't until Nurse Ellen pulled out her first clump of hair that Aiden began to panic.

"Oh, my God! Oh, my God! Oh, my God!" she screamed with a bloodcurdling cry that made Aiden's insides turn and twist into knots.

"Calm down," said Dr. Savage in his eternally even and deep voice. It was hypnotizing in its melodic tone, so much so that even Aiden found himself getting calmer. "Everything is going to be just fine," the doctor assured her. "Now, let me see."

She bent her head down to him. From what Aiden could see, Nurse Ellen had pulled off a chunk of hair from the back of her scalp. In the yellow light, the area looked dark, which he figured was blood, and the skin around it was frayed at the sides. Whatever was wrong, it wasn't natural.

"All right," Savage said. "It seems to me that your hair is falling out due to lack of B12. None of us has seen the sun in weeks, so it is no wonder that we will be seeing issues like this."

"But—" Nurse Ellen said through sobs, "why is my scalp coming off?" She pleaded with him for answers, all the while holding the limp piece of skin and hair in her hand. The sight was horrifying to Aiden.

Is this going to happen to me? He wondered.

"It's a natural thing for our bodies to react to changes like this. It probably won't be the last, and we all need to be prepared for it," Dr. Savage warned. "However, it is nothing to fear, and I promise, it won't be permanent."

Taking Nurse Ellen in his arms, Dr. Savage attempted to calm her. When she wasn't calming down, Aiden watched the doctor hand Nurse Ellen off to Nurse Cindy for comforting. Moving to the back corner of the room, the doctor took out a key to a small lockbox at his feet. It was white and had a red cross on it. Opening it, he placed his hands inside and pulled out a syringe and a bottle of medicine the size of a quarter. Aiden wasn't sure what it was, but he hoped it was something that would calm her. The incessant crying was driving him insane. Continuing to watch, he saw the doctor fill a syringe with the medicine, tap it, and then return to Nurse Ellen. Saying nothing, not even warning her, he stuck the tip of the needle into her arm and pulled it out. Nurse Ellen looked at him.

"What was that?" she asked.

"Just something to calm you."

Within seconds, Nurse Ellen was asleep.

2

It was hard to keep track of time in the basement. With only the yellow light and no windows to the outside, Aiden found it impossible to know if it was night or day. Which was the reason he found himself going in and out of sleep. He had stopped sleeping for long periods; the most he would sleep was four hours at a time. Oddly, Aiden found he was taking these naps frequently, at least more frequently than ever before. It was during one of these periods of rest that the doctor came to him. Feeling a rock of his shoulder, Aiden stirred. Opening his eyes slightly, he saw through the blurred vision of awakening, Dr. Savage's yellow-hued face. Aiden sat up immediately.

"Sorry to wake you," the doctor said.

"It's fine," Aiden reassured him.

"I just wanted to tell you—what I did to Ellen. I did it for her benefit."

"Okay," Aiden responded.

Why is he defending himself to me? Aiden questioned in his mind.

"You know I would never use my medicines or healing prowess on someone just because," added the doctor.

"Of course," Aiden agreed.

"Good. I just wanted to make that clear. I wouldn't want you to worry."

"Thank you," was all Aiden could think to respond with.

"I just want what is best for us all. Go back to sleep now."

Of course though, Aiden couldn't. Instead, he sat up thinking of the doctor's words to Nurse Ellen about B12, wondering if they would ever see the sun again.

3

It was the next day when things got even worse.

One of the other patients from the clinic, Tamera Hagan—who had received a face-lift—began to spit out her teeth. In big pools of blood, small chunks of yellow (the teeth were that color due to the emergency lighting) were revealed.

"What's happening?" she asked the doctor.

"B12," he said to her. "We all just need more B12."

Then, like with Nurse Ellen, he administered a shot, calming her immediately.

Don't let me be next, was all Aiden could think.

4

Complete horror overtook Aiden as he awoke from another of his four-hour naps. Another patient, Rory Allen—who had received liposuction—was sitting on his bed pulling off his fingernails. Once again, the doctor was nearby, consoling his patient.

For Aiden, the scene was just too much.

It's a nightmare, he tried to convince himself, *it has to be.*

So, without even so much as sitting up and asking if the man was going to be okay, Aiden willed himself to go back to sleep, hoping that when he awoke again, everything would be back to normal.

5

Sleep.

Four hours.

Awaken.

Sounds of crying.

Open eyes ... See Nurse Cindy ... It is her cries that awaken him.

Her skin is breaking out in red blotches. Blood is pouring out of them as the skin is breaking.

Dr. Savage is now trying to calm her as well.

Fear building inside.

Need more sleep.

Back to sleep.

Sleep.

6

Sleep.

Four hours.

Awaken.

Another patient, Michael Aimes, is bleeding profusely from his nose. It doesn't seem to want to stop.

The doctor examines it and stuffs gauze inside, packing it.

Aiden feels his head aching. It's horrible ... his vision is full of blinking circular flashes.

Fear building inside.

Need more sleep.

Back to sleep.

Sleep.

7

Sleep.

Four hours.

Awaken.

Nausea.

Stomach pain.

Sitting up and looking around the room. All is calm. Everyone is asleep.

Back of throat squeezing and tightening ... Feels like choking ...
Vomit.

Wrenching pain and acidic taste in back of throat, which is coated with chunks.

Swallow.

Wipe tears from the eyes and breathe in through the nose hard, trying to catch breath.

Look at the expelled remnants of the stomach ...
Chunks of bile ... and blood!

8

"What is that?" Aiden said in a panic. Dr. Savage came into his line of sight. First he looked down at the puddle of blood and gunk spewed all over the gurney Aiden was lying on.

"Don't panic," the doctor stated.

"Don't panic?" Aiden questioned. "I'm puking blood!"

"It's perfectly normal."

"Normal?"

"It's the lack of B12 in your system."

"This is not a vitamin deficiency!" Aiden screamed.

With that, Dr. Savage lifted a syringe and pushed the plunger just a bit, releasing a drop or two of whatever medicine was in it. The doctor had it at the ready, which to Aiden meant things were getting very bad.

"Don't," Aiden pleaded. "I don't want to go back to sleep! I need to stay awake."

"It'll be okay," the doctor assured him. "Nurses!" he called out, "a little help here, please."

Nurses Ellen and Cindy rushed into view. Aiden was horrified to see them. Nurse Ellen had lost more hair and had long rivulets of blood streaming down her face. The patches of missing hair seemed to be skinless, showing what appeared to be her skull. Cindy, on the other hand, had patches of red sores all over. They had come open somehow and were leaking gooey puss.

"Wait!" Aiden yelled. "What's going on?"

The only response he got was a pinch in the arm.

The drug was quick-acting, and before he knew it, Aiden was spinning in a liquified reality.

Then he was asleep.

Again.

9

When he finally came to, Aiden wasn't sure how much time had passed. Unfortunately, what he awoke to wasn't any better than before. Everyone in the room was up out of their beds, and Dr. Savage was forced into a corner. He was screaming and pushing the others off him, attempting to get out of the trap. Nurse Ellen had a syringe in her hands, ready to plunge in the end of the needle.

What's going on now? Aiden wondered.

"Don't touch me!" the doctor screamed. "I'm fine; there's nothing wrong with me."

"Please, Doctor. Let us calm you down," Nurse Ellen begged him.

"I'm fine! I'm perfect! As I always am!" Dr. Savage continued to plead his case as he fought. Yet even Aiden could see he was wrong. The doctor's beautiful and perfect look was ruined. Along the jawline and around his eyes, seams had opened, as if the places he had done work on his face had swollen and popped. Blood was outlining his face like a jigsaw puzzle.

Aiden knew he needed to help.

Slowly standing, he walked over to the open lockbox in the back corner of the room. While the others were still battling Dr. Savage, Aiden filled another syringe with what he assumed was the same medicine the doctor had been giving the others.

The bottle looks the same at least, Aiden reasoned.

Wasting no more time, he rushed over to where the doctor was cornered. Due to the positioning, the doctor couldn't see him sneaking up, and neither could anyone else.

"I'm perfect!" Dr. Savage screamed. "I'm a specimen of the human form! You can't do this to me!"

Just then Aiden stabbed the needle in his arm. The doctor paused, looked down at the syringe sticking out of his arm, and met Aiden's eyes.

"I'm perfection—" was all he said before his eyes closed and his body fell to the ground.

Aiden looked at the group surrounding the fallen doctor.

"Let's get him to a bed," Nurse Ellen ordered. The others in the group helped lift him up and take him.

"What do we do now?" Cindy asked Ellen.

"There's only one thing to do," Aiden responded. "Get the hell out of here."

Sean

1

When Sean was clear from the rubble of the Playpen, he found whatever clothes he could so that he no longer needed to wear the unsightly red jumpsuit from Milford. About thirty miles from the jail, he came upon the first small town, not much more than a few homes and a gas station. Of course, those homes were destroyed, and the only thing left of the gas station was the pump, but he hoped he could at least find a change of clothes. The sign of the gas station still stood and advertised that gas prices were *only* $10.75 a gallon.

No wonder the world has destroyed its self, Sean thought.

A quick sweep of the rubble where a house once stood revealed several bodies, three male, four female, but thankfully no children. They all wore pajamas and seemed to have been caught off guard by the attacks and killed in their sleep. Sean assumed, given the early morning time of the attack, most of the country was killed the same way.

Looking through the rubble, Sean found some jeans, a flannel shirt, some worker boots, and a coat. He figured he'd need a coat given the fact that it was November and only getting colder. The mountain-man look of the clothes was not necessarily his style, but he figured beggars couldn't be choosers. Once dressed, he was off moving south away from the jail and hopefully toward some other survivors. Sean knew he had to start heading west eventually if he was ever going to get back to Michelle and Winnie, but the warmer the climate, the better chance he had of surviving.

Assuming they're still alive anyway, he thought.

Pushing the disturbing thought from his mind, Sean began to walk and think things through. Supposing they were alive, he was sure they wouldn't want to see him again. Despite the apocalypse, he wasn't sure their fear of him had waned. Sure, overnight everything had changed in America—every law, every moral, and every person—but that didn't mean they would accept him back. Either way, though, Sean was going to locate them and find out.

On his journey from Milford, Sean was struck by the absolute destruction of the countryside. Fields were scorched brown from fires. Mountainsides that were once lush with colorful poppies of purple and yellow were now blackened with ash. In the distance he could see Chicago burning; the sight was chilling. Even the roads were affected—no longer flat, they were pushed upward, as if they were an accordion waiting to be played. Only the few overturned cars that had hit the roads early that fateful morning offered protection at night from the howling winds. Snow fell as well; some was natural due to the onset of winter, and some was decidedly unnatural, caused by the fallout of the nuclear bombs. In the air, Sean could also smell the rancid odor of death. It was a horrible smell—one that Sean could feel in his skin, under his fingernails, and in his hair.

What I'd give for a bath! Sean thought, though he would not dare to enjoy the lakes and streams he came across. They were gray with soot and other unspeakable things, like the ashes of burning corpses. Even fish, which were always barely aware of the troubles that affected those who dwelled on land, floated on top of the surface …

Dead.

Sean took this as a warning, like the cartoon face from his childhood … the yellow one with the face spitting out its tongue: *"Do Not Drink! Poison!"*

Due to Milford Pen's placement in the northern wilderness, Sean could see how life had changed on earth. Pine trees once as plentiful as the stars were blackened and crisp. They reminded Sean of pictures he had once seen of a place called Pompeii. Human remains had been forever fossilized in perfect form after the eruption of a volcano. The figures were frozen in time during their death throes. The pine trees in their ash shells were just the same. No birds took to the air anymore, and he hadn't seen so much as even a single deer. From what he could tell, the wildlife was as dead as the trees.

I can't even find so much as a cockroach, Sean realized. *I guess the theory of cockroaches surviving the nuclear apocalypse was wrong.*

Sean laughed at this thought. Quickly, he chastised himself for doing it, though, finding it a disgusting reaction to such macabre sights. But then he heard his mother in his head ...

"Laughter is the best cure," she would always say.

Yeah, right, he thought, but couldn't help but do it anyway. Forcing himself to stop these morbid thoughts, Sean continued to walk along the long, lonely road.

2

Moving from the northern tip of Illinois to the southern, Sean figured he had a good chance of finding other people. He hoped they would have information about what had happened and why. However, a week into his journey, he still had not found anyone.

Is everyone dead? he wondered, but then tried to convince himself they couldn't be.

Yet no one seemed to be around. Not even other escaped prisoners.

Where did they go? he pondered. Deep down, though, he was glad he hadn't run into any. *They're ruthless.*

Still, with each major city he approached, answers to why the populace was scarce became clear. Illinois being rather narrow, but filled with cities, was hit hard. Most of the outlying areas around the cities were destroyed as well. To his surprise, it wasn't just Chicago that had been hit, but Peoria, and as he found out a week after that, Springfield too. This meant that almost all of Illinois was a festering graveyard. Though finding live people seemed to be impossible, coming upon the dead was a dime a dozen. It made the journey depressing and sickening.

Also affecting his escape was the fact that finding food was quite a chore. Surviving on whatever he could from wherever he could, he had to hunt for his sustenance. If a home had been destroyed, he would search it and take whatever he could find—some canned foods, some stale breads, or rotting fruits and vegetables. When nothing else was readily available, he would eat the burned tree bark and dead animals he found along the way—cats and dogs included. It disgusted him, but he had to get to Winnie and Michelle, and starvation was not going to be the reason he didn't make it.

I will eat the dead if need be, he decided early on, but hadn't been desperate enough to yet. As the weeks passed, though, Sean wondered how long it would be before he took that step. The hunger was thankfully dissipating as his body became used to subsisting on less (which had already been little considering he was in jail), but he knew he still needed to eat or soon he would be no help to anyone— including himself. His energy was slowly waning and his weight was dropping at an alarming rate, making him tire more quickly and be less sharp mentally.

3

One night, about a hundred miles out of St. Louis, which was on the border of Missouri and Illinois, the acid rains began. St. Louis, like the rest of the cities he had seen, was also leveled, and the land around it was scorched black. As Sean walked, he could feel his skin burn from the raindrops. He knew he needed to find shelter, so, crawling into the cockpit of an overturned pickup truck, he decided to hold until the rain stopped.

Inside, the driver awaited him. The skeletal remains of Lucas— according to his scripted name on a badge over his right pectoral—were frightening, yet oddly comforting. At least Sean wasn't alone.

"So, what brings you here?" Sean asked Lucas.

"The barbecue," Lucas answered back.

"Yeah, I heard the fat was in the fryer here!"

"You have no idea. Sometimes the cook burns the meat too much, but I love some good ol'-fashioned fried meat!"

"That's all we are these days!"

The conversation went on and on like this for hours. They discussed books, politics, even what their loved ones were doing while they were away. Soon, a regular camaraderie developed between Sean and the decomposing Lucas.

Am I going crazy? Sean figured he must be. *Why else would I talk to a dead man or laugh at the sight of tragedy?* He assumed that after weeks of loneliness, surrounded only by the moribund remains of a fractured reality, some kind of mental break was inevitable.

All he could do was hope that when all was said and done, he could pick up the pieces.

The next morning, Sean continued his journey, trying to forget his evening with Lucas. As hard as he could, Sean tried to convince himself that it had been a fever dream, just a moment of needed companionship. However, the pit in his stomach told him otherwise. It had been real to him, and even with the rise of the overcast sun, that fact wouldn't change.

As he continued to travel, Sean began to play games with himself, hoping to bring his mind back to reality. When he came to towns where only welcome signs remained, he imagined how they would have been portrayed on television.

What kind of genre would they have been?

Ducktown: cartoon.

Beersheba Springs: period piece.

Friendsville: Sitcom.

New Hope ...

4

It was in the town of New Hope, which lay right at the border entering Kentucky, that Sean's existence changed. It was a small, three-farmhouse place. Surprisingly, all still stood. Unfortunately, there were still bodies of the dead strewn about the streets, but in their cases, they had bullet wounds in their heads as opposed to being killed in their sleep. From the fact that these bodies were hog-tied by their hands and feet, Sean could tell they had died just as violently, though, and by some lunatic's hand. For a moment he wondered which was worse. Seeing these murdered people put Sean on edge. Someone might still be there, lying in wait, to kill him.

So much for a New Hope, Sean thought. *How ironic.*

The town was anything but what its name implied. Of all the towns he had come upon in this dire aftermath, New Hope seemed to be even more depressing than the others. Perhaps it was due to the name itself. If a place called New Hope could be so drenched in blood, what hope had Sean of ever finding a new place to call home?

Sean looked to the skies. He wasn't sure why he did that. He certainly wasn't looking for answers from the heavens. Instead, he simply felt compelled to, feeling so small, so insignificant among all the death and destruction. If Sean were the last man on earth, maybe the rules of nature were broken. Maybe simply wishing for the skies to open up and take him away from all this would be enough.

Which is when it happened.

It was as sudden as it was violent. The skies had grown a dark green. Everything around him looked sickly in tone. Despite this, an eerie calm had come across the wind. The air seemed to be sitting still, as if it were a layer of heavy cloth placed over the town. Lightning was shooting across the sky, rolling upon itself like veins of electricity through the thin skin of the clouds. A storm was brewing.

But what kind of storm is this?

Suddenly the wind picked up. It was a spinning wind, cylindrical in nature. Sean could see dust and debris being swooped up into the sky and turned into funnels. It was a tornado, Sean realized, but not any kind he had ever seen before. It was only a few seconds later that a second, third, fourth, and even a fifth funnel came into existence off the main cone of spinning wind. Like an octopus reaching out its tentacles for something to grab, they came after him.

Sean ran for cover. The storm let out a lurching scream of sucking power, and for a moment Sean thought this would be a fantastic way to die. All he had to do was ride the wind. Yet something inside him stirred. He couldn't give up! Winnie and Michelle pulled his mind into focus. He had to survive; he had to live on so that he could find them.

They are alive! He knew it deep down, and nothing was going to stop him from finding them. Not the apocalypse, not Mother Nature, and certainly not himself.

With the wind picking up speed, Sean could feel his clothes and hair begin to whip around. It was only a matter of time before he was sucked up completely. He needed to find shelter. As he moved in search of a place to hide, large chunks of brick were flying by his face, hitting the ground, and splattering apart even farther. Sean figured he had minutes before he died.

Suddenly he saw it: a large door in the ground, sealed by a metal casing.

A storm shelter! Sean realized. This was tornado country, after all, so people were prepared.

Thankfully, it couldn't have been more than forty yards away. He could reach it as long as the funnels didn't change direction. So, he booked it across the town of New Hope, dodging all obstacles. He leaped, ducked, and wiggled his way through the yards of dead bodies, trash, and cars. All the while, Sean could hear the screaming monster behind him. He pictured a face in the storm, opening its mouth wide, revealing sharp, glistening teeth, drenched red with blood and ready to swallow him whole.

When he was only fifteen yards away from the door, the storm started to throw its strength at him. Car hulks were beginning to fly around him; walls standing on their last legs fell and tried to flatten him. The storm was relentless in its pursuit of Sean, as if he were some sort of weather magnet pulling it toward him.

At ten yards, he could see the color of the door: red.

At five yards, he could see the paint that had been pulled away from the metal, revealing the stainless steel below.

At one foot away, he dove and grabbed onto the handles. They were locked! He pulled hard at them, but had no luck; the swinging doors to the bunker would not budge.

"Let me in!" he screamed as his legs were swept out from under him. The storm was sucking him up into the air. His legs flailed around as he held onto the door handles. It was as if he were a cowboy on a bucking bronco trying to whip him off. His fingers were starting to hurt from the strain of holding on, the skin of his fingertips turning red and then to white from the pressure.

"Please! Open the doors! I'm going to die out here!" he screamed again, hoping someone was inside.

Suddenly a click could be heard from inside the structure. The sound of something large and heavy scraping the doorway gave Sean hope, making him hold onto the doors even harder. Still he didn't know how much longer he could last.

Please open the doors fast, he thought; *my hands are slipping …*

With a clang they opened hard, outward, almost flinging him off into the storm. Holding on as hard as he could, Sean could see some figures below. He couldn't tell what they looked like, and he didn't care. Sean just wanted in. Fighting against the sucking wind, he reached up and closed the doors behind him, then locked the door with a clasp. Discovering a stronger metal bolt to the side of the doorway, he placed it in its slot and fully braced the door. The whistling wind could be heard beyond, and the doors shook violently at the roar of the wind, producing a loud rattling sound, but they would hold.

Sean looked around at his new surroundings. It was dark, but lit gently by gas lanterns. Five narrow concrete steps led down further into a room made of all metal. Packed to its ceiling of maybe five feet (he had to duck when standing) were canned food, water, and other amenities. This room was a survivor's paradise.

The discovery of all this would have been shocking enough had he seen it and nothing else, but standing in front of him were two children, one about ten and the other maybe eight. One girl and one boy standing alone in the room. The boy, the older of the two, stood stoically with a gun in his hand, pointing it directly at Sean's surprised face.

"Don't move or I'll shoot!" The boy said. Sean believed him. Then the little girl, with her sad blue eyes, turned to him.

"Mom won't wake up. Can you help her?"

Sean followed her pointing finger to a body slouched in the corner. Just from the look of the slumped-over body, the woman was obviously dead, but Sean knew the little girl was too young to understand.

"I can't," he said in as gentle a tone as he could muster. The little girl just looked at him, anger rising within her. She had a stare so sharp it could have cut a diamond. Sean had never seen a stare like that on a child before. It scared him.

"Shoot him then," she said without hesitation or emotion.

Sean looked from the little girl to the boy, who cocked the gun. With the click of the hammer, Sean found himself wishing he had stayed outside and taken his chances with the storm.

Nell

1

The infection began to set into Mark's left leg a week after the rescue. First the nub that had been created from the leftover skin of the ankle turned black. Then, the acrid smell of rotting flesh perfumed the air. Nell wasn't sure at first that it was a problem—she thought the coloring was simply a byproduct of the cauterization of the wound—but when the smell began, it was clear something was wrong.

2

Nell thought back to the moments after she and Mark had been saved. They were horrible moments. The two men who had helped her and Mark saw the damage to Mark's left side and knew something had to be done. Jerry, the older of the two men, gray-haired and wrinkled with age, was a medic in the war and therefore knew how to take action. Pragmatic, calm, and smart, he turned to her and said simply, "We need to cauterize the wound, or he will bleed to death."

Nell understood this to be true and did not panic at the notion. Instead, she screwed up the courage to be by Mark's side as the two men did the deed. They found a fireplace poker among the rubble, heated it, and waited until the tip of the poker turned red. With a piece of wood in Mark's mouth, they closed the wound. He squeezed Nell's hand hard, making her think for a moment that he had broken it.

With every burn of the poker against his flesh, blood-red smoke floated into the air. The smell of it was unbearable for Nell. Her stomach turned as she lost the little food she still had left inside. However she never let go of his hand. She was proud of that. When her man needed her the most, she was there for him. Jerry came to her in the minutes afterward, sweat beading down from his brow.

"Let's hope that worked."

She could hear the skepticism in his voice but knew it would all be fine. When Mark awakened afterward, he smiled at Nell, filling her with relief.

"Hey," he said, touching her face, "I told you it wasn't good." He laughed weakly as she kissed him deeply on the lips.

"Yeah. Get some sleep, Mark."

3

For the next week, inside a shelter that Nell and the two rescuers fashioned out of the remains of her home, Nell tried to help Mark, but he wasn't getting better. During the days he would barely stay awake, and at night, when his fever raged, he slept fitfully. Nell and the others raided the refrigerators in the neighborhood for food, but it didn't stay fresh long and they ate whatever canned food they could find. What Mark could eat helped him gain some strength to heal, but more often than not, he just threw it up.

To take her mind off the drama, Nell tried to imagine the two of them in their own little home, with four children and a dog. The heat emanating from his body, as well as the growing stench from Mark's wound, however, made it tough to get lost in her dreamland.

When the week had ended and Nell couldn't take it anymore, she went to Jerry for advice.

4

Jerry took a look at the leg. Red veins stretched out from the black skin of the nub and up to Mark's thigh.

"It's septicemia," he said to Nell. Nell had no idea what that was and it showed on her face, which is why Jerry added, "Blood poisoning. It occurs when the bloodstream becomes infected by bacteria through a wound. We need to amputate his whole leg."

Panic and dread took Nell over. She knew that in relationships, people who were beholden to one another sometimes had to make tough decisions for their partners' health, but that was something she didn't expect to have to worry about until way in the future. Yet in this new world, innocence and peace of mind had become a long-lost commodity. Oh, how she wished she could talk to Mark about what decision to make, but he was in and out of consciousness and in no shape to help make a decision. Nell didn't want to think about living in this godforsaken place without him, but that was exactly what she had to do unless she made the right decision for their futures.

"Do it," she said with steely resolution. Jerry nodded.

"I found this in the rubble," Jerry said, lifting an old-fashioned wood and metal handsaw. "The only problem I see with it is that the blade is bent and old. But I can't find anything better."

Nell stared at the tool. Old was an understatement; it had rust on the blade and looked like it could barely cut through a piece of paper, much less bone. Jerry saw her eyes studying the blade.

"I'll clean it and sharpen it as much as I can; most of the rust will come off. But I'm not sure how sharp I can get the blade."

"I trust you," was all she could really say.

5

That night Nell and Mark made love. It wasn't pleasurable. Both of them were too filled with sorrow to enjoy it. Mark fought off sleep and Nell tried to ignore the heat coming off his body so that they could share this moment. The smell of his leg was unbearable, though, making it hard on Nell to continue. Yet she did. It had been only two weeks since they both gave their virginity to each other, but since then, this was the only other time they had shared love. They both knew it could very well be their last time, at least together. So, neither person wanted to deny that moment to the other.

Afterward, Mark slept, and Nell held him tightly in her arms. The contentment she had felt after their first time was gone now. All she felt now was fear and anger. No one thinks they will be the ones who have to endure such hard times, but here she was, without parents and about to lose her first love, all the while trying to survive in a world gone insane.

What did I do to deserve this? she thought to herself over and over that night as sleep never came. When the sun rose into its gray hue (which was the new postapocalyptic daytime), Nell gently held Mark's hand.

"Just fight," she said to Mark, though he gave no response. The fever had knocked him out.

She hoped he stayed that way through the whole surgery.

6

Jerry had set up an operating area. He had boiled water over a flame, and the saw looked pristine except for its bent, dull blade. One could tell that Jerry had tried to straighten and sharpen it, but to no avail. Jerry and Winston (the other of the two rescuers) carried Mark to the table. He was so light now, having lost twenty pounds.

"He out?" Jerry asked.

"I guess so," Nell answered, stroking Mark's head.

"I'm sure once we begin cutting, he'll awaken briefly, but the body knows how to take care of itself. More than likely, he'll go into shock and pass out."

"Let's hope," Nell said.

Jerry grabbed the saw and began to put it in place.

"We will need to quickly tourniquet the wound. You have no idea how fast someone can bleed to death. Be ready for a lot of blood."

"I'm ready," she said, though she doubted that she really was. She watched silently as Jerry prepared to begin. Out of the corner of her eye, she saw Winston turn toward the horizon.

"What is that?" Winston exclaimed.

"What's what?" Nell asked, turning to look.

"That sound."

"Quiet, both of you; I need to concentrate!" Jerry belted out in exasperation.

"Wait, I hear it too," Nell said as a small rumbling sound like that of a motor began to get louder and louder.

"Yeah," said Jerry. "It sounds like a motorcycle."

"It sounds like a lot of motorcycles," agreed Winston.

As they stared into the distance, a gang of bikers came up over the ridge. Following close behind them was a crowd of stragglers. The crowd was plentiful—by the looks of it, hundreds strong.

Two of the riders at the front saw Nell and the others with her. They drove down to where they had set up for the amputation. The riders wore helmets, dark goggles, and red bandanas with skulls embroidered on them. Their mouths were covered, so what they looked like beneath was a mystery. They came to a stop a few feet away.

"What do we do?" Winston said, fear making his voice tremble.

"Stay calm," Jerry reassured, but Nell was scared for her life.

The two cyclists approached, both removing their helmets. The first of them was, surprisingly enough, a woman, though from her build it would have been hard to tell. One look at her, and it became apparent that she could easily take on any fool who might attack her.

Nell thought, *This woman was built for this new world.*

The second rider was a man, one of the biggest Nell had ever seen; he had to be at least six foot five, if not taller. His long hair and beard made him seem bearlike, which Nell found comforting.

"What's wrong with him?" the giant asked.

"Blood poisoning. We need to amputate," said Jerry.

"He's a goner," the tough women said back. She turned to look at the giant, who was clearly in charge.

"Go get the doctor," he told her, which she quickly did.

"You have a doctor?" asked Nell, on the verge of tears.

"Oh yes. And medicine."

"Oh God, thank you!" Tears flowed freely from Nell.

A doctor! she thought. *Mark's saved!*

The giant put his arms around Nell, holding her tightly to him.

"There, there, it's all going to be all right now."

And Nell believed him.

Part Two:

Survival

Sean

1

Sean stood hands up to the sky, staring down the barrel of the boy's gun. It wasn't much, a small six-shooter, like a gangster might have kept in the waist of his pants, but still, big or not, one shot from that gun would likely kill him. Despite all Sean had been through—gang fights, jail, an apocalypse, even that octo-twister—this young boy with his gun was the scariest thing he had ever experienced.

"Please, don't shoot! I have to get back to my daughter!" Sean yelled.

The boy pulled his gun away and then looked over at his sister.

"You have a daughter?" the boy asked.

"Yes," he said, nodding furiously. This seemed to be working. "They live in California. I'm headed there."

"Is California okay?" the boy asked with a twinge of hope in his voice.

"I don't know, but I can take the two of you with me. We can find out together."

"Not without our mother!" the girl screamed at him.

Sean had to make them realize there was no hope for her. If they wanted to save themselves, they had to go with him to find help. This was not going to be an easy task.

"She's dead," he said calmly, putting as much sorrow into the sound of his voice as possible. He knew if they perceived him as any sort of threat to their mother at all, they would kill him.

"No, she's not!" The boy whined, the pain evident in his voice. He pointed the gun at Sean again. To Sean's surprise, however, the girl did not seem nearly as shocked by what he was saying. Though the younger of the two, she was clearly the more mature.

"Are you sure?" she asked him.

"No, I'm not a doctor. But it doesn't seem she's breathing."

The girl looked down at her mother. Sean did as well. Her hair was matted with blood, she had no color in her skin, and from the looks of it, the woman lying motionless in a ball on the floor had lived a hard life. Some bruises on her body seemed older than others, indicating she may have been beaten before she died. She also had leathery skin and calloused hands, showing a life of work. From the way the girl was looking at the body, Sean could tell she had cared for her mother quite a bit. The son too, from the way he was acting. And Sean understood the love for a good mom.

2

Just like these two children, Sean would have done anything to protect his mother. For many years, he watched as his biological father had beaten his mother regularly. He recognized the pain in these kids' eyes, and couldn't help but see himself in them.

Is that what these kids saw? Is that what happened to their mother?

Thinking back on it now, Sean realized Ethan Varley Jr. was an honest-to-god monster. He would beat her, Sean, and his older brother every day and twice on Sundays. Yet he worked hard to help support the family. He was not a good man in the slightest, but he did try to provide his family with a home and food to eat. While Sean's mother would go on to marry a few other men, Varley was by far the worst. Sean was glad when they ran off, leaving the son of a bitch behind. They changed their names (taking his mother's maiden name) and created a whole new life for themselves.

If only my mom was the type of woman who could have stayed alone, she would have saved herself three other husbands' worth of heartache.

Thinking about his mother made Sean feel a twinge of regret. He had hoped one day he might still be able to bring a smile to her face. Now he doubted that opportunity would ever come.

There's no way she survived all this. She simply wasn't that kind of strong.

3

Turning his attention back to the kids, he started to approach the body.

"Hey! What are you doing?" yelled the boy as he closed the distance between himself and Sean, more than ready to pull the trigger. The boy forced the mouth of the gun into Sean's side with some strength. Sean was surprised how much he found it hurt.

"Look, I'm going to check out your mom. I want to take a look at her. Maybe I can help her; I don't know."

"I thought you said you weren't a doctor." The boy pressed the gun against Sean again.

"I'm not, but I think I can tell if someone is dead or not."

The boy looked to his sister. It was obvious who was in charge of the decisions.

"If you do anything strange, mister, I'll have my brother shoot you. You understand?" she said defiantly.

"I understand," Sean calmly replied, sidestepping her brother and arriving at the body. He went down on one knee, turning the body toward him. He pulled back a bit in revulsion; her face was severely beaten in, swollen, and unrecognizable as human. Whatever had done this to her had done a thorough job of it.

"What happened?" Sean asked, repulsed and holding back the urge to vomit.

Losing it won't help these kids, he thought; *stay strong.*

"What do you care?" the boy cried out in a voice filled with pain.

"Did your father do this?" Sean asked, anger filling inside him.

"What?" said the boy.

"Of course not," said the girl. "Our father died when we were babies. Look, mister, is she alive or isn't she?"

Sean didn't really know how to find a pulse. He understood the theory behind it, but wasn't sure he truly knew where to put his fingers conclusively. Feeling her wrist for it, he did notice that her body was cold. This all but guaranteed she was dead. However to make sure, he came up with a better idea.

"Do you have a small mirror?" he asked.

"A what?" asked the girl.

"A mirror? Or piece of glass, something I can check her breathing with?"

He could tell the mother's chest wasn't moving, but her breath could have been imperceptible to the naked eye. Sean had to be able to convince these children of the truth.

"In the old, old days, the days before electricity and holographic 4-D imaging, they used to check if someone was dead by putting a piece of glass to their nose."

The girl walked away, and then came back and handed him a small broken piece of window.

"If it fogged up, it meant the person was still alive, as the breath hitting the cold glass would make it steam; if it didn't do that, then you knew your answer."

Sean took the glass from the girl and placed it underneath the woman's nose. After a few long seconds and no fog to be reported, he dropped the glass and put his head to her chest.

Maybe I didn't have the glass on her nose, he thought.

Sean put his ear down to listen. No heartbeat. No movement. She had to be dead.

Raising himself up on his feet, he turned and looked at the two children.

"Well?" the girl asked with the most emotion he had heard out of her.

"She's dead."

The boy let out a loud cry, while the girl just stood there nodding.

"Just as I thought," she said.

It was impressive how mature this young girl was. It was also sad. If this girl had ever been a happy-go-lucky child, one who enjoyed pigtails and puppy dogs, she wasn't now. Essentially, if it hadn't been for the dirty doll she clutched in her arms, one might think she wasn't a child at all; just a bitter adult trapped in a child's body.

She looked up at Sean suddenly, her eyes full of determination.

"Tomorrow we go with you then."

"No!" her brother said. "He may be like the other one! We can't trust him."

"What other one?" Sean asked, to no avail. The girl simply continued past his question.

"I trust him. And that's all that matters."

Her brother nodded in agreement, though it was obvious the boy didn't trust Sean at all.

"You can sleep back there," the girl said, pointing to the other side of the room.

"You can't put him over there; what about the—" but the girl cut her brother off.

"See you in the morning," she simply stated and pointed again.

Sean took the hint and began to walk away. He probably should have asked their names, but felt uneasy about going back. He could make out the faint sounds of the two talking, whispering, probably about him. Sean knew, although he was to be their guide during their long trek to California, the two could kill him at any moment. While he would have liked to believe the brother and sister weren't capable of such an act, he could tell they were. It was in their eyes.

As he came upon the final shelving unit—where the girl had pointed—he noticed a large clump covered by a sheet at the end of the aisle. The clump had been pushed against the metal wall that made up the room around him. The covered object's shape was awkward, with points of odd geometry jutting out in all directions. Whatever was under the sheet had not been carefully placed there. Sean paused a moment.

They want me to sleep over here?

He looked back at the children. Only the girl remained in view. Her face was stone; no emotion or clues to her thoughts could be gleaned from just looking at her. Sean simply smiled and waved at her, hoping to break the tension between them all. The girl did not smile back.

"Only me," Sean said to himself sarcastically as he walked into the aisle. "Of all the bunkers in all the world, I had to walk into this one," he remarked, riffing on some line from some movie his mother had made him watch as a kid; the line had always stood out in his mind, even to this day. Although he remembered it having to do with a girl and a gin joint and not a person's survival. It was also in black and white, so that was unfortunate. Still Sean remembered that guy's luck was sort of shitty too, as he was always either running from the law—having maybe killed a man—or from Nazis, and he even lost the girl he loved.

Fairly similar lives, he thought.

About halfway down the aisle, he grabbed a can from the shelf and sat down with it. The shelves were filled with canned foods and bottled water. He opened the pop-top of the can immediately. He was so hungry that he didn't care if it was pigs' knuckles; he would eat it to the very last drop. He took a bite, then another, and another. Truth be told, the product had almost no taste. He looked at the can and read the label: Peach Slices.

Better than pigs' knuckles. He laughed to himself.

Sean ate all the peaches, and then he drank the juices in the can. His mind started to come back to him a bit, energy building; it was probably just the sugar in the fruit, but he wasn't going to complain.

After a moment of enjoyment, Sean's eyes turned to the clump.

What's under that sheet? He had to know.

Sean started toward it, creeping along low to the ground, trying not to draw attention to what he was doing. As he reached the clump, he looked back toward the end of the aisle—no one was there. Slowly, he reached his hand out and pulled the sheet back, but only a little, revealing a foot underneath it.

"Oh god," he said out loud without realizing it.

Sean again looked back, now considerably paranoid he might be next. Still, no one was watching him. Sean removed the rest of the sheet. Staring up at him were the blank eyes of a man, about forty-five, graying at the temples, with a bullet hole where one of his eyes used to be. Sean could also see blood on the man's chest revealing another gunshot wound. One thing had been confirmed: unless they had more bullets stashed away, that gun had only four shots left.

4

That night, as Sean tried to get some sleep, he could hear the brother crying about his mother.

"Stop crying!" he heard the sister say. "You're such a baby."

"But Momma's really gone," the brother squeezed out between sobs.

"We knew that, you idiot. What did you expect?"

"Don't talk to me like that. Mom and Dad would give you a good whoopin'!"

"Yeah, well, they ain't here, and we are. So buck up and start acting like the older brother."

They went on like this through the night until they eventually went quiet. It reminded Sean of the sleepovers he had as a child. He and his friends would compete to see who could stay up the longest, eventually drifting off to sleep, sometimes in mid-sentence. Though Sean didn't know whether to feel sorry for these two or scared of them, he knew that tomorrow they would depart this place together, each of them having to trust the others for their very survival.

Of all the places I could have ended up in, why this one? he asked himself.

That one thought repeated in his head over and over until he suddenly drifted off to sleep. Oddly enough, it was in mid-sentence.

Aiden

1

"We can't just leave!" said Nurse Cindy, whose face over the last month had gotten terrifyingly awful. Large chunks of skin had fallen off, only to grow new sores and pustules. To look at her, no one would guess that two months earlier, she was a gorgeous blonde with perfect skin.

"I don't think we have a choice," responded Aiden. "We've put this off as long as we dare. Look at us. Whatever is doing this to us is in here."

"No! It's the lack of B12!" yelled Nurse Ellen.

"Fine. Either way, if we hope to get better, we need to get up top and get out."

"And what if we don't get better?" asked Rory. "What if we get up there, and without any protection from whatever happened up there, we end up dying."

"It's possible," Aiden said, conceding that things might not be any better out of the basement. On the other hand he figured they had a better chance of survival there than staying put. "But if we die up there, trying to help ourselves, that can only be better than dying down here."

Everyone was silent, thinking over the options. This debate had been going on for weeks, and the only person who always kept his opinion to himself was Dr. Savage. Since the moment his looks began to fall apart, his magnetism seemed to die. This bothered Aiden; he had counted on the doctor for support and guidance, and he wasn't giving any.

Hopefully that changes soon, Aiden thought.

"So, what do we do once we're up there?" Tamera asked. "I mean ... Where do we go?"

This had been the question that plagued Aiden's mind for weeks. Frankly, he didn't have an answer. Yet he gave one anyway.

136

"I think we try to go to Camp Pendleton," he explained.

"That's all the way down by San Diego!" Cindy exclaimed.

"Yes," Aiden continued, "it is. But if the military is still there, then they may be able to help us. It's the best option I can think of."

"This is crazy!" Cindy continued to argue. "We're just going to leave what little shelter we have and take our chances out there without any guarantee that we will be able to survive?"

"We're not surviving here!" Aiden lost his temper at her; he was just so tired of arguing. "Listen, do what you want, but I'm leaving."

"You open that door and you could kill us all," Rory said.

"That's a chance I'll take. If anyone wants to join me, you're invited," Aiden said.

"We can't let you just open the door," Rory insisted.

"Then you better kill me, because tomorrow I'm leaving."

The tension in the room was palpable. It was clear that no one knew what to do, and with the lack of leadership, there was no clear direction. One thing was extremely clear, though: unless someone they all respected took up that role, there was a good chance they might all kill each other.

"We go," Dr. Savage suddenly said. His voice was calm and quiet, as it usually was, but there was also a newfound determination in it. When he spoke, the room froze. Everyone was so surprised he said anything that they all listened for more. "Aiden is right; we are slowly dying here in a miserable way."

"But, Doctor—" began Cindy. He raised his hand, cutting her off.

"There's no more discussion. You may stay behind if you wish. That goes for everyone. But I'm leaving with Aiden. For those who want to come, we need to pack up supplies, and we will take the ambulance we have on site. Hopefully the roads aren't too congested. We will see how far the gas in the tanks takes us, and then we'll reevaluate. Any questions?"

No one had any. The rest of the day was spent packing and getting ready. Aiden felt relieved.

Finally, he thought, *a leader.*

The next morning, they were on their way.

2

Once on the road, things got immediately better. Whether it was the fact that they were being proactive or just the change in scenery, all of their spirits were lifted. Which was a good thing. After all, in various forms of the same thing, they were all losing hair and teeth, getting pustules on their faces, and starting to look inhuman, so going on a road trip was just what the doctor ordered.

As they drove south, things went smoothly at first. The roads were ripped up and filled with potholes that they had to avoid, but as far as traffic and stalled cars, there was little to none. Since the attacks happened so early in the morning, most of the cars were off the roads. That made maneuvering easy for this crew. Aiden shuddered to think what it would have been like if there had been a warning or if the attacks came midday. The few roadblocks they brushed against, like fallen trees or the random overturned car, weren't hard to deal with. The trees were so burned to a crisp that it took but a touch for them to disintegrate into ash, while the cars were easily pushed aside to be cleared. The hardest thing for them all to stomach was the sheer destruction around them. Having been blocked from it all this time, it was a shock to finally see what they were contending with.

San Francisco was still smoldering and surrounded by ash clouds. It was leveled and nothing more than flat land. The great hills of the once-glorious metropolis were gone. Not even a building or a bridge remained. Aiden wondered what Alfred Hitchcock would have made of the town now. Once a famous feature of his films, San Francisco was no more. Alcatraz, abandoned to rot years ago when it was shut down as a tourist attraction, was also gone. Now, the whole island was but a few rocks peeking through the surface of the water. In the bay there were dead things—not human corpses, because all humanity here was destroyed—but fish, great white sharks, and even whales floated on the surface. As they got to the outlying areas, the redwood forest, one of the greatest and oldest features in America, was shredded. Only bent-over stalks of half-burned trees remained, and where there once were only leaves for sky, gray, thick air now floated.

"This is unbelievable," Tamera said for everyone.

"I guess we should be thankful we are even still alive. I'd say our looks don't matter as much now," added Aiden.

Continuing on their journey, they steadily passed through the bay area, driving out of their way east to avoid Oakland. After a few hours, they crossed down into the flatlands of the central valley. They had hoped to run into other survivors, but all they found was annihilation. Modesto—gone. Fresno—leveled. Even small towns like Turlock, Merced, and Clovis were barely standing, leaving behind only destroyed homes and dead bodies. Overall, California was a ghost state.

"Do you think there is anyone to find out here?" asked Cindy.

"There has to be," Ellen said in a hopeful but questioning tone.

"Bakersfield is next," said the doctor with dread in his voice, and Aiden understood why. It was the doctor's hometown, and Aiden could only imagine the emotions stirring inside him.

Arriving outside of Bakersfield eight hours after they had left San Francisco—usually a four-hour drive—the doctor had them stop the ambulance so he could see the destruction. Like the other towns, Bakersfield was nothing but ash and ruins. Tears came to the doctor's eyes, which, from his reaction, stung the wounds on his face.

"Seeing one's home destroyed like this ... It's ... sobering," the doctor stated. "It's like my whole life has been wiped away. As if my past never existed at all."

Aiden could understand this feeling. He felt much the same way after Hollywood had been shut down. He thought he handled the emotions of it well at the time. How the doctor would handle this, though, was anybody's guess.

"I've been alive for a long time. I've lived through some horrible things. But this—this is beyond imagining. So many people, so many families I've known. Dead. In an instant. Just ... gone."

This is the moment, Aiden thought. *Depending upon how the doctor recovers from this is how we as a group will go. If he falls off the cliff and gives in to despair, so will we.*

"We need to let go," the doctor continued. "We need to say good-bye to the past and embrace this new world."

Okay, thought Aiden, *this is not how I saw this going.*

"We have all been born again," he said. "Born into this new world, and we must now find a way to survive. I will cure us. I will see that we fix humanity, so that if we are indeed the last people on earth, we will help create a better world so that this ... can never happen again."

Heading back to the ambulance, Dr. Savage put a hand on Aiden's shoulder.

"I will need your help," the doctor said to Aiden. "Can I count on you to do whatever it takes to help fix this world?"

Aiden didn't quite know what to say. *What does he mean by asking if I will help him "fix the world"?*

"Of course," Aiden said.

"Good," the doctor said through a smile. "Now let us continue on to see how much work we have ahead of us."

With that, everyone returned to the ambulance, and they drove on into the distance.

3

It wasn't until they arrived in the mountain town of Frazier Park that they found some other survivors. Situated on top of Grapevine Pass, which connects the Central Valley to the Los Angeles basin, Frazier Park had once been an idyllic place to live the rural life. During the troubles of the last century, Frazier Park slowly became nothing more than a rest stop filled with uneducated poor trash. It seemed that the town had been untouched by the attacks due to its placement in the mountains, but one of the lousy little secrets of this area was that all the pollutants from Los Angeles and Bakersfield traveled up into the town's air, poisoning everyone who lived there. Which is why, when Aiden, the doctor, and the rest of the crew arrived, they found a town full of sick individuals just like them.

The whole town of about 150 had the same symptoms as Aiden's group. The cracking skin was the first horribly painful change. Soon, they all developed the red lesions and pustules. The hard, round, egg-like nodules protruded from where their skin had cracked, creating a redness around the infected area, oozing every few days. Where the ooze soaked into the skin, more cracks would form, followed by more lumps. Eventually, they would fall off, but as Aiden and his group had learned the hard way, they would be replaced by even larger versions. The lesions were purple and tender. They had a texture like scales to the touch. In short, it was becoming very clear that this town and all of Aiden's group were beginning to look like monsters.

In a weird way, this whole process relieved Aiden. He found a certain freedom in no longer having to care about his looks. He also found his mind was clear for the first time in his life. He wasn't thinking about his hair or his complexion, nor was he concerned about his muscular figure. All he kept thinking about was when he would die. It seemed reasonable to think this physical metamorphosis was only a precursor to their bodies completely failing. As it turned out, the people of Frazier Park were thinking the same thing.

They were all wrong.

4

"What are you doing here?" said the police chief of Frazier Park to the doctor as he led the group down the hill into town. The chief had his gun out and badge up, but with the blood coming out of the wounds along his face, it was really hard to fear him. He was no better off than they were.

"Do not fear us," the doctor said. "We are just like you. Hurting, scared … We need a place to stay for the night and hoped we might find you to be hospitable. I am a doctor and these are my companions. We may be able to help some of you while we are here."

"Do you know what's happening to us?" the chief asked.

"I do," Dr. Savage said.

News to me, Aiden thought. *I hope he isn't still thinking it is lack of B12.*

"Please," the chief said, "help us."

"I will."

5

For the night, each person was given a room at a local motel, of which there were plenty. Once there, they were given some water to wash with (it was cold), and some food that consisted of stale bread and soup that was nothing more than water with some sprouts (also cold). Nevertheless, it all helped.

As night fell, Dr. Savage and Aiden met with the chief and mayor of Frazier Park. They sat in the lobby of the motel, which had a fireplace and some old leather armchairs. The fire made the room warm despite the frigid temperatures outside, and the chairs were the most comfortable Aiden had felt since before the surgery. In a way, this was a little bit of heaven.

"So, I want to thank you all for your hospitality," the doctor said to the two men.

"You are very welcome, Doctor," said the Mayor. "If you don't mind, may I ask what your specialty is?"

"I don't mind at all," replied the doctor. "But first, we should probably exchange names. With all the fuss entering town, I don't think we've done that yet."

"It seems we've all lost our manners with the world," said the mayor.

"Yes, it does. I am Dr. Savage."

"I am Mayor Trank, and this is Chief Littles."

"And my companion here you may even recognize; this is Aiden Ross."

The mayor's and chief's eyes opened wide.

"You mean Aiden Ross as in *the* Aiden Ross?" asked the chief.

"One and the same," Aiden responded.

"Wow," the mayor said. "I loved your movies when I was a kid."

"Thank you."

"Well, isn't that just the be-all end-all!" added the chief.

"No," said Dr. Savage, "I think that already happened."

"Yes," the mayor agreed. "I guess it has."

"So," the chief plowed on, "what is happening to us?"

The doctor smiled.

"It's quite simple," he said. "We're mutating."

Aiden hadn't been expecting this response. He was expecting the B12 explanation or something about radiation poisoning, but not mutation. The chief and the mayor hadn't been expecting it either; both men began to get emotional.

"Oh, my God," said Mayor Trank."

"It's not as bad as it sounds," added the doctor. "Things could be much worse. We could be dying of radiation poisoning or already blown to smithereens. As I see it, we are the lucky ones."

"Lucky ones?" Chief Littles remarked. "You have an odd sense of luck!"

"Maybe," the doctor replied. "But as far I can see, I believe I can cure us. I can't do the same for the dead."

Everyone was silent for a moment as they let this last remark sink in.

"Cure us?" the mayor repeated.

"How?" asked the chief. Aiden had to admit to himself he wanted to know too.

"It's a process," the doctor began. "Possibly a long and even painful one, but I will find the cure. You have to trust in me."

"Why should we?" Chief Littles demanded.

"Well, have you seen anyone other than us?"

"No, in fact, we haven't," replied the mayor.

"Exactly. So as far as we know, I may be the best bet for humanity's future. I am a geneticist, after all, and I know a thing or two about what makes us human. Who else if not me?"

Chief Littles looked at Aiden. "Is he who he says he is?" he asked.

"Yes," was all Aiden added to the conversation.

"Then I guess you're right," said the chief. "So what do we do next?"

"Next? We go out there into that world, and we try to find a medical facility where I can do my work from. I promise within months, I will have a cure."

"You want us to leave here?" asked the mayor.

"Of course," said the doctor. "If you don't, you're all going to die."

"Are you threatening us?" the chief asked brusquely.

"Not at all! Right now your town is situated in the worst possible place. The fallout from several nuclear explosions is slowly infecting the air, and at the moment giving you only enough radiation to mutate you. Give it time, and that radiation will kill you."

Aiden watched as the doctor's words sank in. Even he was ready to hit the road running.

"So," the doctor began again, "what's next, you ask? Next, you get everyone in your town together and tell them to follow me."

6

The next day, the town of Frazier Park was abandoned. It didn't take long for Mayor Trank and Chief Littles to convince the 150 people left in town to leave. Once they explained that they were all mutating and eventually going to die, everyone was ready to go. The plan was that they would traverse the Grapevine Pass and see how close to Los Angeles they could get. The hope was that in some of the small suburbs that made up the Los Angeles basin, they might find other survivors and the supplies the doctor needed to begin to work on a cure.

Leading the pack of pickup trucks and SUVs, the ambulance headed down the mountain. When the road leveled out in another town, the sky was gray over this town as well, and the wind from the Los Angeles blast had clearly hit with uncompromising strength. Nothing was left but flattened homes.

"Nothing to be salvaged here," Aiden said from behind the wheel of the ambulance. "Should we go around?"

"Yes," remarked the doctor. "Look in the distance."

All they could see was orange fire and ash cloud.

"It's all destroyed," the doctor stated.

"Well, I'm glad we filled up in Frazier Park," Aiden said. "But if we go for too long trying to get around all this, we're going to run out of gas."

"I understand," said the doctor. "Just drive."

Turning east on another highway, Aiden led the wagon train of cars forward.

7

It wasn't long before they came upon another small town. Keeping their distance, Chief Littles, the doctor, and Aiden scouted what condition it was in, how many might still be living there, and what supplies they might have. The rest of the group was parked out of sight and far enough away from prying eyes that no one would even know they were there.

"Doesn't look like there was much damage here," said the chief, handing his binoculars over to the doctor.

The doctor peeked in.

"It looks very nice," the doctor said.

"I only saw about twenty homes, but there's a grocery store, a hardware store, a gas station, and some other small buildings. This isn't a large place, but there might be some supplies."

"So," Aiden began, "where is everyone who lived here?"

"They're here," the chief remarked. "I saw a few of them through some windows. I think they're just hiding."

"Let's see if we can get them to come out," said the doctor.

8

Entering the town, the three men kept their guard up. It was quiet, which in this world was something to worry about. As they walked, Aiden could feel the blood filling his shoes from all the open sores he had on his feet. The sores made every step excruciating, and with every step he was reminded of what they all looked like. He wondered how that would go over with the people in this town, if, that was, they didn't already look like them.

"Hello?" yelled Chief Littles.

No answer.

"Maybe it's abandoned?" asked Aiden.

"I told you I saw them," said Littles. "This is being lived in. I'll try again. Hello?"

With this second call, a woman holding a toddler came out of one of the buildings. She was going about her day, whatever that consisted of, and singing a tune to her little one.

"I'm picking up my baby bumblebee, won't my mother be so proud of me! I'm picking up my baby bumblebee—*ouch*! It stung me!"

Her voice was appealing, and Aiden was surprised how reassuring the singing was. Until then, he wasn't sure he would ever get to enjoy such simple pleasures again. A small smile crept across his face as the woman suddenly turned and noticed them. Her eyes went wide, and her song stopped.

"Hi," the chief began, "we're—"

But he didn't get to say anything more. The woman screamed at the top of her lungs as if she were seeing monsters instead of men—monsters which, Aiden realized, they closely resembled.

"Please," Littles tried to plead with her, but was unable to through her cries. Suddenly she dropped her baby and ran. The child began to cry as he was abandoned by his mother and hit the ground hard. Aiden went to the child and bent to help.

"I wouldn't do that if I were you," said Chief Littles.

"We can't just leave it there," Aiden replied back.

"If they see you touching the child, they may kill you."

"They who?" responded Aiden. "No one else is here."

That's when a gunshot rang out. Aiden looked up, and a group of about fifteen men, followed by another ten or so women, came bounding up to them. They were armed with guns and other assorted weapons, like knives and even pitchforks. To Aiden, it looked like a scene from a horror movie, but instead of playing the hero, Aiden and the others were the things that went bump in the night.

"Don't touch the baby!" one of the men said, pointing a sawed-off shotgun in his direction.

"Okay," Aiden replied with his hands up, backing away, "I was just trying to help."

Once he was far enough away, the mother ran to grab her child.

You're a bitch to have dropped him in the first place, Aiden thought; *should kill you for that—*

Aiden paused.

What did I just think?

"What do you want?" the man with the shotgun yelled at them.

"We are looking for some shelter and supplies—" the chief began but was quickly cut off.

"Get outta here!" The man pointed the gun at them hard.

"But why?" Aiden responded.

"Have you looked at yourselves?" said the man. "I don't know what's wrong with you, but we don't want you here."

"Please—" began the chief, taking a step forward, but this time the gun went off. The chief was thrown back as the spray from the shotgun hit him square in the chest, opening up a huge crater where his heart used to be.

"Holy shit!" yelled Aiden, looking at the doctor who just stood there, watching, analyzing the situation, and staying perfectly calm.

"That was rash," Dr. Savage said. "We could have helped you, but now we won't."

"Help us?" The man laughed. "We don't need your help, you freaks! Now get out before I kill you too!"

"You need my help more than you know," was all the doctor said in retort, and then he began to walk away. Aiden followed, scared out of his mind.

As they exited the town, Aiden felt like he was going to throw up.

"Well, that was a disaster," Aiden said through gasps for air.

"No, it wasn't. We now know they have the supplies we need, or they wouldn't be protecting it as much as they are. We also know they are turning into us."

"What?"

"Did you see the red spots and small cracks along their cheeks and lips? It's just beginning for them, but soon they will be like us. If we invade the town and take care of some of the men, the women and children will fall in line with us, and we will be able to take this town for our own."

"You have to be kidding. Invade the town? What are we?"

"I thought you knew that already," the doctor said with a smile. "We're monsters."

9

When they returned without the chief and explained the events, the people of Frazier Park were more than ready to get revenge for their fallen comrade. A few among the town had been in the war, and were all too eager to help form a plan of attack. They realized the people in the town were outnumbered and stood no chance of holding them off. Even if a few of them had to die, it was worth it for the supplies in the town.

Entering under cover of night, the group was stealthily quiet. The people who lived there all still had homes and were hunkered down inside them. Each house was surrounded by ten from the attacking group. Once the signal was given, the invaders entered the homes, took the families by surprise, and overpowered them. After that, the doctor had the men of the town brought forward into the street.

With torches blazing, the doctor walked up and down in front of the men. The women and children of the town were being held captive in a huddled mass, crying and watching their men being analyzed. Finally the doctor stepped to the man who had held the shotgun at them earlier that day.

"Where is this man's shotgun?" the doctor asked.

"Here," said one of the invading group and handed it to him.

"Is it loaded?" the doctor asked.

"Yes."

Boom! sounded the shotgun as the doctor killed the man. He had aimed it at the man's face, which no longer remained. It blew apart like a watermelon falling from on high. Aiden looked away in disgust but was smiling as well.

The bastard deserved it, he thought.

"Anyone else want to screw with us?" the doctor challenged the gathered group of men. No one answered. "Good. I am a doctor. I do not like to take life, but I will if it means the difference between survival or death. This man attacked us first when all we wanted was a little help. Now, we have taken over the town. We mean to take what we need and leave. I suggest you do the same. Those wounds on your faces and bodies are just the beginning of what is happening to you. We started off just like you, but look at what we've turned into! You are doomed to become the same. Join us, and I will help you. I am searching for a cure, and I will make every one of us normal again if it's the last thing I do. If you do not agree to go with us, stay behind, but know this: you will die, and there is no hope for you other than me. So think long and hard. It's a life-or-death decision."

With that, the doctor stepped away from the gathering and left everyone to ponder his words. Most of the men eventually agreed to join the doctor's new society.

10

The next morning, the doctor had everyone gather what they needed, fill their cars with gas, and take the new people who agreed to go with them.

Annette

1

The valley in Wyoming was beautiful. Annette suspected it might be the last perfect place on earth. Surrounded by snowcapped mountains and split by a river so calm and replete with trickling sounds, it almost seemed like a recording for relaxation. Annette could only see this place as a heaven on earth. Perhaps the last haven of tranquility for anyone out there, beyond the mountains, needing rescue. She and her followers could call this place home, but first they had to make sure it was truly habitable.

Along with not being some kind of mirage for the desperate, Annette thought. *Plus, assuming it was real, what of the people who actually lived in this town?*

Though the sign on the outskirts of town read "Bastion, Wyoming: Pop. 1,500," from Annette's vantage point, it was hard to tell if anyone was still alive down there.

If there are survivors, how would they react to a group of strangers from the outside? Will they take us in with open arms, or shoot us onsite to protect what was their own?

Unfortunately, there was no way of knowing the repercussions of their actions until it was too late. Annette only knew one thing for sure—and that was contact had to be made.

"I will be going into the town to see if I can work out a deal that allows us to enter and maybe find homes here," Annette said to the group. "I don't want to bring you all in right away—we don't want to be presumptuous—so I would like two other people to join me."

"I'll go," Frank chimed in; it was exactly what Annette had been hoping for. Though Frank had been with them the shortest amount of time, he had shown his mind to be sharp and knowledgeable. True, he said little about his past during their long conversations about politics and life, but Annette could tell he was a man of great intellect.

His mind worked in ways that Annette realized hers never could. Therefore, she concluded maybe he was a scientist in the old world, or even a genius. Either way, he was a boon for her group's future and a great man to have by her side when she approached the leaders of Bastion.

"Thanks, Frank. That would be great," she added.

"I'll go," said Milton, in a way that expressed more about his dread of doing so than his courage.

"No," Annette replied. "You've been sick of late; I think it will be best for you to stay here." He nodded in agreement, and she was thankful her refusal to use him didn't hurt his feelings. The truth was his paranoia was not the energy she needed for this.

On and on they went through the group. Each person who volunteered, she had a reason for him or her not to go. Certainly they were good reasons, but the truth was she knew who she wanted all along. The problem was, Willy would never agree to go unless pushed to do so, and she had hoped this little display would do just that.

"What about you, Willy?" Annette asked. "You've been quiet."

"Awww, hell," he said. "I knew you was going to ask me next."

"You don't want to help the group?" Annette challenged.

"I help the group all the time. I catch us food, I protect us—"

"Which is exactly why I need you. Frank and I can do most of the talking, but we need you for protection."

Willy sighed in discontentment.

"Fine," he reluctantly agreed. "I ain't promising to be Mr. Goody-Two-shoes though. Someone messes with me, I mess with him back—got it?"

"Of course," Annette said and smiled to herself, knowing she had gotten the result she had wanted from the beginning.

Annette realized Willy wasn't all he purported to be. It was clear he had issues and could be violent, but he was useful to her. He could hunt, and he had shown he had no problem in doing what it took to survive. According to him, he was a construction worker before, which was how he had built his muscles up to the mounds that they were. Annette had been around enough liars in her life—her four husbands included—that she knew when someone was lying. So she knew he was hiding something, but his intimidating look and uneasy temperament made him perfect for this mission. She needed someone who showed that they weren't a group to be taken advantage of and could be threatening. Willy hit those marks for sure. So, as long as Willy continued to mind his p's and q's around Annette, then she figured he could say he was a tightrope walker in the circus and she'd be okay with that.

Annette hoped that with these two men by her side, she could secure a safe entrance for her group and hopefully a new home for them as well.

"So, how do we do this?" Frank asked Annette.

"Well, I don't think there is any other way than to just head down the mountain and say, 'Hi, how are you?'" replied Annette. That comment might have come off as sarcastic, but honestly she meant it sincerely. She saw no better way to accomplish her goals than to just go for it.

"I'll bring a couple of weapons," said Willy. "I've got my knife."

"And you can take my gun," added Ted.

"I don't think bringing weapons is the right move," added Frank. "If we are trying to show we are peaceful and not a threat to their way of life, we need to be unarmed."

"Is that safe?" asked Marcy.

"Probably not," added Frank. "But it will send them a message as to our intentions."

"I ain't going anywhere without my Impaler," Willy shot back.

"Then you shouldn't come," responded Frank.

"I don't want to go anyway, so that's fine!" Willy sulked.

Great, Annette thought, *destroy everything I just worked out!*

"No, Willy," Annette said, talking to him like a mother would her four-year-old child who wanted to bring his new toy to a fancy dinner. "I need you to be a part of this. Just leave the weapon this once. It'll be okay."

Willy looked at her suspiciously, searching deep in Annette's eyes for any sign of weakness. Annette didn't show any. She just kept his gaze and tried not to let the worries she had deep down betray her.

"Fine," Willy agreed. "But Ted and Milton need to be armed and watching us as we enter the town. That way, if there is a problem, they can bail us out."

"Agreed," Annette said. "Once down there, we'll ask to talk to their mayor or whoever is in charge, and we'll explain ourselves. I'm sure they are reasonable people. They won't be looking to fight, not after everything that has happened. Ultimately, I think it'll all go great."

"You're a lot more positive than I am," added Alice.

"It's the only way I know how," agreed Annette. "Well, gentlemen, get some rest; we leave in the morning."

2

Descending into the valley with determination, Annette, Willy, and Frank kept an eye on their surroundings. She could feel her anxiousness growing deep down inside with every step.

What if this is the wrong plan? she thought. *What if I get us all killed and fail my group completely? I'm no leader; I've just been thrown into that role.*

However, none of these thoughts were helpful at the moment, so she tried to push them away. She had to do something, and as far as she could tell, becoming a part of Bastion was their best opportunity.

As they reached the bottom of the mountain, Annette and her companions were surprised how clear the air was inside the valley. They had come to accept the fact that fresh air was gone—replaced with oxygenated soot and particles, the contents of which no one wanted to imagine. The fact there was blue sky in the valley was unreal.

"This is unbelievable," Annette said. "The air is so clear." She took a deep breath, savoring the fact.

"Yes," Frank agreed. "This must be due to some kind of inversion layer."

"A what?" Willy responded skeptically.

"It's significant because inversion layers are areas where the normal decrease in air temperature with increasing altitude is reversed, and air higher above the ground is warmer than the air below it. So what happens is, they block atmospheric flow, which causes the air over an area experiencing an inversion to become stable. This can then result in various types of weather patterns. Topography can also play a role in creating a temperature inversion, since it can sometimes cause cold air to flow from mountain peaks down into valleys. This cold air then pushes under the warmer air rising from the valley, creating the inversion. More importantly, though areas with heavy pollution are prone to unhealthy air and an increase in smog when an inversion is present, because they trap pollutants at ground level instead of circulating them away. The opposite can be said with good weather, which is what I suspect is happening here. The good atmosphere is being kept inside, while an inversion layer is keeping the radiation and fallout—well—out."

"How long can this last?" Annette said.

"Indefinitely," Frank stated emphatically. "It's why some cities are more prone to smog and never seem to get better. Once an inversion layer is stable, it doesn't change. Given the surroundings, in a valley surrounded on all sides by mountains, I doubt it'll change for at least a few hundred years."

"Sounds good to me," Annette said back.

"Why you so smart?" Willy asked Frank. "You a scientist or somethin'?"

"Or something," was all Frank said in reply, which Annette could tell rankled Willy. Annette knew these two men didn't really get along, but she needed them to for the sake of their future.

"Okay, guys, let's stow the bull, shall we?" Annette ordered. "We need to stay focused."

"Agreed," responded Frank.

Willy just rolled his eyes.

As they began to walk again, they were stopped in their tracks by a rustling in the forest.

"What was that?" asked Annette.

"Probably an animal of some kind," Frank said.

"Let's check," Willy said, pulling his knife out from under his shirt.

"What's that doing here?" Frank said, exasperated. "We agreed to leave all weapons behind."

"Yeah, well, I do what's best for me, and bringing this is what was best for me."

Annette shook her head. Her plan of bringing these two with her obviously wasn't the best choice.

"Right now, your selfish behavior is endangering this whole mission," Frank chastised.

"Well, suck my balls, Mr. Wizard. I don't care! Now you can stand here and gripe all you want, but I'm going to go out there and find that animal and get us some grub."

Willy turned to head off into the woods, Impaler in hand, when Frank grabbed his arm. Willy turned and looked at Frank's hand and gave him the most dangerous look Annette had seen since her first husband. Bloodlust was in his eyes.

Oh great, Annette thought, *they're going to kill each other.*

"We don't know what kind of people live here," Frank said to Willy. "An act as aggressive as killing an animal could be seen as poaching their property, assault, or worse—an invitation to battle. This is a new world, with new rules. Until we know what those are, we best play this one with the cards close to our chest."

Willy rolled his eyes.

"You're touching me," he finally said through gritted teeth.

Slowly Frank released Willy's arm. "Why, yes, I seem to be. I'm sorry."

"I've killed people for less," Willy remarked.

Annette wondered how true this statement was.

"And you said you were a construction worker before?" Frank questioned. "Now tell me, why does a construction worker need to kill people?"

Willy paused. It was clear to Annette he was thinking things through. *He probably only said that to sound dangerous,* she hoped.

"Man," Willy said back, "do you know how to ruin a party or what?" and Willy put the knife back in his belt, hiding it under his shirt. "Truthfully I don't give a shit if some dumb-asses in some small town get pissed off because I killed one of their animals, nor do I care what would happen in a fight between me and some backwoods idiot. I can take anyone who wants a fight. However, I do care about my further survival, so if that means playing by some kind of unwritten rules until further notice ... fine. But the minute that changes, I'm gonna kill every animal I see in these mountains and get me some fresh meat. If you're lucky, I might even share."

"That's fine. Just don't propagate any issues as of now."

"Propa—what? You know," Willy continued, "you have a great way of making people feel stupid."

"Yeah," Frank nodded. "I've been told that. I try hard not to."

"Try harder," blurted out Annette. She'd had it with this crap from both of them. She knew there were reasons not to trust Willy, Frank too for that matter, but she had to now, and she needed them both to get over their personal disagreements. "Now, if we're totally done, let's go."

3

The three of them continued to walk down the road, following it toward town. Had they been more perceptive, they might have noticed they were being watched, but Annette was too caught up in her worries, while Frank was a man who believed in humanity's best and Willy was too busy thinking about all the ways he could screw society, to care about anything else.

These mental lapses would prove dangerous.

Quentin

1

Quentin "The Killer" Kershaw, as he was known in the 75th Ranger Battalion, had been on watch for the last six hours. His brother, Colin, was supposed to be keeping the watch with him, but had instead fallen asleep three hours earlier from boredom. Quentin was trying to teach his younger brother responsibility, but trying to teach a fourteen-year-old boy anything other than how to get a girl to let him get to second base was like trying to pull teeth. So Quentin was left to keeping himself occupied and aware.

2

Quentin had learned many tricks during his time in the Army to keep his mind sharp and his reflexes quick. The sad reality was, though, that Quentin was finding he was out of practice and struggling to keep his post. Sleep beckoned him. His stamina for these long days and nights was gone, which he figured was a sad indictment of the kind of soldier he had been.

Barely even a year out of the shit, and I'm no better a soldier than my weak, tired, and easily frightened younger brother.

Quentin was not happy being home. Sure, he was happy to be near his on again/off again girlfriend Louise, though they had not parted under the best of circumstances. Louise wasn't exactly what Quentin would call his girlfriend. She was his *best* friend and had been since grade school, but despite the romance and sexual tension in their relationship, they had never made anything official. Probably because Quentin had become a soldier fighting overseas for the freedom of the country, while Louise became an activist against all war. Most of their encounters began with some sort of squabbling about politics, graduating from there to arguments about the role of creativity in society (Louise viewed herself as a Renaissance woman), and then, after all else had been discussed, they would usually spend the evening taking out their frustrations with each other by fooling around.

Before Quentin went off to war, he asked Louise to marry him. She refused. He said he loved her, and she agreed she loved him back but not in the I-want-to-spend-the-rest-of-my-life-with-you kind of way. That night, she took his virginity in a tender and beautiful evening of lovemaking. When it was over, however, they returned to being "just friends."

Despite their continued friends-with-benefits status, Quentin only counted on her so much on a romantic level. For whatever reason, she just couldn't fall head over heels for him. The night of his parents' funeral, Quentin again asked her to marry him. It was odd to Quentin that he found he was scared to approach her. After all, since he'd been through the war, courage was not something Quentin lacked. However, when faced with this red-haired, firebrand goddess, he found nerves were all he felt. Still, on that particular night, he fought through them.

"Why won't you marry me?" he asked, trying not to feel dejected.

"Marriage isn't for everyone. I don't know that I believe in it."

Quentin understood why. When Louise was in high school, her father left her mother for another woman, which in a town the size of Bastion was big news. It broke her heart. Despite the fact the woman later became Louise's stepmother, Louise had to watch her mother struggle with the pain. Her father and mother never could be in the same room with each other ever again. Therefore, familial gatherings of the normal kind, like Christmas mornings or Thanksgiving dinners, were completely lost to her. To Louise, marriage meant heartache.

"True love is real," she said. "I believe that much. However, it happens for some and not for others. Love wouldn't be magical if it wasn't elusive."

That ended the discussion. Early on in their relationship, Quentin learned not to push things with Louise. Doing that only meant she would shut down and leave earlier than he wanted her to. However, since Quentin returned from the war, Louise and Quentin had been spending practically every night together. Though Louise still wanted their relationship only to be considered a deep friendship, Quentin was hoping that perhaps her defenses were finally beginning to break and before long she might finally consider becoming his wife. This possibility did nothing to deter Louise from saying that all flirtations needed to stop while others were around.

All this, and the fact that his brother seemed completely unappreciative of his guidance, made Quentin wonder if returning to Bastion was the right thing to do.

In point of fact, he never really had a choice.

3

Quentin's tour of duty in Muslim-occupied France was not over, and his role in the fight to push the Muslim occupiers out of Europe was hardly done, when fate made other plans for him. A year earlier, Quentin and Colin's parents had died during a vacation outside of Denver. They had wanted to go skiing, but were ultimately caught up in a riot triggered by some gangbanger war, which had spread from the inner city of Denver to its outlying areas. Their car reportedly crashed trying to escape.

His parents' deaths had galvanized the small town of Bastion into writing letter after letter to President Mitchum asking for Quentin's release from duty so he could care for his younger brother. When approval came from on high, Quentin found himself on a plane home. He figured it was a publicity stunt to calm the angered public of an unpopular war.

No, not a war; President Mitchum called it a skirmish.

So Quentin figured he was being used as some kind of public-relations tool, whereby the president could show he had a heart.

See, he's the greatest president this country has ever had!

Which is why politics annoyed Quentin. He wasn't one to get into the meaning of things. He didn't join the Army because he believed in the reasons for the war.

No, not a war, a skirmish.

Quentin simply figured it was a good way to get out of small-town Wyoming, where his friends struggled to stay solvent, with no industry to speak of and booze galore. Many of his friends were full-blown alcoholics by twenty-one, and destitute and depressed by twenty-five. He wanted to be better than them, which was why he joined the army at the outset. Three meals a day, a dry place (usually) to sleep, and money being paid into a bank account. Overall, being in the armed forces was not a bad gig, if you didn't mind the killing. Which is exactly what Quentin had found out about himself: he was good at killing ... and *he liked it.*

No, not liked it ... just was good at it.

In the Army Quentin learned he was adept at killing. No matter the battle, no matter how outnumbered his platoon, Quentin came out unscathed, with souvenirs of his kills. He didn't do what some of his fellow soldiers did, which was rip off ears of the dead or take their teeth. Quentin simply took a token from each man he killed. Something he found to be special about that person, a totem from their lives. Sometimes it was a picture of a loved one, or some kind of memento from home. Whatever it was, Quentin always did it in a respectful manner. To Quentin, their deaths were not something to be celebrated, but rather memorialized so the lives of the men he killed would not be forgotten.

By the time he was sent home, Quentin had chalked up 137 confirmed kills—the most of any enlisted man. To some, that might have made Quentin scary, but in truth, Quentin didn't want to be feared. Despite his nickname "Killer," Quentin was not some madman on the loose killing the innocent. Undeniably, he knew he could never kill anyone outside the war. Not if they were innocent themselves. Quentin had a strong heart and a good soul, something the army could never destroy. This purity in others was important to him. He could never hurt anyone who was honest and true. Wrong him, however, and as all in his army unit knew, he could go off. Which was one of the major reasons he hated Chief Mankins.

Quentin was surprised how much he hated Mankins, especially because he was a police officer, which ultimately meant they had a lot in common. Quentin was charged with holding a gun and protecting the peace. So was Mankins. But Manks, as Quentin liked to call him, was pure evil. He knew from the things his father told him and the way he ruled over Bastion with an iron fist. Now Quentin fully understood not everything was black and white and that sometimes hard, terrible decisions needed to be made—unpopular decisions. Despite knowing this, Quentin had seen too many incidents where Chief Mankins abused his power just because he could.

To Quentin, this just wasn't right.

4

It was these thoughts that Quentin was focused on during the watch in Bastion while his brother slept, when he heard the shuffling of feet on the pavement in the distance.

The forest that surrounded Bastion, Wyoming, suddenly became one of Quentin's war zones.

Frank

1

Frank, Annette, and Willy continued to follow the road as it weaved its way toward the outskirts of Bastion. Everything was quiet except for the sound of a bird or two, creating a song Frank found surprising in this new world. Until now, he hadn't even realized the songs of birds were missing. He was too busy trying to survive. Now though, hearing the chirping, Frank was reminded of the old days and everything they were missing. Oddly, in the months since the attacks, Frank had become used to the new ways, which had become relieving. Listening to these nature sounds now was a dichotomy he wasn't ready for, and it made him feel out of place.

In his old life, however, he often listened to nature's music and the sounds of birds and babbling brooks to calm himself.

Regardless, that was a different time and place, one he was sort of glad he couldn't go back to.

2

Frank had been a science teacher in the years leading up to the attacks, and he knew all too well the scientific data concerning a nuclear fallout. He used to play a game with his students where they would anticipate what it would take to survive a nuclear holocaust. It was always grim. He hoped the lesson they would learn would be to help take care of the world the best they could. Now, he hoped the game served as some kind of survival guide for any of them that might still be out in the ruins of earth.

Survival of the fittest.

That thought quite honestly scared him. Frank never liked the ideas of Darwin and natural selection. Though he had to teach it, he found that the idea was always being warped to fit some madman's idea of how the world should look. As an African-American man, he was experienced with the way genetics could be used to subvert different races.

One only had to look at the recent emergence of the New Ku Klux Klan to see how, even in a country like America, where freedom is supposed to be the right of everyone, being different was still an intolerable crime. The new Klan had spent much of the last seven years creating a presence in the government and pushing through legislation that created jobs only for white men and women. The resegregation of schools in the South was hard enough to believe, but as economic hardships increased, it was becoming all too clear how the new society inspired by the Klan was going to be: Blacks would be starved out of the South, and then America, just like the Jews, Muslims, and Hindus had been years before.

Thankfully, Frank lived in a southern area of Nevada where the Klan was still banned. Since Sin City still existed in Nevada, it meant anything still went in that state. Which meant Frank could teach in whatever school he wanted to, as long as they would hire him. He'd hoped being black and gay wouldn't matter. In truth, though, none of it really mattered anymore. With the world reeling from an obvious nuclear attack on America, Frank guessed the prejudices of surviving Americans might not matter as much.

Or they could matter more, Frank considered. *Would people want to create a perfect society from the ashes of death, or would they embrace a new kind of world? A utopian way of life? Where all were accepted for who they were and what they could contribute?*

Frank hoped for the latter, but knowing human beings the way he did, he suspected it would end up being the former. It all depended on who took charge. Though he didn't want authority, Frank hoped he survived long enough so his opinion could be heard.

After all, how often does one get the chance to be part of creating the new world order?

This was Frank's chance to make a difference, a chance he might not have otherwise gotten. If a positive was ever going to be taken from all this destruction, he hoped it could be that.

3

The three of them came to a brown street sign that read: Town Center.

An arrow pointed forward.

"I guess we go there," said Frank.

"I guess so," replied Annette.

"Thanks, genius," Willy remarked.

They had begun to move forward, when behind them they heard the sound of someone clearing his throat. As they turned to see who had made the sound, they were all surprised to see two men with guns pointed in their direction. One of them was clearly the leader of the other, who couldn't have been older than sixteen in Frank's estimation.

"Hi," Annette began to say. "We're—"

But she was cut off.

"Put your hands up!" the older of the two said. Frank and Annette followed his directions immediately, while Willy hemmed and hawed. This forced the man to take a step forward and point the gun directly at him. "I said, hands up!" Willy finally complied.

"We just want to talk to whoever is in charge," Annette pleaded. "Can you please just help us do that?"

The older man looked at the younger, and they exchanged some kind of moment. To Frank it looked as if these two might indeed be brothers and that they had a close-enough relationship that they could practically read each other's minds. Suddenly the older one looked back at them.

"Follow me," he said, and led them at gunpoint into town.

Althaus

1

Reverend Althaus stood at the podium staring out into the sea of faces that had gathered in the tent. It was a much larger space than the ones they used for sleeping, about a hundred times as big, but it was made of the same fabric and steel. This place had been erected by General Black's men the afternoon they crossed into Oklahoma, in a limbo of dry dirt. Now it was Sunday, and as Black had made Althaus promise, it was time for him to bring hope to the masses.

2

Unlike when he was speaking in front of his own congregation back home, Althaus found he was nervous, even daunted over the task ahead. This nervousness was surprising to him; it had been a long time since he was worried about speaking in front of any kind of group. Granted, the prospect of doing so annoyed him, but with the new feelings coinciding with it, he found he was veritably excited to speak as well.

It was reminiscent of his first time. A young man of twenty-three, apprenticing at the local church, Althaus was finally given the chance to give a sermon when the regular pastor had been ill. Thinking back, he could still feel the pit in his stomach, the cold sweat up and down his back, as he prepared to begin. Althaus was glad to be feeling something similar now.

He felt young again!

Looking out at the faces from his "pulpit," he could see the 250 or so people intently waiting for him to begin. More people gathered outside the tent, around the entrance flap and plastic windows. In all, he thought maybe he was preaching to three hundred. They needed this. They wanted it. Their eyes and ears were wide-open to receive his words. A few people squirmed around, as they were smushed in the tent like sardines, but most were just waiting for him to begin. Althaus could feel the sweat run down his back; the heat in the tent was a bit overwhelming with so many people gathered in one place.

It smells bad too, he thought; *we all need baths.*

However, he couldn't worry about such frivolous things now. Now he just needed to begin.

3

"Good morning," he started, clearing his throat a little with those words.

A boisterous "Good morning!" came roaring back from the crowd.

"It's been a long time since any of us have been to church," Althaus stated. Nods and moans of agreement rose from the crowd.

"I want to thank General Black and his men for giving this to us. General Black is truly a man of faith and deep convictions."

Another time he could hear the crowd agree. Slowly Althaus was beginning to feel right at home.

"What do we make of this new world before us? What does all this destruction and death mean? Is this the hand of God reaching down and smiting us? Is God finally punishing us for our sins? That is one way to look at the events of the past couple of months. After all, the evidence before us shows a very bleak set of circumstances. We have little food, barely any medicines, our cities are destroyed like Babel before us, and we have no connections to the rest of the world. For all we know, the world beyond our borders might still be intact. Maybe only America has been struck? Maybe the rest of world has simply abandoned us to our fate? So, how do we move on from here? What lesson about our future can be gleaned from these tragic events? In truth, I don't know the answers to any of this."

As he said these words, he felt the room's energy fall. An audible groan came up through the crowd. They were disappointed; they wanted more from him—reassurance that God was on their sides. They wanted to know there was hope, but it wasn't the message they were getting. Which meant Althaus had them where he wanted them. Having spent years in front of crowds, probing and prodding them, keeping them rapt to every word he spoke, he knew that any good speech had its emotional ebbs and flows. He knew to get them to their highest emotional peak, he had to drop them low. Once there, they were like putty in his hands.

"God spoke to me the other day." He said the statement simply, putting zero context to it, allowing the words to flow through the crowd, capturing their full attention.

"He came in a dream. God's form was indistinguishable. God could have been a man, woman, or even a child. All I saw was a white light that made up the form of God. It blinded me! But there I stood in my dream, face-to-face with my maker. The white light that came from the figure of God took me to one knee. I had felt a similar feeling only one other time in my life. I know you all felt it as well. When our world changed, when we were blasted with light, that was the same feeling I had in God's presence."

The crowd acknowledged his description. They knew the feeling he meant; it was all too close to them. Raw. Though Althaus was making this up as he went along, the imagery he was setting forth for this new set of parishioners was one he knew would dig deeply to their cores.

"'I am the light,' God said to me. His voice was strong, like a father's, yet caring and motherly at the same time. All I could do in return was nod at the words in some kind of silent understanding. 'I sent the bombs down upon you all. I saved all of you for a purpose. You are my chosen people now.' 'But why, God?' I exclaimed as loudly as I could, feeling my spoken words could not penetrate this white light. 'Because,' God said, 'like Noah before you, it is time to start anew.' What was I to say to that? I had no words to either beg for a better world or ask what my place was within it. I simply asked, 'But why so much pain to get there?' I could sense God smile at me then, though I had no way of seeing this. The light was still blinding me. Painfully so. 'Pain is white,' God replied. 'White is goodness and hope. There is no birth without pain. There is no future without birth. Remember my light? The white light is my hand upon thee; it is my lesson to your world: remember the pain, remember the white light. The light is hope.' And then the light dissipated. The pain ceased. My vision returned. Calm was restored to me, yet God's words were seared into my soul. 'Pain is white ... remember the white light ... the light is hope.'"

The crowd again began to talk among themselves, but these weren't expressions of discontent. No, Althaus could tell that the crowd was with him every step of the way. They wanted more, and Althaus was going to give it to them.

"It is true, my fellow survivors, we are in pain. We have lost loved ones; we have lost all we knew and held dear to us. We may be all that is left of humanity, the only hope for a future for this world. But with this pain and responsibility, we find light. We find a glimmer, a beacon, pulling us toward an uncertain future, where more pain and suffering could be ahead of us. But with that uncertainty, we know that we are in God's hands, guiding us to create a new world ... a better world. For we will get to decide what that world is now. We will set forth the guidelines from which all society will live and future generations will adhere to. We are the heroes, the prophets, and the kings of this new world. We are the children of the light. Though we do not have any idea of where we are going or what we will do or be like when we get there, we have to be strong and take the pain. In the end, a new world will rise around us. We must make the sacrifices willingly so our children, and our children's children, will have a brighter future. That is our mission. That is our destiny. That is what God wants from us."

Althaus paused a moment to take stock of the crowd. They were silent. For the first time in a long time, Althaus felt utter satisfaction. He took a deep breath and smiled.

"Pain is white, remember the white light, the light is hope," he repeated slowly. The crowd began to mutter the phrase under their breath.

"Pain is white, remember the white light, the light is hope!" Althaus repeated again, more emphatically. The crowd began to utter the words back at him.

"Pain is white, remember the white light, the light is hope!" Althaus was practically yelling it now; he was animated while he did it, lifting his hands to the sky in exultation of God. Then the crowd stood around him, lifting their hands to the sky. With all their might and in full unison, they yelled to the heavens: "Pain is white, remember the white light, the light is hope!"

The crowd continued to chant the words as Althaus focused on the back of the tent. Standing at the entryway was General Black. He nodded at Althaus in approval. Althaus nodded back.

4

After the last of the parishioners left the tent, Althaus collected his belongings—nothing more than a Bible he'd found and his jacket—and was headed to the door when Black came up to him.

"Good speech," Black said.

"I just tried to do as you said."

"Oh, and I believe you did. However, you may have gotten more than you bargained for."

"How so?"

Black just smiled and pulled the flaps of the tent open so that Althaus could exit into the street. Once there, Althaus was greeted by a shocking sight. Hundreds of men, women, and children stood in an unruly crowd. They were pushing and shoving, all trying to be the next in line to talk to Preacher Althaus. Althaus felt a sudden pang of regret welling in his gut.

"You're the man who spoke to God," whispered Black in his ear. "Good luck with that."

Black walked away, leaving Althaus to tend the crowd. As people pulled at Althaus's clothes and yelled at the top of their lungs for him to help them, Barrett realized he had opened up a Pandora's box he would never be able to close. Somewhere in the back of the crowd, a chant continued to rise into the air: "Pain is white, remember the white light, the light is hope."

Nell

1

It had been twelve days since Nell had been brought into the giant's group. In those twelve days, a lot had happened. The giant had his followers set up camp within the ruins of Nell's neighborhood. People made hovels out of the ruins of the homes and cleared paths to make the area maneuverable. As far as Nell could estimate, there were at least seven hundred people in the giant's group. Therefore, the neighborhood got crowded and tight quickly. Most people were only inches away from the next, and the shelters they had fashioned were cramped and crude. Nell and Mark were situated toward the back of this improvised camp, just two among a sea of people. Despite this, the giant was as good as his word and made things better for her and Mark.

The doctor he had sent had been a godsend. His case was filled to the brim with medications taken from abandoned pharmacies, and he administered many of them to Mark. Hitting him with every strong, fast-acting antibiotic he could get his hands on, Dr. Brody Sandberg took time to dress the wounds, properly creating a sterile environment for the leg to heal. Dr. Sandberg was a young man just out of medical school. After a few days, it became clear Mark would be able to keep his leg, and his infection was going away.

"Here is two weeks' worth of antibiotics," said Dr. Sandberg, whom Nell couldn't help but find very attractive. He was exotic to her. She hadn't ever seen a man with his coloring. Dr. Sandberg's olive skin, dark brown eyes, and equally dark brown hair made him seem mysterious. More than that, though, the big difference between the two was that Mark was still a boy, while Dr. Brody Sandberg was a man. She could see this difference evidenced in the doctor's actions—the way he confidently moved, knew answers, and made her feel safe.

As well, of course, is the difference where there is a stump now instead of Mark's foot, thought Nell.

"I can only give you two weeks' worth because we are rationing. If he needs more at the end of the two weeks, we will revisit the situation and, of course, do what is best for him."

"Thank you, Doctor," she said, feeling completely relieved. Her boyfriend was going to get better, and this man was her hero.

How silly I must look to him, she thought, *a child caring over her little crush.*

She hoped Dr. Sandberg saw how much of a grown woman she was becoming.

"You know," Dr. Sandberg came back to her with, "I've been giving everyone in the group thorough evaluations. It's taken awhile as there are many people with us, but I suggest you get on the list fast. I'm coming to the end of everyone, so I might be able to get you examined quickly."

"I'm fine," she quickly replied, feeling a bit flush at his offer, which seemed stupid to her; after all, he only wanted to see her clinically.

"I know you're strong," he reassured her. "But things can creep up—infections, small scratches, a cold… Believe it or not, your health can mean the difference between life or death right now. With the way things are, the slightest sniffle could become something far more serious. The sooner we take a look at you, the better."

Nell nodded. "Of course."

"See you soon then." Dr. Sandberg left with this final remark. Nell just stood there, wishing he would come back, feeling like she had lost all assurances with his departure. Quickly, though, she shook off these feelings, returning her full attention to Mark, who would hopefully be himself soon enough.

Minus a foot.

2

As hours turned into days, Mark continued to heal. Nell could visibly see the strength building back up within him. It was day three when he began to eat again, day seven when he was aware enough to hold a conversation, and by day ten he was surprisingly frisky! Nell had to fend him off.

Stupid teenage-boy hormones!

That was the day Nell started to think everything was going to be okay. All was returning to normal—at least as normal as possible.

Except for the stump.

"Thank you," Mark said while trying to snuggle her. It took all the strength Nell had to let him do so. Her mind couldn't help but fixate on his missing foot.

"For what?" Nell asked sweetly, rubbing her hand across his brow.

"You saved my life, Nell. You took care of me. I love you."

"I love you too," she said, while trying to block out questions about their relationship. Nell figured these questions were due to stress, but she also wondered if it was Dr. Sandberg. Nell found her mind wandered to him every waking moment. The stress of these feelings, having to deny them to herself and hide them away from Mark, was beginning to take its toll on her. She was queasy with worry. Constantly tired from all the emotions, she found she was sad all the time. Too much had changed. Her world was destroyed, her parents were dead, and Mark was very sick. It was also because of her feelings for Dr. Sandberg.

And the stump.

Every day she had to unwrap it, clean it, put ointment on it, and rewrap it. Sometimes she even had to pop sores filled with puss. It made her sick. Mark made her sick. He used to excite her, he used to be gorgeous and strong, but now, he was minus a foot. The stump was red, smelly even, though the worst of the rotting flesh had gone away. To Nell, though, this person wasn't Mark at all. He was a patient needing constant attention.

This must be what a baby is like, Nell thought. *Thank God I don't have one of those!*

Even though he tried, Mark could barely move. If he had to relieve himself, Nell had to practically do it for him, and his attitude was extremely negative.

"Why don't you just leave me?" he said nightly.

"'Cuz I don't want to. I love you," she said in return.

"You'll be happier without me," he added.

"Don't tell me what makes me happy. You make me happy. You just need time to heal."

Unremitting it continued. Night after night, and day after day. It was exhausting. Nevertheless she had spoken the truth: she did love him, she knew that. The question she kept coming back to, however, was …

What kind of love is it?

3

It was day fifteen when Nell noticed she had come to the end of Mark's pills. At first, he seemed fine without the medications, but by the next morning, his fever had returned, along with the pain.

"I'm never going to be okay again!" Mark yelled with frustration.

"Of course, you will," Nell replied. "We just need more medicine, that's all. It just wasn't enough."

"What if it's never enough?" Mark's eyes filled with tears. "What if I die?"

"Stop it! Just stop. You need to have confidence. Be positive. It'll help you recover."

"Right," he agreed, but in such a way that Nell got the feeling he just wanted her to shut up. So she did. Besides, negative attitude or not, Mark needing more medicine meant she would have to go see Dr. Sandberg again. Excitement blazed through her at the thought of this. She hadn't seen Dr. Sandberg since he gave them pills and fixed Mark's leg. She was almost unable to contain her excitement at the thought that she would get to see him now!

For Mark, of course.

4

Before the attacks, when she would dress for a date, she would put on makeup and an outfit that would get her noticed. Now she no longer had that luxury. Like many of the women in their group, Nell found that she wasn't as concerned with her looks anymore. On this day, however, knowing she was going to see Dr. Sandberg, she found herself wishing for a mascara or at least some lipgloss.

The doctor's quarters, which were nothing more than the lower level of the remains from a house that hadn't been wiped out in the attacks, were on the opposite side of the camp. Guided by Dr. Sandberg himself, the followers of the biker gang put some mattresses recovered from the ruins in the room. They had covered the open ceiling with as many blankets and tarps as they could find, and created two separate areas, one for serious patients and one for examinations. The serious-patient section was always clear because if someone was in a serious state, he or she usually died quickly. Everyone knew it wasn't the best of "hospitals," but it was good enough to examine patients and administer medicine.

When Nell arrived, there were only eleven people waiting to see Dr. Sandberg. This was a small line; usually it contained up to thirty or forty people. After a short forty-five-minute wait, she was called into the back examining-room area, which consisted of a sheet as a partition and a mattress. Dr. Sandberg had a medical bag, but other than that, there wasn't much in the way of equipment. This bag reminded Nell of the books she read in school, like *Little House on the Prairie,* where doctors made house calls with everything they needed in their leather satchels. Dr. Sandberg's medical bag wasn't exactly like that—his was instead a backpack with a red cross on it—but in theory it was similar.

"How are you today, Nell?" Dr. Sandberg asked politely.

"Good. You told me to come by for an examination, so I did." She hoped that didn't sound too desperate. Yet the feeling of undeniable guilt consumed her. In her mind, there was but one image: *Mark's stump.*

Which reminded her.

"Oh, and I need a refill of Mark's prescription. His fever has returned, and so has the pain."

Something quickly changed within Dr. Sandberg; Nell could tell immediately. It reminded her of how her father would act when he was given particularly bad news about something he didn't want to do, yet knew had to be done. There was suddenly a sense of regret in his eyes. His body seemed limp and slow.

"Really? And Mark is struggling without them?"

"Yes. He was pretty sick, I guess, from the start … I mean, you would know, you're the doctor." She smiled as she made this lame comment.

"He was pretty far gone."

"Thank God you saved him."

"I didn't do anything; it was all your boyfriend. He has a strong will to live. That, coupled with antibiotics, and you have the recipe for survival."

"Still, we were going to cut off his leg. He would have died, bled to death or something. You saved him from that."

"True. Well, thank you." He smiled at her. This action and the sight of his cute, dimply smile gave Nell goose bumps all over.

I've "got it bad"—as the saying goes, Nell thought, *and that ain't good.*

"Nell, I'll submit an order to get more after I examine him again. We need to be sure he needs more meds. If he has a fever, it could just be his body fighting off the remaining infection. From there, if more medicine is needed, I'll see what I can do. The problem is, as you know, we are rationing all supplies. Medicines especially. Unless someone needs something for life or death, each case is taken on its own merits. Stonehenge decides who gets what. So I just want you to understand that this is not a sure thing; he may not get anymore."

"Oh. What happens if he doesn't get it?"

"If Mark doesn't receive more meds and he does beyond question need them, he may never return to the boy you once knew. There is an outside chance the infection could heat up again, at which point he might die. But it's a small chance of that."

All Nell heard was "the boy," which was exactly what Mark was. Still he needed to get better, and Nell wanted that medicine for him.

"We need the medicine, Dr. Sandberg."

"Okay then. As soon as I have an answer, I'll let you know. I'll come by tonight and check on him, and right after I'll go see Stonehenge."

Stonehenge was the nickname of the giant who first rescued Nell and Mark. He was the leader of the camp, and equal parts feared and respected. As far as Nell understood it, no one knew Stonehenge's real name or why he was called that. Most just assumed it was because he was so mammoth a figure, and thus an immovable object, like the stones after which he was named.

"Thank you," Nell said as she stood, readying to go.

"Wait!" he said with excitement. Her heart skipped a beat.

Maybe he will grab me and pull me near, kissing me passionately on the lips? Nell's imagination was getting the better of her.

"Didn't you want an examination?" he asked.

"Oh, yes. I forgot." She sat down on the bed.

"Right," he said, opening his supply bag and removing a wooden tongue depressor.

How many mouths has this been in? she thought, but lost all strength to complain as he moved his head close to hers and said, "Say ahhh."

She complied and lost herself in his dreamy chocolate-brown eyes.

5

The shock from the doctor's words hadn't worn off yet. She kept hearing them.

"Nell, you're pregnant."

Over and over. In truth, she wasn't sure how she felt about that.

As Nell returned to the ruins that now represented her homestead, she found she was overcome with guilt. Her heart felt hollow, as if she had cheated on Mark instead of just having thoughts for another man.

How could I have ever allowed myself to think about leaving Mark? How could I have ever envisioned being with someone else? There are days that change one's life, she thought, *and lately I'm having my fill.*

The day of the attacks had certainly changed her (she wasn't as innocent anymore, or quite as helpless), but she still saw herself as a child. Now, though, even the mere idea of childhood was gone.

It's okay, she rationalized. *Mark and I love each other, and if I wasn't certain of that before, I am now.*

Which meant Mark's survival needed to be assured, whatever it took. Nell would do whatever was asked of her to keep her "family" together. Warmth coursed through her body as she came to these realizations. As if the assurance of knowing that Mark and she would always be together was all she needed to feel safe. Days were not going to be easy in this new world, she knew that, but armed with the information she now had, she knew nothing could come between them.

Arriving at their hovel, she took a moment to catch her breath and calm her pounding heart.

Am I excited or nervous?

Probably a lot of both, but she knew she had to tell Mark the great news. The blood ran out of her body, though, when she got a good look at him. He was paler than before and beaded with sweat. He looked up at her, very dazed, his eyes barely open to take her in.

"Any luck on the medicine?" he asked with a croak.

"Uhm, yeah. The doctor will be here tonight. He will examine you, and then he will look into it."

"Good." He cleared his throat of phlegm as he finished his one-word answer. From the looks of him, Nell could tell things were beginning to get desperate again. She had to do something about it.

"Everything else okay?" he asked. Despite how he felt, he wasn't too into himself not to care about her.

Another reason to love him, she thought.

"Perfect," she said.

"Thank God. I don't know what I'd do without you." As he said this, she realized she felt the same way.

Without Mark, I would simply be lost.

"So," she began, "is that why you keep asking me to leave?"

"No, I'm just being stupid," was his response.

Tell him, she thought, *quickly, before he isn't able to understand my news.*

"Mark," she began.

"Yes, babe?"

Mark tried to make himself strong for her, to open his eyes wide to take in whatever it was she wanted to say. Nell couldn't help but find this endearing. In spite though, she could tell his composure was fading.

"Nothing; get some rest." She placed a hand on his forehead and felt the fever building inside him. He smiled at her and kissed her hand. Slowly, he shut his eyes and began to drift off to sleep. Nell felt that pit in her stomach return as he fell away.

I should have told him. But it would have been just so unfair to do so. Adding another weight to him as he tries to recover.

She just couldn't do it.

Why worry about it now, though? After all, I have nine months to figure it out.

Frank

1

Frank, Annette, and Willy were marched through the town at gunpoint. Frank could sense that the two men behind them were ready to pull their triggers if the strangers made any sudden moves. So Frank began a conversation, trying to relax them if possible.

"Have you all heard anything about the outside world?" Frank asked. Annette gave him a glance of concern, but Frank just gave her a charming smile in return.

"Not really. We tried sending people out to obtain whatever news we could, but they never returned," the older of the two men stated.

"Ah," Frank replied.

"Is it as bad as it seems?" the younger one asked.

"Worse," Frank said. "It's truly Armageddon."

Frank could sense the younger one tense up.

"How about you not frighten my brother?" the older one said.

"How about you lower your weapons?" Frank struck back. "We're unarmed and we're not here to hurt anyone; we just want to talk, that's it."

The older man lowered his weapon, and his younger brother followed suit.

Men of reason, Frank thought. *Good sign.*

"Thank you," Frank added. "Now we can be much more comfortable."

"Don't try anything stupid," the older brother remarked.

"I wouldn't dream of it," Frank said through a smile. "I'm Frank, this is Annette, and my charming friend here is named Willy. And you two?"

"I'm Quentin. This is my brother Colin."

"Well, Quentin and Colin," Frank stopped and put out his hand.

"Nice to meet you." Quickly he and Quentin shook. Annette gave Frank a large smile. Frank smiled right back.

After a moment, they all began to walk again. Quentin and Colin remained behind them, but the tension was lifted now that guns were not directly involved.

"So, there isn't any sign of the government?" Quentin asked. "No military or control of any kind?"

"Not that we've seen," Frank stated.

"It seems we are on our own," added Annette.

"That's hard to believe," Quentin stated.

"Why?" Willy spoke up. "They abandoned most of us before this anyhow ... Fucking government!"

Great! Frank thought. *We just got them comfortable, and Willy goes and makes a statement like that!*

"Well," Quentin began to speak again, "I can't disagree with you there, but still, under these circumstances, protocol would mandate at least executive action."

Phew, thought Frank, *Quentin is a moderate.*

"You sound like a soldier," Annette said. "Were you in the Army?"

"Yes, ma'am. Served in Europe. Came back a few months before all this happened," Quentin replied.

"Well, welcome home," Annette stated.

2

As they walked, Frank tried to focus on the town. Main Street was filled with mom-and-pop shops. From diners to package places, this was a self-contained province. Probably one of the last in America. Even the grocery store was family owned. From what Frank could tell, not one chain restaurant or national corporation did business in Bastion. The look of it all was out of time, like a town from the last century, before industry and government took over, before the selling out of America to the corporate world. Frank, who had been an antique collector in his former life, picked up on all the tropes of the 1960s, his favorite era from the past.

"One hundred years ago, they had style," Frank would say about the sixties, as he referred to them.

The town was rustic, filled with homes and buildings made with an assemblage of wood and nails. It wasn't full of cookie-cutter homes, as was the norm in suburban America. The neighborhoods that extended away from Main Street were filled with distinct and original homes, some built on hills, giving them a ladderlike look, and some jutted outward in odd geometrical configurations because that was how the land wanted them built.

These homes have flair! Frank thought.

Overall, Frank thought the town seemed normal. As if nothing at all had happened here.

Not in the attacks or in the last hundred years.

As they walked, Frank, Annette, and Willy began to see the townspeople peeking out of windows and doors, taking the strangers in, sizing them up. Frank considered that the three of them, each in their own ways, had been outsiders to society, Frank because he was an African American, Annette because she was a single mother, and Willy because he was ... whatever he was. Frank for sure knew he wasn't a construction worker. Yet Frank had never felt as outside of normal society as at this moment.

As they walked, no one would acknowledge them other than to stare. Annette said "hi" to a few people as they passed, only to be shocked when they turned away or spit at the ground. It was clear the inhabitants weren't going to make it easy for them to join.

3

Finally they came to a building made of concrete. The sign above the door would have glowed, but even in the dark, the words Bastion Police were still legible. Quentin opened the door to the building.

"Inside."

Frank and Annette did as they were told, but Willy was a bit more reluctant.

"What happens when we go in there?" Willy asked. "You all gonna ass-rape us, lock us up, and swallow the key?"

"Willy," Annette said, trying to calm him.

"What?" he said to her. "Why are we trusting these assholes?"

Frank knew Willy had an issue with authority—he could tell from his tattoos that read "Kill the Prez" and "F-U America"—but from the way he was beginning to act about going into the police station, Frank realized he didn't know how deep that issue was.

With luck it won't become a problem.

"Listen," Annette said to Willy, "the calmer we are, the calmer they will be. It'll all be okay."

Willy considered this. He looked Quentin in the eyes, trying to intimidate him. Quentin didn't even blink.

"Fine," Willy said. "But one wrong move, and I'll kill all of you."

"Sure," said Quentin. "It might be kind of hard without this." Quentin quickly reached behind Willy's back and pulled Impaler from his belt.

"Hey!" Willy shouted, trying to get the knife back.

"Listen," Quentin said, pointing the tip of the knife out defensively, "I get it; you want to protect yourself. That's fine. However, the chief of this town is a tough guy, and if he finds this on you, he'll kill you. Believe me. I'll hold this with me, and after the meeting, I'll give it back. I swear. Just trust me."

"Why should I?" Willy spat back.

"Because I hate authority as much as you do, but I'm just trying to save your ass."

Willy considered his words. Frank couldn't help but smile at someone putting the head case in his place.

"All right," Willy finally agreed and went inside.

Passing through the glass-paned double doors, Frank caught eyes with a police officer sitting behind the front desk. The name on the tag was Officer Tymes. She was a tall, muscular blonde who looked like a model mixed with a wrestler. Frank realized she could probably take him in a fight, Willy too, maybe even both at the same time. She stood up quickly as they approached. Shock was written across her face; her eyes were wide with wonder.

"Where did they come from?" she said in a tone that sounded masculine.

"Found them coming off the ridge," said Quentin. "Need to take them to see Manks."

"The chief, you mean?" she said pointedly to Quentin.

"Sure," he replied back sardonically.

"Of course; go right back."

As Frank, Annette, and Willy were marched past the front desk into the main office area, they saw two more police officers, one fat and tubby, the other tall and wiry. The officers watched the two men walk by in astonishment.

"They must not be used to seeing black people," Willy joked to Frank.

"Don't talk," Annette interrupted. Frank wondered if she was regretting her decision to have Willy take part in this.

Finally, they were escorted down a hall toward a door with "Chief Mankins" stenciled on it.

"Go on," pushed Quentin. They followed orders, but from the way Willy kept tensing up, Frank could tell it was only a matter of time before he blew his top. As they came to the door, Quentin moved into a place where he could keep an eye on the three of them while being able to knock on the door at the same time.

"Who is it?" a gruff voice exclaimed from within.

"Its Kershaw. We brought you some strangers."

"Strangers?" The voice sounded exasperated, almost annoyed, to have to deal with the problem. The chair scraped the floor, and with the shake of a handle, the door opened.

Frank had to look down. Chief Mankins was a short but hairy gentleman. He was no bigger than five foot two, but was thick as a lumberjack. Willy let out a chuckle at the sight of him, though Frank tried to cover it up by putting his hand out. Annette spoke first.

"Hi, my name is Annette Bilkins. We come as representatives from a group that has emigrated east from California. We have been wandering the deserts of California and Nevada for months. From what we can tell, most of the area we have traveled is destroyed. Including army bases and most places that might hold shelter. It was by total accident that we happened upon your town. Quite frankly, I was shocked to see it hiding both up the mountains and in a valley. Honestly, it seems like providence has sent us here."

The chief looked them up and down, refusing to shake their hands. He cleared his throat and finally answered them in his gravelly deep voice, "Come in. Let's talk."

They walked into the room. Quentin began to follow, but Chief Mankins stopped him.

"Leave them with me," Mankins said. "You and your brother head back to the watch. There may be more where they came from."

"We just got off a six-hour shift," Quentin reminded him.

"So, stay another six hours. You're the best, aren't you?"

Quentin bristled at Mankins's challenge and was reluctant to leave, but leave he did as Mankins ushered them out of the office, shutting the door on their faces.

"You two say you are representatives from a larger group?"

"Yes, sir, we—" Annette began.

"Look," interrupted Willy, though Frank gave him an agitated look. He continued anyway, "We need a place to stay, us and our friends. You seem to be sitting on a paradise here! We are only fifteen people. What do you say you give us a place to stay, little man?"

This last comment seemed to strike Chief Mankins hard. As he squinted his eyes, he began to walk slowly, wonderingly, to his desk. He sat down and pulled out a gun from the desk drawer. This got Willy's attention.

"I say," the chief began, "you give me the due respect this badge requires, limp dick. You think you three can walk in here and begin ordering me about?"

"That wasn't our intent at all, sir, we—" Frank came in quickly.

"Listen, dark fella, I know your kind. We haven't had any survivors pass through here, but I've seen desperation before and it makes people do strange things. You want to stay here? Live here? Become one of us? Then you need to pay me a little goddamn respect! You understand?"

"Yes," Frank replied.

"What about you, momma?" Mankins asked Annette.

"Understood," she said.

"And you, Limpy?" he said to Willy.

"Whatever," Willy dismissively replied.

"See, I don't like guys like you, ones with all the tattoos, all the pent-up hatred toward the world. As I see it, whatever mess we're in as a country happened because of people like you. I've spent twenty-three years protecting this town from the world around it, and if you think you deserve some sympathy just because the world ended, you've come to the wrong man." The chief took a moment, tapping his gun again. "Do I make myself clear? Or do I need to speak in words you three might actually understand? Small words, like fuck and you."

Frank took a deep breath. He had been hoping this would go a lot better. Looking at Annette's face, he could tell she was feeling the same way.

"No, sir," Frank said. "We understand perfectly."

"Good," Mankins said heatedly. "Now get the hell out!"

With that yell, Quentin and Colin came back into the room.

"Listen, Manks," Quentin blurted out, "you can't just throw them out there again!"

Mankins's face turned red, Frank could tell this whole meeting was about to get out of hand.

"What the hell are you two still doing here? Didn't I tell you to go back out on the watch? Goddammit, just like a Kershaw to disobey!" Mankins ran his hands through his hair, straightening out the mess he had created from his agitation.

"I don't take orders from you!" Quentin snarled back. "Listen, we've talked to them; they seem like good people."

"Do they?" Mankins remarked. "Is that true? Are you good people?"

"Yes, we are," Annette spoke up crisply, grabbing Mankins's full attention.

"Okay, little lady." Incredulity poured out of Mankins's every word. "Why should I trust you?"

"This is a whole new world, Chief Mankins. It is hard for any of us to predict what needs there are or will be. Among my people, we have skills. Teachers, musicians, even a banker. I am sure your people also have similar skills. Pooled together, we can begin to recreate a society. One where we and others in our situation can survive."

"And who may I ask would lead this brave new world?" Mankins slyly asked.

"Is that what this is about? Power? I see no reason that should even be an issue. We would, of course, fall under your jurisdiction and follow the rules you have set forth for this town. We would blend in. Listen, I don't want to be in power. You think I like having people look to me for answers, for guidance? I don't want that pressure at all, and I would gladly give it over to you. But only if that meant the safety of my people."

Annette finished. She could tell from the look in Chief Mankins's eyes that her words had zero effect on him. She braced herself for his response.

"God! A woman leader … What makes you think we need you? From where I'm sitting, the only ones in need of anything are your people, not mine."

Frank knew he was right. A group of starving, sick, desperate people would barely make an impact in a town that was, for the most part anyway, untouched by the disaster beyond the mountains.

"Fine," she agreed. "We need you. Now what is it going to take?"

Mankins wiped sweat from his brow. Frank watched as Annette scowled at this.

Bad move, Annette, Frank thought. *If he saw it, he might take offense. No matter how gross this little man is, he wants to be treated with respect.*

It was too late though. Mankins did see her scowl, and he looked angrily at her.

"Something about me bothering you, little lady?"

"Not at all," she said.

"Sure," he replied, with a chuckle of disapproval and a shake of the head.

"Look," Frank spoke up. "Tell us what we can offer you to gain entry to Bastion. We'll do whatever it takes."

"Bribery? Is that what this is? Are you trying to bribe me?"

186

"That's clearly not how I meant it," Frank quickly added.

"How did you mean it then? America or no America, bribery is against the law, especially in this town. What? Did these two Kershaws tell you otherwise? Did they tell you I could be bought?" Mankins was standing now, yelling at the top of his lungs.

"We didn't say a word, Manks!" Quentin said.

"Don't call me that, Kershaw! I hate that!"

"Don't turn these people away, Chief!" The title slithered out of Quentin's mouth with all the respect vomit has for a toilet. "They need us. And quite frankly, with all that is going on, we need to be helping people, not turning them away."

"Get out," Mankins ordered. Colin turned to leave, but Quentin simply moved closer toward the desk.

"You can't do this. Turning these people away would be murder."

"What did you just call me?"

"I didn't call you anything." Kershaw seemed confused, but he stood his ground.

"I'm not a murderer!" Mankins yelled.

"I never said you were."

"You are all banished!" Mankins suddenly decreed as if he were a monarch on a throne.

"You can't do that!" Quentin looked like he was about to attack, but Frank and Colin grabbed him.

"I can and I just did." Mankins smiled as he said this. "Now get out before I have you killed." Mankins walked to his door and yelled down the hallway, "Hey! Backup! Get these fuckers out of here!"

Moments later, the footsteps of the other officers could be heard rushing down the corridor toward them. Quentin was being held back like a wild beast, while Mankins sat in his chair sweating, rubbing his head profusely, caring neither to control the situation nor send it over the rails. The whole event was absurd and chaotic.

Frank tried to speak out again to calm the situation, but his words were lost in the din of yelling, the loudest voice of which was Mankins's.

"Get out!" he yelled as his police officers escorted them all out of his office. As they all walked down the hall, they could still hear him yelling, "Understand this: it's my duty to protect the survivors inside this town's borders! If I see you in this town, I'll kill you! If I see you leaving full of stuff, I'll kill you on the spot! There's no trials here anymore. I am the only law that's needed!"

Frank thought his point was well-taken.

4

"That son of a bitch!" Quentin screamed as the group of them walked through the forest toward the camp. "I could kill him!"

"Could you?" Annette broke in. The remark stopped everyone. Annette and Quentin linked eyes.

"I only ask," she said, "because that may be what needs to happen if there is going to be peace in this valley."

"You can't be serious?" Frank said.

What am I hearing?

"Why not?" Annette said. "How many people have we seen dying out there—or already dead? How much longer do you think we can survive? I'm not sure we have very long. Many in our group are tired, getting sick due to the cold. Things look bleak to me. If killing that disgusting excuse for a man allows us to live and keep peace in the town, why wouldn't we do it? For all we know, it is the last safe and perfect place on earth. Why should we allow that madman to hold it for himself?"

"Because it's wrong," argued Frank. "Killing a man? It's ... it's desperate. And it completely breaks the laws of humanity. We can't just kill him. That makes us as bad as him."

"I'll do it," Quentin said.

"What?" Colin asked.

"I've killed before."

"Yeah, but that was in a war," Colin pleaded with him.

"And what do you think this is?" Quentin said. "This is a war! But it's a war that actually matters. It's a war for survival. Out in those Paris streets, those French countrysides, I didn't know what I was fighting for. Mostly it was for the guy standing left and right of me.

But now, Colin, we have no choice. Mankins is a bad man, and one thing this world doesn't need right now is bad men."

"I'm glad you see it my way," Annette said.

"Hell," Willy said. "I'll help if you need another hand. And if it'll get me my knife back."

Quentin reached for the knife and handed it over.

"Thanks," Willy said.

"So, we're actually planning this? We're actually going to kill a man?" Frank asked in shock.

"Yes," Annette said. Everyone was suddenly quiet. What else was there to be said?

The five of them walked the rest of the way to camp in silence.

Colin

1

Colin Kershaw wasn't anything like his brother. Quentin was a tough guy, a warrior, who was unafraid of facing down any obstacle. Colin, however, was quite the opposite. He was scared of everything.

As a little boy, he and Quentin would watch horror movies, and while Quentin hardly seemed bothered by them, Colin would have to sleep on his brother's floor for the better part of a week. When Quentin went off to war, Colin had sleepless nights of worry for his brother, while Quentin's messages from the front relayed a cold calm that Colin couldn't understand. Had it been Colin at the front, he would have pissed himself twelve times before lunch every day. While Colin's friends would jump from cliffs into pools of water, or do stupid things like car surf, Colin played it safe, out of fear of what might happen if he didn't.

It wasn't that Colin was yellow ... exactly. He was just appreciative of life and the beauty in it. He was an artist—which was a way of life long since abandoned in this world. Society saw the arts as useless and most museums had been abandoned to neglect, the artwork in them either destroyed or sold for cash by governments to private collectors. Most governments and communities found putting money into keeping the arts alive was a useless and expensive enterprise. For Colin to experience art, he had to look in the books that Louise had stolen some years back from the town library before they could be burned.

"Here," she said, while handing him the books, "I wanted you to have these."

She handed him a pile of great books of art. He looked at them in astonishment. He was only eleven at the time, and it was right before Quentin had gone off to war.

"I saw you drawing the other day," she added. "I wanted to help you see what art is before everything is gone and you never know."

That's when Colin's eyes noticed another book that she still held in her hands.

"What about that one?" he asked, hoping it was his as well.

"Oh, that one's for me," she said with a smile. "I need art in my life too."

She left him alone with the books after that, and soon he found himself inspired to become an artist. Sure, he drew all the time and liked to doodle, but he wasn't anywhere near as good as the artists he read about in these books. From that day on, Colin taught himself the knowledge to be an artist: form, structure, and perspective. The idea of going to an art class was laughable. Even to speak of such an idea would get a person ridiculed by his peers. Nonetheless every time he saw Louise after that, she pushed him further; and over the years while Quentin was away, she was the only person who acknowledged his talent.

"That's beautiful," she said while looking at a piece of his work. He usually would go after school to her house, where the two of them would sit on the porch looking at the drawings. "If you keep on like this, you'll be as amazing as any artist in those books I gave you."

To hear this from her, a woman who understood what art was, made him feel awesome.

"Thanks," he said. "I could draw you a picture of my brother if you want."

She laughed. "Now why would I want that?"

"To remember him. In case he doesn't come back."

A sadness came over Colin. He was only twelve and a half at the time and Louise eighteen. They had bonded during Quentin's time away. Essentially, Louise had become an older sister to him, and he hoped when and if Quentin returned, it would stay that way permanently.

"I don't need a drawing to remember your brother," she said. "He's always in here," she added, pointing to her heart. After a brief pause, she went on, "but I'd love it if you did."

A few days later, he created a likeness so close to Quentin that it brought tears to her eyes.

2

During one of Colin's boring days at school, his little secret of being an artist was finally discovered. One of the other students, Sebastian Kreuk, the son of Bastion's mayor, spied some of Colin's drawings. Colin had a hard time focusing during class. This often prompted him to draw in the margins of his books or notepads. When Sebastian saw the drawings, he grabbed them and spent the rest of the day showing Colin's drawings to everyone he could, teasing him to no end.

After school that afternoon, without thinking, Colin did the unbelievable. He summoned up the courage to go to Sebastian and try to get his artwork back. When he found Sebastian, he was surrounded by his group of leeches and suck-ups. Being the mayor's son made Sebastian the most popular kid at school and granted him latitude from teachers, which meant no one was going to stop Sebastian from treating others badly. He was a bully, and his behavior was tolerated. Despite this and how scared he was that Sebastian would kick his ass, Colin cherished every piece of art he had ever created and needed to get his work back. Scrounging up every ounce of courage he had, Colin went to confront Sebastian.

"Give them back to me!" Colin yelled as Sebastian dangled his drawings out in front of him.

"Or what? You want this little ... What even is it?" Sebastian asked mockingly.

"It's the moon."

Sebastian let out a big laugh, and his "friends" followed in suit.

"The moon," Sebastian mocked again. "How beautiful. Did you have to ask your mommy if you could stay up late to see what it looked like? Oh wait, that's right, your mommy's dead!"

The group laughed at Colin again. Colin tried not to link eyes with any of them; he didn't want them to see his fear or the tears that were welling up in the corners of his eyes thanks to the comment about his mother. Yet he couldn't avoid one in the crowd, a girl he had known his whole life. She lived next door to him, and she was everything Colin ever wanted. She was the sweet and beautiful Kimberly Cooper. She wasn't one of Sebastian's normal followers, so he was surprised and dismayed to see her there.

Kim and Colin's eyes met. She looked away, saddened about what was happening.

"Look, Sebastian, I just want my artwork. Give it back, and we can just act like it never happened."

"Never happened, huh? You want your 'artwork'!"

"Yes."

"Then take it from me."

Sebastian pushed hard, and Colin went flailing backward, hitting his head on the brick wall of the school. Colin could hear his skull crack hard. If he didn't know better, he could almost swear he had felt his brain squish inside. The group laughed hard again as Colin groaned in pain. Looking back at them, he could see the faces of the group mad with laughter. Only one looked at him with any compassion at all … Kim. She was sad.

Suddenly, deep within him, Colin felt rage. Fear trickled away while he felt his fist curl. Quicker than even he could register, Colin's fist collided against Sebastian's jaw. Blood squirted out from between his lips as Sebastian fell to the ground.

The laughter stopped.

"Give me my art, Sebastard!"

With that, Colin grabbed his pictures and walked away.

3

Colin always felt bad after using "Sebastard" to insult the mayor's son, but it was one of the few ways to get Sebastian's attention. As sore spots went, it had to be one of the sorest for him. Everyone in town knew Sebastian was a bastard. It was widely known the mayor's wife couldn't get pregnant, so one winter, he and his wife went away from town. At the time, the mayor's wife was still wearing a size two and therefore clearly not pregnant. When they finally returned five months later in the spring, not nearly enough time to have gotten pregnant and had a baby, it was with a ten-month-old baby in hand.

In the new American black market, if a couple with means really wanted a child, all they had to do was go into one of the big cities, find a poor family willing to sell the wife's body or even a baby for the right price, and buy one. This was Sebastian's story. He was tanner, had more angular features, and his lips were wider than the Kreuks'. Although his eyes were the same color as his father's and his hair matched as well, his mother was blonde and blue-eyed. Supposing this were not evidence enough, the fact that none of his facial features looked like his mother's probably was.

Most people assumed that a few weeks before the mayor's exit from town, he had bought a woman to give birth to his seed. Therefore, Sebastian was his bastard, a babe born from a mother not married to Mayor Kreuk. For the mayor's enemies, it became sport to tease Sebastian for what was really no fault of his own. Ultimately the nickname Sebastard was coined, and it stuck indefinitely.

4

On his walk home after his fight with Sebastian, fear gripped Colin from within. He could feel shivers, and cold sweat spread throughout his body. It was all he could do to get himself home.

That night, sitting in his bedroom, he heard a small crack against his window. He could see Kim bending out her window. The windows were adjacent to each other, though Colin would never dare look into hers.

He walked to his window and opened it.

"Hey," Kim said.

"Hey," Colin squeaked.

"Good job today. He deserved it." Her smile was the best reward Colin had ever gotten for anything.

"Thanks," was all he could say back to her.

How stupid can I be?

"Sebastard ... now that was funny," she giggled as she pulled back inside her window, closing and locking it.

5

The next morning, the world collapsed.

6

Once Quentin and Colin had safely returned Frank, Willy, and Annette to their camp, the two brothers found themselves off in the forest helping to gather some wood for a fire. They were banished now, but thankfully Annette's group was willing to take them in.

Colin was not worried about being banished, though. Quentin knew how to survive in the wilderness. Without him, Colin knew he didn't stand a chance, but with his brother, he knew he'd never have a problem. Even so, that fact didn't make him feel any better about his brother at the moment.

Colin was surprised to realize just how uncomfortable he felt around his brother after that conversation about killing the chief. He had always loved Quentin despite knowing the truth about what he had become in the war, but now, standing next him, knowing what he was planning to do, he realized he was frightened by him as well.

"You're not saying much," Quentin said.

"What do you want me to say?" Colin asked. Quentin was always insisting Colin learn not to wear his feelings on his sleeve, but that now seemed impossible.

"For starters, you could tell me who beat you up a few weeks back."

"Why? You going to kill them too?"

"Come on. That's not the kind of person I am."

"Oh, really?" Colin was pushing. He knew he probably needed to back off, but as far as he was concerned, it wasn't his task to temper emotions—that was what Quentin needed to do. "You know, Quen, I knew you had it in you to be a killer in the war. But I never thought you'd bring it home."

"Colin," Quentin said, grabbing his brother by the shoulders, trying to get him to calm down a bit, "I'm doing this for the safety of all of us."

"If that's what you have to tell yourself. But murder is murder." Colin broke free of his brother's grasp.

"No, it's not," Quentin said. "It isn't always that black and white. The truth is, people kill for different reasons and for different levels of acceptability. I had to learn that lesson before I could kill in the war. See, killing an enemy during battle is acceptable because we are fighting for different ideals. If I don't kill that person, then he'll kill me. This thing with Mankins is the same. If you don't think he'd kill us in a second, you're badly mistaken. I'm going to kill him because he and I are in a war of differing ideals and he is flat-out wrong. And it's revenge for killing our parents."

"You don't know that for sure," Colin added.

"No, but it's about time I found out."

"Well, tell yourself what you need to, I guess."

"Don't confuse the issues, Colin," Quentin said. "There are different types of killing; it's that simple. This one is right. It's a needed execution."

Colin blocked his brother out and just headed off deeper into the woods.

"Where are you going?" Quentin yelled after him.

"Anywhere away from you."

"You're being naive!" Quentin called out, but Colin simply kept walking deeper and deeper into the woods.

"This is the world we live in!" Quentin tried again, but Colin just ignored him.

Colin hoped perhaps this fight between the two of them would make Quentin feel guilty, perhaps create second thoughts about the plan.

Yet Colin knew better.

If anything, this scene would make his brother dig in even more. Quentin was nothing if not stubborn. Colin was certain his brother would just continue building their shelter, all the while planning the way he would kill Chief Mankins.

As Colin walked deeper into the woods, thinking about Quentin and the possible assassination of Chief Mankins, his mind wandered to the fight Quentin had been referring to. Oddly enough, it happened in these very woods. Though Colin tried to concentrate on finding good kindling wood, he couldn't help but think back on that day.

7

It was only a month after the attacks. Colin hadn't had much time for art, and he needed to get away. All he found time to do was follow his brother's instructions and learn to protect himself. After a while, all that training had become too much. Not that he was any good at it anyway. So, sneaking away, Colin sat against a tree in the woods and sketched.

Colin always carried paper and pencil, but with his brother around all the time, he had been unable to find an opportunity to draw. In the serenity of the chirping birds, brushing leaves, and streaming sunlight, he drew a picture from memory. With each curve of the line, each stroke of shading that created shadow, Colin developed a perfect resemblance. Not only was his picture taking form; he was finding his fear of the unknown future dissipating within him.

This is paradise.

As he finished his sketch, which for anyone else would have been a masterpiece, he looked down at what he had finished. It was her, of course—a picture of Kim, every blemish and perfection. Just as Colin was getting lost in her eyes drawn in lead, he felt a sudden and sharp pain in the back of his skull. With it, he found himself falling forward onto the ground.

Turning over, he saw Sebastian staring down at him, with three other boys behind him. Sebastian looked pissed and held in his hand a rock now dripping with Colin's blood.

"I've been waiting to get you back!" Sebastian said with his teeth gritted into a menacing snarl. "Only problem has been your brother wouldn't leave you alone. We've kept an eye on you, waiting for the right moment. And now here it is."

Colin grabbed the back of his head. He could feel the small wound leaking blood. He was dizzy, which probably meant a concussion.

"I think it only fair we warn you," Sebastian continued. "We're going to kick your ass, and you're going to take it. Oh, and if you ever call me Sebastard again, we'll kill you. You understand? Don't think I'm not serious."

"I—" Colin tried to speak but found vomit was all that came out. The three boys recoiled away from his spewing instantly. As if his vomit had been laced with poison.

"Now that's just gross," Sebastian said with a disgusted face. "Hey, what's this?" Colin realized Sebastian had found his drawing. He watched helplessly as Sebastian picked it up. "Not bad, Colin. It really looks like her! She's mine, you know? She's agreed to be my girlfriend. So you just stay away from her. Don't talk to her; don't smile at her; don't even breathe near her! Got it?"

With that, Sebastian nodded to his "friends," who promptly began to kick Colin over and over until they were satisfied.

All Colin could think was, *Maybe self-defense would be a better skill.*

8

As night fell on the group from the mountains, Colin tried to sleep. He tucked his hands under his head and sat as close to the fire as he dared. He watched as the others tried to shut down for the night, either unrolling blankets or snuggling close to another person in the group.

Off in the distance, just away from the camp, Colin could see his brother talking with Annette, Willy, and Frank. He knew they were hatching a plan to dispatch Chief Mankins. Though he could not hear them or read their lips, Colin could understand what they were saying, and it hurt him to know what they were talking about. He wondered what his parents would think of what Quentin was about to do.

Would they approve?
Would they stop Quentin?
Should I stop Quentin?

He didn't know for sure. What he did know was that he and his brother were completely different people, and he hoped they stayed that way.

Stonehenge

1

Stonehenge felt he deserved all the treats he got. After all, he was helping so many people and making their lives better. So what if he asked for a little something in return? Some people he'd helped just out of the kindness of his heart, like that girl, the one with the boy friend whose leg was going to get cut off. He didn't ask anything from her in payment, did he? No, he only got a hug.

That wasn't so bad, he reasoned.

Lost in these thoughts, Stonehenge could feel the woman on top of him performing only the necessary moves to achieve her end of the bargain. As he lay there below her, his mind wandered. She was attractive and okay at sex, but overall, she wasn't good enough to lose himself in.

"Am I doing this right?" the woman asked.

"Sure," was all he said in return.

As she continued to gyrate, Stonehenge could hear a ruckus going on outside the tent. He wasn't surprised by it nor worried. He tried to just finish quickly, but knew he wouldn't have the chance.

Juanita was coming.

"Should I stop?" the woman asked with a tremble in her voice.

"You might want to, though you're screwed either way."

Entering in a blaze, Juanita grabbed the woman by the hair. She screamed in pain as Juanita threw her to the ground.

"That's my man, you bitch!" Juanita screamed as she jumped onto the naked woman, her fists landing hard across the woman's face.

Stonehenge wondered if he should stop her, but he just stayed in bed enjoying the show. This was probably disconcerting to the woman, but who cared? A self-proclaimed womanizer and sex addict, he never felt the need to defend his actions.

I am who I am.

Even when he tried to change, the fact was he just couldn't help himself.

Juanita is a saint for understanding this, he often thought.

Just as suddenly as the fists began to fly, Juanita stopped. Blood was dripping from her knuckles as she pulled herself off the woman.

"Now get out," Juanita demanded.

The bloodied and battered woman just stood there. Her face was a red pulp now, and what little beauty she had would be gone for at least a few weeks. Juanita stepped back, taking in her work, and as she did this she began to undress.

Stonehenge finally stood, his gigantic frame throwing a shadow over the small woman. He tried to help her steady herself with his hand, which was so big her whole forearm rested in his palm.

"I'll call for you soon," he said. "In the meantime, I'll make sure your children get some new clothes to keep them warm. Heal up—I don't want you with a face like that."

Bending over, quite a ways down, Stonehenge kissed the woman's forehead, and then let her exit the shelter. His and Juanita's shelter was rather large, made of broken walls from different homes. It was rectangular, twenty feet long by eight feet wide, and they had been able to fashion themselves a bed inside. It was a mattress that survived the destruction. With some blankets they recovered and even some singed pillows, they had fashioned a very comfortable resting place. Yeah, perhaps he should have offered these amenities to some of the others, but he figured he was the leader and the leader needed to be comfortable.

So screw them!

"Weren't you bit hard on the poor girl?" Stonehenge asked.

Juanita grunted in response. She was naked now and lying on the bed.

"You want to finish or not?" she bluntly asked.

Stonehenge just smiled and got on top.

Thankfully for him, this was the way of their relationship. He'd cheat and she'd forgive—at least him. The women he strayed with often got Juanita's rage. Stonehenge supposed he should have stopped her, but he didn't. Maybe that was cowardly, but as he saw it, every woman he was with knew about Juanita.

It's their own stupidity if they didn't realize she'd come after them.

Plus, how could he stop her? He loved Juanita too much and didn't want her to hate him. So this was the bargain they had. He got with other women, but didn't stand in Juanita's way of getting her revenge. *That doesn't make me a bad person, does it?*

Stonehenge looked at it like he saw his newfound leadership. These things were thrust upon him. He didn't ask to be the leader, just as he didn't ask to be a sex addict. The truth was, he was just good at both. He knew how to lead people naturally, just as his natural need to feel good sexually often took over his every action.

It could be worse, he thought; *at least I'm fair.*

2

Stonehenge believed in giving everyone the chance to take the lead. In his life, he had been on the kicking end of many so-called leaders' boots, and he couldn't stand any of them. To him, leadership meant being humble, allowing those who might disagree with him the chance to stand up and be heard—even when those people were wrong. He insisted that while he was the one in charge, anyone among them could challenge his right to that.

They just have to be okay with the repercussions.

Stonehenge was gruff, he knew that. He could be short-tempered and at times downright violent. However, if he really wanted the power of leadership, he wouldn't allow people to stand up and try to take that power away from him—he could lose it! As Stonehenge saw it, he was very fair to the people he protected. After all, he never forced them to follow him; they just did.

Why me?

He figured it had something to do with the way he made people feel safe. Which in turn was because of his enormous size.

However, it hadn't always been that way.

3

When Stonehenge was a kid, his name was Escobar Montoya. He grew up in a poor Mexican border town, where his mother sold him to a drug cartel for dope. Stonehenge was made into a mule, taking drugs back and forth across the border—up his ass or swallowed in his stomach—because he didn't have a choice. He was small for his age and therefore was made to do plenty of things he didn't want to. That was until the day he hit puberty. Practically overnight, he awoke to find he had sprouted like the beanstalk Jack ascended to the giant. Only now, *he* was the giant. No longer was he some small runt of the litter. Instead, he was a two-ton tanker, ready to be feared.

This realization gave him the idea he should build up muscle mass and become a stronger individual in mind and body. At night, when the other cartel slaves slept, Escobar worked his body into shape. His arms got thick, his chest popped out of his shirt, and even his legs became gargantuan. Soon, everyone in the slave shack kept their distance from him. By age fifteen, he was 250 pounds of pure muscle.

Noticed by the head of the cartel, Juan Avila, Escobar was moved up from mule to hit man. From there, he was given a Harley Davidson and a monthly stipend of $100,000, and he was sent into America to settle the cartel's debts. No one argued with him; if they saw him coming, they knew they either paid up or died. He was given the name Stonehenge by the fearful because they understood he was a monument that would stand for all time. In the end, Escobar enjoyed the name, so he adopted it fully, wiping away his history and becoming something more: a symbol to be feared.

That implacability didn't mean that Stonehenge had no heart. As far as he was concerned, he was filled with love. Having been brought up under less-than-ideal circumstances, Stonehenge found he had a weakness where the downtrodden were concerned. If he found a person who needed guidance and that person came to him for help, he would do just that. Like the dons of the old Mafia, he would do a "favor," give the petitioner a leg up, so to speak. Most of the time, it was a broken leg, but who was being picky? After he helped that person get on his feet, the word of his deeds would spread, endearing him to the people.

When in Mexico City or the outlying towns of San Diego, Stonehenge could blend in and be protected to avoid the authorities. Eventually he was so powerful and had done so many things for so many people, he was on the verge of starting his own cartel. If he had wanted to, he could have taken over the whole South American drug industry. Yet he never took that next step. All he did was kill those they asked him to and collect little favors from the people he helped, like shelter, food, or sex. In return, he gave them his continued protection, which in that part of the world might as well have been gold.

4

This style of living was perfectly suited to this new world. If anyone could make a living in a world destroyed by the apocalypse, it would be him. This he had proved immediately after the attacks.

The night before the attacks, Stonehenge was hiding out in a town at the Texas border. He had just finished a job to "take care" of a man who had stolen a shipment of cocaine from the cartel. It had been a simple job, but now Juanita and he needed to lay low until the heat died down. Which meant he couldn't cross the border for a few weeks. The town he was in was made up mostly of Mexican-Americans who were paid off by the cartel to help hide things if needed. In this case, they hid Stonehenge and his girl.

Stonehenge and Juanita had slept through the attacks, as did most of the town. It wasn't until they checked the border crossing that they realized something was wrong. No one was at the job that morning. Not a single guard or police officer. Stonehenge couldn't believe it. Getting on their bikes, Stonehenge and Juanita decided to cross into Mexico. Manually lifting the crossbar and driving through the empty streets, they made their way to the outskirts of Mexico City. It was destroyed, along with all the shantytowns that surrounded it. They couldn't get very close, as the remnants of a mushroom cloud still adorned the sky. With this sight, Stonehenge understood one thing for sure: Mexico had been attacked and the cartel was destroyed. America was his best bet for survival now. If, that was, America hadn't been attacked as well. To his shock, it had been.

What about the rest of the world? Stonehenge wondered but never could get an answer. All communication systems seemed to be destroyed, making it impossible to assess what was happening in the outside world. For now, it was a journey into America that presented his best chance for answers.

It was during this journey back over the border, into the southernmost towns of Texas, up north toward Dallas, that he collected his followers. They were mostly people who had already revered him from his history with the cartel, but for those who didn't know him, they attached themselves easily to the group. They needed and wanted help, and everyone who was already following him seemed safe.

There's nothing like peer pressure.

Consequently with every new person taken in, one thing was made clear by others in the group: if the new person wanted to, he or she could also lead.

It just meant one had to challenge Stonehenge. Which didn't happen—until it did.

5

The day in question began like any other. New survivors were brought to Stonehenge's gang and society. A man among them brought with him his wife and two children. Despite being an intellectual man, one who obviously had never been in a fight in his life, he challenged Stonehenge because the giant had attempted to take liberties with the man's wife in exchange for water. Stonehenge couldn't understand the big problem.

I gave them water. All I wanted in return was a little poke.

Since the man refused and dropped a challenge of leadership, all Stonehenge could do was oblige the request and kill the man.

Let's see him protect the woman's honor from six feet under, Stonehenge thought.

A crowd gathered to watch. It must have been the whole zoo—about six hundred. They watched as the two men did battle, egging them on like the crowds in Rome that once cheered the gladiators. Both men entered a makeshift ring formed by motorcycles and cars.

It made escape impossible. Entering for battle, the men shook hands, but that was the last of the pleasantries.

The first blows came slow and weak from the challenger. Stonehenge did not react to his punches; instead, he just laughed them off, encouraging the little fellow to keep coming, to not slow down. Stonehenge believed in the little people.

Better not let this fight end too fast, Stonehenge thought; *they will think I'm a brute.*

The challenger fought on, punch after weakening punch. Stonehenge equated each blow to the power of a large puppy jumping up on a person.

It might knock you off balance, but it doesn't really hurt.

After about three minutes of doing everything he could to draw the fight out, it was clear the challenger was too exhausted to continue. Stonehenge backed away and looked the man straight in the eyes.

"It's not too late to change your mind. You've fought well. But you know I'm going to kill you. There is no shame in backing away and giving me your wife."

"No," the man said through the wheezing sounds of desperate huffing and puffing. "I ... will ... not ... let ... you ... have ... her."

Stonehenge nodded in understanding. Yet a twinge of sadness overtook him. He didn't *want* to kill the man, but what choice did he have?

I can't look weak.

"Your children will speak of this day," Stonehenge said. "And they will know their father fought well. But I will have your wife anyway."

The challenger's eyes widened with rage and fear, but it was then that Stonehenge finally struck back. Taking both hands, he swooped them down across the man's face with all his might. Stonehenge squished the man's head like a fly inside his two big bear claws. Some say the man's eyes popped right out, others say brain oozed from his ears; either way, the challenger was killed instantly. No matter what the details were, a message had been sent: *Death awaits any man who chooses to fight Stonehenge.*

6

Stonehenge was buttoning his pants when Dr. Sandberg was let into his tent.

"Why, Dr. Sandberg, what brings you here this fine evening?"

Stonehenge could see the doctor's eyes flick over to the bed, where a woman lay naked. It was not Juanita, and Stonehenge could see how uncomfortable it made the good doctor. Stonehenge took a sort of joy in knowing this.

"Uhm, I came because there is a girl in the group who needs some medical assistance." Sandberg got the words out through waves of nervousness. The effect of Stonehenge's presence on people always made him feel powerful. He'd be lying to say he didn't enjoy it.

"Is the treatment for her?"

"No," Sandberg blurted out. "Her boyfriend."

Boyfriend? thought Stonehenge. *Excellent.*

"How young?"

"Seventeen."

"Hot?"

"She is ... what you would call attractive."

"I would call?" Stonehenge challenged back.

"Anyone would call. It's the girl whose boyfriend's leg needed fixing," Sandberg added.

"Ah, I see." Stonehenge smiled at him. "Well, bring her here. I'm sure we can work something out."

"Okay." And with that, Dr. Sandberg exited the tent.

Stirring the girl from her slumber, Stonehenge went to his most recent conquest. Stonehenge was sure the doctor had recognized the girl; it was, after all, the challenger's wife.

"Who was that?" she asked.

"The doctor. It seems someone needs my help."

"Oh," she replied, understanding full well what that meant. She was to be abandoned.

Even she wants to stay in my presence! Stonehenge thought. *Despite the fact I killed her husband. I'm that good.*

"I guess I won't be needing you anymore."

Stonehenge stood and walked out of the tent, smiling as he went.

Mankins

1

Chief Mankins hadn't taken his antidepressants in six weeks, which was probably why he had such little patience for that presumptuous bitch and her friends. He was not in the mood for her crap, or for those damned Kershaw brothers.

Screw the Kershaws! he thought.

They were a reminder. A reminder of all the dirty deeds he had ever done. In this new world, he saw a chance to forget, to rebuild, to become a new person ... a better person. Yet every time he looked at those two kids, he was reminded of who he truly was ...

A murderer.

As he sat in his office, with night having fallen across Bastion, Mankins ran his fingers over the temples of his skull. His head ached with agony.

Damn meds! Mankins thought. *Or lack thereof.*

The first symptom of his withdrawals from the meds had been the dizziness. It was overwhelming. Mankins's head would grow light and disoriented, and then the world would spin around him until he would black out. Which became the second symptom. The blackouts would sometimes last minutes, other times hours, and when he woke up, he would find he had developed a splitting headache. The pain would run from the base of his skull all the way to his eyeballs. It was debilitating. Severe vomiting would take Mankins to his knees—a place he wasn't used to being—followed by the shakes with cold sweats.

This must be what heroin addicts feel like when they are cleaning up, Mankins thought.

As if on cue, he could feel a blackout coming on, but he needed to be strong a few minutes more. He was about to have an important meeting.

The sudden knock on the door sent pain through his brain like a pin through its cushion. Mankins growled in pain. Trying to rub away his headache, he said, "Come in."

Entering his office were the three biggest bullies in town, Winston Deerdorff, Brooks Nolan, and Clifford Montgomery, as inseparable as they were stupid. Mankins had enough on them to arrest them ten times over. So when he needed little deeds done around town, like vandalizing a store to scare someone or creating a threatening situation to keep people in line, he would use them to keep his hands clean. Now he needed them again.

"Hey, what's up, Manks?" said Deerdorff, who was the ringleader of the group. He was a putz, out of shape and beginning to bald, but he was a nasty son of a bitch, and Mankins liked the way he could come up with horrifying things to do to people.

"Ya ain't lookin' so good," added Montgomery, who was the dumbest of the group. "Ya got the clap? Hey, Brooks, maybe he got the clap!" Montgomery laughed at his joke hysterically, and Mankins was convinced that if this man ever took an IQ test, he would be borderline "special", but Mankins tolerated him.

"Shut up, you douche bag," was Mankins's response. This shut him up immediately. Montgomery was doe-eyed and skinny, and his crooked buckteeth made him a comical sight, but when he realized he had done wrong, he often broke into tears. Mankins could see them stirring already.

"Can you please stow the waterworks," Mankins said. "For Chrissake, you're my tough guys; act that way, will you?" He heard Montgomery sniffle and try to collect himself. Mankins went on, "Listen, you three, I need you guys to do me a solid."

"We're always doin' stuff for you," said Brooks Nolan. "What do we get out of it?"

"How about not going to jail?" Mankins attacked back.

"Yeah, I guess that's something.'" Brooks was the real smart-ass of the group, who never knew when to keep his mouth shut. He was relatively handsome and might even have been a fighter on the circuit, but drug use got him kicked out of high school and his life was now just an endless stream of bingeing.

"Can I get to the point now?" Mankins asked.

"Sure," replied Deerdorff.

God, my head hurts!

"Good," said Mankins. "I want you to find the Kershaws and kill them."

"What?" asked Brooks Nolan in surprise. "I mean, we done a lot of things fer ya, but we haven't ever killed—"

"Well, now's as good a time as any to start," was Mankins's response.

"You sure about this?" Deerdorff asked.

"I wouldn't be telling you to do it if I wasn't."

"And we won't be implicated in any way?" Deerdorff wanted assurance.

"After this," Mankins said, "I'll make you just below me in the power structure of this town. There won't be anything you can't get away with."

Deerdorff and his friends smiled at the thought of this.

"Consider it done. I hate that fucker anyway," added Deerdorff while he and Mankins shook on the deal.

Althaus

1

"Hello," Althaus said as the newcomers were brought into his tent. About twenty people in all, they had been examined by the medic and given their tent pouches; now it was his turn to see them. "Pain is white, remember the white light, the light is hope," he added in greeting.

Since the speech, Reverend Althaus had been kept busy. General Black had been sending out scouts in all directions. They were using some of the tanks and were told to bring back any survivors, food, medicine, or any other supplies they could find. Black also had them searching for a more suitable place to live, though so far none had been found. Black's instructions to Althaus were to give each battalion a blessing before they left and take any soldiers' final confessions in case they did not return. However, all the soldiers who left did return. Triumphantly at that. Some brought food, some brought medications, some even brought along more survivors, which made Althaus even busier. The general made him the conduit to the camp, the first person of authority newcomers met. Which was why he was greeting the new group of twenty.

The routine of the induction process was simple but important. As usual, when Althaus was finished saying the greeting, "Pain is white, remember the white light, light is hope," everyone in the room stared at Althaus as if he were crazy. Sometimes he even felt that way, but he tried to push those feelings away and do what was asked of him. The truth was that Althaus had never thought or intended those words to stick like they had. He was just trying to come up with something snappy for people to say that could signify their new spirit. Intended or not, though, it was now commonplace around the base for people to greet one another by saying, "Pain is white, remember the white light."

The reply back was, "The light is hope." Then they would continue with their conversation.

In these meetings, though, he was just expected to bring the new people in and make them feel comfortable about this new place and its rules.

"Don't be alarmed," Althaus continued his speech to the newcomers. "What I just said is a little saying we have around here. It simply means that though the attacks of the white lights may have brought us pain, there is hope in the new world created by the attacks. We can build anything from here, and that is what we intend to do."

The new group was calming now. They were happy to be here, Althaus could tell that, happy to no longer be stuck out in the world having to fend for themselves, but the new people were always nervous. Especially when they heard what Althaus had to say. That nervousness would usually dissipate as he went on.

"Let me tell you all what is expected of you in our camp," Althaus continued. "Here we believe in positivity. We want to help you feel at home. We expect you to add to this positivity. Sure, life isn't easy here, but we want you to be productive. Therefore, please find a way to be as content as possible. I am here to listen to all your worries and concerns, and as a man of God, I believe I can bring faith to your soul. If I am not around, there is another man of God, Reverend Solomon, who can help as well. Which brings me to another expectation of ours. We want you to believe in God."

This was always the part of the speech that was the hardest to say. He still wasn't sure how strong his own faith was, but this is what Black wanted. As the general would say, "Belief in God brings hope."

So, Althaus did as he was asked.

"Do any of you have any problem with what I have said so far?" he asked the new arrivals.

None of them spoke up; they just nodded their heads in agreement.

"Good. Now the next part goes back to the saying I spoke earlier. Pain is white, remember the white light, the light is hope. It's really more our new belief than just a saying. It is everything to us; it represents our hopes, our dreams, even our way of life. In order for you to be a part of the new society we are creating, you need to be able to say it and believe in it." Althaus spoke these next few words carefully; he hated to alarm the newbies, but they had to understand. "If you cannot say those words or believe in their meaning, then you cannot be a part of this camp."

He paused a moment, letting this sink in. Althaus hated saying this part, and once he even questioned General Black about the democracy of forcing such rules upon those that were found. General Black simply laughed off Althaus's concerns and said, "This world is where liberty and democracy led us," and Althaus let the issue drop. After all, who was he to argue with the general?

General Black was a willing leader. Since Althaus met him, he had seen nothing but his constant push to create a stable society for the ever-growing population of people living within the borders of the camp. Not many men would take on such responsibility, but it was clear to Althaus that Black not only fought for his own survival, but for the survival of everyone under his care. If that meant a few liberties needed to go by the wayside for the greater good, then so be it.

So, after the dramatic pause, Althaus began again, "If you choose to not be a part of this camp, that is fine. We have rules to govern us because we want to feel safe. If that is not something you are interested in, we ask you to return the tents we have given you, and on the way out, we will provide you with water enough for a day's journey. However, if you would like to stay and become one of us, then repeat after me ..."

Althaus looked everyone in the eyes. He could tell none of them would refuse the rules. They wanted to stay.

"Pain is white, remember the white light, the light is hope," Althaus stated boldly.

"Pain is white, remember the white light, the light is hope," the group said quietly. They always started off embarrassed to speak up.

"You can do better than that," Althaus remarked. He hated sounding like a cheerleader, but ultimately that was what this job had become.

"Pain is white, remember the white light, the light is hope," they said again, this time with more confidence, but not quite enough.

"Better," Althaus told them. "Again!"

"Pain is white, remember the white light, the light is hope!" This final time the group yelled it. Althaus smiled at them.

"Now you're ready. Please, feel free to roam about the camp and make it your home."

Althaus signaled for the soldiers to escort the new arrivals from the tent.

Finally, he was alone again. Alone, that was, except for the soldier that was posted to help guard the new church.

He was intimidating. The uniform was an imposing black color, stealth in its way of blending into the dark of night. If not for the shine from the composite armor, one might not even notice the soldiers were there. Althaus tried to eye the uniform as much as he could on such occasions, realizing upon closer examination, each section was fitted to the other, like a suit of armor from the feudal days. Unlike the knights of old, however, these suits of armor were light in weight. Each soldier could still move quickly and quietly. Below the armor was a one-piece bodysuit made of chain-link, but not the metal kind. Instead, it was the same composite metal that made up each flap in the armor.

As far as Althaus could tell, there was not one weakness to be found in the suit. He did wonder what it was like inside one, though. From what Althaus could tell, weather, cold or hot, did not disturb the soldier who wore it. Truthfully, until the day the war began, he assumed a soldier was invincible inside.

2

The dreadful day in question began like any other day for Barrett Althaus. He woke, left his quarters to use one of the showers in the officers' area, and once he was done with his cold shower, was off to have breakfast.

Quickly, he ate his increasingly diminishing rations; eating didn't take long, as there wasn't much on the plate. Rumors around the base had it that if any more people were found, they were going to start to have numbered groups that instructed survivors on which day was theirs to eat. As far as food was concerned, things were beginning to turn bad. Eventually they would run out completely, and until they found a permanent place to call home, Black asked them to refrain from trying to grow crops.

"It would waste the seed," he said. "We won't be here long enough to see if they do grow."

Althaus hoped that was true. He knew some of the soldiers sent off on reconnaissance missions were looking for a permanent home for the camp; however, he wasn't sure they would find one. A place where blue skies could still be seen and where the sun came down, sprinkling plants with photosynthesis, seemed like a pipe dream. With the sky above them growing increasingly dark as the ash and nuclear winter from the attacks spread, Althaus was unsure where that better place was. If there was still an inhabitable part of America, Althaus figured they better find it soon or the little world that he and Black had created would dwindle and die.

In addition, leaving the country seemed like a fantasy.

Besides, he thought, *the rest of the world might be destroyed as well.*

After breakfast, Althaus went to his church. There, a line had already formed. Every day, people of all kinds wanted to come to Althaus, to ask what God wanted of them, to find out how to contend with difficulties in this new world. Often he didn't know what to say, but he found if he repeated his now famous slogan—*or was it infamous?*—they would repeat it back and find comfort.

It's all so stupid, Barrett Althaus often thought to himself. Though he never shared this thought with others, especially General Black. He liked Black and he trusted Black with defense of the base, but he feared Black and what he might do if he realized Althaus was a doubter. If he could kick people out of camp for not believing, what would he do to Althaus for lying?

It was about midday when the news began to spread and the camp filled with panic. Elvin was now Althaus's assistant at the church, and he came running in like a bat out of hell.

"Rev … Rever …" the poor boy struggled to get the word out.

"What is it, Elvin?" Althaus said with patience. He really liked Elvin; he had become a great help around the church, and Althaus had even begun to see him as, if not a son of his loins, then a son of the church. Almost like Quasimodo was to Notre Dame.

Hopefully, though, without the tragedy, Althaus thought.

"Sol ... so-durs have re ... re ... re-tun!" he finally spat out.

"Well, they return all the time," Althaus said with a smile, trying not to dismiss his young friend's words.

"One of ... of ... 'em ... 'i ... 'i dud."

The words shot through Althaus's whole body.

Dead?

For the first time he considered the soldiers could die, fully realizing people were inside that black armor. Men with real souls.

"Take me to the soldier, Elvin. Take me now!"

3

By the time Althaus and Elvin arrived outside the general's tent, a crowd had gathered outside. News had obviously traveled fast, and the throng was concerned.

"You go back to the church, Elvin; people may need help. I'll be back there soon. If you need to, go find Reverend Solomon to help you out," instructed Althaus. The boy just nodded in reply. Weaving his way through the crowd, Althaus came to the front of the tent, where two guards were posted outside.

"May I help you?" one asked curtly.

"I'm Reverend Althaus. I came to offer my services to the fallen soldier."

The soldier nodded and let him pass. With that, Althaus entered the tent.

Inside, things were chaotic. The medic of the camp was over the body of the dead soldier, who had been placed on the ground. Other soldiers were helping to remove the man's armor. Two others, the ones who brought him back, were standing at attention in front of the general, who was just staring at the dead man on the ground. Althaus looked at the mangled body below. His armor was broken and his undergarment torn. Dry blood clumped in the cracks of the uniform's armor shells, while chunks of flesh, even some brain matter, were exposed from underneath the broken helmet. Whatever had happened to this soldier was violent and thorough. He was dead; there was no doubt about that.

The only question was: what had killed him?

Black looked up and linked eyes with Althaus, noticing him. "What are you doing here, Reverend?" he asked with clear distress in his voice. This took Althaus aback; he didn't expect the general to be so emotional.

"I came by to offer any assistance—" but Black just cut him off.

"What happened?" Black asked the soldiers.

"We were attacked," the first soldier said. "Outside of Lubbock, Texas, sir. We made it that far. Found the city mostly abandoned. We could see Houston burning in the distance, but Lubbock hadn't been hit by any of the bombs. It was heavily looted, though, sir. From what we could tell, everyone abandoned it after. We were able to find some supplies. Food, medicine ... we stashed away as much as we could. It was on our way back when it happened."

"What happened, Lt. Turner?" It was obvious Black was growing impatient.

"Sir, we decided to move through west Texas," Turner added quickly. Our theory was there might be survivors in all the small towns ... in the rural areas." From the way the soldier was talking, Althaus began to wonder if they had acted against orders.

"They just came out of nowhere. As if they had been waiting for someone to come along. They were all around us, sir. We were lucky we got away. They grabbed Sgt. Dawson, grabbed him and tied him up with chains. They dragged him for miles until he was no longer fighting and was dead. After that, they ran him over, sir. Several times."

"Where were the two of you?" asked Black as calmly as he could.

"Sgt. Guitierez and I were cut off from him, sir. When they had initially attacked, there were fifteen men. They were excessively armed. We took cover behind the tank, sir, and fired upon them. We took most of them down, but Sgt. Dawson had been immediately surrounded and captured. Once the group around us was dispatched, we gave chase to the group that was dragging Sgt. Dawson. Opening fire, we were able to recover his body and take down most of the rest of the enemy force. In all, only five remained from the initial attack. Even though the sergeant had been overwhelmed and dragged, he was able to take several down before he died himself. He fought valiantly."

Lt. Turner finished his report. In the soldier's voice, Althaus could hear the grief inside.

"You say they ran over him, son," said Black. "What did they run over him with?"

"Motorcycles, sir. They were on motorcycles."

Black stood up from the dead soldier and looked at one of his men.

"You know you disobeyed orders," Black reprimanded. "Your orders were to scout the Houston area and report back."

"Yes, sir. When Houston was destroyed, we felt a more thorough recon of the area was necessary."

"But those weren't your orders!" Black erupted now. The men became even more rigid as he began his admonishment. A long silence overtook the room as the general thought through the situation.

"We will deal with the repercussions of disobeying orders later. Call the officers together. We're going to track those men down and kill them."

"What if there are more of them, sir?" asked the lieutenant.

"Then we're going to war!" Black said and walked away with a fierceness Althaus had never seen out of him.

Althaus now knew what should have always been obvious. General Black was a stone-cold killer.

A sleeping dragon.

Now the dragon was awake.

Aiden

1

The doctor thought he was the perfect candidate to lead the expedition.

"People are familiar with you," he said. "They recognize you from your movies, and that makes you someone they can trust."

Until now, they had kept on surviving. Moving down the West coast, the weeks turned into months, and they had gathered an even larger group of survivors, all with the same malady. The doctor theorized that in some way every one of these survivors had been protected somehow from the full blast of the radiation, and therefore instead of dying, they were turned into mutations. As the weeks dragged on, they had come across fewer and fewer "normal" people; everyone seemed to either be in a full-blown stage of mutation or in the beginning throes of it. Most normals ran off when they saw them. Which is what prompted Doctor Savage to initiate his new plan.

"I have been thinking things through long and hard," the doctor stated. "We're all infected. Our reproductive organs are failing. For sure, the women won't be able to have any more children."

"I don't understand. What does that have to do with anything?" Aiden asked. Honestly, he didn't know what the doctor was getting at, but this was how it was now. Every night the doctor would come to him, wherever he had found shelter that night—be it in an abandoned car or destroyed home, on this occasion it was down a sewer drain—and he would babble out his ideas. Aiden seemed to be the doctor's closest confidant, and therefore his favorite ear.

"I know," the doctor said. "At first I thought I could cure us ... but I was wrong. We haven't been able to find the resources. Now as we find more and more people inflicted with our same sickness, I can't help but wonder about the future of the human race in general. If in some way we are able to reproduce, what would men like us and the women we have in our possession create?"

Aiden had never thought of it, but now that he did, he was horrified. The fact was, their collection of people, the Tribe as the doctor had affectionately begun to call them, were deteriorating. In health and sanity. Many were miserable, and many more were slowly going crazy. They grunted more than communicated with language, and they had fits of rage from the constant pain. If two of them could create offspring, who knew what mess would come from that? Humanity was being lost—Aiden could see that now—and the doctor was saying he wanted to fix it.

"So," Aiden asked, "what's your plan?"

"We need to replenish the world with proper and healthy humans."

"How?"

The answer was astonishing—and quite frankly more than a little insane—but in truth there was a logic to it, a logic that Aiden could not deny. So he was sent out into the wilderness, away from the Tribe, to find an answer. He was given a small contingent of men, strong and wild—they were no longer right in the head—to help him achieve this goal. He had specific instructions from the doctor on what to do once he had found out what he needed.

"With any luck," the doctor said to Aiden, "you'll be back before next spring, triumphantly displaying your treasure!"

So, as leader of the expedition, it was up to him to begin to carve out a future for the human race.

2

By the time they crossed the border into New Mexico, their group had grown twofold, from ten men to twenty. Having left the Tribe a month earlier, Aiden had found it was easier to send groups in different directions to find the treasure they were searching for than going out as one big lump. Up to this point, they had found quite a few of the intended goal. It had been quite easy to do. Most "normals" were scared of them on sight, so Aiden, being well-versed in the school of acting, directed the others to put on a show, hooting and acting all crazy, to make the unaffected more vulnerable. The plan worked to a T.

Looking out on the display at their New Mexico base, Aiden knew the doctor would be happy with his returns. In the back of several pickup trucks, now lined with fencing and mesh, there sat normal women. Women who still looked like humans, showed no signs of infection, and could still reproduce. Which was the whole point.

The doctor felt the only way to fix humanity was to breed humanity. While the mutated women could no longer carry children, the non-mutated ones could, and coupled with the mutated men's seed, the doctor figured humanity could be saved.

Aiden smiled thinking about the future. He knew the world would be set right again. The doctor was a great man, and he just needed as many "normals" as possible to make it happen. Which was why Aiden couldn't quit now.

No, Aiden thought. *We need much, much more.*

Nell

1

Dr. Sandberg arrived at Nell and Mark's hovel around what Nell believed to be eight o'clock in the evening. It had been hard to keep track of time without clocks, but Nell found if one kept an eye on when the sun went down, it could be approximated how the hours passed. Due to it being January, the sun went down early, around five thirty. Mark usually fell asleep once the sun went down, giving his body the rest to fight off the infection. Which meant that Nell would stay up and watch over him.

Was this what the olden days were like? she wondered. *The ones before technology and other distractions, the ones where man lived by candlelight, reading books to one another for company?*

Nell remarkably found it quite peaceful at night, and enjoyed spending these quiet hours next to the man she loved and father of her unborn child. Still, she contemplated how much of her new resolve toward loving Mark was brought on just due to her situation, as opposed to it being real. Which was why, when Dr. Sandberg came by, she found it a much-needed distraction and a punch to the gut.

He knocked on the leaning wall that represented a door to her home. Mark stirred a little at the sound, but Nell rubbed his forehead, which sent him back to sleep. His head was dripping wet from fever, so she hoped Dr. Sandberg had good news for them.

Quietly, she walked out of the ruins and into the cool night. Nell had come to realize it was colder than usual in Texas for this time of year. It could routinely drop into the forties, but this cold felt more like the twenties. She wondered if they might wonderfully get snow. Folding her arms around herself, trying to keep warm (she didn't have a coat), she gave Dr. Sandberg the universal sign to keep quiet by placing her pointer finger on her lips.

"Everything okay?" Nell asked Dr. Sandberg quietly.

"He wants to see you," Dr. Sandberg said.

"This is good, right?"

"Yes," he replied. From the tone in his voice, though, Nell could tell he was worried about something. "Just do as he asks, and it'll be fine."

2

Ten minutes later, they arrived at the bonfire, the flames of which rose high into the air. Around the bonfire sat Stonehenge, his men, and their skank women. These were the people Stonehenge had been riding with since he became an enforcer for the cartel. There were thirty of them in total, and they were the ones the giant leaned on to do the dirty work at the camp. The survivors called them the "Inner Circle," and though they had no power, they helped Stonehenge create a gang mentality, forcing people to come to him with their problems. Fights were always breaking out among survivors, and there was no real law and order to speak of. With the Inner Circle as the aristocrats, the actions they took were irresponsible and helped to make the camp feel like a jungle.

On top of the food chain sat the giant, who was considered the biggest, baddest carnivore of them all.

The giant insisted on few rules to govern them. He believed in anarchy and the will of the people, unless that will of the people clashed with his, and then he would let everyone know who was boss. At first, Nell had felt safe because of him. However, the longer they stayed part of the camp, the more she learned to fear him. Every night he scoured the streets for a new concubine. Every night he would get drunk with his Inner Circle, filling the time with debauchery and swill, until they passed out. Nell later came to learn everyone called the giant "Stonehenge," presumably because he stood so tall and mighty. His wife's name was Juanita.

Of the two, Nell feared Juanita the most. Nell had once seen Juanita come up behind a woman and slit her throat.

It was horrifying.

And Nell had no idea why she did it.

So while Nell liked Stonehenge for the safety he provided, she was trepidatious about getting too close because of Juanita. She did not want to be indebted to Stonehenge, that was for sure, or look like she was coming between Juanita and him. She could only imagine what would happen then.

Hopefully Dr. Sandberg has the whole thing worked out, she thought. Perhaps she would owe Stonehenge nothing in return for the medicine, and that would be that. Why then was she so worried?

As she and Dr. Sandberg approached the Inner Circle, her guts started to turn. Nell could see Stonehenge standing in front of five men from his Inner Circle. They were on their knees, beaten. Stonehenge had a bat in his hands and was screaming at them.

"What the fuck did you do that for?" he screamed at them.

One answered back, with his arms up blocking any further hits from the bat. "There were only three of them! They were an easy mark! Besides, they had a tank and guns!"

"We don't need tanks and guns," Stonehenge hollered in reply. "I sent you all out there to find supplies, not to kill people who might strike us back!"

"We're sorry," another of the men said. "But we did it for you!"

"No, you didn't," was all he said back. Stonehenge turned away from them and thought for a long moment. Nell could tell he was contemplating things—what to do perhaps? "Two of them got away, you say?"

"Yeah, but one of them we killed."

"But the others. You said they were soldiers ... do you think they had a base to go to?"

"I don't think so," the second man said. "They were in these all-black uniforms; they didn't have any badges or anything. I couldn't even tell who they were soldiers for. If it wasn't for the American flag on their vehicles, we would have just thought they were normal people like us."

"Do you think they have reinforcements? Or were they just nomads?" Stonehenge asked, his head down as he listened to their answers.

"Nomads!" one answered in haste.

"Definitely nomads," another answered with panic.

"For your sakes, I hope you're right," Stonehenge responded. "It's bad enough they killed ten of us, which to me says a lot about their training. I hope to God they don't come after us, because if they do and there are more like them, I don't think we can win that fight. I should kill you for this!"

The men shook in fear at his statement. Stonehenge paused and looked at each of them.

"But I won't. You have taken a beating for this and you will have to live with the guilt of their blood on your hands. So, you are forgiven of your impudence. Do it again and I'll kill you, got it?"

"Oh, yes!" one said.

"It'll never happen again," said another.

With that the five beaten men stood and left him behind. Stonehenge, meanwhile, sat back down and draped over another woman that was not his wife. Juanita was across the circle watching them. She looked disgustedly in their direction. Nell was worried for a moment that Juanita might attack, killing all of them in the process, but as Nell watched her, she seemed disconnected emotionally and in control of her latent rage. As for Stonehenge, he sucked on the girl's neck, slurping her up like a Big Gulp from 7-11.

Is this really the man I have to ask to save my lover's life? She had thought better of him and was surprised by the events of this whole dark scene.

Just as she finished this thought, Dr. Sandberg grabbed Nell and brought her close to him. For a moment, her feelings for him came pouring back. Nell reminded herself of what was growing inside her and pushed the feelings away.

"Listen," he said in all seriousness, "I can't protect you. I wish I could. These people ... they want what they want, and they'll do anything to get it. Just do as they say. Do it for Mark. Do it for that baby, but whatever it is they have you do for the medicine, forget it after it's done. Don't let it eat at you. This is a messed-up world right now. We don't have the luxury of wishing things could be perfect. We all have to do what we have to do to get by. Do you understand what I'm saying?"

Nell thought she did, but at the same time, fear was creeping over her.

"Just forgive yourself," Dr. Sandberg said.

Nell nodded while peeking over at Stonehenge and the woman below him. His massive body engulfed the poor girl. That's when she realized exactly what Dr. Sandberg was trying to tell her.

Oh God! she thought.

Sandberg grabbed her by the hand, taking her to the giant. Stonehenge cleared his throat as he stood. For a brief moment, Nell wanted to change her mind.

Mark doesn't really need the medicine, does he?

It was too late, though; the giant had spotted her. He wiped his mouth with the back of his hand, looking down at Nell. Nell quickly averted her eyes, staring at the girl who had been underneath him. She was pulling her shirt back above her shoulders. She looked ashamed of herself. Nell knew that sad stare was what she, herself, was doomed for. Scrounging up her courage, Nell looked back up at Stonehenge.

"Is this the girl?" the giant asked.

"You know it is," Dr. Sandberg said with a surprising amount of contempt. Nell found this made her respect Dr. Sandberg even more.

"What can I do for you?" Stonehenge's big eyes peered through his bushy eyebrows.

"I need medicine for my ..." This stopped her for a moment. *What is Mark to me?* "For my husband," she said with confidence.

"Your husband?" Stonehenge said skeptically. "How old are you, girl? I remember you from that day you were going to cut your man's leg off! You looked like a little girl. Lost, needing a daddy. Is that what this is? Do you need a daddy, little girl?"

Stonehenge placed his gigantic paw on her shoulder. This touch sent chills up her spine. Nell could remember the first hug she gave him and wondered how she could ever have been so trusting.

"I'm not a little girl! And I'm not leaving without the medicine." Nell was suddenly proud of herself. This was the most courageous moment of her life.

Stonehenge reached into his pocket and pulled out a vial of pills. He twirled it around in his hand.

"This is a precious commodity ... little girl. What do you think it's worth? Something like this, around here, is worth a price. And money, well, money isn't worth a damn anymore. We trade in things now. So, what do you have to trade for this?"

"I have nothing," she said, lowering her head.

All is lost, she thought.

That's when she felt his finger, like a fishhook, snaring her in his trap, below her chin. He slowly lifted it up, forcing her eyes to again meet his.

"Oh, I think we both know that's not true. Come with me, and let's figure out how to make this work for both of us. I'm sure we can come to some kind of agreement."

With that, he put an arm around her, walking her away from the bonfire, away from the Inner Circle. Nell took a moment, looking back for Dr. Sandberg, but he was nowhere to be seen. He had left her alone to fend for herself.

He's a coward! she thought. *Which is just the way of the world now. It's full of scared, cowardly people, more concerned with their own survival than helping a friend.*

As she began to turn around, back to her fate, she caught a glimpse of Juanita. Her dark eyes were burning a hole through Nell's soul. That was when Nell knew the future was no longer bright.

Not for her.

3

Two hours later, Nell returned to her hovel. Mark was up, waiting for her. She felt guilty, dirty, and sinful. She knew Mark could see that something was wrong; it was written across her face. She simply hoped he wouldn't ask how she got the medicine. Telling him would kill her.

"Where've you been? I was getting worried," Mark said.

"I was getting you medicine!" These words came out like razors. *Can't he just appreciate the fact that I helped him?*

"Sorry, I didn't mean to—"

"I know ... I'm just ... tired. Just take the pills, and let's get some sleep."

She handed him the pills; there were only twenty of them. She watched as he swallowed three.

Slow down! she thought. *If he keeps going at this rate, how soon will it be before Mark's taken them all? How soon before I have to go back to Stonehenge for more? What will I have to do then?*

All these thoughts raced through her mind as they both lay down on the blanket they used for a bed. Usually he held her tightly all night, but not that night. She wouldn't let him.

I don't deserve his embrace.

Instead, Nell turned away, unable to look at him, unable to be held by him.

Dr. Sandberg's words of wisdom came pouring back to her: *forgive yourself.*

His voice repeated that over and over in her head. Yet it was too late. Nell knew she could never forgive herself. Her pain would never be penance enough.

"I love you," she heard Mark say.

She said nothing back.

Quentin

Having grown up around Bastion his whole life, Quentin knew all the secret ways back into town. He knew every wooded hideaway, hidden path, back road, and alley. It was easy for Quentin to position himself at Mankins's home without anyone being the wiser. Once he broke in and planted himself in the living room, it was just a matter of being patient and waiting.

Slow the blood, clear the mind, take the aim, and fire.

His sniper instructor drilled these words into his head. He always ran them through his mind during the long seconds of waiting for the right moment and setting up for a kill. He found them preferable to what his brother had just said, that was for sure. If he let his mind focus on Colin's misgivings, he could soon find himself losing resolve.

Not that Quentin was rationalizing the work ahead. He didn't question the need for this murder or if he should be the one to do the dirty work; it was obvious this was the right thing to do. The chief was unstable and an evil man, he had to be killed, and no one else had the balls to do it but him.

It's my duty!

Some might say that Quentin was a man of low morals due to his willingness to perform this act. He knew that Frank guy probably felt that way. Maybe Frank and even his brother saw him as a man who either had no heart or was imbued with death. For sure he had become desensitized to it; the army after all had transformed him into a killing machine.

However, Quentin knew that wasn't exactly accurate either. It wasn't that he cared too little that allowed him to kill; it was he cared too much. Unlike others, he did not kill for the thrill of it or the need to feel powerful like a god. In his case, it was his need to see justice done that allowed him to put aside his conscience. As long as Quentin knew the right side had won, it was a-okay by him if it went down bloodily, for freedom, justice, and the American way.

As Quentin waited, he checked and rechecked his rifle. It was odd doing this sitting in the living room of the man that he was about to kill. Usually he prepared from far away, not in the confines of a person's home. On the battlefield, surrounded by death, and the enemy in the distance was how he was used to having to perform his task. Tonight, though, he brought his skills home.

Despite the accuracy of his weapon from long range, Quentin wanted to be up close and personal, even though it was safer and more pragmatic to kill Mankins from a sniper's perch. For this, Quentin did not want to be too far away; he wanted to see Mankins's eyes as he pulled the trigger. Not out of some sick sense of joy, mind you, but because he wanted to make sure no mistakes were made. From far away, a sniper could assume the kill had been made, only to find out the target had survived to live another day. For Quentin, he knew there had to be zero question that Mankins was dead.

There was also another reason he wanted to be close. Quentin had a few answers he needed from Mankins before he left this world, and no matter what, he was going to get them.

2

It was a little before eleven o'clock when Mankins finally pulled his car into his driveway. He exited the vehicle, a police cruiser, and entered his home. What he didn't know was that Quentin was sitting in wait.

When Mankins moved through his house, he lit candle after candle. There was no electricity since the attacks, and for most people, candles were all they had. To Quentin, the fact that Mankins was lighting every candle he had seemed wasteful. Though some places, like the hospital or police station, ran on gas generators, the common townsperson was now living like it was the dark ages. Soon the candles would be gone too, unless they made more. Still, despite Quentin's disapproval, he found the way Mankins was lighting the candles to be helpful. He was creating a pathway to the kill. With every candle lit,

Quentin could see the hallways illuminate a little more, illustrating just how close Mankins was getting.

"I was wondering when you'd show," Mankins said with resignation in his voice. Quentin realized he was exposed by candlelight as Mankins finally reached the living room. "Anything I can do to get you not to kill me?"

"Not really," Quentin replied coldly.

"That's what I figured. Just do it then."

"I need answers first."

Mankins laughed hysterically. "You want to give me a pop quiz before you kill me?"

"Did you have my parents killed?"

"Now why would I admit that?"

With Mankins's evasion of the question, Quentin fired his rifle. A bullet lodged into Mankins's knee. He fell hard to the ground, writhing in agony.

"I thought you were going to kill me!" Mankins yelled, spit flying from his mouth as he gritted his teeth trying to bite back the pain.

"Oh, I will, but only after you give me the answers I want. You see, along with training me to be a sniper, the US Army taught me how to torture someone to get the answers I need. So as I see it, we can make tonight quick and painless, or we can drag it out as long as it takes. It's up to you."

Quentin prepared to fire again.

"No, don't ... please!" Heedless of Mankins's cries Quentin fired the gun again. A bullet tore through the air and planted itself in Mankins's foot. He screamed as blood began to gush from the chunk of meat he once called a foot. Quentin tore pieces of a sheet he had left by the couch. He took these long pieces and began to tie off the bullet holes in Mankins's body. Stifling the blood in the leg was easy; however, the foot, now resembling hamburger, had to be clumped up and fastened hard.

"There are more than twenty-five places I can shoot you on your body that won't immediately have you bleed to death," Quentin explained. "There are also chakra points that I can take a knife to that will give you the maximum amount of pain, yet leave you alive for hours."

"Jesus, Kershaw, you're ruthless."

"I can be when I want to be. I can also be very compassionate. You're not a good man, Mankins. You know what you've done. As I see it, you have a final chance to come clean. Did you have my parents killed?"

"What if I did?" Mankins spit out. Quentin could tell Mankins had never been in so much pain.

Getting answers will be easy.

"If I tell you, how do I know you will make my death quick and painless and not drag it out even longer for revenge?" Mankins asked.

"Because I'm not you. My word means something. I promise I'll make it fast."

Mankins looked into Quentin's eyes, studying his sincerity.

"Fine. Yes. I had them killed."

"How?" Quentin quickly asked.

"I had a few friends of mine run them off the road. Your father died on impact, but your mother lived. As she walked away from the crash, the same men ran her down in the road."

Anger boiled up in Quentin's blood, and for a moment, he wished he had not given his word to this man at all. But he had, and he was not going to allow Mankins to change the kind of man he was.

"Why did you do it, Mankins?"

"I had no choice. Your father knew I had been paying judges. He had paperwork that proved how corrupt I was. His vacation to Denver was to talk to an informant. I had that rat killed too."

Quentin nodded in understanding. He had the answers he needed.

"Sorry, kid. In truth, I liked your father. It wasn't personal, you know. It was just him or—"

Bang!

Quentin "The Killer" Kershaw had pulled the trigger a final time. The bullet went straight through Mankins's skull. Though the chief's body twitched on the ground, Quentin knew Mankins felt no pain.

He was dead. Revenge obtained, yet there was no justice or satisfaction in the moment.

Nothing can bring my parents back.

Suddenly, sirens rang through the night. They were in the distance, but Quentin knew they were coming for him. As quiet as the town was since the attacks, Quentin was sure the loud gunshots were heard all the way to the police station. The police were on their way; it would take awhile to place where the shots came from, but when they arrived, Quentin would be gone. The officers who were left behind in the wake of Mankins's death would be angry they lost their leader, but without him, Quentin hoped they would fall in line with Annette and her group easily.

Maybe they hate Mankins as much as we did, Quentin hoped.

As Quentin raced away through the woods, he realized to others—his brother included—he would be a murderer. To himself, however and those who knew about sacrifice, he knew he was a hero.

Maybe not the kind they wanted. Maybe not the kind they would ask for. Instead, Quentin knew, he was the kind they needed.

The kind of hero who could pull the trigger.

Sean

1

The children took Sean to their parents' truck, which had been stocked with emergency gasoline. Together they stocked it with other supplies and headed west.

Thank God for paranoid middle Americans, Sean thought.

The truck was a faded red pickup, rusted on the wheel flaps and beat-up from a seemingly long existence of hard work. For five long days, they traversed the broken country before Sean even learned the two children's names. He had attempted to have them reveal their names earlier, but it wasn't until he saved their lives that things between them all began to change.

They had been traveling west along the highway; Sean's plan was to cut through the western corner of Tennessee, head through Arkansas and Texas, and perhaps meet up with the old historic Route 66 around New Mexico. It would take them all the way to California, while not taking them too far off the beaten path in case they needed to stop somewhere to get supplies. Sean also hoped staying near the highways might help them find other survivors.

As they got close to major cities, the highways filled up with burned-out cars, stuffed with the bodies of those that didn't make it out. Though Sean was still not sure about what killed everyone, from the looks of cities like Memphis and Dallas, whatever hit them made it impossible to get close. Ash clouds were still thick, making breathing the air dangerous. This forced Sean to guide the kids north of Dallas, into Oklahoma.

Every ranch or outcropping they came across had been abandoned. Some of the smaller cities, like Durant and Lawton, were completely picked through and bare. However, whether that was due to the attacks or they had been like that prior was uncertain. What was certain was no one seemed to be around. Mile after grueling mile was just empty, desolate landscape.

Sean kept wondering, *Where is everybody?*

Thankfully they had stocked up well before leaving the bunker, especially with water, so the fact food was hard to come by wasn't a death sentence. The back of the truck was a veritable feast for someone who hadn't eaten, but to the three of them, it was survival. Sean just hoped nothing ever happened to the truck. They were making surprisingly good time across the country, detours and all; there just wasn't any traffic.

Despite the crowded city byways, once beyond the leftover metropolises, it was as if no one had the opportunity to escape. This made Sean realize everyone was just like he had been, caught by surprise during the attacks. There must have been zero warning, even on the outside. Another reason they were making such great time was also the most distressing: there was an utter lack of distractions to stop them.

This doesn't bode well for finding other survivors.

At night, the kids slept in the cab, locked in for their own safety. Whether that was protection from Sean or from some unknown danger was never made clear. The little girl wanted it that way, and what she wanted she got.

Sean found he liked sleeping in the back of the truck. The evenings were quiet, the weather was cool (but not freezing), and though the skies were clouded with ash, he could just make out the stars beyond them.

It sure is better than staring up at a prison ceiling, he thought.

While lying there, his mind would wander ...

Is my mother still alive?

Did Michelle or Winnie make it?

Where are all the airplanes? Sean hadn't noticed it before, but there was a complete lack of air travel.

Is this due to the attacks? Were flights grounded around the world until further notice? Or is it because there's no one left to fly?

Even scarier: *Are we the last three people on earth?*

It was the fifth night when he got his answer.

2

They had crossed back over the Texas border, stopping to sleep for the night somewhere near Amarillo. It didn't take long for Sean to fall asleep, as he had been doing all the driving and he was exhausted. He had no idea how long he had been out when he awoke with a start. Sitting straight up in the bed of the truck, his eyes took a moment to adjust to sheer blackness around him. They darted about, taking in every inch of the desert around him, though nothing could take formation. His eyes were still too tired to comprehend his surroundings. Suddenly he heard something ... a sound ... he was sure of it. Sean tried to place the sound, but due to being awakened from a dead sleep, his mind was too disconnected to place its origin.

By instinct, Sean looked to the children first. They were sound asleep, holding each other. After realizing they were fine, he scanned the horizon.

Nothing.

Just the endless black of night. He looked back to the cab of the truck and could see the gun clutched in the boy's hand. Sean wanted that gun. Especially because he was the one sleeping outside in the bed of the pickup. But he knew it was going to take more than five days on the road to pry that gun from those little buggers' hands. Finally, after a minute of no sound, he tucked himself back under the wool blanket he was using and closed his eyes.

Rattle.

It was small and quick, but he heard it clearly this time. It came from below the truck. Sean jumped to his feet. He had packed an ax in the back of the truck, which he grabbed. Holding it in his hands, poised and ready, he waited. Whatever was making the noise would have to come out from under the truck sometime. Sean just hoped it was an animal and not something else—though he had no idea what that something else might be.

Panic fell over Sean.

From the corner of his eye, he could now see the kids were awake. They must have stirred when he jumped. They looked scared.

Silence fell around them again.

"What is it?" Sean heard the muffled yell of the girl from inside the cab.

Sean did not answer back. He put a finger to his mouth, signaling for quiet. For once, she followed his instructions.

Sean waited, but everything in the night was calm now. It was possible that whatever had been under the truck had crawled off, but Sean thought he would have seen it. Besides, Sean could sense it, waiting down there, in the dark, for the right moment to strike. Sean's imagination was going wild on what it could be. Creeping into his mind were images of animals, infected by nuclear fallout, mutated into some kind of hideous beasts.

It's out of fiction, the worst kind, but really, how else would you explain it?

That's when he heard it.

A laugh. It was deep, almost a growl, but it was a laugh all the same. Sean's mouth fell open in shock. If it was a laugh he heard, which it had to be, that meant one thing: this creature was not a creature at all—it was human!

Only humans laugh.

"Who's there?" Sean yelled but got no answer. "Come out, you gutless freak!"

Suddenly another laugh emanated from below the vehicle, followed by another, and then two more, until it was a chorus of laughter breaking the silence. Sean looked at the children. They hugged one another, each trying to protect the other. Sean too found he wanted protection, but hiding wasn't an option. His job now was to protect the kids, and he couldn't do that hiding.

So, he jumped.

Rolling forward on the dirt, his eyes caught a glimpse of four shadowy forms under the truck. It was too quick a glimpse to make out what they looked like, but Sean knew it didn't matter. He needed to get them away from the truck. Once on his feet, Sean ran at full speed.

Behind him, the shadows hooted like wild animals. He had the ax to fight if need be, but from the power and strength of the sounds the creatures behind him were making, he somehow doubted it would be enough to stop them. He could hear their loud footsteps and howls getting closer. They were gaining on him. It was time to stop running and turn to the offensive.

Sean saw a boulder ahead, a big one. He quickly ducked behind it. They saw him do this, of course, but he wasn't trying to hide; he just needed an upper hand. During the few seconds, maybe five, he had to prepare, he moved the ax into striking position. Sean gripped it hard, steadying himself, calming his fears.

This is it, Sean thought, *better to go out fighting.*

Finally one of the creatures jumped around the boulder. Sean swung down the ax, hitting the creature square in the forehead. Its body convulsed as it let out some kind of guttural scream. Its arms and legs flailed in all directions, sending the other two creatures scurrying away into the night.

"And don't come back!" Sean yelled after them.

Analyzing what he'd seen, Sean thought they reminded him of apes who had lost their alpha male. Without leadership, they were nothing. Still, Sean could have sworn there was a fourth laugh. He looked back at the truck and saw he was right.

Another one of those things was hitting the truck, circling it, trying to get inside. It snarled and hissed; all the while, the kids screamed. The boy had his gun pointing at it the whole time, his hand shaking from fear. Without thinking, Sean ran toward the beast, ax above his head. As he arrived at it, he swung down, smashing the head of the ax into the back of the now-whimpering creature. Sean pulled out the ax and turned the creature over. Their eyes met. The thing had very human eyes. Sean could have sworn he saw fear sweep across its face. Yet Sean did not hesitate. He swung the ax down once more, burying it deep in the thing's skull. It twitched a few moments, then stopped.

It was dead.

Sean approached the cab of the truck. The kids unlocked the doors. They both dove into his arms, where he held them for a few long moments. Sean realized he hadn't been hugged in a very long time. He doubted they had either.

"Shhhh," he said softly. "It's okay now."

"Amy. My name is Amy."

"Okay, Amy, it's all right now."

"And he's Charlie."

Charlie and Amy.

At least, if nothing else, he now knew their names.

3

The light from the truck illuminated the remains of the thing that had attacked them. Sean, Amy, and Charlie stared down at the deformed figure, studying it.

"What is it?" Charlie asked, his voice still shivering from fear.

"Well, whatever it is, it's human. At least it was," Sean said.

"But it attacked us like an animal."

"Or a monster," Amy added in her usual joyless tone.

"Maybe it's a little bit of all three," Sean concluded. "Maybe it's what we become when we have nothing but desperation left. That and the effects of radiation."

"Shouldn't that just kill us?" asked Charlie.

"It should," Sean answered. "But only if it's enough radiation to do so. Otherwise, I suppose we become sick in other ways. Which, looking at this, is exactly what I'd say happened."

"A mutant," Amy agreed.

"He's gross!" Charlie looked away.

"Yes, he is," Sean agreed as he took in the semblance of the mutant monster below them. His head and face looked completely human, except for the bulbous growths protruding from his forehead and right cheek. His eyes were droopy, and his hair was falling out in patches, revealing bald yet brown skin, which was also peeling in thick chunks. Dry blood coagulated around the open sores where hair had once been. The clothes the monster wore were torn and revealed pale skin, spotted with more growths and festering wounds. The hands of the beast were gnarled, while fingernails were either completely missing or hanging torn away from the cuticle. Barefooted, the feet were dripping pus from infected wounds on the bottom, and the bridge of the foot itself was also ripe with growths. It was clear to Sean, this being had started off as human, but what it looked like now was pure monster.

"You think there is more of them?" asked Charlie?

Sean nodded.

"I only killed two, and there were four total, so we have to imagine where there are four, there are going to be many, many more. My best guess is these were survivors like us, just far closer to the blast sites than we were. Anyone close enough to be affected by the radiation may look like this. The reason they attacked us was probably for the food in our truck."

"Or they saw us as food," Amy said creepily.

"Well, aren't we cheery?" Sean struck back. "However, we can't discount it. We were targeted, that much is for sure. And if it is true that these ... people ... have turned cannibal, then it's safe to say the radiation from the blasts isn't just affecting their bodies, but their minds as well."

"We should have stayed in the bunker," Charlie whined.

"Shut up, Charlie," Amy attacked. Sean found he felt sympathy for Charlie. He was scared, understandably so, and his closest surviving relative treated him like a redheaded stepchild.

"Stop it, you two," said Sean. "I know you're both scared, but fighting with each other does nothing to help us."

"Then tell him to stop being such a baby about everything!"

"I'm not being a baby!"

"Good God, shut up!" Sean broke in. "You're both babies. Hell, I feel like a baby. Right now the only people we can depend on are each other, and if this monster shows us anything, it shows us we may be up against more than we can even imagine. Our survival depends on us staying clear of mind. Focused. We need to stay wide of the blast sites, and as far away from radiation as possible. We need to protect what we have. That begins with us, got it? So, let's drag these corpses away, turn off all our lights to not attract more of them, and get some sleep. I'm sure we have a big day ahead of us tomorrow, and we need to be prepared."

With that, the arguing stopped. Charlie and Sean moved the bodies, while Amy began to create a small area for them all to sleep in the truck. Staying within eyesight, no one went too far so that the others could come running if they screamed. Before long, they were all stowed back safely in the truck. Sean was surprised that he was invited to join them, but he supposed the children understood there were more dangerous things than him out here. After a few moments of calm, they all returned to sleep despite being scared out of their wits.

4

Sean was shaken awake. His first thought was the monsters had returned, but that wasn't it at all. To his surprise, Amy was looking down at him with tears in her eyes.

"Is everything all right?" Sean asked.

"I had a nightmare ..."

"Okay," Sean said, wiping sleep from his eyes.

"Can you please stay up with me?" she asked, for the first time acting her age. Sean was in even more shock from this question.

"I'm scared," Amy continued. "I don't want to go back to sleep, but I don't want to be up alone either."

Sean could see the fear in her eyes. He now realized the arguing and strong exterior were just a front. She was compensating for the fear deep within. He needed to remember Amy was still just a little girl, living in a world of unimaginable horrors.

For a moment, Sean wondered if he'd still be as put together as she was if their roles were reversed. When he was her age, Sean was tough, but not like her.

"Sure," he said.

They both sat close to each other. Quickly he looked over at Charlie, who was thankfully still fast asleep.

Thank God, Sean thought, *the last thing Charlie needs to see is his sister like this.*

The relationship between the two, as odd as it was, reminded Sean of the kind he had with his mother. She was always so tough, never allowing herself to look weak in front of Sean or his brother. The worst moment of Sean's teenage life was the time he walked in on her crying. After that moment, he realized she was just as vulnerable as he was. Sean assumed if Charlie saw his sister like this now, his already-weak defenses would crumble.

"I'm sorry for almost killing you that first day," Amy said.

"That's okay," Sean said. After all, what could he say about it? "You were both frightened. I could have been anyone. I get it."

"No, you don't. You know the man, the one you found dead in the bunker?"

Sean smiled at this.

She's a sly one, this Amy.

He never told them what he had found, but she had sent him down that aisle for a reason. She wanted him to find the body. *To intimidate me.*

"Yes," he said.

"He was like us, you know? He lived past the big explosions ... and came by the bunker, like you. Mommy was still alive then. The man was nice ... but then he changed. Mommy tried to protect us. She did all sorts of things to keep him away from hurting us. And she was scared of him because he killed everyone in town. Mommy had found that out when she tried to get help. But there was no one left to help us. So my mommy tried to be with him ... to make him happy. The man slapped my mom around, got her to do whatever he wanted. Charlie said it was because the man wanted me. I still don't know what that meant, but from watching what he did to my mommy, I really don't want to know.

"Anyway, one day, the man knocked my mommy around so hard she ended up ... well, you saw her. That was the night before you came. And right after she stopped moving, he grabbed me. I kicked him, pushed him, tried to get him away from me. Charlie couldn't do anything; he just sat there watching. He couldn't help me at all. He just sat there, on the floor by our mommy's body, crying over her. I yelled for him to help me, but it's like he wasn't there. The man held me so strong I couldn't get away. But that's when I saw the gun in his pocket. As he was opening the doors to the bunker, I pulled it out fast. I knew if the man got me out, I'd never see my mommy or my bother again. So, I killed him. The gun went off, and the bullet went through his side. Blood was everywhere. He dropped me and I fell down the stairs, but I got right back up and shot again. I shot him in the head. In his eye ... I don't know how I did it ... but he fell to the ground ... dead."

She stopped talking suddenly. Tears welled up in her eyes. Sean didn't know what to do. He stopped himself from reaching out to touch her. After what she had been through, he didn't want to scare her.

"That won't ever happen again," Sean said. "I'm going to protect you. You understand me? No one will ever harm you again."

"Okay," she said. "But that was what I was dreaming about. I do it every night. I dream about the way his face looked after I killed him. He was surprised."

"It's over now."

"I know." As she said this, she curled up next to him, putting her head on his shoulder. Within minutes, she was asleep. Sean held her the rest of the night, never moving, allowing her to sleep safely next to him.

That was the moment he realized there was no way he could take them all the way to California. They'd never survive, and he'd never find Michelle and Winnie with them in tow. He had to find a safe place for Amy and Charlie to live their lives.

Soon.

Willy

1

It's a compulsion, simple as that.

Willy knew he enjoyed killing things, and he didn't mind that fact. No matter what he did, he had a hard time controlling the desire, so most of the time he just gave into it. This was why on the night he first entered Bastion, Willy traipsed through the woods looking for an animal to kill; he hoped it would not only quench his hunger for food (he was starving), but also for the insatiable need to kill something.

He could feel that need building up inside him. First it started in his balls, as if he were becoming sexually aroused; then he would feel it in his gut, like a hunger for food; and soon it would make his whole body shake like he were detoxing of a drug. Willy knew he couldn't let it get to that point, not because he didn't want to kill anyone, because there were a few people in the group he did want to kill, but because he didn't want to screw up his chances of staying in Bastion and surviving.

As he continued to move through the woods, he realized that he wasn't much of a hunter. He had never tracked an animal in his life, so even though he followed people from time to time, tracking an animal was far different. The people he followed were part of the concrete, gray, city landscape, with trackable habits and homes. They were cold, pretentious, and unaware of the everyday dangers positioning around them for the kill. However, in nature, Willy felt like the hunted. He didn't know the animal tracks, he didn't know how to leap from tree to tree, and he didn't know how to use the hedges to hide his presence. He didn't know where a deer went to bed for the night or to feed. Though Willy, to some extent, knew he too was an animal, he was one that had been removed from his habitat and was therefore at a disadvantage.

With the moon shining through the trees, Willy could see bits of landscape around him. Nothing more than shadow and parts of trees, but occasionally, he would hear something rustle or leaves crackle like paper being torn. His head darted back and forth as he would try to place the sound; alas, though, he found it impossible. To him it seemed to be coming from everywhere and anywhere.

Suddenly he heard a laugh. This stopped him in his tracks.

What the hell was that? he thought. *It certainly wasn't an animal.*

More laughter broke out. Finally he was able to place it. Deeper into the woods he went, just beyond the hedges. With every step, the giggles got louder and were easily attributable to young girls.

If not a deer to kill, he thought, *how about them?*

Walking slowly, he started to see the girls' silhouettes take shape. They were at the road, each one pushing the other to enter the woods, daring each other.

"You go in!" one said.

"No, you!" said the other. Then both erupted into laughter again. Not because it was funny however; it was nervous laughter because they were frightened.

If only they knew how frightened they should really be. Willy smiled to himself at the thought.

"Scaredy cat!"

Yes, Willy thought, *scaredy cats! His little fluffy pussies. Let me get close enough to pet you.*

2

While a gangbanger, Willy killed seven people, three totally innocent and just because he didn't like the look of them. Two were from rival gangs, and the other two were women he had fallen for and stalked. Eventually, he had to kill them too, so no one else could have them. Unlike the ones he killed as part of his gangbanging ways, the two women were experiments. The most notorious of American gangs, the Leviathans automatically made Willy dangerous. He had to be. If you were a member of the Leviathans, the only way to rise up through the ranks was to show that you could kill. Willy had no problem showing that. Thus, he was a protected man, and the more despicable acts he did, like holdups, beating old fogies, or rape, the more protected he became. By the time he had been in the Leviathans a year, Willy was in the upper echelon of gang leadership. Having never been caught or gone to jail for any of the crimes he had committed, Willy had begun to feel invincible.

During his formative dating years, Willy had found he enjoyed women whom he could control and manipulate. The more he could push his will onto them, the more he found he got off on the feeling. The same could be said as to why he liked to attack innocents as a gangbanger—the rush made him horny. Often after a stickup or a home invasion, Willy would need to find a girl to end the night with. Sometimes they'd even come willingly. Sometimes not. In those cases, he had no problem paying for it. That way, they were forced to do whatever disturbing things he could think of, and he could think of a lot. Not too long after these habits started, Willy realized this probably made him some kind of sicko.

Still, as he figured it, he liked what he liked, and he'd be damned if society was going to tell him it was wrong. Especially with so much wrong with society!

As a gangbanger, he broke every law around, just to fit in. As a survivor, he kept his head down and did as he was told—that way he could keep on surviving. That was Willy; he was a chameleon. He knew how to blend in so he could survive. Which was probably why no one ever seemed to see him coming.

Now though, as a hunter, he felt in his element at least emotionally, if not physically.

3

Suddenly he was on them. Breaking from the woods. The girls both screamed, and the sound echoed off into the distance, bouncing off trees and dissolving into the night sky, too far from the town to be heard. Willy smiled as he realized they were truly all alone.

Oh how I love that sound, Willy thought. *Screaming makes me hot!*

"Whoa, whoa, don't be scared," he said. "I'm not going to hurt you."

"Geez, sir … You scared us half to death!" the first girl said while trying to catch her breath.

"Only half?" Willy spoke with charm in his voice and laughed. "Well, I suppose that's good. I'd hate to be responsible for fully killing you!" He let out an even louder, more uproarious laugh, which began to set the girls at ease. "What are you two doing out here, alone, so late at night?"

"We heard there were people in the mountains—" the second one replied, but was cut off by her friend.

"Shhhh," she said. "He could be one of them."

"That's true," he nodded, "I could be."

"Is it true?" the second one asked. Willy could tell she was excited by the danger of it. Which in turn excited him.

"Yes. It's true. I am one of them."

"Oh, my God—" the second girl said with a giggle.

It would be so easy, Willy thought, *just to reach out and grab the two of them, take them into the woods, and do what I want with them. They are so young, so pure.*

Willy smiled a crooked smile and began to reach for them. Then he noticed the dark town in the background. Bastion: the group's last hope. *His* last hope. Taking a deep breath, Willy calmed himself as Frank's warnings of poaching danced around in his head.

No need to start a war over two missing girls, Willy thought, allowing a cooler head to prevail. *After all, if I wasn't careful, I would have been caught years ago. And if I get caught here, I'll get thrown out … or worse, killed.*

Which, of course, he couldn't risk. He enjoyed life too much, which was one of the main reasons he had linked himself to this group of jokers in the first place. He needed them for his own survival. Deep down, he knew he would ditch them at his first opportunity.

Especially that black dick Frank, he thought.

Seeing people like Frank, people he deemed beneath him but who somehow had advanced further in life than he, made him sick. Willy just wanted to take a rock and bash his face to a pulp. No matter how much he tried to fit in and ignore his feelings of hate, he knew it was only a matter of time before they pegged him for what he truly was. Which would be disastrous.

In the old world, gangbangers were not viewed popularly by society at large. By respectable people—whatever that meant—he was seen as something evil, which Willy knew wasn't far from the truth. Willy supposed that was why he was able to lie so easily to the old lady about his past. There was no guilt left inside him.

But I had to lie, he reassured himself, *to protect myself!*

Willy knew if his past were revealed to the group, they would leave him behind, as a penalty for his crimes.

Which is why he decided to let these girls go.

"You two should get back home," Willy suddenly said with a stern quality to his voice. "You don't know what else might be lurking out here in the night."

He gave this last comment a tone of mystery and just a smidgen of danger. From the look the two girls gave each other, he could tell it had the intended effect.

"Go on now!" he added. "Go!"

The two girls immediately turned and ran off. He watched them as they went, listening to their intoxicating giggles.

They're not my style, Willy assured himself. *I like them older, more ripe for the picking.*

Willy reentered the woods, searching the area for an animal. Any animal …

It would be the only kill tonight.

He began to whistle as he searched.

Soon though, Willy promised himself, *soon blood will be on my hands, and the fire within me will be out.*

Althaus

1

"Will you take my confession and give me your blessing?"

Reverend Althaus had been closing the sanctuary for the day when General Black arrived saying those words.

"I'm not a Catholic priest. I don't usually do confessions," Althaus replied.

"Does it matter these days?" Black said with a smile. "You're everything to everyone. Anyway, you're all we got."

"There's always Reverend Solomon," Althaus said, but General Black just made a grunting sound, which Althaus realized indicated how he felt about Clarence. "I'll listen to whatever you have to say, and of course, I'll give you God's blessing."

Althaus sat in a chair. General Black sat across from him. Each man stared at the other, linking eyes, waiting for the other to start.

Black finally began, "So, how do we begin this? You say you're not a priest? Well, I'm not much of a Catholic, either. But I figured I should do this. Considering we are going through Judgment Day or whatever." Black was flippant about this last remark, which surprised Althaus. Though he had not known the general long, Althaus assumed he was a religious man, a true believer. Now it seemed quite the opposite.

"I'm just here to listen, General. Begin whenever you are ready."

"When I'm ready, huh?" Black paused for a moment. He stood and looked around the room, coming to a pause before the cross that now dwelled above the tabernacle. Neither the cross nor the tabernacle were much to look at, made of whatever wood could be found. Still, they got the idea across.

"You want to know what the hardest part of being a leader is?" Black finally continued. "It's making a decision. I've made so many decisions. Often they involved sending young men to their deaths. Just like I'm doing now. I'll be leaving with a group of men tonight.

Strong-willed men who are willing to lay down their lives because I'm ordering them to do so. They are unafraid of death, unquestioning of my judgment. Does that make them brave or stupid? You want to know the truth, Barrett? Sometimes I don't even know."

Black raised a hand and laid it upon the cross.

"I've killed so many young men, though most not by my hand. And every time one of them died, I ran through my orders, relived every mission I'd sent them on, and wondered, *What did I do wrong?* ... 'But it's war!' I would tell myself, rationalizing. 'Soldiers are going to die!' But I can't help it; I always feel like I've failed somehow. Failed their mothers and fathers, wives and children. Or just failed myself and the mission, and yet I continue to make these terrible decisions."

Black turned away from the cross and back to Althaus, looking for some sort of answer. The reverend remembered his training, kept his silence, and revealed nothing of his true feelings about the conversation.

"I sent out some soldiers for some recon. They found the camp of bikers. I know who killed my men, and I know what I have to order my men to do. Today I'm going to ask these men to fight," Black continued, "fight for a fallen comrade, against an enemy that we—only months ago—probably fought to protect. Our own people is what we are going to find out there. And I'm going to ask these men to kill them. What kind of order is that? This isn't an enemy. This isn't foreign soil. I feel like Lincoln ordering brothers to kill brothers. But what choice do I have? This is for our very survival. We must survive! Otherwise, everything is lost. We can't simply let wild animals kill our troops or attack what is left of the American ideal. These enemies of ours killed a soldier for sport. We can't let them get away with such an act, can we?"

Althaus could tell Black wanted his support, wanted him to say it was okay, but Althaus knew it wasn't his blessing to give. Black needed to find the right answer within himself.

"You don't have to go," Althaus said. "You have two choices you can make. God has given you the free will to do that."

"Yes, that's true, but I'd be letting the people down. Our people, the people who look to us for safety."

"Maybe not. Maybe going off on this mission is letting them down more. We are running out of fresh air. The pollutants from the fallout have killed the land around us and poisoned our water. Maybe leaving us now is worse than letting some bikers who killed one of your soldiers get away."

"Is it?" The general paused, lost deep in thought. After a few moments, he returned to the conversation. "I am sending you away," Black said with sudden conviction.

"What do you mean?" Althaus asked.

"Tomorrow, after our departure, you are to guide the camp to better surroundings."

"Where would I find that? I don't even know where to go," Althaus protested, but he could tell Black was unmoved and resolute in his decision.

"Follow the blue of the sky. Where there is blue sky, there is fresh air and sunlight."

"How will you find us again?"

"If we survive, we will do the same. God willing, we will end up together again."

"Will you leave some soldiers with us for protection?" Althaus hoped his answer would be yes. Deep down, he was afraid of what might be in their path. Althaus realized that with Black and his armor-clad men, he had fallen into a false sense of security.

"Stick together as a group, and you won't need my men. But yes, I will leave you with some."

Suddenly Black turned to exit.

"Wait, I haven't given you a blessing," Althaus said.

Black looked back at him and smiled.

"I don't need it."

With that, General Black left Reverend Barrett Althaus alone. While a great pressure may have been lifted off the general, a new one had been dropped upon Althaus. How was he going to lead this group, a thousand and some strong, into an uncertain future? Was he to be like Moses, leading God's chosen people into a new promised land?

What if there is no new promised land?

Althaus turned and looked at the cross. He slowly walked to it. He took in its jagged shape, made of old wood from a destroyed house and tied together with frayed string. He placed a hand against it.

If they are to leave tomorrow, this cross needs to be protected at all costs. It's the only tool from God left to guide us and protect us.

Feeling the rough wood of the cross against his skin, Althaus had the oddest thought:

I'm about to be crucified.

Part Three:

War

Nell

1

In the three months since Nell had gotten the medicine from Stonehenge, she'd had to ask Dr. Sandberg for refills six times. The operation to get the meds had become routine. Sandberg would take her to Stonehenge, and the giant in turn would make her work for the meds. Each time the acts required got worse, while the doses got smaller. These horrible moments of depravity haunted her, continually replaying in her mind, over and over, until Mark was forced to ask, "Where are you? Because you're not here."

"Sorry," she would simply reply.

Honestly, she had no other answer for him. Nell's mind was too busy thinking of all the ways this was going to end. Eventually her pregnancy would show, and then Stonehenge would no longer find her attractive. At that point, the supply line would stop, and Mark's recovery would come to a halt.

Maybe I should tell everyone about the pregnancy, she would think. *Maybe then I can be taken care of.*

Nell was relatively sure Mark would insist on her taking it easy and then he would be forced to be a responsible man.

It's his fault I'm in this predicament!

Perhaps even Stonehenge would show some pity and allow her to stop her "payments" for the medicine.

Maybe he would just give us what it would take to get Mark better. For the sake of our child.

As much as she hoped for these things, however, she knew it was only a fantasy.

To Nell, the longer she could hide her pregnancy from both men, the longer she had to create a plan that would save Mark, herself, and the baby. If Mark realized she was pregnant, he would push himself too hard to take care of her, likely killing himself in the process. If

Stonehenge realized she was pregnant, he might assume it was his, panic, and decide to do something foolish.

Like kill me, Nell imagined, *just to rid himself of the baby. No, I have to do whatever it takes to keep my situation a secret.*

2

On this particular morning, Nell woke to the sound of engines all around her. The Inner Circle would often go on runs for gas, which they siphoned from stations, cars, and trucks—anywhere they could find the stuff. Her guess was they had found a large cache of it somewhere and were off to get it. She sat up out of the uncomfortable bed (if that's what you wanted to call it) and saw Mark perched on a slab of debris, watching the world around them.

"What's going on?" she asked.

"They found more fuel. About ten minutes ago, the camp went nuts." Mark was watching the surroundings intently. To Nell, Mark looked stronger suddenly. His color filled her with hope.

"Should I go find out?" Nell wiped the sleep from her eyes as she said this.

"No, let's just stay in here. Let them deal with it. I am sure if they need us, they'll get us. Lot of help I'd be anyway."

Mark hobbled around, positioning himself back down on their painful excuse for a bed. He put his arm around her, tucking Nell in close to him. While that should have made Nell feel safe, it made her stomach lurch. She wasn't sure if it was the guilt or the pregnancy hormones, but either way, she felt awful.

After a few moments of trying to pretend nothing was wrong, Nell gently lifted herself from Mark's grip.

"What's wrong?" Mark asked.

"Nothing. Just feel a bit nauseous."

Big hint! she thought.

Yet she had been throwing up for weeks, and yet he was oblivious to what was happening to her.

Stupid boy!

"You sure that's it?" Mark reiterated. "You've been distant from me for weeks."

"Have I?" Nell tried to play it off, but found it hard to lie so continually. She felt if she couldn't start telling the truth, she was going to explode. "I'm not doing it on purpose!"

Another lie.

"I didn't say you were." Mark held her hand. "Just remember, we're a team. I'm here for you. I can help."

"Right," Nell said, fangs bared. She hated herself for speaking to him this way, but all the anguish was starting to add up.

"What is that supposed to mean?" Mark attacked back, anger starting to build underneath his calm exterior.

"Nothing. Just, I mean, you're hurt, you know. What can you do?"

That had to sting him, she knew. *What a bitch I am!*

Mark looked down at his leg, and she could see the pain beyond his loving eyes. Mark shifted his gaze back up at her. Tears were welling up in his eyes, as the guilt hit her anew.

"I didn't mean that," Nell quickly added, but it was too late. Mark was devastated.

"You think I want to be like this? I used to be able to do everything!" Mark was screaming now, no longer in control of his feelings. "I was an athlete, for God's sake! I was attractive. Now I'm—well, I'm this! I wanted more for us, you know? I want to do more for you! But what am I supposed to do?"

She hugged him tightly. "Stop. I'm sorry. Don't do this. I didn't mean it. I'm just tired."

For a long time, she just held Mark, hoping her arms around him could help hold the pieces of their lives together. The truth was, no amount of binding was ever going to stop them from crumbling. Their relationship was like the world around them ... in shambles.

"How many more pills do you have?" Nell asked with artificial concern in her voice. She was scared of his answer. Deep down, she was only thinking of herself and what she would have to do to get more.

Mark pulled away and returned to his prone position, covering himself with their blankets, trying to hide.

"I don't know. I don't care." Self-pity had overcome him. Nell had seen this quite often recently. He was constantly fighting bouts of depression. She supposed it was only normal considering everything they had been through, but it angered her.

With all I'm doing to keep you alive, it only seems fair that you should be happy.

"Fine!" she said, anger piercing her voice. "I'll check."

She walked over to the envelope that held the medicine. They kept it behind a rock, which was, in turn, fitted into the wall for safety. People were desperate, they had reasoned. *Who knows what they would do if they found out we have meds?*

Nell wiggled the rock free of its encasement, revealing a small boulder-shaped enclosure. She grabbed the envelope within. Just from feel alone, Nell could tell the contents were light. She looked in.

Three pills left.

"Damn," she said. "How many of these have you been taking?"

"I don't know," he said. "Three or four a day."

"You only need one or two."

"I'm trying to get better!"

"Your body is probably building up a tolerance to this stuff. You should be better by now."

"So, what? We need more?"

"Yes." Anxiety fell over Nell, like a heavy blanket that was not made of cloth, but instead iron, wrapping her up.

"I'll be back." Nell stood, finding the strength she needed.

"Want me to go with you?" Mark said. Nell could tell he wanted to protect her. She could tell he knew something wasn't right, but his help was the last thing she needed.

If he knew, she thought, *he would probably die of shock.*

"No, don't worry, I'll be back soon." She bent to him, kissed his lips lightly, passionlessly, and walked out.

Mark

1

Mark allowed Nell to get twenty yards away before he started following her. The good thing about being a cripple was that people underestimated you. The reality was, Mark had gained enough strength to keep an eye on Nell. Even if he couldn't move as quickly as he wanted to, he had at least developed a way to move.

Over the past couple of weeks, Mark had made what amounted to a peg leg. He whittled it out of some wood, attached some straps to it, and uncomfortably tied it to his stump. He had spent some time practicing on it, giving him full confidence he could follow Nell.

The first steps were excruciating as the wood dug into his sensitive, healing skin, like a thousand pins into his leg. He could feel the end of his bone pressing onto the hard and unforgiving lumber as splinters broke away, wedging into his flesh. All he could do was grit his teeth and bear it.

Can't stop, he thought. *Turning back is not an option. There is something wrong with Nell, and I need to find out what it is.*

Mark followed slowly behind. He figured there was no need to hide. For one, Nell would never guess he was following, and two, he was moving so slowly it was hard even keeping her in his line of sight.

Mark fumbled his way down the streets of camp, bumping into people as he went. No one said boo to him about it, though, as they felt sorry for him more than mad. He had to divert his gaze from people's stares. He hated being judged by their prying eyes.

Oh, look at that poor cripple, I know they're saying. No doubt about it. After all, isn't that how I used to judge people in the same predicament?

Uncomfortably, Mark recognized in his pre-cripple days, he was a starer. He couldn't help himself—handicapped people made him leery. He was scared their problem would rub off on him. Destroying his athletically perfect body. He laughed at the irony of that now. Thoughts of his mother often saying things about not judging people came to mind, but it was too late. He had judged people, and this was his punishment.

Mark turned a corner onto another street. He could not spot Nell at all. He had lost her in the crowd. Mark paused a moment, catching his breath, feeling the sweat that had broken out all over his body. Cold coursed through his tingling body. This was more exertion than he had done in months. His body was shaking from the work, and he was afraid he wouldn't be able to make it back home. Still, he had to find her. Mark had to know where she was going.

Fighting the aching pain in his stump, Mark trudged on. He figured it was better to keep going straight than to try to veer from the course they had been on. His hunch was right, because from out of the hospital came Dr. Sandberg, with Nell.

Mark froze.

He was right out in the open, only feet away. Nell looked over his way, but thankfully didn't notice him.

The mind only sees what it wants and expects to see, realized Mark. Since Nell didn't want or expect to see him, she didn't.

Walking behind a brittle wall, he was able to hide from view, all the while keeping an eye on Nell. The two of them were on the move, headed toward the center of the camp. Again, Mark followed.

2

He arrived at the campfire site. It was still soiled from the party the night before. Mark had known something had been going on night after night. He could hear the sounds all evening long, but now he was seeing the evidence with his own eyes. Empty beer bottles, ripped clothing, and trash were strewn everywhere. Disgusting things, like vomit and used items that were not supposed to be out in public, just lay all over the landscape for all to see. The whole graphic scene sullied the destroyed world even more. Mark hoped he didn't lose his balance and fall into the ground of slop. Worried about just such an occurrence, he stopped to gain his balance and watch Nell from afar.

Nell was outside a hovel at the far end. She waited alone, head down, seemingly ashamed. She was certainly not the confident and strong girl Mark knew. Among these ruins, she seemed so small, just one more piece of rubble among a world of destruction. Dr. Sandberg emerged from inside the hovel and nodded at her. Nell took a deep breath as the giant arrived in front of her.

Stonehenge placed a hand on Nell's cheek. To Mark, he was touching her far too familiarly to make him comfortable about this situation. The giant opened the entrance to the tent, and Nell walked inside. The hulking mass of a human followed, with a disturbingly lustful look on his face. Mark was about to say something, scream for Nell, when he saw Dr. Sandberg apparently debating whether to walk into the tent or not.

Maybe Dr. Sandberg would help, Mark hoped.

For a moment it seemed so, but then out of fear, or maybe just lack of empathy, he turned on his heels and walked away.

There will be no help from him, Mark realized. *I'm alone now.*

With a violent wobble, Mark started forward, carefully balancing on his peg leg. He could feel the ground beneath him squish, pulling his wooden leg inches into the ground beneath. Mark struggled to free it with every step, making him increasingly unstable. On the side of Stonehenge's ruin, Mark could see a window. To look inside meant danger, but despite the fear of being caught, he had to see what was happening. Looking around, he noticed the coast was clear. The giant must have sent his whole gang out to get oil this morning, and now he was alone. The time for Mark to do this was now.

Mark arrived at the window and peered in.

What he saw broke his heart.

Annette

1

"We are here today to bury a beloved member of the Bastion family," Pastor Pemberton said, standing over the coffin of Chief Mankins. A hole had been dug in the cemetery, and most of the town had come to the graveside memorial to pay their last respects to the divisive man. Annette and the rest of her group decided to go to the funeral in an attempt to show solidarity with the town, hoping to ingratiate themselves with the Bastion populace. She also hoped that being at the funeral would take the suspicion for his violent death off of them.

"Chief Mankins was a man who gave his all to Bastion," the pastor continued. "He spent his life making sure everyone in Bastion was safe and protected."

Annette could hear some people in the crowd crying, but most were silent. Despite the hate Mankins had stirred up, it seemed he was also dearly loved. Annette hadn't counted on that. Off to one side, she saw Quentin and his brother Colin. Quentin looked emotionless and stared at the grave, trying not to betray himself. Colin, on the other hand, seemed nervous. Annette hoped he could hold it together for all their sakes. If it got out how the chief was murdered, things would get really bad for all of them.

"So now we send Chief Mankins's soul into the arms of God. There may he finally find the rest and peace he never allowed himself to feel on earth"

Annette began to zone out on the pastor's speech. She began to look over the faces in the crowd, trying to discern their allegiance. She was beginning to realize her rash command to kill the man might have been the wrong decision.

Of course, that was to be expected, she thought. *I'm not a leader. I've been forced into this position. I did what I thought was right.*

Finally the pastor finished his speech, and the remaining officers from the police station began to lower the casket into the hole. As they did this, the crowd began to disperse. Quentin and Colin came to her and the rest of her group.

"Good turnout," Annette said to them.

"It's to be expected," Quentin said. "Most in this town are still scared of him. They probably thought if they didn't show, he'd come back from the grave to get them. I'm sure the fear of reprisals doesn't help either."

"Will there be reprisals?" asked Annette.

"There's a good chance."

"We better prepare then."

Out of the crowd, three men stepped forward. One of them began to point and yell in their direction.

"Murderers!" he yelled.

Annette paused, unsure what to say back. She looked at the rest of her group, and they looked uncomfortable. Frank shook his head.

What have I gotten us into?

"We know it was you!" the man added for good measure. "No one here could have killed him! It was all of you!"

"We—" Annette began, but wasn't sure of what to say.

"Get out of our town!" yelled another person in the crowd. Then more joined in as well. Things were beginning to get out of hand.

"Stop this crap, Deerdorff!" Quentin yelled back.

"Oh, yeah?" said the man who responded to that name. "What you going to do?" The man stepped up to Quentin, followed by his two friends. "Kill me?"

"Back off," was all Quentin said back.

"We know you killed him," Deerdorff added. "In fact, the chief wanted us to kill you first."

"Did he?"

"Oh yes. In exchange he was going to give us power in this town."

"So you're admitting to collusion?" Quentin challenged. "Smart!"

"Smarter than you. Your new friends better watch out. You too, Kershaw. We're coming to get you."

As Deerdorff finished this, he stepped back and began to incite the crowd.

"Chief Mankins was the best thing that ever happened to this town! Without him, we would be lost! But the chief, in his infinite wisdom, told me the day he died to protect this town. He said if anything should ever happen to him, that I should stand up and protect it! I will do that now for his memory!"

The crowd was cheering him on now, accepting what he said as fact.

"This can't be good," Annette said.

"I agree," Quentin added.

As Annette and her group began to walk away, she could hear the crowd chanting: *Get out! Get out! Get out!*

So much for blending in, she thought.

2

It did not take long for rumors to take root in Bastion. Everyone was on edge looking for the perpetrator of the crime, which was quickly splitting the town in half. One half was glad he was dead and thought the killer should be commended, while the other half saw Chief Mankins's death as a tragedy and wanted the killer to be brought to justice. All this made the political climate very hard for the new arrivals. They couldn't blend in as they had originally hoped.

It was assumed by those who lived in the town that the group from the mountains (as they had begun to be called) had something to do with the chief's untimely death. Word had spread that if one were accepting of these strangers in their homes or business establishments, they would be seen as sympathizers and be dealt with accordingly.

So, wishing things would calm down, Annette had her people stay out of Bastion for the time being. Her hope was that within a few weeks, as things calmed, they could move in. About a week after the funeral, her hopes seemed well placed. Innkeeper Mary Anne Silva opened the doors of her award-winning bed-and-breakfast to the group from the mountains.

"Listen," she said, "unlike these savages, I like to get to know people before I judge them. I figure the best way to do that is to invite you to stay with me. I have food, nothing great, just some canned things and fresh vegetables from my garden, and I have water we can boil to get hot. When was the last time any of you had a bath?"

"Months," Annette said.

"Come to my house, and I will make sure you aren't bothered."

Mary Anne Silva was blonde, busty, and beautiful. She was in her thirties and full of sunshine. Annette liked her immediately.

"Well, I'd like to say yes—" Annette began, but was cut off by Mary Anne.

"Then say yes!"

"I need to talk to everyone else from my group."

"Let me do it for you." Mary Anne turned to the group, who had all been standing by, listening. "Who thinks my house sounds way better than another night on dirt and dead leaves?"

Everyone responded affirmatively.

3

That night, everyone washed, ate, and put on some extra clothes that had been donated to the group by one of the local clothing stores. Annette, to her astonishment, found she was relaxing. Sitting in Mary Anne's beautiful living room, decorated in a rustic, turn-of-the-century cabin style, lit by candlelight and fireplace, Annette sat on the plush couch and covered herself with a blanket. Despite the fire, it was still cold in the house, as a gentle snow was beginning to fall outside. Even before the attacks, she had never lived in such luxury.

Mary Anne came in with a tray piled high with teacups, a kettle, and a closed box made of wood.

"Tea?" Mary Anne asked.

"Sure."

"I already heated the water. Thank God for gas stoves and matches; we can still cook a little. Until the gas runs out anyway."

Mary Anne began to pour the hot water into a cup. Annette had never been a tea drinker, but she was just glad to have something fresh and warm to drink.

"What kind should I have?" asked Annette.

"Depends on your mood. Usually at this time of night, I go for something calming, like chamomile, but you may want a kick, so in that case I suggest a black tea. Like Earl Grey."

"The chamomile sounds fine," Annette replied.

Mary Anne opened her wooden box and removed a tea bag. She began to steep it in the water, which created a sweet smell that Annette found refreshing. She breathed it in and found it made her even more peaceful.

"Thank you for all this," Annette said.

"Of course. Hospitality is what I do. It's why I opened up this bed-and-breakfast," Mary Anne said and handed Annette the tea. "I suppose there isn't a point to such an establishment now, so I figured helping you all was its best use."

"Well, thank you." Annette drank the warm tea and was immediately infused with the sweet spicy taste of the chamomile.

I'll need to become a tea drinker, she thought.

"Well, everyone else is settling in," Mary Anne said. "You pick a room yet?"

"Yes, I'm going to stay with one of the other women in that purple room of yours."

"Dark orchid," Mary Anne corrected.

"What?"

"Dark orchid. That's the name of the color. I'm not trying to correct you or anything; I'm just proud of my color choices."

"Ah," Annette said, feeling like the biggest white-trash Okie ever. Okie is the nickname for the people who went to California from the dust bowl in the 1930s. Most famously, they were featured in Steinbeck's book *The Grapes of Wrath*. Annette's grandparents were some of those unfortunate people. For the first time in her life, she couldn't help but have an understanding for their plight. The group from the mountains were the new Okies, the Calis. "Well, purple or dark orchid, it's pretty."

"Thank you." Mary Anne smiled at the compliment.

"However," Annette added, "I'm not sure I'll make it up there. This couch is so comfortable I may fall asleep right here."

"You wouldn't be the first guest to do that. Even I have a tendency to fall asleep on it."

Willy entered from the hallway. He was shaven and looked clean. Even Annette had to admit he looked relatively handsome, at least compared to the rat-looking man she had first met and come to know.

Now if he'd just get a new hairstyle.

"Hey, Willy," Annette said.

"Hey," he said quietly.

"You getting comfortable?" Mary Anne asked.

"Yeah ... very," he said while licking his lips. Annette saw this and found it odd, but that was Willy: odd.

"Anything you need," Mary Anne said, "you just tell me."

"Will do," Willy said.

As the night went on, the three of them were joined by increasingly more of the group. Soon, they were all having a grand old time in that intimate warm living room. For sure, it was the best time they'd had since everything changed. The only peculiar thing that Annette noticed was how Willy kept staring at Mary Anne as if she were a piece of meat on a plate. It made Annette very uncomfortable, but she tried to dismiss it.

It's just who he is, Annette reasoned, *nothing to be concerned about.*

Soon the group headed to bed. One by one they left the living room and went off to slink under the blankets on the plush mattresses of Mary Anne Silva's bed-and-breakfast. However, true to her word, Annette did indeed fall asleep on the couch. Before Mary Anne blew out all the candles, Frank covered Annette with a blanket and watched a moment as the fire bounced off her skin—red, orange, yellow, then red again.

Annette, dead to the world, didn't move an inch the rest of the night—not, that is, until the window broke and three flaming torches were thrown into the house.

4

The crashing noise of the windows was all Annette needed to jump up from her deep sleep. Quickly she surveyed the area around her. At first she thought the light in the dark room was coming from the fireplace, but as her wits began to gather, she realized the drapes of the windows were on fire and even the rug in the room was burning.

What is going on? she thought while jumping to her feet. *This whole place is going to burn!*

Annette ran from the room and looked out the front-door window. Three men were standing there preparing to light more torches. She recognized them as the ones from the funeral who had threatened them.

Shit! she thought. *We're dead.*

That's when the fire alarms began to ring.

Thank God fire alarms run on batteries, she thought.

That's when the men outside broke the windows in the dining room, setting that room ablaze.

Jesus, Annette thought, *everyone better wake up soon.*

"Wake up!" she yelled at the top of her lungs. "Get out of the house! We're being attacked!"

Realizing she should run out the back door, she instead ran up the stairs. She couldn't leave everyone else behind. If they died, she could never live with herself. So, running up the stairs, she yelled havoc trying to wake the others.

"Wake up! Wake the fuck up!" she yelled over and over.

Finally, people were coming out of their rooms, rubbing their eyes and asking stupid questions like, "What's going on?" and "Is that smoke?"

"Come on, everyone, run out the back door. We're being attacked, and they're waiting out front! We can't go that way!"

Mary Anne came running out of her room, her eyes startled open into two big zeros. Taking the whole scene in, she screamed. Annette could tell she was losing it. Willy was standing right near her, so Annette called to him.

"Willy! Throw her over your shoulder and come on!"

He did as he was told, though she struggled the whole way down the stairs.

"Come out! Come out wherever you are! You murdering bastards!" one of the men yelled from outside the house. "We want to talk, that's all!"

Bullshit! Annette thought.

As everyone scrambled toward the back door, things were getting crowded and crazy. The flames were nipping at their heels on every side, and the door just wasn't big enough for them all to escape. Frank quickly ran to a stool that was in the kitchen, where the back door was. He threw it into a large window, cracking it into a million pieces.

"Come on," Frank yelled. "Out the window!"

Which was how several of the group escaped, Annette included. Quickly they ran from the house, which was now disappearing in the flames. The fire was beginning to get out of control, jumping to some of the trees outside the house and becoming dangerously close to setting other houses ablaze. Sirens could be heard in the background as the fire truck was racing toward the house. Annette could see the red lights in the distance, but it was too late. The house was a goner.

That's when she saw the three men jump in their truck and drive off.

Chickens, she thought.

Finally they all arrived at the woods, finding cover under the trees and the dark.

"Quick," Annette yelled. "Count everyone ... make sure we're all here."

"We're all here," Willy said.

"No, we're not!" yelled Alice. "No Marcy ... Where's Marcy?"

Annette looked around the scared crowd trying to spot her, but indeed, Marcy wasn't there.

Looking back at the house, she watched as it burned.

Oh, Marcy, Annette thought, *you died in flames after all.*

5

Events got worse as the first week of integration went on. The more townies that came to the aid of the group from the mountains, the more extreme the atrocities became. Pure, unadulterated hatred had taken control of the town. Annette worried it would not yield until everyone was either dead or the town was wiped off the map.

Mitch Mularky, the town historian as well as third assembly member, opened the high school for the group from the mountains. He intended it to be a neutral place for them to call home. He set up cots and had frozen school meals prepared every day (thankfully the school had working gas ovens and was one of the places still being powered by a generator), in hopes the displaced people (now including Mary Anne Silva) would at least feel comfortable. He also hoped this might allow the townies time to simmer down.

It didn't work.

Two days after the opening of the school, he was attacked. Strapped to the back of a truck on long lengths of ropes, Mitch Mularky was dragged nine miles through town. He was left, still alive, in the town center, where he was taken to the doctor's office, now run by a nurse only, for recovery. The closest full hospital was over an hour away in Cheyenne, though due to conditions, no one was even sure it was in operation. Though his body was covered with large scrapes, his skin was imbedded with stones and glass from the street, and large gashes were gushing blood, none of the injuries were going to need surgery. However, even with that blessing, the consensus was that Mitch would never be the same.

Witnesses of the event pegged Brooks Nolan, Clifford Montgomery, and ringleader Winston Deerdorff as the men who took Mularky on the "joyride." Yet they were not arrested or even as much as questioned. Now that Chief Mankins was gone, this group of men—Nolan, Montgomery, and Deerdorff—were the men in charge. With the police in their pockets, because Mankins had told them to do as these men said in case something happened to him, they were able to do whatever they wanted.

Desperation truly seems to make people the worst versions of themselves, Annette thought as things got worse.

More of the townies joined her group in the school for protection as things were just getting out of hand. The clothing store that gave the group from the mountains clothes was looted, forcing the owner and his family into the school. Quentin and Colin were attacked, beaten, and forced to take refuge with them as well, and Louise also joined them. She feared that due to her connection to the brothers, she would be targeted. She was probably right. But she was also just the type of person who wanted to be with those who needed help, no matter the circumstances. Even the town nurse, who was called in to treat some of the group's wounds from the fire or beatings, was attacked on her way back to the office. They broke both her hands and legs, rendering her useless to not only the group from the mountains but the rest of the town.

Idiots, Annette thought.

The violence, originally enacted perhaps in the hopes they could just scare the group from the mountains out of town, needed to be stopped. Which meant stopping those who started it: Nolan, Montgomery, and Deerdorff. Annette realized a battle for the control of Bastion was brewing, and she was all too willing to bring it to a boil.

If a civil war is what they want, then a civil war is what they will get.

6

On the evening that the first shot of the war was fired, Annette was meeting with what she had come to think of as her cabinet. In attendance were Frank, Willy, Quentin Kershaw, recovering town assembly member Mitch Mularky, and town librarian Wilma Garrett. They were all gathered around a table in the school library. Each had a long face and a quiet demeanor. It was clear from the mood in the room how serious this meeting was.

"So, what are our choices?" Annette asked.

"We don't have any!" exclaimed Kershaw quickly. "I know these guys—they'll kill us if we just sit here!"

"Maybe," added Frank, always the voice of reason. "It's just as easy for us to talk to them and try to come to an accommodation."

"Like what?" interrupted Willy. "There is no talking. We killed their chief, they know it, and they want us gone or preferably dead."

"You did kill him?" asked Wilma. She was older, mid-sixties, never married, and all too innocent for this type of direct talk. Annette knew she wasn't the ideal person to be on her cabinet, but she was well liked in town, which Annette figured could be a coup for them if war did erupt.

"I killed him," Kershaw admitted with stoic dignity. From his demeanor, one could tell that while he wasn't proud of the act, he wasn't ashamed of it either.

"Quentin! How could you? I've known you the whole of your life—" More admonishment was coming from Wilma, but Quentin cut her off.

"He was a bad man, Wilma, you know that! It needed to be done. Besides, he killed my parents. He admitted as much to me. Justice was done."

With that Quentin defended it no more. Wilma stopped arguing too. Whether out of fear or because she had known and liked Quentin's parents was never discussed. Either way, she stayed at the table.

Annette turned to Mitch, expecting him to say something, but he just sat there, staring at the table, lost in his post-lynching fear. He was useless to Annette on an opinion basis, but as a figurehead, his presence on the cabinet was crucial. His agreeing to be part of it spoke louder than his words ever could. If there were people remaining on the fence, perhaps they would see these two townies and realize the group from the mountains wanted to include everyone.

Frank spoke up again. "I say we send them a communication. We ask for a meeting. In the meeting, we offer them whatever they want to stop the violence. If we can just have some moments of peace, maybe they will allow us to set up a camp on the outskirts of town."

"No!" yelled Willy, but Frank kept speaking over his protests.

"We need to show them we are not a danger to their way of life. Right now, we are killers. How would you feel about us? Maybe if we develop a small community outside of the proper town, they will invite us in after some time."

"This is ridiculous! We need a safe place to stay. What are we going to do? Chop down trees and build log cabins?" Willy was being a bit reactionary, but he was right.

What are we going to do? Annette thought, hoping her doubt wasn't plastered across her face.

Annette didn't like the prospect of being back out in the elements. None of them were survivalists. It was amazing they had lasted this long.

"We need to go to war." Quentin spoke up again.

"Yes! That's what we do!" Willy jumped out of his chair with excitement at the prospect. It was as if he were itching for a fight, which he probably was.

"We're outnumbered; they'll kill us all." Mitch finally added something to the conversation, though the shaking in his voice made it hard to take in.

"He's right," added Frank. "There's no way we can take on a whole town of hunters. They are hunters, aren't they?"

"I'd say most folks in this town own a gun, yes," agreed Wilma.

"There you have it," concluded Frank. "Discussion over."

Except it wasn't.

"We don't need to take out the whole town," spoke up Quentin. A quiet confidence exuded from his calm demeanor. In Annette's eyes, these types of conversations were when Quentin was at his best. "During the war, the army had a special unit. Their number was the Eighth Special Forces Group, but during the war, they were known by codename: Flatscans."

"What? Is this from some kind of science-fiction story? What the hell is a Flatscan?" asked Frank.

"They're soldiers. The best of the best," Quentin continued. "These were the men everyone in the war were afraid of on both sides. Don't get me wrong, we were glad they fought for us, but if we saw them in town, at a bar, or at a USO show, we let them be. They were scary guys who knew how to kill. They could go into any town, infiltrate it, take it over, and stop an insurgency within days."

"Except we're the insurgency," Frank said.

"True," retorted Quentin. "Still ... you want to know how they did it?"

"How?" asked Mitch.

"They found out who the leaders were, got close to them, and killed them. They stopped at nothing! Their task was to kill the leaders of insurgent groups in such horrible ways that the fear of God was put into the grunts. After that, the desire of others to take on the leadership role was zero. Cut off the head, kill the body. It worked every time. See, it wasn't just the murder of the leadership that got the job done, it was the strength the Flatscans showed in doing it. It was clear to everyone, good, bad, or otherwise, these men would not and could not be stopped. Why even try to fight them? Peace was easier."

"What are you implying?" asked Annette.

"That we become them, the Flatscans." Quentin said this with ultimate confidence.

"So, you want us to become killing machines?" Annette added.

"Not all of us. Just the ones unafraid of doing what needs to be done."

"I've heard all I need to hear." Frank stood up from the table. "Annette, I trust in your judgment, but realize if we keep doing this—keep killing everyone in our way—we won't be able to stop. Ever."

"I know," Annette said. "But what choice is there?"

"None," finished Quentin, and silence befell the room.

7

After the meeting cleared, Annette asked Kershaw to stay.

"You really think this is the only way?" Annette asked.

"Yes, I do. They'll kill us if we show any weakness."

"And you're going to organize this?"

"Yes."

"Who will you take with you?"

"Just Willy. We don't need more than that. I'll be doing most of the dirty work." Quentin seemed very confident of his plan, and given how he handled the Chief Mankins mess, Annette felt very confident as well.

"All right. When will you start?"

"At oh-dark-hundred."

Willy

1

Willy was literally hopping with excitement!

As he and Quentin walked into town, he couldn't help but have a bounce in his step. Quentin kept eyeing him, but Willy didn't care; he was way too jazzed knowing he was going to be able to kill.

And it's allowed! Willy thought. *I'm killing for a purpose. For the betterment of the world. I like that. I'm being a* hero *and doing what's right for the world.*

So what if he enjoyed the kill while doing it?

No big deal.

"Hold up a second." Quentin grabbed Willy by the arm.

"What's up? Why are we stopping?"

"What's your deal, man?"

"What do you mean?" he asked, hoping he hadn't made Quentin too nervous.

"You're walking louder than an elephant! We need to sneak up on them. Why are you acting like a teenager about to get some ass? Slow down."

"Sorry. Just nervous, I guess. I'll stop."

"You've done something like this before, haven't you?" Quentin asked directly.

Can I tell him?

"Not like this, no," Willy said, deciding not to.

"I thought you had a mean streak in you. That's why I picked you. I wasn't wrong, was I?"

Fear crept up in Willy's mind.

If he continued to act like an inexperienced douche bag, he knew Quentin would send him home and do all the killing himself. He couldn't let that happen.

I need this!

"You made the right choice," Willy said calmly. "You won't regret it."

"Good," Quentin nodded. "Then let's get to it."

With that, the two men walked quietly toward the town.

From then on, Willy kept his excitement in check.

2

Once inside the Deerdorff home, Willy was shocked to see how girly it was. Doilies on the mantle, little statues of angels, and horrible paintings of mountains and streams were everywhere.

"Is he married?" Willy whispered to Quentin.

"No, he lives with his mother," Quentin whispered back.

Willy swallowed a laugh at that. Even though Willy went through years of being unemployed, never once was he forced to live with his mother. That was one of the great things about being in a gang: they took care of their members. No matter what.

"Which reminds me," Quentin said, "try not to wake her."

Great, Willy thought, *we've come here to kill a man, but we have to act like mice.*

They walked quietly up the stairs to the long upper-level hallway. Two doors sat at opposite ends. Willy assumed one of the rooms belonged to Deerdorff and the other to his mother. Just that realization alone made him chuckle again. It was out loud this time.

"Shut up!" Quentin whispered sternly.

"Sorry! I can't stop laughing about the fact he lives with his mother."

"Get over it!" Quentin said. To Willy, the tone had more anger in it than the situation called for. Upon examination, Willy realized why. Quentin himself lived in his parents' home—when not hiding out at the school, that was. Though it was not exactly the same situation, Quentin probably felt a bit like Willy was making fun of him too.

"Oh, nut up," Willy said to him, tired of hearing Quentin's bluster. "Just tell me which room he's in."

"That way," Quentin said, pointing right.

Together, Willy and Quentin crept down the hall, which due to the creaking floor, seemed like the longest walk of Willy's life. It was ironic to Willy how each noise the floor made seemed as loud as a truck backfiring, even though in actuality they were probably no louder than a fart under a sheet.

Reaching the door—finally—they entered the room. In sharp contrast to the rest of the house, the room was that of a man's man. There was a gun rack with rifles, hunting gear, even nudie mags, which were so old they had gone yellow around the edges and crusty.

Gross, Willy thought.

Looking down at Deerdorff asleep in bed, Willy thought about taking his knife out and running it across the sleeping man's throat. He could picture the blood spilling from the gash and seeping out onto the white sheets below, creating the effect of food coloring turning pure water into a colorful array of pinks and purples. Willy was intoxicated with the vision when he realized Quentin was snapping at him.

"Sorry," Willy mouthed so as not to make any noise.

Quentin pulled out his gun and gently cocked it. Willy pulled out the duct tape. Quentin nodded. Quickly the two men moved. Willy placed tape over Deerdorff's mouth while Quentin pointed the gun at his head.

Deerdorff opened his eyes in a flurry of fear and rage. He tried to yell out, but all the sound he could make was a muffled cry.

"How ya doing, Winston?" Quentin stated, no different from how he might have had said "hello" in church. "You're coming with us."

Willy smiled to himself as he began to tie Deerdorff's hands together.

Now it's gonna get good.

3

The three men walked through some back alleyways of town and headed back into the woods. Willy was getting impatient. He was promised a kill, and he wanted it bad. Furthermore, it was getting late, and they had two more men to find. Something needed to be done.

Stick him! Willy kept hearing over and over in his head.

Stick him! Stick him!

"When are we going to kill him?" Willy said straight out. He heard Deerdorff moan under the tape as he learned the true fate that awaited.

"God, Willy, really?" Quentin said.

"What? It's the truth; we might as well tell the man."

Whimpering started to fill the night as tears began to roll out Deerdorff's eyes. The sounds were more pathetic due to them being covered up by tape.

"What?" Willy asked Deerdorff. "Were you as sorrowful when you attacked us?"

Willy kicked him. Deerdorff fell to the ground.

"Willy, stop," Quentin said. Yet Willy continued on, and so did Deerdorff's tears.

"You are one sniveling little shit, you know that?"

Willy began to kick Deerdorff, who couldn't protect himself. Quentin tried to grab Willy and stop him, but it was too late.

"Just shut the hell up!" Willy stated as he revealed his knife: sweet old Impaler! Just holding it in his hands gave him a sense of power.

Swinging it into the air, he smashed it into Deerdorff. Up and down it went. The metal color became covered in a red hue that looked black in the night.

Stick him! Stick him!

Up and down, over and over, red, red, red. Quentin looked on in shock as Willy did his worst.

Stick him!

Then suddenly, as fast as it started, Willy stopped. The night was silent again, except for Willy's heavy breathing. Deerdorff's whimpering was gone, and all that remained was a twitching body bleeding out into the dirt below.

Willy had a smile on his face, as well as spots of Deerdorff's blood.

That's better, Willy thought.

Turning toward Quentin, Willy quickly wiped the smile away with his forearm, taking with it the blood that had splattered against his chin.

"What?" he said to Quentin. "We were going to kill him anyway."

"Not like that."

"Who cares? It's as good a way as any."

"I had a plan." Quentin sounded very angry. Now Willy feared for his own life.

"We can still do your plan," he said. "But the man deserved it. Besides, he wouldn't stop crying—it was irritating."

Quentin just stared at him in disbelief.

"Come on, let's get the others. I promise I won't stab them. We'll do it your way."

4

After hiding the body, Quentin and Willy went to get Deerdorff's comrades. This time, though, the fire was out. Willy's thirst was satiated. All he felt was ... *relief.*

Quentin

1

Morning rose on Bastion, Wyoming. The sun had to break through some thick clouds, which had descended into the valley overnight, covering it in a fog. The town stirred slowly, as was its custom. Even before the attacks, being a small town meant the business day started on the residents' own terms, as opposed to when corporations deemed it was time. With the end of the world and civilization as the residents knew it, the days got started even more slowly.

It was past ten o'clock before most of the town decided to venture past their front doors. Given the violent nature of things lately, people had begun to keep to themselves. Trust in thy neighbor had fallen to an all-time low in Bastion, which was why the display Quentin and Willy had set up had not been noticed until noon. However, once it was, news of the scene spread like wildfire.

In the center of town stood a great oak tree. Having stood for almost three hundred years, the tree had been made into a historical monument. When an out-of-town company wanted to tear it down and replace it with a strip mall, the Bastion Historical Society took up the cause of preserving the tree for future generations. It took the Historical Society all of twenty-four hours to come up with a thousand signatures needed to name the tree "protected." It was quickly fenced in, creating a small garden area around it, and a plaque was placed on the fence.

It read: "For the future of Bastion."

The tree was very large, with thick, heavy branches that extended out from it in all directions, like hundreds of gangly fingers. It was on these branches that Quentin created his message. At twelve fifteen, with streams of sunlight finally cutting through patches of clouds like tendrils from heaven, a shocked group of spectators began to gather at the tree. When the clock turned 12:35, the number had tripled, and by one o'clock, most of the town had arrived to see what was hanging there.

Brooks Nolan, Clifford Montgomery, and Winston Deerdorff swung from the larger limbs as if the branches were hands holding marionettes. Rope extended from their necks, and their bodies were stripped bare, showing every part and crevice, including the new ones given to them by Willy's Impaler. Placards were placed around each man's neck, each with a different word written on it: Coward, Follower, Bigot—in that order. Another sign was posted on the tree below, with one word clearly printed on it: Justice.

Time would tell if this message worked and whether others would rise to take these men's places and continue their mission to keep outsiders from finding sanctuary in Bastion, but for now, all was silent. Quentin, who watched the whole scene with the emotional distance of a warrior, thought the message could not have been better sent; just from the reaction of the onlookers, he knew it had been received loud and clear. People stood there for hours on end, shocked, scared, and utterly quiet. He assumed they considered their own mortality, contemplating if rising to avenge these three men's deaths—men who most in Bastion would admit to truly disliking—was worth losing their own lives for. As each townie left, Quentin could see the answer was no.

When night fell again and the crowd had long since dispersed, Quentin and Willy cut the bodies down from the tree. They were careful to not be seen. It was one thing for the townspeople to suspect who did it and another to be seen out in the open admitting guilt. Once the bodies were down, they took them deep into the woods, setting them out for the wolves to eat.

With that, the war for Bastion ended as quickly as it began. Peace took over the town as both groups—the townies and the group from the mountains—began to live as one.

Aiden

1

Aiden was dumbfounded. Two of his men had been killed while attempting to take their treasure.

Standing over the bodies of his fallen comrades, Aiden felt sick. Angry even. He wanted revenge. He wasn't sure what had gone wrong between this group of Tribesmen and their intended prey, but whatever it was, he wanted revenge.

"What happened?" Aiden asked the two surviving brothers.

"We found a truck with three normals inside. One was a treasure. We couldn't take her. They fought us off." Aiden looked away from his dead comrades in disgust.

"Fought you off? How many of them were there?" Aiden asked, anger spitting from his voice.

"Three," said one of the brothers.

"One man and two ... children," said the other reluctantly.

With that Aiden spat in disgust.

"What should we do?" another of the contingent asked.

"The doctor would want us to complete the task," Aiden said confidently. "We need to follow them and take what is ours. Get in the trucks! We're chasing them down, boys!"

With that, the Tribesmen screamed with pleasure. They sounded like demented cowboys—a posse—yahooing the hunt! Aiden went to the main truck and got into the passenger seat.

The driver looked at him.

"What do we do with them?" He pointed back at the bed of the truck. Inside were "normal" women of all ages, held captive like roosters by wooden gates and chicken wire. They were too weak and dehydrated to even attempt to escape.

"We bring them. Soon, they will have a new friend."

With that, they rode off into the distance to track down the killer of their brothers.

Black

1

When they found the camp, General Black positioned his men strategically. He had them do absolutely nothing but watch. For days they watched, gathered intelligence, and began to understand their enemy. They watched as their enemy rode around on their motorcycles. They watched as they stole gas from cars, raiding gas stations, and hijacking any kind of supply truck that survived the apocalypse. This allowed these bozos to do a very smart thing: stockpile gasoline.

That will come in handy, Black thought, *after we kill every last one of you and take it for our own.*

Black and his men also watched as the motorcycle gang went back to their base camp. Black's men observed that inside this camp, they had survivors with them that were weak and undisciplined. Black's men had discerned every crack in the defenses, making the impending invasion seem easy for soldiers as experienced as Black and his *Flatscans!*

At least, that's what they called them during the war.

The Flatscans watched as people in the camp fornicated, starved, or were beaten. The Flatscans assessed and reported to Black that this was a savage group of people. Black figured he'd rescue those he could, put out of their misery the others, all the while putting the fear of the devil in those that dared to stand against him.

Was there any doubt this group housed the men that attacked his soldiers? None whatsoever that he could find. If the motorcycles didn't give it away, the GPS coordinates on his KIA (Killed In Action) soldier's uniform did. The PRU (Positional Recorder Unit) proved it. The PRU was tasked to provide the exact location of a trooper in the field. At any moment during battle, a general could better position his soldiers by using these beacons as a guide. The PRU recorded each soldier's exact location, so if a battle were lost, the Army could easily see if men were disobeying orders, causing the defeat, or stranded behind enemy lines. The Army spent millions on the development of such sophisticated weaponry. The suits his men wore represented the pinnacle of American hubris. Misguided though it may have been for the technology's usage to be for war instead of some greater good, the suits were still extremely effective. The PCU also showed that the camp Black and his Flatscans had been watching was placed not thirty miles from where his men had been attacked.

So, while he figured there must have been other groups of survivors in the desolate, barren leftovers of America, this was the one they were looking for. Besides, in their long trek from base, they had not run into a single other soul. That reinforced the assumption that this ridiculous outcropping of metal machines, lost souls, and desperation had to be the target.

Yes, Black thought, *I'm sure of it. These are the men. This is their camp, and in a few short hours, they are going to feel the wrath of the most-feared unit in all the defunct US armed services.*

This wouldn't be a battle. It would be a massacre.

Sean

1

Sean had been running with the kids for days. They were being followed by more of the "things," or as they had now named them, "mutants." After he had killed the first of them, he hoped that would be it, but they had returned and in larger numbers.

The mutants attacked them every night, preventing them from getting any sort of extended rest. REM sleep had become an idea of the past. This made driving during the day nearly impossible. The long hours of travel on straight passes of roadway became hypnotizing, lulling Sean into a half-asleep, half-awake consciousness, where if others were on the road, they would surely get into an accident. Thankfully, there were only the few and far-between random stalled cars, which he was able to avoid as he could see those miles away. If it wasn't for the fear of death at the hands of those relentless demons—the mutants—Sean would probably have fallen asleep at the wheel, killing himself and his little companions. However, adrenaline and his own survival instinct made his eyes stay open like they had been sewn that way.

Sean had no idea when this terrible race would end. He figured eventually they would either run out of gas or steam, whichever came first. Then they would be taken by the mutants. Sean wasn't sure why the mutants wanted them so much; the mutants were clearly delusional, but something kept them coming. No matter how fast Sean drove or for how long, the mutants were always somewhere behind. The mutants followed in wrecked hunks of junk that were only shells, taken from the mass of abandoned cars, trucks, and SUVs left to rot on the side of the roads. While they didn't get good speed on these skeletal structures, they moved. Maybe slowly, maybe even unsteadily, but as the old story goes: slow and steady wins the race.

At night, Sean and the children would huddle in the truck and watch as the beasts danced around them in the dark, hooting out their desire for blood with horrible, painful cries. Every night, the sounds got louder as they approached ever closer to their truck. The suspense was driving the group of them insane. Still, inside the protection of the car, they tried to sleep, even if only for a few hours.

On the final night, the three sat up listening to the disturbing catcalls of the mutants.

"What do they want?" Charlie asked.

"I don't know. I wish I did," Sean replied.

"They want us. They want us for food," Amy added in a frightened tone that did not help calm Charlie. "They're just waiting until we are too tired to fight back."

As the night went on, they all did eventually drift off to sleep. It wasn't restful nor was it deep, but it was sleep. Sean awoke before the children and considered their options.

Keep running until we can't anymore or deal with these lunatics once and for all?

He felt he had only one choice in the matter, and while he knew he was outnumbered, he figured if he could kill enough of them, then maybe the children stood a chance. His life was no longer important if it meant the children would survive.

With a decision made, Sean finally drifted off to sleep yet again. This time, with his soul decided and at peace about it, he fell so deep and hard that the world could have ended around him, again, and he wouldn't have known a thing.

2

"Wake up!" Sean heard the cry wrenching him out of the land of dreams. "Wake up! Amy is gone!"

The words echoed around his head as his eyes trembled, straining to open. The voice was clear, though, and so was the meaning. It was Charlie's voice and Charlie was shaking him, begging him to awaken because Amy had been taken in the night. "She's probably dead!"

Sean finally sat up straight, eyes wide-open, panic gripping his guts.

"Where is she?" he muttered out of a daze.

"I don't know. They just opened the door and took her. I woke up and tried to fight them off, but it was too late. You didn't even stir! I've been yelling for five minutes!"

"Why didn't they kill us?"

"Maybe they just wanted her?"

This seemed plausible. They got what they came for and left them alone.

But why?

"Quick, buckle up, we're going to get her back!"

In seconds, the truck was screaming down the roadway, swerving between debris and dead animals. Time was of the essence if they were going to save her. Sean didn't quite know where they went, but he headed back the way he and the children had come from. For all he knew, however, the mutants were headed in the opposite direction. Sean simply had to hope he had chosen right.

A few miles down the road, he saw them.

The mutants!

The headlights from their vehicles were waving in the heat lines drifting up slowly from the hot desert sand. The mutants were no longer driving, as they had pulled over into the dunes that surrounded the roadway. There was a large wagon, as ragged-looking as the rest of their vehicles, led by some sickly looking horses. Sean slowed to not alert the mutants to their presence.

Sean grabbed the gun and opened the door.

"Where are you going?" asked Charlie.

"To get a closer look."

"But what if they get me?"

"If they wanted us, they'd have taken us."

Sean got in as close as he dared, ducking behind cars for coverage. Soon he had a good view of all the vehicles in the group and the details of what was going on.

The mutants were all grotesque. At the moment, they were all sound asleep, not even protecting themselves from the elements. Winter or summer, the Texas desert was unforgiving. In the wagon, there seemed to be people, not many, but a few, captured and slowly freezing to death. The temperature was low, maybe in the forties, and they would all eventually get sick. Winter or summer, the Texas desert was unforgiving.

They were women, Sean realized. *That's why the mutants only took Amy. They want women.*

Sean shuddered to think of why. They varied in age: one older—perhaps a grandmother. Another in her mid-twenties. A teenager with purple hair and the tattoos of the street gangs. Finally there was the two youngest—one a little older than Amy, and Amy herself.

Sean began to creep over, figuring a rescue would be easy as long as the mutants were asleep. He stood up from behind the car, knocking over the door from its destroyed frame. He hadn't realized the car was so fragile. The door landed on the ground with a large thud. Suddenly the mutants were up on their feet, surveying their surroundings. Sean ducked down just in time not to be noticed.

Damn! Sean yelled at himself.

Realizing there was no further hope of rescue, Sean slowly crept back to Charlie and the truck. Again, Sean realized he was going to need a plan if there was any hope of getting Amy back. The only problem was at the moment his mind was blank.

Willy

1

Supposedly this was their last night in the school. After tonight, they were going to mix with the general population outside and become one with the town of Bastion's populace. This left Willy with one more night to make his move on one of the women who had come to stay with them at the school.

Mary Anne Silva.

She was the one who owned the now-destroyed Emporium Bed and Breakfast. During their time in the high school together, she and Willy had formed an unlikely bond. It was odd; she wasn't his normal type. She was a goodie-goodie, blonde, and had no tats or piercings. However, while she might not have been like girls from the Leviathans that he banged, she did remind him of the *other women*, the ones he had kidnapped, raped, and killed. Willy was surprised to find this made him even more excited at the prospect of being with her.

The only problem was, until this point, their relationship had been one based on protection. Mary Anne saw him as a strong man, one who could save her from danger, but not one she'd want to save her from frigidity. Every sexual move he made, Mary Anne either did not pick up on or ignored. The problem for her was Willy didn't take hints. He got what he wanted, even if it meant getting it by force. All Willy needed to do now was wait for an opening.

It had been hard to get away from the group at large. They were all stuffed into the cafeteria together, cot to cot, forehead to asshole, like matches in a box. It was annoying, especially because Mary Anne had taken the bed right next to him. She was so close the whole time. He watched her while she slept, seeing her breasts rise and lower with every breath. Her ripe-smelling, unclean body odor, lofting on the air over to his nostrils, was like the aroma of fresh-baked cookies.

I just want to munch!

2

Despite Willy's trying to control his every instinct, one night he lost that battle, almost getting caught in the process.

Reaching over to the sleeping Mary Anne, Willy had the intention to just gently touch her skin. Feel the oily silkiness of her body and maybe lick the salt of her from his fingertips. As he was just about to reach her greasy hair—it hadn't been washed in some time—a movement behind him distracted him enough to turn from her.

Standing there, paused in shock, was Colin. Colin and his brother had chosen to take up residence right across the row of beds from Willy and Mary Anne. Quentin, like the rest of the room, was asleep. Colin, however, had his eyes wide-open watching Willy.

"What?" Willy asked the boy, challenging and trying to intimidate him.

"Nothing." From the shake in Colin's voice, Willy could tell it worked.

"Well, what the hell are you even doing up?" Willy asked with even more ferocity.

"I had to pee," Colin replied.

"Well, you better just head back to sleep, kid."

"Right."

With that Willy watched as Colin tucked himself under the stiff, wool blanket and tried to ignore Willy's stare.

Damn, Willy thought. *This is precisely the kind of attention I don't need!*

He couldn't wait to have his privacy again, and with it, the ability to do whatever he wanted, when he wanted. The only problem with that was, once he was away from Mary Anne, he wasn't sure he would ever get another chance to have her again. Opportunity, like an open window, was closing fast.

3

Around seven o'clock on that last night in the cafeteria, Mary Anne excused herself to use the restroom.

Willy smiled. The moment had come.

Mary Anne was his.

Colin

1

Colin watched as Mary Anne left the room. Like most nights, the refugees who populated the school gym were doing whatever they could to occupy themselves. Some slept, others played card games or even checkers, while the chosen few, like Quentin, Frank, and Annette, met together to discuss plans for the future. Often, Colin felt left out. Since there were no other kids at the school, he didn't have a group to belong too. His brother never let him in on the big discussions, and most people didn't want him hanging around. They didn't want the responsibility. So, mostly Colin kept to himself.

Sometimes Louise would hang with him to pass the time.

"You still drawing?" she asked.

"Sometimes ... if I get the chance. But since Quentin's been home, I haven't really had the time."

"Don't let him stop you," Louise pushed. "You have real talent. Sometimes those that don't have talent like you do can't see the use of it."

"Oh, he has a talent," Colin said. "Just not one we'd like to talk about."

"Yeah," Louise said, suddenly distancing herself from the conversation. "I suppose he does. Anyway, though, you draw when you can."

"Thanks. I will."

As he finished this conversation, Colin saw Mary Anne cross in front of him and exit the room. He watched her curiously as she went. Ever since the night he caught Willy doing to her whatever he was doing, Colin had been watching her.

As Mary Anne left the gym through the two metal double doors, Colin watched as she passed by people unnoticed. One thing Colin had realized about the refugees was that they zoned out the world around them. If someone got up to go somewhere or do something, they didn't take notice. Whether it was because they wanted to respect others' privacy or because they didn't care, Colin wasn't sure, but he did realize he was the only one watching as Mary Anne left the room. Knowing what he did about her—that she was a fiercely religious and staunch woman—Colin was sure she would want to be looked after. Also knowing what he did about Willy—Quentin had told him everything that happened when they captured Winston Deerdorff—he was also sure Willy wasn't a man to be trusted. So when Colin saw Willy go off after Mary Anne, he couldn't help but feel the need to alert someone.

"I'll be right back," he said to Louise and tried to think of whom to tell. The only problem was there wasn't anybody really. In the back corner of the room, Colin turned his eyes on his brother, Quentin. He had been busy all day with Annette and still was. From the looks of things, Quentin, Annette, Frank, Mitch Mularky, and a few select others were still deep in discussion. Colin thought about interrupting them, but what would he say?

Quick! That Willy guy is a creeper and is going to do something to Mary Anne! No one would listen to him, especially because Willy had been such a help to the cause. They'd probably just dismiss Colin and tell him to go. So that wasn't an option, and really everyone else seemed too shell-shocked from the events in the town to be able to handle anything more. To Colin, this meant he had to pursue this himself.

Too bad I'm so scared.

2

Following in the direction the two went—at least the direction he thought they went; the high school was rather large—Colin created a picture in his mind of what might happen to him if he was caught. He imagined Willy grabbing him by the arm, breaking it, and beating him silly. Once that was done, Willy would return him to his brother, who in turn would feel the need to protect Colin, forcing Quentin to fight Willy. Down deep, Colin knew his brother would win such a battle;

however, Colin also knew Willy was sneaky. He would do whatever he needed to in order to win. Therefore, Colin wasn't sure his brother would be prepared to take him. All these thoughts created a pit the size of the Grand Canyon in his stomach. For a moment, Colin wondered if he should turn back, but then he heard it!

A small scream—

Colin's breath escaped him. He was frozen in place.

Which way had it come from?

He looked around the hallways of the school. They were dark and long, made of concrete brick and painted the school colors of red and black. Sound seemed to echo off every brick, making the scream bounce around the school in all directions.

Damn! he thought. *Scream again so I can find you.*

Another scream! It was coming from the other end of the school. Colin ran—his guts twisting inside, the long hallway extending forever in front of him. It was as if he was in a dream where the hallway kept getting inexplicably longer.

What am I doing? he asked himself. *I'm not a hero!*

Still, he went on! His desire to help was overwhelming him, but his feet weren't carrying him fast enough. Which perhaps was a good thing. Danger lay ahead—what hurry was he really in to get there? Sweat began to drip down his temples. His stomach was rumbling, which made Colin hope he didn't crap his pants while trying to come to the rescue.

That would be classy, he thought.

Suddenly he came upon them.

Willy was getting off Mary Anne Silva as Colin came around the corner of the hallway. He was pulling up his pants while she lay sprawled against the wall, her legs unceremoniously spread apart, with her jeans pulled down around her thighs. Willy stood, buttoning his pants and then bending over to pick up his knife. The knife was large, dangerous-looking. Colin swallowed hard in fear just seeing it. Frozen in shock, all he could concentrate on was the satisfied look on Willy's face and Mary Anne's crying. For a moment, Colin was so petrified he thought he might release his bladder, but he pulled his butt cheeks tight and held it in. A moment later, he almost lost it again when Willy looked straight at him.

Their eyes met. Colin's mouth went dry.

Willy saw me, Colin thought. *I'm dead now!*

Willy's smile left his face slowly. For a moment he did nothing, but then he gripped his knife tight and started toward Colin.

I should run, Colin thought but couldn't move. *I should really, really run.* Still he couldn't go anywhere; he was too frozen with fear. Then it was too late.

Willy grabbed the collar of his shirt and pushed Colin against the lockers in the hallway. Colin could feel the tip of the knife pinching the skin between his chin and Adam's apple.

"What did you see?" Willy asked with urgency.

"Nothing! Nothing!" Colin replied in panic.

"You sure about that?"

"I swear."

"You breathe a word of this to anyone and I'll kill you. You understand me? I will ... you know I will."

"Yeah, I know," Colin replied, beginning to tear up.

"Don't cry, kid. I like your brother too much to hurt you now. But if you tell him ... or anyone ..."

Colin could feel the knife pierce his skin; it was a slow entry, and it felt like twelve bees stinging him at once. Then he was suddenly released and falling to the floor. Colin put his hand to his wound and found that it was barely a scratch. His mind made the wound hurt more than it deserved. Nonetheless blood was on Colin's hands, as the small poke was gushing quite a bit, more than he would have thought for its size.

"All right then," Willy said, calm and cool as a cucumber. "See you around."

As Willy walked off, Colin turned to Mary Anne, who was trying to pull herself together but uncontrollably crying. Colin went to her.

"Are you okay?" Colin said, reaching his hand out to support her. Her legs were shaking, tears were running down her cheeks, and she had zero control over her balance. She looked as if any second she could topple over. Then she did. Right into his arms. Colin didn't know what to do. He was just a boy—well, a teenager—but surely he wasn't prepared to handle this.

"Why?" she asked. "Why did he do that to me?"

"I don't know," was all Colin could say in reply.

As the time slowly ticked by, Colin continued to just stand in the hallway with Mary Anne in his arms.

She cried for over an hour.

Althaus

1

"Pain is white, remember the white light," Reverend Althaus heard behind him.

He turned and replied, "The light is hope."

Standing before him was a haggard woman. She was probably in her mid-thirties, but from the way she appeared, one might assume her fifties. Althaus had seen many in this kind of shape. Especially since they began their exodus north. Mile after grueling mile, different campsites every night; it took a toll on a person. Every night, Althaus would walk around the camp, talking to as many as he could. During these talks, Althaus discovered there were so many new kinds of miseries in this world. Often, they were problems he could not solve.

Though General Black left him with a medic, Althaus was helpless to provide medications (they didn't have enough) or ointments (they had none). He did not have a roof to put over these traumatized people's heads, nor hot water to bathe them in. All Althaus had was the comfort of the Lord, which even he had to admit wasn't much comfort at all.

"They're so sick," the woman said.

"Who?" Althaus replied, adding the appropriate comforting tone for good measure.

"Why won't God help them?"

This took Althaus back. He always hated these moments—the ones where the miserable come to him and asked why God had not acted for them, expecting him to have an answer. In the past, he might have said, "God acts in mysterious ways" or "God only throws at us what we can handle," but even then he barely believed his own words. Now, given all that had happened, he was sure anything he could say would simply sound trite.

"Who won't God help?"

She looked up at him, her eyes filled with tears. "The children."

The words hit Althaus like a ton of bricks.

What children? he thought.

He had seen a few among the crowds as they walked, but they seemed okay to him (as okay as everyone else, anyway).

Are there more in camp that I don't know about?

"I'm not sure," Althaus added. "Are they still with us?" He trod lightly. After all, it was just as likely that this woman was insane or suffering from some sort of delirium brought on by the lack of good medical help or nutrition as it was that there were sick kids with her. These children might have been in her imagination.

"Yes!" she screamed at him. "You don't even know about them, do you? They're a part of your flock, and you don't even know they're alive."

Althaus felt a shiver go down his spine.

There are so many survivors, how can I be expected to know every one of them? That's why I insisted on having Clarence help me. It's just too many! Are we both failing by not knowing these children?

This woman, whom he was sure he had never met before, knew him and his words, but she obviously had a life he knew nothing about.

How many more sad stories are going on like this? he questioned within himself, chastising himself for the job he was doing as a leader. *I was appointed to spread hope, but from the looks of this woman, it's not spreading fast enough.*

There was only one thing he could do. "Take me to them," he said. "I'll help if I can."

The woman hugged him tightly.

"Thank you! Thank you!"

For a moment, Althaus felt some relief; maybe he could somehow help this woman.

He was wrong.

2

The tent was on the far side of the temporary camp. As he arrived, he could sense the overwhelming pain that was contained within its vinyl walls.

What's inside? he wondered. *What have I gotten myself into?*

The woman ushered him forward as dread overtook Althaus's insides. She opened the front flap to the tent, and Althaus entered. His eyes could not believe the sight before him: children of every age filled the area. They were practically on top of one another and surrounded by loved ones, either parents or stand-in parents these children found along the way. The stench inside was awful—a mix of feces, vomit, and death. The sound of buzzing flies was incessant and annoying. The longer Althaus's eyes took in the sights, the more he realized where the stench was coming from: the children.

They were dying.

As he walked along, greeted by parents hopeful he would be able to help them, he looked into the eyes of the dying. The children's skin was being eaten by lesions. Their hair was falling out in clumps, leaving bald, round patches of skin where hair used to be. Their eyes were sullen, yellowed by failing kidneys, while their skin was sickly green. Althaus could tell whatever was eating these children alive was irreversible. Eventually, they would die. All Althaus could do was pray for sooner rather than later.

"What's happened to them all?" he asked the woman who brought him to this sight.

"Radiation from the attacks. We are all from the same town, just outside of Dallas. They were caught in the blast. The children were at school, which was positioned far enough from ground zero not to kill them immediately, but too close to really let them survive. Most of the parents who survived were even farther away ... but it would have been better if they had not lived at all."

Suddenly the woman's words made sense to Althaus.

Why won't God help them?

These words echoed inside his head as he continued to walk around the tent.

Why won't God help them? he questioned. *They are suffering! Is this God's plan? Is the intense torture of children what he wants?*

As much as Althaus wanted to explain it away, he was finding he couldn't. Finding God's meaning in these children's fate was impossible.

"What is it you want me to do?" Althaus said helplessly to the room. "I can give them last rites to send them to the next world with—"

"No," the woman said with strength and determination. "We want you to help us end their suffering."

"I don't understand," he said in reply, even though he thought he really did.

"We want to *end* their suffering," she said pointedly. Obviously she didn't want to alarm the children, but from the looks on their faces, as well as their parents' faces, it was clear they were all in on the plan.

"No," Althaus said. "I mean, I can't. How could you even … I mean … that's against God's will!"

"Is it?" she asked. "Because as we see it, he's torturing them to death already."

Horror swept through Althaus. How could these parents ask this of him, for his blessing to murder their children? Was this even murder?

Or was it something more than that?

"How will you do it even?" he asked in his disaccord.

"We were hoping for your help with that too. Inside the army med tent, word is that there are pills, tablets … saved in case of a soldier's capture and torture. Bite on one and it releases a painless toxin that kills within minutes. We want those pills, and you can get them."

Disbelief overtook Althaus. He didn't know what to say. All he did was look into the eyes of every dying child-all the time wishing for a sign from God.

3

During Althaus's long walk back to his church, his mind considered every angle of the sad parent's request.

Wouldn't I be helping carry out God's work by sending these children on their way to his kingdom? Wouldn't it be better that a man from God oversaw the deed to make sure the devil's hands were not a part of it? Still, isn't the act of murder alone an act against God? Is the fact that this is even being considered, proof of the devil's hand already? Alternatively, is this really murder at all? Maybe this is pity. These children are already dead; by helping them, wouldn't I really just be taking away their pain?

Anger began to overwhelm him. Blasphemous questions formed in his head:

How could God do this to them? How could he test such innocents like this? It's no wonder people are being tasked to make such horrible decisions as killing their own children. The world, God's world, was destroyed, and they had to go on living in it. Yet isn't this precisely what the Bible said would happen? That those left behind would have to fight evil to prove their heavenly worth? But what had these children done to deserve such horrible deaths?

Somehow Althaus doubted the tribulations humanity was experiencing now had anything to do with the Bible's book of Revelation.

Where's the Second Coming? Who's the Antichrist? No, this isn't "Judgment Day." This is just the way the world came to destroy itself. It was inevitable with or without God's help.

Althaus walked into his church, but it was nothing more than a tent. The place was an illusory setup, made to look like a place where God lived. A cross made of scraps left from destroyed homes, a wooden table recovered from an abandoned furniture store, even a Bible stolen from the remains of a church helped with the scene, but it was all just a façade—an unhallowed space created by man to remind people of God's presence.

But what answers are there?

In order for there to be answers, there had to be a God—a fact that even for Althaus was finding harder and harder to believe.

"You seem distressed, brother," said Clarence, who stepped out from behind a small partition that was set up to serve as a meeting place in case people wanted to speak in private. Althaus turned and looked at the man. Clarence was the last person he wanted to see.

"You're here late," Althaus said.

"Well, we hadn't seen you all day, so I decided to put in some overtime," Clarence said with an air of superiority.

"I've had a lot to think about."

"Have you found the answers you were looking for?"

"Not really."

"Would you like me to pray with you about them?" Clarence asked, with the same superiority as before. It was making Althaus's skin crawl.

"Pray?" Althaus repeated.

"Yes," Clarence said. "To God ... for answers."

"He has none," Althaus replied.

"What?" Clarence asked back with shock in his voice.

"God has no answers."

"You're talking blasphemously."

"I suppose I am."

"You 'suppose'?"

"Don't you feel God has abandoned us? Left us in this world ... to rot?"

"What has happened to you?" Clarence asked. "You are a man of God. You are supposed to be an example, not to mention a teacher of his words. Have you forgotten the gospels? Have you forgotten Revelations?"

"Don't talk to me like I don't know the scriptures," Althaus snapped back, his annoyance thoroughly on display.

"Then act like it!" Clarence responded. "God is testing us. We are the people left behind! We are the ones that will fight for good as evil attempts to conquer the world. As the scripture says, in these end-times, some of us will abandon God, while others will rise up and fight for his glory. Which will you be, Barrett?"

Althaus didn't know what else to say. What was the point in arguing with the man? Althaus thought he sounded ridiculous and like a fanatic. Althaus hated fanatics and knew they were impossible to reason with.

"Maybe you need to pray on that," said Clarence, who didn't bother to wait for an answer. He just turned and left Althaus alone.

For a moment, he stood in the middle of the room, assessing the chairs, the podium, even the cross hanging on the back wall. Its presence was condescending to him.

"You've abandoned us," he said to the cross. Of course, there was no answer back. There was no sign from above like a burning bush or pillar of salt, either.

"We are no longer the children of God, are we?" More silence returned his question. "No, we are the children of the light."

For a long moment, he stood silently. He thought about his lack of faith, his religion, and his place in it. He thought about the very idea of God's existence. Althaus had begun to doubt God before the white light, but now that doubt was turning into rage. Althaus was beginning to realize his old religion was no longer what the world needed. Christianity was a belief of the old world—along with Islam, Judaism, and any other religion that led to this end. It was time for something new.

Reaching up, Althaus wrapped his hands around the cross and removed it from the wall.

"Your time is done."

Throwing the cross to the ground, he waited for some kind of intervention, like a heart attack or lighting strike, taking his life away and condemning him to hell. Yet nothing happened. Not even a roll of thunder like one might have expected to see in an old movie.

Althaus now knew his place in this new world. It was time to begin.

"Pain is white," he uttered aloud to himself. "Remember the white light." This would be the first doctrine of the new religion. "The light is hope."

With that, Althaus made up his mind on how to relieve the sick children of their pain. Finally, he would deliver them to the light.

Mark

1

Mark had hardly spoken to Nell for a week. Nell was beginning to argue with him about that fact. In reality, it was more of an argument with herself than between the two of them. Mark, still in horrible emotional pain, was simply devoid of responses, so the whole thing was rather one-sided. Despite a great desire to tell her what he knew, he chose to keep her in the dark. Perhaps if she had known he knew, her words to him, which came out like stilettos, would not have been so sharp. Yet before Mark could confront her and ask why, he needed to digest the pain he was in.

"Why won't you answer me?" she yelled again. This had become a familiar refrain. Over and over she was saying it, as if it would break him from his silence. Mark though was too stubborn for that. Silent he remained.

"I don't understand what's going on. It's been a week like this. What have I done? All I do is take care of you, be here for you! Do you know how hard that is? Do you know how many people would've left you by now?"

So why haven't you? Mark thought, even though he supposed he knew why. She loved him; her behavior proved that. Nell was hurt by his silence. This was counter to what Mark thought would happen. He had assumed that in pulling away from her, he would make Nell happy again. He thought needing her less would relieve her stress. He was quite wrong.

This has to mean something, right? But maybe it doesn't. Maybe it just means we were foolish to believe children as young as us could ever make an adult relationship work, Mark thought. The fact their relationship was failing wasn't necessarily their fault, though. Life and events were conspiring against them. No matter how much they tried, it was hard to deal with all the drama they had endured since the night they lost their virginities. Even adults would have a hard time with all they'd been through. Unfortunately Mark couldn't see these facts; he could only feel the heartbreak and pain.

Nell's mood suddenly changed, which broke Mark from his reverie. Instead of yelling, she was bending down, grabbing Mark's face in her hands. She linked eyes with his. There was an almost pitiful look in them.

She's hurting, Mark could see that. If Mark allowed it, he knew he could feel sorry for her. He just loved her so damn much.

Which is why he finally spoke.

"Why?" he simply said.

"Why what?" she replied. "Why speak to me? Because we're together, that's why! Because we're all we have. I should ask you why!"

"Because I saw," he said.

Her face went blank.

"Saw what?" she asked, trying not to seem worried.

"I followed you ... to his tent—"

"You can't walk," she said. Mark grabbed his peg leg and threw it down in front of her feet.

"I made that. I followed you. I had been sensing things were wrong with us for some time, but I wasn't sure why. Now I know."

Mark could see panic set into Nell's eyes. She grabbed his hands, but Mark pulled them away.

"It's not what you think! You don't understand."

"What don't I understand? That you went to him because he's huge and strong, and I'm ... this?" Mark lifted his stump into the air. She looked at it.

"No," she said, tears starting to flow from her eyes. She placed a hand on the stump. "I love you."

"Then why?" Mark pleaded with her.

Nell took a deep breath and walked away from him, turning her back in shame.

"Because if I didn't, he wouldn't give me the medicine that was keeping you alive. I did it for you. I didn't want to lose you; I had no choice."

Silence filled the space between them. Now Mark was feeling like a bastard. Of all the reasons he had come up with for why she was doing it, this wasn't one of them.

"Oh, my God," he finally blurted out, unsure of what else to say. "I had no idea."

"I didn't tell you because I didn't want you to worry about it. I will do whatever I have to do to keep you with me. You are my everything! I'm sorry I hurt you. I am *so* sorry."

Mark saw her speaking to him. He vaguely heard the word "sorry" in his ears, but it wasn't registering. Anger was sweeping through him, and all he could think about was what he wanted to do to Stonehenge.

What kind of messed-up people have we met? Mark thought. *I have to do something!*

Mark grabbed his makeshift leg and began to attach it.

"What are you doing?" Nell asked.

"Taking care of this."

"No, you can't! He'll kill you!"

"Better that than you whore yourself out so that I can live!" Mark was up on his wobbly leg now. Gaining his balance, he walked out into the streets. Nell quickly followed, grabbing his arm, attempting to stop him.

"Please, don't do this! It's fine! I can handle it! I'll stop! I won't go back. You're better now. We have enough pills to last awhile—"

Mark stopped and grabbed her, pulling her to him. He kissed her on the lips. It was the most passionate moment they ever had. After, he put his forehead on hers. He could taste the salt on his lips from the tears running down Nell's cheeks.

"Don't do this, please," Nell begged him, her voice breaking in and out between the sobs.

"I have to. I'm sorry I have put you through this, but either I end it or I won't be able to live with myself."

That's when Nell said it: "I'm pregnant."

Mark pulled back a bit, looking deep in her eyes. Nell could tell that questions of paternity were filling his mind.

"It's yours. I've known awhile. Before Stonehenge and I … I didn't tell you because I wasn't sure you could handle it."

One final time, Mark kissed her. The kiss lasted a long time. For Mark, it was possibly the final kiss of his life, and he wanted to remember it in the world beyond this one.

Mark finally released her. All Nell could do was watch as he walked off toward the giant.

Stonehenge

1

Wham!

The blow took him by surprise.

It went across the back of his skull, cutting a gash open across it. Lifting his hand to the cut, he pulled it back into eye view and looked at the blood.

Lucky shot, Stonehenge thought.

Had he been ready for it, he would have ducked or braced himself at least; however, he didn't have the chance, as some coward had snuck up behind him and laid one on him so fast and hard, he was now seeing stars.

That's a first, Stonehenge thought as he wiped blood away from his mouth.

Turning around, he looked at where the blow came from. Standing there was some crippled kid. He had a crutch in his hand—which must have been what hit him—and across his face was the look of a man intent to kill. Stonehenge knew the face well.

Dumb crip kid, he thought as he recognized Mark, *he's that bitch's one! The one who needed medicine to save him. This sucks! It isn't worth it. She wasn't even good in bed!*

"You're going to pay for that," Stonehenge said while standing to his full size again. He looked down at the kid, who, even though he was six feet tall, Stonehenge still towered over.

"I challenge you for leadership!" the kid yelled at the top of his lungs. A few gasps went up from the crowd that had begun to gather around them. They were in the center market area of the camp, which meant there were lots of bystanders to see the fight.

Good, thought Stonehenge, *more to see him die!*

"You sure you want to do this, boy?" Stonehenge said, collecting himself for battle.

"You have no idea." The challenger smiled back.

"Dumb kid."

Stonehenge pulled his fingers to his palms tightly, forming two massive fists. He felt the power and strength in him. He was ready to unload.

"I'll give you a chance," Stonehenge said while holding back his anger. "Throw all the punches you can, and I'll just stand here and take it."

The kid smiled.

"Fine."

He started firing away. One left, then a right, then another left, an uppercut, even a few large hits to the ribs. Stonehenge barely winced. The kid, fresh from healing, was weak, leading each punch to land like a feather. Finally, the hits stopped. Stonehenge linked eyes with the young man. All energy and hope had drained from him.

"You finished?" Stonehenge patiently asked.

The boy, exhausted, nodded.

Stonehenge smiled.

"My turn."

With a mad punch, he began.

Nell

1

Nell didn't see the fight, only the aftermath.

Dr. Sandberg returned Mark's body to her possession an hour after he had left. From their home, Nell could hear the sounds of the crowd cheering as the fight ensued, but she could not will herself to go watch it. She could tell from the sounds of the crowd the fight didn't last long. There was cheering for several minutes, then silence. Yet despite knowing how quickly the fight ended, she was surprised by the damage done.

Mark's face was swollen beyond recognition. Blood was seeping from multiple wounds. One of his arms was bent in such an awkward way that it could only be because it had been broken in half. The peg of Mark's leg had been removed and thrust into his chest, where it jutted out from inside a grotesque wound that enfolded it. More blood leaked from there. One of Mark's eyes was open wide with terror, yet it was also bloodshot from broken blood vessels in the brain that were bleeding internally.

While some might have cringed from this sight, Nell took it in. She memorized every horrifying inch while her tears began to dry. Strength of will overtook her.

"We can have the body disposed of," said Dr. Sandberg.

"No," she said. "I will bury him."

"Are you sure?"

"Yes, he was my family and family should do it."

"Did he know?" asked Sandberg.

"I told him. Right before the fight."

"He was brave," Sandberg said in a quick kind of eulogy.

"Our child will be too."

With that, she bent to the body and began to wash it clean.

Colin

1

Colin was relieved that he and his brother were able to return to their own home and leave the school behind. The confines of the school cafeteria did nothing to calm Colin's already-overactive nerves, which had increased substantially after what he experienced with Willy and Mary Anne. Even though Colin hated the fact that his brother had been involved with killing three local men, he just pushed those thoughts out of his mind and tried to feel glad to be home.

Since his parents' deaths, walking into their house had become quite a task. Every room had memories of wonderful times, making the rooms now feel empty and cold. No matter what Quentin did to try to make them feel like a family again, it failed. Which made the house feel like nothing more than a rotting carcass, devoid of a soul.

When Colin and Quentin walked into the house, Quentin lit a candle for light and walked straight for the kitchen.

"You want some food?" Quentin asked Colin.

"I guess. What canned treat will it be tonight?"

Quentin looked into their almost-empty pantry. Since the attacks, they had been able to restock it twice with food they found that was either canned or dried out. Beef jerky had been the choice for a while, but the two local grocery stores had run out long ago and now Colin and Quentin were forced to eat only canned goods. Colin worried this wasn't good for their long-term health, but what choice did they have?

Quentin handed Colin a can of peas.

"Mmmmm ... savory." Colin took the can from his brother and started to walk toward the stairs to his room.

"Tired?" Quentin asked.

"Yeah, I haven't slept very well lately."

"Well, you should sleep well tonight. It's safe now, you know. I made it that way. For you." Quentin wasn't saying this for some kind of thanks. Colin could tell he was simply trying to reassure him.

"I know," Colin answered.

Please leave out the details, he thought.

"Good. Now eat up and sleep. Tomorrow we get back to your training."

"Right."

Just what he wanted.

2

Once Colin was in his room, he lit a candle and ate the peas. He took them down slowly. He was starving all the time, which was not ideal, but it sure did make him appreciate every bite. Despite the awful taste of the canned peas, Colin ate every last one.

For a moment, he thought *maybe I should go back to the school, where we got to eat frozen school meals.* He knew eventually they'd run out, but for the time being, it was better than canned peas. That thought only lasted a moment. All it took was sitting on his mattress to remember it was way more comfortable than the cot he had been sleeping on.

Colin sat on his bed looking at the drawings posted around his room. As Colin saw it, this was his museum. Each picture was his very own copy of older—and at one time famous, even revered—works of art. The *Mona Lisa* by Da Vinci, *Guernica* by Picasso, and *Water Lilies* by Monet, all forgotten now by the general public but cherished by Colin. To him, these were all the most important visions ever created by man. Among these were his own drawings. More than a few of these were of Kim. He hoped she never set foot in his room; he'd be embarrassed if she saw all of this.

As Colin got comfortable in bed, the unkempt sheets on the mattress ruffled as his slender, seventy-five-pound frame tried to settle in. Once stowed away in the sheets of his bed, Colin took a deep, relaxing breath. His mother always told him that to clear the mind, one had to breathe deeply. He lived by that notion. As he exhaled, his mind began to clear of all the disturbing thoughts of the day.

That's when he heard it.

Klink!

Colin sat up from his bed quickly, and his eyes darted about the room, trying to locate where the sound was coming from.

The window! Colin realized.

Colin quickly moved to his window and sheepishly looked out. Across the way, he could see a light coming from the upper window of the house next door.

Kim's room.

Colin could make out the gentle form of Kim silhouetted against the light from the house. She was staring out at him. He lifted his window just as she pulled back her arm, ready to throw at his window again.

"Hold it!" Colin yelled before she could throw again.

"Oh, sorry!" Kim lowered her arm.

"What's going on?" Colin asked with confusion in every word.

"I saw you came home," Kim said.

"Yeah."

"I'm glad you're okay. Things have been so weird."

"Yeah, they have."

Like you talking to me right now, Colin thought but did not say.

"You need something?" he asked.

"No. Yes. I mean. Well, no ..." Kim's voice trailed off. Colin couldn't see her face well, but even in the darkness, he could make out that worry was creased across her brow.

"You, uh, want to come over?" Colin offered.

Why did I say that? Colin chastised himself. *I'm only begging for another beating from Sebastian. Plus, she can't come into my room. Anywhere but here!*

"Yes, actually," she said.

Colin gulped at the thought. His throat dried up instantly, and he barely croaked out his next word.

"Okay," and he quickly cleared his throat.

"I'll have to sneak over. My dad isn't letting me leave the house after sundown."

"Um, well, I can meet you in the backyard."

"No," she quickly replied. "I can't get out that way. Hold it; I'll be right back."

She disappeared into her house. This momentary break gave Colin the time to assess what was happening.

Kim Cooper is coming to my house, Colin thought.

"Oh, my God!" he yelled aloud.

Scrambling around his room, Colin began to remove all of his pictures. He had to hide them, especially the ones of her.

If she saw them, she would think I'm a freak.

Finally, with every piece of artwork down, Colin went back to the window. By this time, she had returned.

"Why are you out of breath?" Kim asked. It was at this point Colin realized he was panting.

"I was, uh, cleaning up. Wouldn't want you coming into a messy house."

"Okay. Here!" she said while throwing a rope over to his window. He barely caught his end, leaning so far from his window he almost tumbled out.

"What are you doing?" Colin asked.

"I'm coming across! Tie your end up tight."

From his viewpoint, Colin could tell she was already tying off her end. Colin quickly looked around for something to tie off his end of the rope. He decided on the leg of the bed. He began to tie a knot with the rope but immediately found it difficult. His brother had taught him some knots out in the woods, survivalist stuff, yet faced with needing to remember one, he couldn't for the life of him do that. In an ugly version of the kind of knot one uses to tie shoes, he double- and triple-knotted the rope around his bedpost.

"You done?" he could hear her calling out. Colin stood up quickly and nodded.

"Done!" he replied.

"Good."

She brought out a piece of tilted metal, like handlebars of some kind. She sat on the ledge of her window, letting her legs dangle down the side of the house. She looked back into her room, apparently making sure no one was coming, and then finally prepared herself.

Colin looked at all this in wonderment.

"Ready?" she asked him.

Am I ready? he wondered.

"One," she said as she placed the handlebars above and on either side of the rope; "two," and she gripped the bars tightly; "three!" and she threw herself out the window. Kimberley Cooper zip-lined across the ground twelve feet below. Colin could see her long blonde hair blowing from the wind she was creating in her glide. Finally, she arrived at Colin's window. He grabbed onto her and pulled her straight up into the room. They both tumbled over, down to the floor with a great *thud*! She was on top of him, only inches away from their lips touching.

"Thanks," she said, giving him a sly smile.

"What was that, Colin?" Quentin's call up the stairs moved Colin to his feet. He quickly yelled back down.

"Nothing, Quen! I just fell!"

"Again?" Quentin yelled back. Colin caught a laugh coming from Kim. "You need to stop doing that, bro!" Embarrassment crept across Colin's face in a red sheen.

"I like your room," Kim said, looking around at it. "It's very bare."

"Yeah," Colin spoke up. "I don't like things on the walls."

"Hmmm. Strange because I've looked over here before, and it seemed like you had a lot on the walls."

"Uh ... yeah, I guess so." Colin's voice cracked as he said this. Kim laughed again and gave him a sly smile. Kim then sat on his bed, while Colin kept his distance.

"How did you know how to do that?" He pointed toward the window to indicate the rope.

"Well, when your father owns a hardware store, you pick up a thing or two. I am an expert at tying knots, for instance."

Oh, great! Colin thought. *She's gonna see my knot and laugh at me some more!*

"Me too; my brother taught me," he said, trying to sound macho. He doubted it was working.

"I can tell." Her head bobbed, pointing out the hackneyed way he tied the rope to his bed.

"So, what can I do for you?" Colin asked, trying to quickly change the subject.

"I'm just lonely over there. My parents are being so protective. This 'end of the world' thing has them really freaked out. I keep telling them it's not that bad! That it is a do-over, you know? A time for new ways and new opportunities."

"Makes sense," Colin answered back, trying not to reveal how badly his hands were sweating.

"But all my dad can do is think of all the negatives. All the things that are going wrong." Colin could now see the worry in her eyes. This made her seem far older than her age. "He tells me his store is almost out of everything needed for survival—rope, tools, weapons."

"That's not good," Colin said.

"No, it isn't, especially since there are no more deliveries coming to replenish the stock. My dad says there is stuff out there, you know, en route to us, that either never made it before the world blew up or is in other stores where no one lives anymore. But he says no one wants to risk their lives to get it here, especially after no one returned the last time. Everyone's too afraid."

She slowly lowered her head now, and for the first time, Colin saw she was just a scared little girl, just like he was a scared little boy.

"My dad also says we are all gonna starve to death, and soon, unless someone does something about it. He says the troubles we've seen in this town will pale in comparison to what it will be like when everyone is starving."

Kim was quiet suddenly. Colin wanted to comfort her. Moving, timidly to the bed he sat next to her, not sure what to do next. He debated putting his arm around her and almost went for it, but froze at the last moment. Kim looked in his eyes.

"You think we're all going to die?"

"I doubt it," Colin reassured her. "Not as long as people like my brother are around. He'll go out there if asked. And if not him, the people who came from the mountains, they seem pretty all right. I know they would do something too."

Kim considered this.

"My dad says we need to fear them."

"Your dad says a lot," Colin spoke up. This made her laugh.

"He really does," she agreed.

"We'll be fine," Colin said. "I promise."

"You know," Kim began again, "we're the future of this world ... the kids our age. In the dark ages, thirteen- and fourteen-year-olds were grownups. They got married," she began to whisper, "had sex. Even had kids! A girl my age was prime for the picking. We might be headed that way again, you know. To repopulate and all. Soon, we might not be kids anymore."

Colin realized just how right she was. The time for childish things was gone.

"Don't think so much." Colin placed his hand on her shoulder. "No one knows the future. Besides, maybe we shouldn't be so quick to repopulate. I think that's how we got here."

Kim suddenly stood up.

"I gotta go," she said, grabbing her handlebars. As she arrived at the window, she stopped. Something above it caught her eye.

Oh, no! Colin thought. *I missed one!*

Above the window a piece of paper was hanging. On it was a picture of Kim at her window. The one time he had actually watched her there and sketched her.

Now she knows! Now she will never talk to me again.

Kim gently pulled the drawing from the wall. She looked at it, analyzing it, taking it in. Colin scrambled in his mind for something to say but drew a blank. She walked over to Colin; he prepared himself for the worst. However, instead of slapping him or yelling at him, Kim leaned in and gave Colin a gentle kiss on the lips. She then moved away, leaving Colin standing in utter shock.

"I'm taking this."

She folded the picture and put it into her pocket, and just as quickly as she came, she left. Before Colin was able to break out of his stupor, he saw her climb back into her window, and then she signaled for him to untie his side of the rope. He did so. After a moment, she pulled the rope out his window, across the yard, and back up into her room. Once the rope was inside, she shut her window and closed it up.

Colin was alone. After a moment of stunned silence, he sat down on his bed. That was his first real kiss and the first piece of art he ever gave away.

Aiden

1

It hurt to pee. It was as if shards of glass were being shot out the tip of Aiden's penis with the urine. Never in his life had he felt so much intense pain. The problem was, even his penis wasn't exempt from the lesions and pustules that had now come to decorate his body as if he were some kind of living pepperoni pizza. Sweat dripped down the back of his neck and beaded on his forehead as he tried to evacuate his bladder. Unfortunately, he was never able to fully empty it. The pain from the acid in his pee stung the open sores around the mouth of his junk, making urinating an impossible task. Bowel movements were even worse.

Hemorrhoids have nothing on this, Aiden would laugh to himself, though really it wasn't that funny at all.

In the end, he would always release what he could, then take a moment to collect himself and go back to the group as if all were totally normal. They were all going through the same things, but there was no point in letting the pain show. It already put them in the worst moods possible; the more they could hide the pain from one another, the more likely it was they could sustain ranks.

Today, though, while trying to collect himself from the pain, he found himself watching the sunset. Moving north, there was a great patch of blue sky that extended deep into the distance. Due to this, it was possible to see the sky change color instead of just showing gray and black due to the soot in the air. It was amazing!

Orange! How wonderful a color it was. Its luminescent glow! He thought, *No one ever knows how beautiful something like color is until you haven't seen it in a while. I need to stop taking things for granted.*

Following the blue sky, which was rapidly descending into night,

Aiden walked forward, studying every fluffy cloud and daylight star.

Yes! Stars still exist despite the fact the earth was all but destroyed. The universe lives on! Humanity's fate is not even a blink in its existence.

With the daylight fading, Aiden came to a stop and looked longingly into the distance. He had watched the blue turn to orange, red, purple, and finally black. How he wanted to walk on, leave this disturbing mission behind, and find peacefulness in the rest of his painful life. However, he knew he could never abandon the doctor and his plans to repopulate the world. Aiden knew helping the doctor to achieve his work might be the only way for Aiden to leave an everlasting part of himself on the world. The idea of being a hero intoxicated Aiden.

I want to be remembered! Perhaps that was why I had originally become an actor, he thought.

Turning back toward the group, he spied the hold that held the doctor's treasures. Each woman they had captured was of equal import. Nothing could happen to any of them. They were to be used as the doctor saw fit in helping to create a new Eden.

They are so beautiful, Aiden thought. *So pure and clean.* Without any of the lesions that covered the mutants, they were perfect specimens. Aiden hoped he would be given one as a reward for his service. Aiden wondered how many more normals there were. He knew they needed more normals to achieve their goal.

I have to find them.

One of the other Tribesmen came to him.

"What's the plan?" the man asked in his choked-off voice. Some of the survivors had lost full use of their vocal cords due to lesions growing on them. This gave a growl-like texture to their words. They spoke slowly and sounded almost like they were deaf bears.

"I want to split up. Keep ten or so here, and I'll take the rest with me. I need you to stay with the group here and keep an eye on our guests."

"Where are you going?" the man asked.

"I'm going north. I'm going to follow the clear sky. Where there is clear sky, there will be other normals. We need more."

2

Within the hour, Aiden had split the group in two and left for the North, hoping to find even more treasures to bring the doctor.

Sean

1

Night had fallen on the desert where the mutants were camping. As far as Sean could tell from his distant vantage point, the captive women were being left alone. Sean had been watching them nonstop for the last twelve hours trying to come up with a plan. If he could find a chink in the armor and figure out a way to exploit it, he could save Amy easily.

The good news was the women who had been captured by the mutants had been taking care of Amy. The bad news—or maybe not bad, but an added complication—was that it meant he would have to rescue all of them, not just Amy. It was only right. When Sean considered it, saving all these women might be the best possible situation. Once he had them all saved and settled, he could leave Amy and Charlie with them and go after Michelle and Winnie by himself.

However that was a decision for another day, Sean thought; *for now it's all about saving Amy and staying alive.*

Charlie was scared and hanging back with the truck. That was fine. Sean didn't need him to distract from the task at hand, and with only Charlie for assistance, Sean couldn't risk hurting him to save Amy. That would be counterproductive to his goal of protecting both of them. There was only one way in which Sean visualized being able to get her: go in headfirst, guns a-blazin', and kill all the mutants until there were none left.

By his count, there were twenty-five mutants total; however, most had left when one group split off. He didn't know where the other group was headed, but he also didn't care. The fewer there were, the better for him. That left only ten. Sean had a gun, extra bullets, an axe, and hopefully the element of surprise. With any luck, he could free the women at least before the mutants could overtake and kill him. Perhaps during the confusion, the group of women could escape with

Amy and Charlie. The only problem with that plan was it did not take into account Sean's survival. Sean figured it was probably just as well, as his chances of making it out alive were slim to none.

Sean turned to the truck, which he had placed around a ridge so it was out of view of the mutants.

"I'm going to have to go in there," Sean stated.

"No, you can't leave me here. Not by myself," Charlie said while on the verge of tears.

"I don't have a choice," Sean said reassuringly, even though he knew it would do little to calm Charlie. "I can't risk taking you with me."

"But I can watch your back. Protect you," Charlie pleaded.

"And who protects you? No way. If I have to watch over you out there as well as myself, I'll never stand a chance. The odds aren't great as it is. If I go alone, they won't know you're here, and I won't have to be worried." This last part was a lie because Sean knew he'd worry about Charlie anyway, but what use was there in telling that to a scared boy? "I promise you'll be better off here. Now, Charlie, hand me the gun and find as many bullets as you can."

Charlie dug in the back of the truck through all the supplies they had loaded up. He found Sean not only the handgun and its bullets, but a shotgun with shells as well. Two guns made Sean feel a tad better, though no matter the amount of weapons, once the mutants' aggression got going, he was screwed.

"All right, I'm going. Stay hidden. No matter what happens to me, don't get caught. If I die, you may be your sister's only chance. Be ready for anything." Sean gave Charlie a hug. Charlie lingered a bit too long for Sean's taste. Sean was already emotional enough; with Charlie's bear hug, it was getting even harder to leave. "See you soon."

Sean pulled out from the boy's grip and began to walk toward the mutant camp.

2

The mutant camp was set up in a circle. The few trucks they had made up the perimeter, keeping the mutants inside. The truck that held the women was inside of this circle, and just off center was a fire. The mutants rested around the fire. They laid sprawled out on the ground with blankets over them and shirts tucked under their heads as pillows. So all Sean had to do was get into the circle, through the mutants, and save the women.

Walking into the night, Sean didn't try to hide; it was dark enough they probably wouldn't notice him coming until he was right on top of them. Still, the walk felt like a long arduous journey, filled with all sorts of emotions. Sean had time to consider how he'd gotten here and think of loved ones like his mother and Michelle and Winnie. Even some of the people he had met in jail. This was his life flashing before his eyes. Sean could feel his palms sweating against the body of the shotgun. His legs were liquefying, making him wonder if he could even will himself to cross the terrain at all. Yet he marched on somehow, each slow, measured step taking him closer to the mutants he wanted to kill.

The light from their fire was beginning to shine on Sean as he cocked the shotgun as quietly as possible. The mutants were huddled closely together by the fire. They were restless, constantly jerking about. Sleep did not seem like something that came easily to them. Instead, they were hyperaware, like pigeons bouncing on the pavement. Their closeness, however, gave Sean an advantage; if he got a lucky shot, the spray from the gun might take out several of them.

Sean was almost visible; if the mutants looked his way, they would see him and attack. Thankfully they were all asleep, which allowed Sean to take quick aim. He locked onto the thickest bunch. Sean stopped in his tracks and lifted the gun.

Now or never, Sean thought to himself.

His finger tightened on the trigger, and the cool metal surprised him for a moment, but not enough to stop him from firing.

Boom! screamed the shotgun as two shells exited the muzzle, spreading wide, over the distance to the mutants. Two mutants hit the ground immediately as the spray from the gun went farther than Sean expected. Screams began as the mutants scrambled for safety. Sean cocked the gun again and fired!

Boom!

Only one went down with the second shot. The mutants were no longer in a large clump, which meant they weren't sitting ducks anymore. Still, he got three, so the whole rescue operation was going far better than he could have hoped. A path had cleared to the wagon, and Sean made a run for it. Just as he was about to get to the prisoners, a mutant jumped out from nowhere and knocked Sean to the ground. Suddenly the monster was on top of him, clawing and drooling. He was so close Sean could see the pus oozing out of his infected wounds and smell his rotten breath.

Sean couldn't fire the shotgun at this range. He would likely hurt himself if he did. Instead, Sean reached for the pistol from the back of his pants and fired.

Bang!

The mutant collapsed, bleeding out all over Sean. This prompted Sean to wiggle out from underneath and throw up. The momentary pause gave the six other mutants time to regroup. They were charging him from multiple directions, all in full run, teeth shining in the firelight for all to see. Sean just let loose. He didn't aim; he didn't reload; he just tried to hit something.

Bang! Bang! Bang! Bang!

Finally the pistol was out of bullets. He had hit two more, but not nearly enough. The last four were on top of him now. The first mutant to arrive lunged at his legs, knocking him to the ground. They wrestled as Sean tried to poke at an eye. Another mutant dropped on him, then another, and another, until it was like a game he used to play with his mother and brother.

Pile on Mom!

This version, however, was far less fun and with no way to yell "uncle" to make it stop. After a few minutes, when he had stopped struggling, the pile cleared and two mutants held him by the arms. Their grip was unreal.

They are so strong! he thought.

Sean didn't know if this strength was part of their mutation, but it was clear they had grown stronger than any normal human. That fact did nothing to console Sean when one of the mutants planted a hard right across his face. Knowing this mutant had extra strength couldn't prevent Sean from almost passing out due to the pain. It felt like a brick hit his face, not a fist. As blood poured from what had to be a broken jaw, Sean could hear the women's voices screaming, Amy among them.

"Stop! Don't hurt him!" she screamed.

One of the mutants came forward to Sean and pulled back on his hair to lift his face.

"Why are you here?" The voice from this creature was garbled, animalistic, but his intonation was clear: *I'm going to kill you.*

"I came for my daughter," Sean said, spitting blood in the mutant's face for good measure. The words through his swelling cheeks were hard to understand and the pain was electrifying, bringing tears to Sean's eyes. However, it didn't seem to prevent the mutant from understanding him, probably because the mutants were used to having to discern their own words, which were garbled even worse.

"Your daughter?" the creature asked, wiping the blood from Sean's cheek and licking it off his fingers.

"Which one of you 'normals' lays claim to this man?" The leader was having Sean dragged in front of them, Sean's failed rescue mission now on clear display.

"Speak up, or he dies."

"He's mine!" Amy spoke loud and clear. She was proud of Sean, he could tell. There was pride in her voice.

"Come forward," said the leader.

Amy came out from behind the small group of women. Sean lifted his head enough to see her. She was unharmed. This was a relief to him. In his estimation, her good health would be the last happy thing he'd ever see.

"Well, breeder, what do you have to say to your father before we kill him?"

"Why?" Amy asked Sean.

"Because I love ya, kid," Sean said. Though due to the broken jaw, it came out, "Eee-cu ... ssss I leeeew ya 'iiii-d."

"Take him away! Kill him where the animals can feast on his bones."

With that, the mutants ushered him away from the group into the darkness beyond the light of the fire. Once they had arrived at a destination, they threw him on the ground. Sean's eyes were closed, expecting the pain in his face to be gone any second as death took him. Yet all he heard was two large *phoomps!*

As he saw the two mutants' bodies fall around him, he wondered, *Is this what heaven looks like?*

Sean was in shock as his body was turned around. The last thing he remembered seeing was Charlie's face looking down at him, behind which were two men, dressed in all-black armored uniforms.

Sean smiled up at Charlie. Blood spilled out from between his now-red teeth. One of the soldiers grabbed him and began to examine his injuries.

"You're going to be okay!" the soldier said to him.

Sean wasn't sure he believed that.

Althaus

1

The pills were white.

Which seemed appropriate to Althaus.

Pain is white, Althaus thought.

It took some persuading to get the medic to release the pills into his possession. The medic wanted to know what Althaus needed them for. Althaus didn't lie about his reasons for wanting the pills; he told the medic straight out his intentions and why. They had a long philosophical discussion about euthanasia, society's opinion of such an act, and the right of the patient—or in this case, the parent—to determine the ultimate treatment. The big question was if this would be considered some kind of murder. It was decided this was a brand-new world, and therefore the old thinking had to be erased for the betterment of those still around. The children were suffering, and worrying about the ramifications of the act to the society in which it took place no longer mattered. As far as Althaus was concerned, there was no more society anyway.

With pills in tow, Althaus decided to wait on giving them to the parents. Instead, he allowed a day to pass. In his time as a pastor, he would often tell those who had come to some kind of large epiphany to sleep on it, and if in the morning the decision still seemed the best one, then and only then should they make it.

What kind of hypocrite would I be if I can't follow my own advice?

So, he slept on it.

When morning came and the tents were struck, he was still convinced he had made the right decision. However, just to be sure, he pondered it even more as they continued north. Hour after hour, following the blue of the sky, hoping to outrun the bad air they had left behind, Althaus still pondered. He always came to the same conclusion: this *must* be done.

As night fell, the tents were lifted. The group had to be well across the panhandle of Oklahoma, still headed in a northwesterly direction. If Althaus had his geography right, they would cross the border of Oklahoma tomorrow and into Colorado. Perhaps the bad air would be far behind them by then. If that were the case, Colorado seemed as good a place as any to call home. The only issue with that was no matter how many miles they walked, the air they left behind them always seemed to cloud over and turn the dark gray hue they had all grown accustomed to calling daylight.

How long will I have to lead these people? For Moses, it was forty years in the desert! Althaus thought about it, and doubted they had that long. If the nuclear fallout kept coming, if the animals all died, if water became contaminated, they would all end up like those children ... or worse.

Most likely, they would starve or dehydrate. Neither of those deaths appealed to him. So he hoped when his time came, he would be allowed to make his death one of his own choosing.

Just like the children.

2

As the camp sank deep into the night hours, Althaus packed up all the pills and walked to the tent. It took him time to find it, as it had been placed in a completely different location from the evening before. A new campsite meant new tent positions. When he finally found it, the parents welcomed him. Desperation and pain were clearly in their eyes, which made it hard for Althaus to focus.

No parent should have to know the pain of losing a child, Althaus thought.

Though he had never had time for a family of his own, he had seen many a parent face the horrific grief of living a life once a child had passed. It wasn't something he would wish anyone to suffer through.

The woman who had originally approached him stepped forward.

"Well?" she asked.

Althaus handed her a bag. She looked inside, and tears began to well up in her eyes.

"Oh, thank you. Thank you!" She hugged him tightly, which made Althaus very uneasy.

Is this really something to hug over?

He pulled back after the long awkward moment and nodded. He had no words of wisdom to impart, no prayer to make the act a blessing before the Lord. This was a purely human moment, one not to be mixed with religion.

Then she said it: "God has truly answered our prayers."

"God?"

"He sent us to you, and you delivered."

Althaus considered this for a moment.

Am I really a messenger from God? Some form of miraculous answer to a prayer? Doubtful. In response he said nothing of it.

"May God bless you," she added for a final good measure.

"No, may God bless you."

Walking out of the tent, Althaus could hear no words being spoken between anyone. That seemed appropriate to him. No words needed to be uttered. This wasn't a time for useless posturing. It was a moment for silent reflection of a better life and a time when decisions were easier to make.

3

Althaus couldn't sleep that night. Nightmares of dead children poured through his brain. He woke up thirty-two times—once for each child.

4

The next morning, the tents came down. Althaus could see everyone cleaning and preparing for another long day. He could see from across the landscape, there was no movement from the tent that housed the now-dead children. This was predictable. He doubted the parents would be joining them for the rest of the journey. While Althaus felt that leaving the grieving parents alone was the best option, for some reason he felt compelled to see if they needed anything before the rest of the camp departed. When he arrived outside the tent, he could hear crying. The whimpering carried grief and on a subconscious level he thought that the crying sounded too high in pitch for parents.

Maybe it's the mothers, he thought.

Althaus took a deep breath and walked through the entrance of the tent. What he saw shocked him.

The children were all still alive. They were the ones crying. The parents had all taken the pills and were lying draped on the ground, lifeless. They had abandoned their children to a horrible fate of sickness and eventual death to take their own pain away.

After all, parents should never outlive their children, Althaus thought.

God's blessing indeed.

Black

1

Unbeknownst to Stonehenge and his gang of sycophants, General Black had his men in attack positions. When dawn came, Black would send his troops into battle. He expected to have full control of the biker camp by noon. His plan was simple: they would start the attack in a full-frontal assault. Of his 250 men, he had left ten behind with Althaus, and he had sixty set for the first wave of the attack. When most of the biker gang came out to fight, he would send in his second wave around to their flank. The second wave consisted of another thirty men. He had sent this deployment to battle positions twelve hours ago, and they had confirmed combat readiness this morning. Black sent the confirmation of battle stations at nightfall. All of this was done with runners, like the old days of the Revolution and Civil War. Black found he kind of liked it; there was no need to worry about transmissions being overheard or codes being cracked. All his plans were written on paper, sent by messenger, and then burned. Because of this, even if the battle were harder-fought than anticipated, the bikers would have no idea about the two-pronged third wave of soldiers, known as a Pincer Movement, positioned to the sides of the camp to squeeze the final life out of it. In short, they were surrounded, with no way out.

The only issue Black saw with any of his plan was the civilians. He instructed his men to be deliberate in their attack and not to get bogged down with the masses. Black felt they had little to do with the leadership of the camp and therefore deserved to be spared. However, as unfortunate as it was, he still expected there to be collateral damage of noncombatants. There always was. Projections stated maybe a few hundred of the camp's inhabitants would die in the attack. There were approximately two thousand occupying the cramped compound, so to Black, two or three hundred civilian casualties didn't seem that bad. Besides, after the battle, Black assumed he would have to take the survivors with him and his men.

A few hundred less of those people won't be the end of the world, he thought.

The surprise of the night came when two members of the Flanking Unit came rushing in with three survivors and a prisoner of some kind. The people they brought with them were a young man, his two kids, and a deformed enemy combatant. Had they still been able to call it in to Black's quarters, the general would have told them to hold off returning to base until after tomorrow's attack, but they had no long-range communications. Black would now have to deal with this distraction immediately. Given the soldiers' need to bring these people in, they obviously felt it was important. Black was intrigued.

2

Upon arrival, the returning soldiers had the father of the two children taken straight to the medical station. He had been beaten within an inch of his life. The two children insisted on being with him, and the hostile was brought into Black's quarters.

Black had no idea what to think of the thing brought before him.

He was a large humanoid, but deformed. Black was not a squeamish man, but the blistering skin and yellow pus seeping out of the open wounds made even Black gag. The stench of rotting flesh that seeped from this thing's every pore didn't help.

"What is that?" Black asked his men as they stood beside it, guarding Black from any attack.

"From what we can tell," the higher-ranking of the two men said, "it's a man, sir."

"I can see that." Black placed a rag to his nose, hoping to blot out some of the pungency of the smell. It didn't work.

"The children we brought in called him a mutant, sir."

"And how are they and their father?" Black was genuinely concerned.

"He's too young to be their father, sir." The soldier spoke out of turn. Black didn't need that information.

"Thank you for your opinion, Corporal. However, if they say that is what he is, in this world, who cares if he's not?"

The corporal nodded. "Yes, sir. He should be fine, sir. Broken jaw, lacerations, but nothing that shouldn't heal with time."

"So," Black turned his attention to the mutant. "What's your name?"

It grunted. Black walked toward it.

"Tell me your name. You were human once. You still are, I guess. So, I want a name."

"Thaddeus," it said through a grinding larynx that made its voice sound like a growl.

"You don't look like a Thad," Black opined. "But you don't really look like much of anything, do you?"

"I suppose I don't." There was a touch of rebellion in the way the mutant was answering the questions. Black liked that.

"Why did you have those people in your possession? What were you planning on doing with them?"

The mutant simply let out a short laugh.

Black pulled his firearm from his belt holster and pointed the gun at the thing's skull.

"Tell me or I'll kill you," Black stated matter of fact.

"I'm already dead. How much longer can I expect to live like this?"

"Longer than not if you answer my questions. Maybe we can help you if you cooperate."

"Only the doctor can help us."

"Who's the doctor?"

"A hero."

"Tell me more about him, and I'll have my medics treat you for your injuries."

"You're not a very good liar."

Black pulled back the hammer of the gun. "How many of your kind are there?"

"More than you could count."

"Why did you have the women?" Black asked.

"They are our breeders. Members of the Tribe can't birth babies."

"That's sick," Black spat out.

"Even we hope for a new generation to repair our world."

"Hmmmm," Black thought. "Thank you for your cooperation." With that, he shot a bullet straight into the mutant's head.

He turned to his men.

"Keep this quiet. The last thing we need is any of our survivors to know these things exist. Until we know more, no one is to talk about this."

Both soldiers said, "Yes, sir!"

"Get rid of the body."

They grabbed it and took it out of the general's quarters. In his time alone, he considered all he had just learned.

How many more surprises like this one are there going to be? Is the world going to be filled with mutant survivors and healthy survivors vying for control over the small amount of resources left?

Black did not know what the future held, except for tomorrow. Tomorrow he could predict. Tomorrow, there would be victory. Tomorrow, there would be revenge.

Tomorrow, there would be war.

Nell

1

Since Mark's death, Nell had been unable to function. She would spend the long days and even longer nights of loneliness thinking of his touch and swearing she could still smell him. Some days she could barely even move. Eating was unimportant, and keeping hydrated was impossible considering she could hardly remember to do anything, much less drink. The fact that she still had a baby growing inside her was amazing in and of itself. Truthfully, if breathing were not an involuntary action, Nell might have stopped doing that too.

Dr. Sandberg thankfully did not forget about Nell, or the baby. When Nell was only weeks away from delivering, Dr. Sandberg went to visit her every day. He would check her vitals, make her eat something, anything, and force liquids down her gullet. At night, he would often stay until Nell was asleep. Eventually, even this helpful attention wore on Nell.

"Night after night you come here!" Nell said. "Can't you leave me alone?" Loathing for life was deep in her eyes as she said this. She wanted no one's help and no one's kindness.

"Death of a loved one is a hard thing. I am here to make sure you know you're not alone," Dr. Sandberg said firmly.

"I don't want you here! Don't you understand? I want to be alone!" she screamed at the top of her lungs.

"Too bad. It is my religious tradition that we do this, stay with those who grieve! So don't expect me to leave."

"I've never heard of anything like that."

"I'm Jewish," he said. There was a long pause. The fact seemed to shock her. "Sorry if that makes you uncomfortable. You've probably never seen one, huh? Bet I'm not quite what you thought."

"I didn't know." She tried to say more, but she was clearly shocked. The new information calmed her.

"You didn't know any of us were left?" he added. "Oh, we are ... or at least were, but who knows now? I know most of us, including my parents, left America during the Iran-Israeli War, back when I was a kid. Even though my parents chose to take me with them to protect Israel, I came back. I wanted to know the country I was born in. It's true not many Jews survived the American Religious Purge, but there are some Jews still left within these borders. We just don't advertise it."

There was silence between them. Finally she spoke.

"My father hated Jews," she stated.

"Did he know any?" Sandberg asked.

"Probably not. The way he described them—you are definitely not like that!"

"Most of us aren't."

"So why come back to a country that got rid of religious freedom?" She was genuinely curious; the hate of her family had not been imparted on her.

"In Israel, we felt the same hate. Since we survived the Iran War, I thought maybe it was time to fight for freedom again in this country. Many American-born Jews were coming back to try to make a go of it. We knew we'd have to register our religion with the government, but we thought it might be worth a try. Then this." Dr. Sandberg gestured to his surroundings. Nell knew what he meant.

"Wow," she simply said. "Great timing."

"Yeah, right," he replied as they both chuckled. He could see her relaxing a bit.

"Dr. Sandberg, you said your people stay with the grieving as a tradition. Why?"

"It's considered a great mitzvah ... uh, a good deed, to sit with the grieving. We call it 'Sitting Shiva.' It is an act of kindness and compassion. It means we understand. Sitting Shiva lasts for a week, Nell. After that week, tradition states it's time to get on with life. So mourn for Mark. Judaism says you have a year to do so. Then life goes on. Understand? It's already been a month. I say let's Sit Shiva this week and say good-bye."

Nell nodded. She seemed suddenly relieved.

"Thank you," Nell said.

"Of course."

Dr. Sandberg and Nell sat every night talking about Mark, who he was as a person, and of the great times he and Nell shared. On the seventh night, Nell asked if there was a prayer Dr. Sandberg could say to bring an end to the week of mourning. Sandberg nodded, and began to say the Mourner's Kaddish.

When the sun came up the next day, Nell felt renewed. Just in time for another test of survival.

2

The attack began as many in the camp were beginning to eat whatever rations they still had left for breakfast—mostly canned food or stale bread found in the ruins. Most of the survivors were losing weight at an alarming rate, but they somehow found the energy needed to continue on.

When the first mortar shell hit the camp, it landed in an unsettled area. It was mostly open fields, thereby missing people completely and allowing everyone to scramble to safety when they realized they were under attack.

By the time the fourth mortar fell, the survivors in the camp had gone insane. They ran in different directions, clogging the streets and byways, making it impossible for anyone to get anywhere. People who were less able-bodied got trampled fast, while those who could run found themselves in a quagmire of bodies all trying to do the same thing: escape.

The fifth mortar hit like an arrow to a bull's-eye, right in the middle of all the commotion. Instantly, everyone within fifty feet of the blast radius was killed. The injured were left to die by the rest of the scattering hordes; the sixth mortar shell thankfully took the injured out of their misery in quick fashion.

During all this, Nell ran from her "home," and into the streets away from the direction of the attack. It seemed to her like she was a fish swimming upstream. The others all seemed to be running *to* the danger, which she figured was because Stonehenge and his gang were that way. To them, the Inner Circle still represented protection. Nell realized the attack was intentionally directed at the Inner Circle. This pleased Nell to no end. With any luck, the attack would wipe out Stonehenge and the rest of his crew.

Running with all her speed—which due to her condition wasn't very fast—Nell found the crowd was thinning out. Though there were sounds of more bombing and screams from victims polluting the air, Nell did not look back.

Better not to know what is happening behind me, she thought, *better to stay on course.*

Just beyond the border of the camp, Nell could make out desert. Realizing she had no water to help her to survive, she stopped.

Water ... I need water!

If she could make it as far as Dr. Sandberg's, she could find what she needed. He had plenty of fresh bottled water in his medical center. Realizing this, she knew she had to move fast; things were not improving.

Bombs were going off in more areas of the camp; no longer were the mortars only targeting the center areas. They were beginning to land everywhere. As Nell ran through the streets, bodies upon bodies of the dead mounted. Blood was running red over the brown mud, and her shoes had gone from dusty brown white to dark purple, forever stained with the life force of the innocents. Shells were landing closer, while debris landed all around her. All she could do was continue to run for her very life.

As Nell turned a corner, the wall of some house that was barely standing to begin with toppled over on her. Flames spewed out from around it as a large piece of concrete hit the right side of her body. Pain was all that was registering. Stabbing pain in her ankle, knee, head, and abdomen.

Please let the baby be okay, she thought, *it's all I have.*

Nell tried to focus her vision, but no matter what she did, her eyes wouldn't see clearly. Her ears rang, even though there was only the sound of silence around her. She could see people screaming, more bombs exploding, yet she could hear nothing.

Am I deaf?

Nell moved a hand to her ear and felt blood oozing out as if it were a nosebleed.

That's not good, Nell thought, echoing Mark's sentiments when he saw his leg.

Yet she had no time to worry about it. Focusing her eyes as much as she could, Nell realized where she was. Only steps away, she could see Dr. Sandberg helping some of the wounded into his clinic. Nell knew she could make it over there if she could only find enough strength.

Digging deep, she moved her arms, lifting herself out of the rubble. Slowly she got her legs under her, putting as much weight as she dared on them. Once she had her bearings, she slowly moved forward, one step, then another, and another, until she was only thirty feet away from her destination.

That's when Dr. Sandberg saw her.

"Nell!" he yelled, placing a wounded person on the ground and moving in a dead heat toward her.

Nell wanted to answer back, but she couldn't; it was all she could do to keep moving. Sandberg grabbed onto her. To Nell, it was the strongest grip she had ever felt. With it, all strength seeped from her body. She weakened in his arms. Gently yet firmly, Dr. Sandberg moved her over to the clinic. He examined her immediately. Nell could see he was speaking to her, but she had no idea what he was saying. She still couldn't hear. Despite this, though, she was happy to be near him. She finally felt safe.

Suddenly Sandberg's head turned from her. He was distracted by something. Nell looked to see what it was. Outside the clinic walls, she could see some of the biker gang running away. They were petrified of something coming toward them.

With no sound, Nell thought the whole thing looked like some kind of strange pantomime: bikers went down, blood shooting out from their chests in violent straight lines of red liquid, fire flew into the sky as people ran in fear, and misty dust flew out of dilapidated walls as bullets hit them. A few moments later, a group of men wearing strange black uniforms, looking more like robots than people, walked by. They turned their heads toward the clinic as they went. She couldn't see any faces inside their tinted masks; instead, they just looked dark and lifeless. A shiver ran up her spine.

The attackers walked through the streets for what seemed like forever. It was an invasion force, well-trained and well-coordinated. Clearly, these men had no interest in her, Dr. Sandberg, or the injured. They knew their objective and wouldn't be distracted from it. This made Nell's heart leap.

Stonehenge is going to get his! May it be an awful death—long and torturous.

Sandberg looked into her eyes with a light. She blinked. He looked in her ears, wiping away blood. The bleeding was stopping, but her hearing didn't seem to be getting any better.

"We have to leave," Nell said, or at least she thought she did. Without being able to hear her own voice, she wasn't sure anything was said at all. Sandberg came into her view, nodding in agreement. Her words must have come out fine.

She read his lips: "Let's go."

Then they were both up on their feet. Sandberg grabbed his medical bag, which she hoped had at least a little water in it. As they exited the clinic, they ran into the oncoming soldiers. Again, the soldiers couldn't have cared less if they were coming or going. Nell and Sandberg were not their targets.

Nell watched the soldiers march as she ran; they were almost reminiscent of an ant colony, going out, searching for food, working as one to achieve their goal. They were frightening in their uniformity, yet awe-inspiring in their sheer determination. Nell hoped if they were captured by the soldiers, they would treat them far better than the Inner Circle had.

Suddenly, something hit Nell hard across her chest. It stopped her in her tracks. It was Sandberg's arm. He was protecting her, as her father had many times in the car when they had to stop short. Nell looked at him. He was staring at something in the distance. Nell turned her eyes to see what it was.

Juanita.

She was bloodied and battered, but had a look on her face that could kill. From the knife Nell saw she was tossing in between her hands, killing was exactly what Juanita had in mind.

Juanita approached them. She was yelling things, but Nell couldn't make them out. Juanita's lips were moving too fast to read. Looking back and forth between Juanita and Dr. Sandberg, Nell could see there was an obvious disagreement. She figured it was that Juanita came to kill her and Dr. Sandberg wasn't going to allow it.

Juanita, who had made her way closer to them, was jabbing the knife in their direction. Nell wished she could explain it to her, calmly and rationally, but that was a wish on a star. Juanita meant to kill, so unless Nell got extremely lucky, Juanita was going to do just that.

Juanita was now close enough that Nell could see that the blood on her was not her own. For a moment, Nell was elated about this.

Maybe Stonehenge is already dead!

If Nell had to die, at least she might get to take solace in that. Nevertheless, Nell knew she could never be sure unless she saw his body, which would never happen once Juanita's knife pierced through her skin.

"Is it his baby?" Nell suddenly heard. It was muffled and distant, but she knew she heard it. Nell wasn't deaf after all; her hearing was coming back, and now she knew why Juanita was upset.

"No," Nell said.

Juanita looked at her oddly. She hadn't expected Nell to say a word.

"It's not his baby. It's Mark's. I know the exact night it was conceived. It's my dead lover's, and thank God for that." Nell hoped the words sounded right, but she couldn't be sure; though they sounded right in her mind, she had no idea whether they sounded right in the world.

Juanita stopped her arguing. She looked Nell in the eyes, probing for any sign of a lie. Nell stayed completely deadpan. She had said the truth. She had nothing to hide.

Tears welled up in Juanita's eyes. Nell was never more surprised in her life.

Who knew that this woman could cry?

As if ashamed of her tears, Juanita bolted away, into the thickening crowd of people. Nell took a deep breath. Danger averted. Sandberg gave her a look. Nell smiled. Sandberg in response grabbed her hand, leading her toward the invading army.

Why is he doing this?

To Nell, it seemed like the wrong direction. Going this way, they were heading into more danger.

Except they don't want civilians, Nell realized; *the soldiers want the gang. So in actuality, Dr. Sandberg is taking me to the safest place ... among the invaders. Within the safety of the enemy, there would be no more mortar shells, gunfire, or any other secret weapons this group had up their sleeves. They wouldn't kill their own, would they?*

Sandberg stopped a moment and tore a piece of his white shirt off. He waved it into the sky, signaling their peaceful surrender. Some soldiers came up to them, took them by the arms, and tied their hands together with some kind of metal handcuffing device. It was beyond any technology Nell had ever seen before, but it was clear Nell and Dr. Sandberg were now captives. It was comedic to Nell that she felt safer like that than she had her whole time in the camp.

Nell looked back upon the battlefield. Sandberg had gotten them a safe distance away before surrendering. She could see smoke billowing up from destroyed areas and fire spreading throughout the remaining homes, while people were running out of the borders of the camp in all directions. Some were waving white cloths as well, while others ran for their very lives. Every so often, a person would fall to the ground, shot by one of the soldiers. Through the smoke and fire, Nell looked for Stonehenge. He was nowhere to be seen. For a moment, Nell prayed. She prayed for his death, she prayed for the revenge of the man she loved, and she prayed for a happy ending.

Althaus

1

As Barrett Althaus stood behind the podium, the reality of what he was about to do finally hit him. Unlike other times he had spoken, this moment was not going to be in praise of God's glory. Althaus did not intend to tell his flock to give their problems to God and wait for them to go away. This moment was something else entirely.

Althaus could see the questioning looks on the people's faces. The story of the dying children's parents had spread around the camp like a disease. He had moved the camp, hoping a change of scenery would squelch any further worries about what exactly happened in the tent that night. Once they had all resettled however, the rumors took hold of the camp and wouldn't let go. Rather than allow these rumors to spread out of control, he decided to call all five hundred in the camp together. Althaus had answers to give.

Right before he began, he looked over to the tent once more. This time he linked eyes with Clarence Solomon, who looked at him with a scowl.

You're going to hate me most of all, Althaus thought, and then he began.

"Good morning, everyone," he said, having to clear his throat first. He was nervous about what the crowd would do to him once he finished his speech.

"Good morning," replied the crowd. He could hear a tone of underlying confusion in their response.

"Pain is white," he said like it were a prayer. "Remember the white light."

Back to him they said, "The light is hope."

Confidence was growing. The people had already adopted the most important saying of his new religion; persuading them to join him on this endeavor probably wouldn't be as hard as he was anticipating.

"We've come to a turning point. We have struggled for months, fighting for our very survival. Trying to carve out some kind of new world for ourselves, all the while trying not to forget the world we left behind. This has been a hard task. To survive, we've had to try to forget those we've lost. It's the only way to keep moving. Along our journey however, we have been met with new tragedies."

Althaus looked over the crowd. They were rapt to his every word.

"A few days ago, a woman walked into this very room, questioning God's motives." A murmur started across the room; Althaus couldn't tell whether it was in agreement of the woman's question or condemning it for heresy.

He continued.

"She wanted to know why God had seemingly abandoned all of us to fates worse than death. She took me to see these children."

At this point, in a display of grand showmanship, Althaus had the children walk out across the front of his pulpit. They were a sight to behold, very dramatic in its effect but also very tragic. Some could walk, some strength left in their legs, while others had to lean upon these other children for support. All were on death's door. All had agreed to help Althaus.

"They are dying. They have radiation poisoning from the initial attacks. They have been dying a slow, very painful death. The woman, one of these children's mothers, begged me to help them end the children's suffering. She asked me to obtain pills to help them cross over to heaven."

The room erupted in arguing. Some in the crowd condemned the act, while others supported it. The argument was becoming contentious, with strong feelings on both sides of the issue. If the crowd was reacting to this so terribly, Althaus could only imagine what the reaction would be to the next piece of information.

"I agreed to help them."

The outrage grew. Some members of the flock were beginning to grab each other. A fight was only moments away. Althaus had to calm them.

"Quiet, please. Let me explain." The noise slowly began to

fade, though he could tell the room was still a powder keg ready to explode.

"I had a choice: let these children continue on in the horrible condition they were in, one where they would never recover, or help ease their pain, to perhaps usher them to a better place. It wasn't easy, but as I saw it, God *had* indeed abandoned them."

A few people in the crowd yelled, *"No!"* or *"How could you?"* Yet Althaus could also tell some agreed with him.

"I prayed that night. I prayed hard, trying to come to some understanding of what was going on. That's when I realized none of this is God's plan. It couldn't be. God would not leave these innocent children to suffer like this. And if he did, what kind of God did we believe in anyway?"

The room was silent. They wanted to know where this was going.

"And it occurred to me that if I was thinking that, then my faith in God had vanished. With that realization, I agreed to help them in their desire to relieve their children's pain. Those parents felt my helping them was God's will, but it was anything but. In fact, it might seem like I was acting out against the Lord. But I wasn't. I was simply trying to do what our supposed God was too weak—or scared—to do himself. Or worse, was never around to do in the first place. So, I gave the parents the pills they had asked for. And in the name of God, they took them from me, to help their children."

Althaus paused here. He collected himself. Feeling the anger building inside him, he knew he had to stay in control. Showing his emotions would only make things worse.

"You can imagine my surprise when I returned the next morning to find the parents had ingested the pills instead. In their cowardice, they doomed their children, and using God's name, they arranged it so they no longer had to feel pain. In God's name, they acted decidedly ungodlike. Oh, you may be saying, 'But that was only the work of humans; they used God's name in vain.' You would be right, but that is how our world has ended up like this. Humans taking God's name in vain and producing hateful acts instead of righteous ones. How much longer can we continue on like this, hurting each other? Why has our belief in the antiquated systems made us so selfish? If God turned us into this, then we must abandon the old ways so we can make a better world. If the old beliefs brought us here, doesn't that obligate us to do something different? Don't we owe it to the future generations to change?"

Althaus paused again. He let the drama of the moment sink in. Then, taking a deep breath, Althaus prepared to drop the bomb.

"We need to abandon God as he has abandoned us. We need to leave our old religions behind. We need to start anew, just as this world has. We need to heal from the past mistakes to create a utopia on earth. Forget waiting for the next life to find salvation. We need to find it now! We need to make this life heaven. It's time to start over. We have found a new God, one that fits this new world ... the God of the White Light."

Everyone in the room was dumbfounded. They all looked at each other, waiting for someone else to react first. Clarence Solomon shook his head in disgust. Quickly Althaus began again before he lost the crowd completely.

"The white light we all saw was that God. It was his voice, his action to destroy the old religions. Our old God is dead now, and we must embrace our new one. There will be doctrines to follow, rules and laws implemented, but for today, the most important one is the phrase we have already embraced. 'Pain is white, remember the white light, the light is hope.' Repeat that."

Slowly the crowd began. Clarence Solomon pushed his way out of the tent and took a few chosen people with him.

Screw you then! Althaus thought about his ex-colleague.

Then the sound built in confidence and power. The phrase was repeated again and again, like a chant. Althaus smiled.

Perhaps I've done it. Perhaps there will be no violence or pain. Maybe they will just accept it.

As the chant took on a deafening volume, groups of dissenters exited the tent, anger clear in their remarks and actions. Althaus worried for a moment, thinking everyone would follow, but to his surprise, most stayed and continued to scream out their support. Althaus raised his hand to silence them. They immediately quieted down.

"I was asked by General Black to give all of you hope. The hope I give is a new start. I give you hope in the form of a new religion, the devotion of the White Light!"

Loud applause broke the silence of the room. Althaus felt a moment of achievement: he had just ushered in a new era. Unfortunately, as with any kind of change, some would resist.

As the cheering continued, a firebomb flew into the tent, igniting it. Everyone scrambled in any direction they could, running through the canvas of the tent and making it fall to the ground. Althaus found himself trapped by the flames. He could see the children were also unable to escape.

A death like this would make them martyrs for the cause, Althaus thought.

As the children's screams began to spread through the collapsing tent, Althaus realized he was about to become a martyr too. Althaus stood in the center of the tent, raising his arms outward, preparing to greet the burning embrace of the flames. Starting with his leg, he could feel the flames grab onto him, their touch spreading up his left side, spreading excruciating heat against his skin. Finally, when Althaus could take no more, he screamed out in anguish, hoping his scream would possibly awaken some God to pity their immortal souls.

The last thing Althaus could see was the roof of the tent falling down on all who remained inside. Through a tear in the fabric, he saw Clarence Solomon staring at the burning tent, and Althaus realized where the firebomb came from.

Look upon your dirty work, Althaus thought. *The violence of your God!*

With that, Althaus shut his eyes and hoped for death to come swiftly.

2

Leaderless and confused, the survivors of the camp began a religious cleansing that would only end after a whole lot of death.

Part Four:

Reconstruction

Annette

1

Now that Annette and her hardy band of survivors were officially part of Bastion, they set out to explore their new home. Though they were all receiving lukewarm greetings from the townies, they did not let that deter them from enjoying the relative calm of this new community.

The group from the mountains' first task was to find better and more permanent housing than the school. Though a descent stopgap, the school wasn't exactly the most comfortable place to live. If they were really going to start calling Bastion home, they needed to find places to live. So they set out into different directions attempting to understand the layout of Bastion: who lived where and what houses were abandoned or had rooms available for occupation. They even looked at the few motels around, asking the owners what they would want in exchange for the rooms; money meant nothing anymore. The goal was not to force anyone to put them up, creating impositions, but instead make fair deals for the service. In the new world, deals were for the making.

As Annette searched the town for a place to hang her hat, she found she liked the town more than she initially thought she might. Given the way they had been greeted by the townies, she had begun to wonder if she had even made the right choice bringing her group there. Considering how much time she had spent fighting to get a place at the table, it was odd to realize that it wasn't until now that she was even sure Bastion was a place worth fighting for. Now she could enjoy the quaintness and solitary atmosphere.

Bastion had been almost entirely unaffected by the destruction of the outside world. There was an overall sense of perfection as well; the way the mountains surrounded it, the perfect blue of the sky, the green beauty of the surrounding nature, all made Bastion a better home than anyone had the right to hope for.

No wonder everyone in the town felt they needed to protect it, Annette thought. *If the world was falling apart, then Bastion could very well be the last paradise on earth.*

During her exploration of the town, Annette found the town had two of everything: two motels (each with ten rooms), two churches (one Catholic and one Methodist), two Italian restaurants (Momma Lucia's and Little Italy), two Main Streets (Main St. north and Main St. south), two schools (the high school, which began at eighth grade, and the elementary school, which went up to seventh), two grocery stores, two hardware stores, even two dentists and two lawyers.

Maybe this town should change its name to Noah's Ark, Annette thought.

Though Bastion wasn't a large place, Annette could see there were enough basic needs covered within the surrounding mountainous confines that the town could be a place where humanity could start over.

Although the idea of starting humanity over is a little too much responsibility, Annette thought.

Annette knew she should forget the needs of the new world and instead concentrate on herself. Over the past months, Annette had made some tough decisions that, when it came down to brass tacks, she was not proud of.

Annette thought, *With any luck, once all is calm, I will never have to make another life-and-death decision as long as I live.*

For now, though, she walked the streets of Bastion.

2

As she wandered, Quentin accompanied her. He introduced her to anyone he felt she needed to know. From the way he talked about her to others, Annette could tell he thought she was practically the second coming. Which was odd since she really hadn't done much other than tell him it was okay to kill a few people for the betterment of Bastion. Clearly he held her on a pedestal, perhaps assuaging his own guilt for killing the other men. She wasn't sure. What she was sure of, though, was that Quentin was going to want her to take over the leadership of the town. She hoped he'd understand when she declined.

Stopping at the Catholic church, Annette met Priest Toller, who explained to her the need for a strong religious base in town, and how, since God's wrath had struck, perhaps there could be a return to basic family values. The Methodist pastor, Izekial Pemberton, reiterated many of the same beliefs, except he insisted the Methodist church take the reins on such a movement, relegating the Catholic church to the gutter. "Where they belong!" he added.

How very Christian of him, Annette thought.

After Annette received blessings from both men, Quentin led her to the grocery stores, where she was greeted by a disturbing sight: empty shelves. She wasn't sure what she had expected. Obviously deliveries had ceased, but the overall bare nature of the stores was unsettling. She realized in her whole life, she had never been in a grocery store devoid of food. Even in earthquakes, there was some food to be found, even if not the freshest. Quentin explained to her that many within the town limits had taken to hunting in the woods, but if that continued, they would soon find themselves out of deer, squirrels, and even bugs. A shiver ran down her spine—though that could have come from the thought of eating bugs.

3

Moving on, Quentin took her to meet the mayor of Bastion, Harlen Kreuk. From the look of him, he was a man who had once been overweight but was quickly losing the pounds, probably due to starvation. His clothes were three sizes too big, and his skin hung off him like he was a shar-pei puppy. Annette was beginning to reconsider her evaluation of the town yet again.

Maybe this isn't such a paradise, she thought.

"It's so wonderful to meet you," Harlen said. "Finally!" He let out a small, awkward giggle at this.

"So you're the man with all the power here?" Annette asked with venom. "Where were you when all hell was breaking loose in town?"

"I was, uh ... I ..." He kept fumbling for an answer, and Annette just watched the appalling display in disbelief. She wasn't sure she had ever met a man this weak before.

"Next time we come under fire, I hope you will stand up and lead the town out of it," she fired at him again.

"Of course ... of course, I will."

"Well, I'm sure it was just all the shock of the situation, right? I mean, you'd lost your police chief, and the town was out of control." Annette tried to placate him a bit, realizing she would eventually need his help.

"Yes ... that was it ... shock!"

Wow, Annette thought, *he'll agree to anything. He could have struck back and called me a murderer, but all he's doing is agreeing with whatever I say. What an easy mark!*

Which was why a man like Chief Mankins would have liked him. Annette concluded there was no way this man was going to be able to lead this town into the future.

Retirement will have to wait, dammit!

Overall, Annette realized, the man was affable, to a fault, extremely friendly, and seemingly unaware of the fact he could accomplish great things with the power of his office. To her, he just seemed like a puppet.

"Anything you need," Harlen suddenly added with a smile. "You just speak up, and I'll take care of it."

"Thank you very much, Mayor, I appreciate it," Annette said, deferring to his position.

"Of course. We are just so glad to have you here," he added. "I know it was rough at first, but I promise you, Bastion is a wonderful town, a great place to live! You'll be glad you stayed." He sounded like a salesclerk or a tour guide hoping to sell her some land.

Annette decided to test his grit.

"Mayor Kreuk, maybe you can tell me—"

"Anything!" he hurriedly answered back, not dwelling on the possibilities of her dangling sentence.

"What is your plan for restocking the town with food?" Her words landed like a slap in the face. Kreuk simply gave an awkward smile and began to stammer.

"Well, we have to ... I mean, there is food ... it's just ... not ..." he trailed off, his eyes moving toward the sides of their sockets, as if the answer to the question were written on a TelePrompTer just off to his side.

"Not? Here?" it was all she could do to not yell at this man for his incompetence. "We have to do something about it, you know; we can't just let everyone starve."

"Of course." The mayor seemed scared of her. Annette realized that to him, she was probably the one in charge, just as Chief Mankins had been before her. "I'll see to it, whatever you want," he quickly added, obviously hoping to bring the discussion to a halt. With Annette, though, he wouldn't be so lucky.

"It's not what I want," Annette added. "It's what we all need."

"Of course. Of course, it is."

"We'll talk soon, Mayor. Maybe by then you will have a plan in place." With that, she shook his hand. His palm was moist with sweat—another characteristic Annette realized would drive her crazy about this man. As they walked away, Annette turned back to look at Mayor Kreuk. He stood on the sidewalk, barely moving, almost confused on which way to go.

"He always like that?" Annette asked.

"Pretty much. He depended on Mankins for orders. Now he has no clue."

"I guess he'll have to take orders from me now."

Black

1

Black couldn't believe all that had happened in his absence. When he and his men caught up to the rest of the camp, they were shocked to find what was left of their group. From the first glimpse, Black knew something had gone terribly wrong. He had hoped leaving Althaus in charge would be the right decision, but from the initial sight of the devastation, Black realized he had been wrong.

Despite General Black having so many plans for Althaus's future, the reality was that his hopes had been dashed. The few soldiers he had left behind quickly got the general caught up on the tragic events that had occurred after Reverend Althaus's shocking oration.

"It was an amazing speech, Sir." Said one of his soldiers, who was not prone to exaggeration. Truth be told, none of his men were, he wouldn't allow it. Black slapped that kind of behavior out of them in training so that on the battlefield they could be clear of hyperbole. "He told us everything we all needed to hear. Everything about the new god and about the white light—it all makes sense now, why we are here, Sir."

"Really?" General Black asked. He was shocked to hear such talk.

"Once the tent was attacked and it went up in flames, those that believed fought off the aggressors. Though many went with Clarence Solomon, the ones that stayed fought for the camp's survival. They were women, children, even the frail, but they fought with all their might. It was amazing to see. It was like Althaus gave them strength. And after what happened to him, he's become that much more inspiring, Sir."

"Hmmmm," was all Black could say in return. "Give me more details, soldier," Black pried.

"Well, once the first firebomb hit the tent, Sir, the rest of the camp erupted into chaos. Three groups quickly formed in the following days: the Neo-Christians, led by Clarence Solomon; the Religion of the White Light, Althaus's new belief system; and the people stuck in the middle. Though we tried to quell the unrest in the camp as quickly as we could, the Neo-Christians proved to be far too much for just the ten of us, Sir. That's when the White Light population stood fast. More violence broke out as we were attacked and some even killed. Overall, we only had three casualties. Eventually, we were able to fight off the insurgency. Solomon left, taking most of the rations and his people with him. Some of the neutrals wandered off as well. The last two hundred of us were told by Solomon to 'rot in hell,' sir."

Black's anger built inside him, but it wasn't for Althaus, though the general's disappointment in him was palpable. It was for those cowardly people who saw the general's exit from camp as an invitation to stir the pot. Starting with the parents and their plea for the death of their sick children—and their cowardly exit—and ending with those whose hatred for change was so great they'd rather kill than face the idea of something new. There was just never a shortage of people who hated just because hate was easier.

In his heart of hearts, Black had hoped this new world might have changed some age-old human tendencies. Apparently, it had not.

Some instincts come as natural as breathing and eating, Black thought. *The hatred of difference is humanity's purest instinct.*

He would change that though. He would change everything or die trying.

2

In the end, Black concluded Althaus had been right to want to change things. He just handled the announcement wrong. So, while Black's feelings toward Althaus were between anger and pity, Black could do nothing about what the reverend was going through now. The general knew Althaus was now paying the price for speaking his mind without fully understanding the consequences. Burned and crippled, lying in a hospital bed in the medical tent, Althaus was being kept alive by machines. He couldn't talk, he couldn't move, and even if his mind were aware, that only meant the pain was probably unimaginable. If this was punishment for his actions, Black felt it was an unearned sentence. As far as he was concerned, General Black would use all his power to make Althaus's pain worth it.

The Religion of the White Light would not end with this man, Black decided. It was too important. It gave so many survivors hope when all else was lost, and there were so many as-yet-unfound people who needed to hear those words, to understand their meaning in this new landscape of death and destruction. Black knew he couldn't let that die. He made a pact with himself: before the general's own life ended, he would do his part to make Barrett Althaus's beliefs the reason for world peace.

It will be a simple thing to do, Black thought. *From now on, it will be my mission to take Althaus's words and spread them to whatever survivors can be found.*

He knew that at times he would have to be prepared for blowback—like that of the Neo-Christians—but he was sure he could handle that. After all, he had his soldiers. What was more important than dealing with the naysayers though, was having to protect those who accepted the new word of the White Light. Then the religion could grow. Like the old Christians before them, they needed to be able to multiply and populate the world until all believed what they did.

So protect them he would.

Black would take them under his wing and deliver them to a place where they could start anew. Once there, safely nestled into a new Jerusalem based on Althaus's ideas, Barrett, if he survived, could rise again and guide them all into a better future, a future full of peace and whatever the word "prosperity" meant at that juncture.

If someone got out of hand or disagreed?

Well, Black knew it was better if they didn't. If they did, they would be dealt with—harshly. In the end, Black would get them all to agree or simply be silent.

Before any further steps could be taken, however, the scarcity of food had to be resolved. How could they start a new world order if everyone was starving to death?

Thankfully, Althaus had brought the camp to the border of Wyoming.

Providence or White Light, be kind! Black thought.

3

Wyoming was full of hidden US government bunkers, built and kept to perfection in case of global nuclear war—or worse. Fortuitously, the general knew where they were. Since Black was a high-ranking Special Forces officer, he had information no else had, and he knew how to use it. Once he got the camp into Wyoming and located the bunkers, he knew that the key to survival awaited inside them.

Each bunker was equipped with enough rations to provide for hundreds of people for fifty years maximum. If they could reach even one of them, they could take what they needed and still leave plenty for if they had to go back for more. Maybe it wouldn't last them fifty years, but it would be a start. In a world where growing their own food might be next to impossible, this information was powerful and meant the difference between the society of the White Light surviving or disappearing into the night.

As for the Neo-Christians?

Let them starve, Black thought. *Live by the new world order, or die.*

Furthermore, there was another reason for Black to find these bunkers. In times of crisis, the government's full archives were sent to every bunker in the United States, so that each one could become the new center of the government if the need arose. Theoretically, all information from the United States of America was now stored at each of these sites. With any luck, the answers to Black's questions about how this all happened would be there. It was also quite possible some in the government had also survived and were trying to rebuild the United States even as Black made all these new plans.

Wouldn't that be a relief, Black thought, *to have President Mitchum underground creating an American resurgence with his joint chiefs?*

In the meantime, though, Black would rest his troops, see to it that those survivors who had stayed with Althaus would be taken care of, and start to develop the new society. He would slowly bring along those they had taken prisoner from the biker camp and search the new prisoners for anyone who might create a problem. With any luck, Black could ferret out any within the camp who might fight against him or the new Religion of the White Light.

It's time for a cleansing.

Some old business needed to be taken care of as well. Black never did find the leader of the biker gang. The general suspected he was hiding in plain sight, perhaps being protected from prying eyes by other prisoners.

The general knew there was much work to be done to make the world safe for a bright future. Some would perish in the months ahead, but Black didn't fear death or the toll it could take, especially when it was for the greater good.

Nell

1

Nell was thankful the general had stopped his march north when he did. Nell and the rest of the prisoners from the biker camp had been walking for weeks before they finally came upon the remnants of some kind of mobile military fort. From the reaction of the general and his men, she figured it was where they had originated from. It had been destroyed and seemed like a pale ghost of the camp it might have been before. It saddened Nell to see this. Thankfully, though, given they had come to a stop, it was at this time her body decided to pop.

The next day she gave birth.

2

"Push!" Dr. Sandberg yelled, as Nell dug deep within for the strength of another agonizing squeeze. She could feel herself tear, but she couldn't stop. As much as she wanted to just quit, leave the baby inside her, and do something else entirely, she realized that was not an option.

"I can see the head!" Sandberg yelled again. Nell knew he was trying to help, but all his yelling and constant updates on the position of the baby were driving her crazy. Nell looked to her right at Juanita, who was dabbing Nell's head with a wet rag.

Juanita had become close to Nell since the camp had been destroyed. It was as if Juanita had latched onto her because Stonehenge was nowhere to be found or because they both shared something in common—their complete and utter hatred for that monstrosity of a man.

"Push again!" Sandberg insisted, angering Nell to her core.

I know what I'm supposed to do; stop reminding me!

"Shut up!" Nell said with a growl. The sound of her voice scared even her, as she never imagined she could sound so disturbing. Her voice had the sound of some demonic creature pushing itself out of hell by way of her body. Scary voice or not, though, it got Sandberg to stop talking.

Again, she dug deep, feeling the need to push the child out of her. Juanita grabbed her hand, which gave Nell the ability to bear down hard with all her might. Nell could feel the skin below her vagina tear yet again, with even more force, but she no longer cared what damage she did to her body. She just wanted the baby out!

Dr. Sandberg was cheering something, encouraging her, but Nell's brain couldn't register his words. She didn't care either. All she could do was concentrate on the task at hand.

That's when she saw it.

From between her legs, Dr. Sandberg pulled up a pale-skinned baby, covered in blood and gunk and not making a sound.

Oh no! Nell thought. *My baby is dead!*

That's when Sandberg slapped the baby on its back, ejecting all sorts of odd fluids from its lungs. This forced the child to cry. The sound was the greatest Nell had heard the whole of her young life.

Juanita immediately took the baby from Sandberg's hands and wiped it clean.

"It's a boy!" Sandberg continued in his excitement.

"It's a boy!" Juanita repeated as she smiled down at the baby.

Peace washed over Nell as she couldn't help but think this was the happiest she had ever seen Juanita. Yet Nell could feel neither excitement or calm; she simply felt exhausted. All she wanted to do was hold her baby, close her eyes, and sleep.

"Give me my baby. Give him to me!" She reached out, practically trying to stand.

"Take it easy," Dr. Sandberg said. "He's right here."

Juanita handed the baby over, still attached to his mother by the umbilical cord.

"I have some work to do on you," Sandberg said. "So, just feed him and maybe come up with a name."

Isn't it obvious? Nell thought to herself.

"Mark, you're Mark." She kissed Mark's forehead as she moved him to her breast. Although she wasn't exactly sure of what to do, instinct seemed to be taking over. Before she knew it, the baby latched onto her breast and began to eat.

Beautiful, she thought.

As the baby suckled on her, Nell fell fast asleep.

3

Nell's biggest fear after the birth wasn't so much for the baby, but worry the general might force them to move on. She was in no condition to walk, and though the general had his men treat them all decently, giving them rations and shelter, they did not give the prisoners the freedom to stay or to go. She couldn't help but wonder what kind of man the general would become when faced with defiance.

Would he hurt the baby and me if he wanted to keep going and we couldn't because I'm still recovering?

She figured worrying about such things was warranted. After all, if she had learned anything in this new world, it was that no one could be trusted. With this lesson in mind, Nell realized she had to trust her instincts now more than ever. Those instincts at the moment told her: *don't trust anyone!* And she wouldn't.

However, from what she could glean from rumors the other prisoners were spreading, it seemed the general planned to stay put for the time being. Which was perfect for Nell. Every day, Nell watched the soldiers repair the damage to the camp from what must have been some kind of hellacious battle. The camp was mostly abandoned, torn apart, and smoldering from fires. Only two hundred people still remained from what had been described as a group that was five hundred or more. Something had happened, though it wasn't clear what. Only the weak seemed to remain: the sick, the old, some young, and even the mentally handicapped. All of them seemed happy upon the general's return.

Yet once Nell had the baby, the whole world around her dissolved away. She didn't care about the fires that burned in the camp or the tragedy that had struck the place; the baby—Little Mark—was the only thing that mattered. So much had gone wrong in her life during the past ten months, it seemed almost impossible that everything could be as blissful as it was now. Yet that was exactly the feeling she had: bliss.

The baby's presence alone had washed away all her grief. She began to realize there was a future worth living for. Admittedly, it was a different future from the one she had imagined as a child, but it was a future all the same. The baby was a reason to keep going, a reason to survive.

And I will survive!

4

A few days after the birth, Nell was given a surprise visit: it was General Black himself. Word about the birth of Little Mark had gotten all the way to him, and now he wanted to pay his respects. Nell was surprised by the compassion in his voice and the gentle touch he displayed as he held the baby.

"I had a grandchild," he said. "My only daughter had given birth about six months before the attack of the White Light. I never got to see the baby because I was stationed away." The general's eyes were joyful as he took in the new life. "I so wish I could have held the baby once before all this."

"Maybe they're still alive," Nell added, knowing she sounded naive.

"Doubtful," the general said. "This birth is an amazing thing, Nell. You know that, right?"

"Yes," she agreed.

"We should spread the word about this child," Black added. "We are a world in despair, and new life gives everyone hope. We need that. Would you mind if I had a few of my soldiers tell everyone that a new child has been born healthy and strong?"

Nell considered what he was saying.

Does he want to use my baby as some kind of symbol?

Hearing this made her uncomfortable. After all, what could she say.

"Feel free," was her only response.

"Thank you," he replied. He handed the baby back to her and began to exit. Before leaving, he turned back.

"You know," Black said with a sadness to his voice, "you remind me of my daughter. She was strong. Like you."

"Thank you," she said, unsure of whether that was appropriate.

"Anything you need, you just tell me," Black said and left the tent.

Nell sat in surprise at the conversation. She had never expected anything like it.

5

About two weeks later, when Dr. Sandberg arrived for his daily check-in, things looked busy outside the tent. There seemed to be dozens of people milling about. Nell thought nothing of it, however. All she could do was feed her baby while looking deep into his innocent blue eyes.

"Hello, Doctor," Juanita said as he entered the tent.

"Hello, Juanita, and how is the patient today?" Sandberg asked.

"She's healing very well. She's a tough girl, a lot tougher than I gave her credit for." As Juanita finished, Nell broke in.

"I'm right here, you two. I can talk for myself."

"Of course, you can," said Sandberg. "So, how are you doing?"

"Perfect, Doctor," she said in a contented tone.

"You know, Nell, we've known each other for a while now. I've helped you give birth to a baby. I think it's okay for you to start calling me Brody."

Nell laughed. He was right. In the past, she had been so scared to call him by his first name because of her feelings for him that she just forgot that his first name even existed. Now, though, after he had literally seen every inch of her body and what it could do, to call him anything else just seemed silly. If that didn't get them to know each other on intimate terms, she did not know what else would.

"I suppose you're right … Brody."

"There, that's better, isn't it?" He leaned down to look at the baby. "You mind if I take a look?"

"No, go right ahead."

Nell removed the baby from her breast, revealing her pale skin and pink nipple. She couldn't help but notice that for even the briefest of moments, Brody looked at it! He quickly turned his eyes away, but the moment happened. Nell smiled. Juanita must have also noticed, because she covered Nell up immediately. As much as Juanita's help over the past few weeks had been appreciated, Nell couldn't help but resent her a little bit for her overprotection. It was like suddenly having a mother again. This time, however, the annoyance only lasted seconds. Nell couldn't take her mind off of what had just happened between her and the doctor. It seemed odd that he would find her even remotely attractive or desirable after having watched her give birth. Yet desire was what she had seen in his eyes, and she was flattered.

From afar and a bit nervously—as any new mother would be—Nell watched as Brody looked over the baby. To Nell, the child was perfect. She hoped Dr. Brody Sandberg felt the same.

"Everything looks good. He's getting the appropriate nutrients and gaining weight, from what I can tell—I don't exactly have a scale. Is he going regularly?"

"Yep. Doing all he's supposed to do. Eat, sleep, pee, and poop," she replied, taking the baby back from him, smiling as she tucked him into her body, rocking him back to sleep.

"Good. Listen, Nell," the doctor's tone changed in his voice suddenly, "there's something you should know."

"I thought we agreed not to tell her," Juanita spoke up, agitation plainly in her voice. She was still one of the most intimidating people Nell had ever met.

Thankfully she's on my side now, Nell thought.

"I know. It's starting to get out of control now," Sandberg shot back. "Have you seen it outside this morning?" Juanita gave him back a dismissive look, but she relented.

"What?" Nell was worried now. She had just gotten so comfortable in her happiness that the very idea of bad news was enough to make her burst into tears. *It also could be my dissipating hormones*, she thought. "What's happening outside?"

"I'm just warning you. There isn't anything you should do about it, but keep out of sight."

"No," Nell replied. "I want to see."

With trepidation, she began to stand, painfully. There was fire between her legs, and the stitches holding her torn lady parts together were poking into the tops of her thighs.

"I don't think that is such a good idea," Brody quickly advised, though Nell was intent on ignoring whatever advice he gave.

"I need to see this, to understand," she said. "Now, are you going to help me or not?"

Brody exchanged looks with Juanita. Nell could tell they were both concerned but ignored their look. This was something she needed to do. So, gently, with Sandberg's guidance and Juanita's help, she walked out the front flap of the tent. She could never have been prepared for what she found.

A large group of survivors had gathered. When they saw her exit the tent with the baby, they all fell to their knees in exultation. Silence befell all of them as they began to praise the baby; they threw their hands up to the sky, and their bodies moved back and forth in a strange, fast-paced rhythm. The absurd display shocked Nell to the core.

"What are they doing?" she asked, frightened.

"Worshipping the baby," Juanita said.

Nell walked forward into the crowd. As she passed by each person, one by one, they stretched for the baby, grabbing onto anything they could. Whether it was Nell, clothes, or hands, they seemed satisfied. Instinctively, Nell clutched Little Mark hard to her breast, to protect him, and Brody did the same to her, placing his arm around Nell. As they continued to walk, Juanita began to swat the people's hands away.

"Why are they doing this?"

"Your baby is the first new life since the attacks. No one was even sure a baby could be brought into this world, given the radiation. They all see your child as some sort of … miracle."

In truth, Nell felt much the same about Little Mark. However that was a mother's prerogative.

Wasn't that what all mothers felt about their children? That they were little miracles? What right do all these other people have to view my son like that?

"Brody, I'm scared." She leaned up against him.

"I know. I tried to warn you."

Trapped on all sides by the horde, the three of them managed to turn around and head back the way they came. It was among this chaos that Nell's eye caught something familiar, a figure in the crowd, towering above all others. It loomed large and dangerous and stopped Nell in her tracks.

"Nell? What is it?" Sandberg asked.

Nell's eyes scanned the crowd, but she couldn't place the figure again. It was as if it hadn't been there at all.

"Nothing. It's just my imagination. Take me inside. I'm tired; I'm just not seeing things right."

With that, they moved forward to the tent. The crowd parted, allowing them free access back. Each person dropping to one knee as Nell and the baby passed.

6

Nell couldn't sleep that night, but for once it wasn't the baby that was keeping her awake. It was the fear. The fear of the figure she knew she had seen.

It could only have been him, she thought; she knew in her soul it was. Nell had hoped Stonehenge died during the attack on the camp, but that was seemingly too much of a blessing to ask for.

If it was him I saw, what then? What can I do about it?

Juanita slept silently on the other side of their tent. She clutched a knife to her breast like Nell held her baby. Juanita was always prepared for anything—Nell knew that.

But would she be prepared for this?

Nell wasn't sure. Juanita and Nell were family now.

What will happen when Juanita finds out he is alive? Will we return to being enemies, or will our newfound friendship be stronger than the love she feels for that monster? As much as I know Juanita hates him, she does indeed love him—odd how someone can feel both ways for a person.

Nell had so many questions fluttering through her mind and no obvious answers. As much as Juanita could be abrasive, even overbearing, Nell had to admit she had never felt so safe as these past few weeks in Juanita's presence. Nell simply wasn't prepared to lose her.

All night, the internal debate raged on. What was she going to do about seeing Stonehenge alive?

As the sun rose, so too did Juanita. Nell was sitting on her bed, nursing, when Juanita walked to her.

"I'll get us breakfast," Juanita said.

"Thanks." Nell was distant—she knew it—but if she spoke too much, she knew she'd squeal.

"You look tired."

"I was up all night."

"Newborns will do that."

"Yep."

"Funny, though," Juanita added, "I didn't hear him at all."

"Just lucky, I guess," said Nell, trying to act like nothing was out of the ordinary. "You probably just needed the sleep."

"Hmmmm. Maybe. I'll be back in a few." With that, Juanita left. Nell had done it. She got through talking with her without telling of what she had seen. Confidence that she could deal with this without involving Juanita was high. That's when she decided exactly how she would solve the problem.

Stonehenge was out there, she was sure of it. She needed to tell General Black that they missed one. Then they could capture him and kill him, and Nell could watch with glee.

Aiden

1

During the first two weeks of his journey north, Aiden and his fellow Tribesmen had come across many small towns, most of them completely abandoned. Only a few treasures were able to be found. Most of the women they had come across (only five) had been with other men or people Aiden had to get rid of. It was easy most of the time. They just scared the men with their grotesque appearance, feigned erratic behavior, and unrelenting drive. Those who didn't run off were eventually killed.

Aiden never felt bad about it. This was a dog-eat-dog world now, survival of the fittest, and Aiden would do whatever he had to to accomplish the doctor's goals, even if it meant slowing the expedition down a bit to take in more people like themselves. The Tribe could only continue on if they added to it, and given the fact that all their women were barren, for the Tribe to become a larger group, either the doctor's plan needed to work flawlessly, or they had to find more infected survivors and bring them in. Which was what Aiden did in the town of Canon City, Colorado, population: 10,570.

2

In this town 120 miles outside of Denver, only three hundred survivors still lived. Apparently, the town was caught downwind of the bombs that hit Denver. That nuclear fallout took out most of the population, and gave those who did survive the same kind of radiation poisoning that created mutants. The reason the three hundred survived the initial blast was because they had all been able to make it to the school gymnasium when the bombs hit. Old Albert Einstein High School Stadium was built in the 1940s and never rebuilt as the town simply didn't have the money to refurbish it. Therefore, the building was still lined with lead and concrete. It protected them enough not to kill them, though in the end, it made them less than human.

This proved to be the single largest group of infected humans Aiden or the doctor had come across. Though the Tribe had grown large, it grew that way slowly by incorporating small pocket groups they found of survivors. This new group Aiden had found was important to the world's future and needed to be initiated quickly. During a town-wide meeting held in the same stadium that had saved their pathetic lives, Aiden explained what life in the Tribe meant.

"The Tribe means never feeling like a freak!" Aiden yelled at the top of his lungs. Since Aiden had been an actor, he had a true flair for the dramatic. "The Tribe means being one with the earth! The Tribe means finding love and connection. All of you feel disconnected now, destroyed, lost to your own humanity, but I am here to tell you there are more like us out there, and once you find them you will feel part of the world again! You will be part of a Tribe!"

With that, the stadium erupted.

"Come with us. Leave this old life behind and see what being a part of the Tribe has to offer. A man leads us, and he is unlike any you have ever known. He is a doctor, and he has a plan! He has been sent to us by some kind of grace, chosen to survive the blasts and chosen to lead us out of the destroyed wilderness. Of all the survivors we have found, of all the members brought into the Tribe, none has been a doctor like him. Some have been soldiers, or cops, or teachers, but none has been a brilliant scientist who can cure us and save humanity. His survival can only be seen as providence, a gift of fate, that will not allow humanity to end! This doctor, he has invented a way to fix this world for future generations; and we, the forever changed, will be able to look back and see how we were not monsters, but the heroes who changed the course of the future."

Again, the room cheered, all their pain and anguish turning to rapturous joy.

"We have a long journey ahead, filled with unknown obstacles and perils. Some of us will not make it to see this new world, but our actions will be remembered as the reason the world rose from the ashes. The simple fact is, the more of us there are on this mission, the higher the odds of success. We are stronger as a whole than apart. I am finding there are more of us left than the normals we pursue. Soon they will be the minority, fearing for their lives, and we will be their masters creating the new society."

Aiden wasn't sure about this last bit, but he knew he had to make them all feel important. They had to know just how right their cause was. If there were even the slightest doubt among them, they would fail.

"The doctor is a smart man, a man who understands how to continue in a world such as this. He understands what has to happen to make a future. The only thing he needs are strong followers, willing to fight for their belief, their belief that the world can be good again."

Applause.

This was an amazing sound for Aiden—or any actor really; he had forgotten just how much he needed it. The sound alone spurred him on further.

"Join with me in praising the doctor's resolve. Say yes to joining us!"

"Yes!" the crowd yelled.

"Say yes to a better world!"

"Yes!" the crowd yelled again.

"Say yes to the Tribe!"

Spontaneously it started. It only took one person in the back of the crowd to start the chant: *Tribe! Tribe!*

Slowly at first it started, but then it picked up momentum.

Tribe! Tribe!

Louder and louder the chant became until it was deafening within the enclosed structure of hardwood flooring and metal ceiling.

Aiden smiled. He knew exactly what to say next.

"Welcome to the Tribe!"

The cheers after that took hours to die down.

3

The same speech was given in the town of Colorado Springs, where they added another twenty-five to the Tribe.

4

And in Black Forrest, fifteen.

5

Fort Morgan, forty-eight.

6

Sterling, 101.

7

Wellington, thirty-two.

8

All said, by the time they crossed the Colorado border into Wyoming, they had amassed a group of 521.

Now they just needed to find more normals to fill the doctor's quota.

Sean

1

Sean had recovered nicely from his wounds. It took seven weeks for his jaw to heal enough for him to be able to chew soft foods, and another month to begin to put on some of the weight he had lost. Despite the severe beating he took, he supposed he had come out on top.

At least I'm alive, he often thought.

Though he was skinnier and weaker than before, Sean was reminded of that old remark, *You should see the other guy!*

Sean wondered what made him fight so hard to live. During his recovery, he could have died many times. He was malnourished, had lost a lot of blood, and was constantly fighting infection. Yet no matter what, he somehow found the strength to fight. Deep down he knew it was because of Amy and Charlie—*and Michelle and Winnie*—but he refused to dwell on the exact reasons for his survival. The important thing was he *did* survive. So with his health and his two children by his side, things were looking up. Even if the rest of the world had gone to hell in a handbasket, he was content—if not happy.

Sean wasn't sure why, but something kept nagging at his guts. Even when he was enjoying the day with Amy and Charlie, walking along the small creek adjacent to the soldiers' camp, or regaling them with stories based on old movies he'd seen, Sean found he was anxious. If he was honest with himself, he knew why. However, he had spent weeks of recovery trying to block those honest thoughts from his mind. They were of his mother, and of course, Michelle and Winnie. When those thoughts came flooding in, even the most tender moments among Amy, Charlie, and him were ruined.

The questions in his mind were always the same:

Are they still alive?

Do they miss me?

Am I needed?

He supposed he would never know.

It was comical to him how he used to think this was such a small world, packed to the brim with people and technology, but now that it was all gone, he realized just how vast the landscape of earth truly was.

Even if I wanted to find them, how would I? If any of them had survived, they could be anywhere. Striving to make it somehow, just as I did.

A more likely scenario was they were dead, under the rubble, rotting away and never to be found for a proper burial.

Even worse-though Sean tried not to imagine it—*they could be mutants!*

2

When General Black settled the camp, Sean had hoped to find that they would be at an army base, filled with survivors and even some semblance of a working government. That was not the case, however. Instead, they were brought to a destroyed outpost that didn't garner much in the way of feeling safe. Sean was sure, whatever had happened in this place, wasn't good and it made him feel decidedly unsafe. Still, he felt there was strength and safety in numbers, and being a part of the general's entourage could only help.

Take, for instance, the way he handled the prisoners from the biker camp. They had been cordoned off using electrical laser fencing that the soldiers had with them. This fencing created a barrier that would hold the prisoners or fry them if they attempted to escape. Sean, Amy, and Charlie were not placed among these people. They and the rest of the women Sean had attempted to rescue were put into tents and allowed to roam freely through the camp.

Along their many strolls, Sean and the kids met many of the other survivors who had been a part of the camp before it was destroyed. Though it was in the process of being reassembled, Sean could not believe the happiness with which both the soldiers and the people of the camp went about their work. They had a hop in their step and they never stopped, even when it was quitting time. They just wanted to keep going.

Apparently it had something to do with a man named Reverend Althaus and his Religion of the White Light. Supposedly this new religion gave them all hope and made them want to work harder for the betterment of the world. Sean thought the whole thing sounded a bit hanky, but he didn't care; he just enjoyed having the pressure off himself so he could heal.

3

Almost every day, Sean, Amy, and Charlie would walk down to a little stream that was by the camp. Here, Sean would wipe away any tragic thoughts from his mind and enjoy watching Amy and Charlie play. Especially Amy.

She acted like a child now, picking flowers, jumping into the seemingly uncontaminated creek, and getting dirty in the mud. While he enjoyed seeing this, Sean's mind would play tricks on him. Instead of just seeing Amy, he would also see Winnie. The way Amy's demeanor had changed since they joined the army brigade made her seem like a completely different child. Her spirit had risen, and Sean couldn't help but draw a correlation to the only other child he had ever cared for. Though he tried not to compare, when Amy smiled or giggled out loud, the revealing and honest sound of the laughter that only a child could make hit him deep in his heart. With a pang of deep regret, he realized just how much he missed Winnie. Though it truly surprised and pleased Sean that Amy could be this way, it made him consider Winnie's fate even more. Which is why he started to hope beyond expectation that Winnie might indeed be fine.

Plus, what of my mother? He also wondered.

It still stung his heart to think the last she saw of him was inside a courtroom. If the image of Sean in jail was the last one in her mind as she died, Sean felt complete hatred for himself.

She deserved better than that! his guilt would tell him. *She deserved a son who would, no matter what, come after her and save her. She deserved a hero—not a criminal. How can I be that hero now?*

Trying to be a hero almost got him killed. He might have very little fear when it comes to helping those he cares about, but the outcome of those bouts of bravery hadn't really gone well for him.

Really, what more can I do? Walking off into the barren wasteland of this world alone does not seem like a very wise decision. Besides, if I left, what would happen to Charlie and Amy?

This question troubled him the most. He knew they couldn't come with him; it was far too dangerous, and it would be hard enough taking care of himself. They were safer among the soldiers or inside the prisoner camp. Either way, though, raised by soldiers or by prisoners, Amy and Charlie were better off versus following after him on a fool's errand.

How to make them see that? There lies the rub.

This much was certain: leaving wouldn't be easy; even if they accepted what Sean had to do, it would tear him apart. The fact was he had grown to love them, as much as he did Winnie and Michelle. They were his family now, and he couldn't imagine abandoning them as his father once had abandoned him and his mother. He couldn't simply go on wondering the rest of his life. He would always regret doing nothing about finding Michelle and Winnie, and therefore one day he would grow to resent Charlie and Amy for making him stay. Ultimately, that would be the worst outcome possible. Even if he died trying to find the others, it would be better than staying and growing to hate everyone he loved. Sean knew no matter what, he had to go. The only questions that remained were when would he leave and how?

4

"Everything okay?" Amy broke into his thoughts.

Sean looked at her and gave her a huge smile.

"Everything's perfect," he lied.

Althaus

1

Every nerve in Althaus's body screamed at him, and his bones stabbed every muscle. Althaus had hoped he would die in the fire, but the soldiers pulled him out, saving him for the medic to treat his wounds. The only problem was, his life, given what it now was, wasn't worth saving. Shriveled up like a burned piece of meat, barely able to communicate, Althaus was a shell of the man he used to be. Acutely aware of his surroundings and his pain, he was still unable to do anything about his predicament. Althaus hoped eventually he would just drift off into darkness and die.

What have I done? was the thought he kept asking himself, over and over. General Black had left him in charge, and he had succeeded in destroying the camp. He split the survivors, creating a religious war among them. Add to that the death of all those children in the fire, and Althaus knew he was deserving of the fate that had befallen him.

From top to bottom, Althaus's body was a disaster. Third-degree burns extended up his entire left side. The skin was covered with damp cheesecloth. Twice daily, the medic would spread ointment on his crusted skin. He smelled like rotting flesh and of a faint smell that Althaus could have sworn was bacon. The right side of his body had somehow survived without even the faintest discoloring, but unless one only talked to that side of him, Althaus knew he was a disgusting monster to behold.

What have I done? Is this some kind of punishment from God for my abandonment of him? No, I no longer believe in God. I have created a new religion, something for the new world! The true believers of the White Light know that this isn't punishment from some all-seeing, all-knowing being—it's just happenstance—just as the world destroying itself was happenstance. Besides, what can I do now, in this state? How can I be of use like this?

In his misery, Althaus wondered if he had the guts to do what those parents had done. If he could stay awake for more than moments at a time, would he be able to talk to the medic and convince him to hand over the white pills? He hoped so, but the fact was he didn't have enough energy to do that. All he knew was pain. Every second was agony, every minute torture, and every hour hell on earth. Honestly, Althaus couldn't understand what kind of future he could have, especially in this world—the broken world—in his broken body.

2

"He just woke up," Althaus heard the medic say.

"Is he aware?" another voice asked; Althaus recognized the voice as General Black's.

Thank God! he thought. *Black is here; he can fix what I have ruined!*

"So, how long has he been in a coma?" Black asked the medic.

Coma?

"Two months."

That's when Althaus heard it.

"Pain is white, remember the white light." Althaus heard this in his good right ear. He could tell it came from the voice of General Black. Since his return to camp, Black had come to visit Althaus several times a day.

In Althaus's mind, he answered back—*The light is hope*—but he couldn't vocally reply.

"The doctor says you are getting stronger. He says you stay awake for longer periods of time. That's a good sign, Barrett."

Althaus answered back with a moan.

"No whining now. The doctor says you are making fantastic progress. He says you're going to make a full recovery, except for the scars, of course."

Althaus listened, not sure whether the general's words were an attempt to make him feel better or some sort of exercise in torture.

"I've talked with most of the people left in camp, the refugees of your war." Althaus could hear contempt in Black's voice. "I think I have a good idea of what happened in my absence."

Althaus wished he had more energy to talk, so he could explain his side of the events. Unfortunatley he didn't. All he could do was think: *It's not my fault! I didn't throw the bomb. How could I have known the reaction of the people?* Althaus knew he did nothing wrong, but still, one aching thought kept ringing in his head: *What have I done?*

"I'm so sorry this has happened to you," continued Black. "I know you only wanted what was best."

Yes! Yes! Althaus shouted inside his head. *Maybe he does understand after all.*

"Your new Religion of the White Light is exactly what this world needs. I support it 100 percent."

Althaus couldn't believe what he was hearing; this wasn't the reaction he expected at all.

"I told you your power was bringing hope to the masses, and for those who stayed, for those who believed, they have found hope in your words."

Althaus groaned again.

"No, no, friend." Black grabbed Althaus's good hand. "Don't try to speak. Just listen. We will bring your new religion to this decaying world. We will make this the religion of everyone who stays. They will either accept it as their future, or they will call down the wrath of my army. I know that this sounds ominous, but this is the world we have been left and we must take control. If a few people die—people who deserve to—and in the end we have a better world, well, then the ends justify the means, don't they? Barrett, you have brought hope to so many, and I commend you for it. That is why, I promise you, I will hunt down every deserter from our camp, I will ferret out those responsible for the terrorist actions that led to your condition, and I will kill them. This I will do in the name of the White Light."

Wait, Althaus thought. *That's not it at all. That's not the meaning of the White Light.* Yet Althaus could do nothing to stop Black. He was in too much pain!

Black bent down to Althaus's ear and whispered, "The world will accept the White Light, or they will die."

Althaus began to shift around in his bed. He wished he could somehow find a way to communicate with Black—to tell him this wasn't the way! To stop Black from making even greater, graver mistakes. All he could do though was moan and writhe.

"Doctor," the general said, with deep concern in his voice, "please, he's in pain. Can you give him something?"

"Of course." The doctor quickly filled a syringe with medication.

Please! Althaus thought. *God help me explain to him—*

Unfortunately though, it was too late. The doctor injected Althaus with morphine.

As Barrett drifted off, he thought one last time to himself:

What have I done?

Aiden

1

The mountain range extended all around him. The isolation of the area alone was surprising, but finding the gas station still stocked with food and supplies, as well as the abandoned delivery trucks on the road at the base of the mountain, made this stop along their trek north perfect. Compared to the other stops on their trail, this was a paradise.

They had barely eaten anything since they left their brothers. Most of the places they found that might have had food had been scavenged already. Aiden and his companions subsisted off of rats and cockroaches mostly. Cats and dogs had become delicacies.

Given how we look, Aiden figured, *who are we to say rats and bugs are too gross to eat?*

If there had been anything good about the trip north at all, it was that they were able to take hold of more treasures. They carried with them twenty-five stolen women, all within childbearing years and all seemingly healthy. Aiden's theory about the normals along this path of fresh air and blue sky was correct. While not plentiful, they were there to be had.

Now the question was: *Are there more?*

2

Setting up a camp inside the gas station (it had a back storage room that was perfect for storing their prisoners), Aiden and his men got a good night's sleep—one of the first with a roof over their heads. Aiden found he dreamed of mating with the normal women, taking them each one by one and impregnating them with his uncorrupted seed. By the end of his dream, he had six wives with twelve children who were as healthy as could be. This had become a recurring dream for him. Being around the women he had captured had become a slow form of torture, which only let up at night as he slept. It was also more than that. He dreamed of this because he knew what they were doing was right. These dreams were his subconscious's way of telling him to hold the course—happiness was coming.

True, each day it became harder and harder to hold onto that, not just because of the ever-growing temptation or because of the added number of treasures they kept finding, but because his wounds and sicknesses were worsening. More often now, his lesions became infected and his growths were exploding. His eyelids had become hard to open due to the amount of inflamed tissue around them. His eyes were constantly stinging and yellowed from pus. Swallowing was revolting, as he could feel the growths inside his throat, and his fingernails had all but fallen off completely. Looking at the others in his condition, he was certain death would come for them eventually, which meant consummating with one of the normal women was of the utmost importance. It was his only guaranteed way of leaving a part of him behind. However, the fact was, not one of them had yet died.

Which is odd, thought Aiden.

Many of the people who lived in some of the small towns they had stumbled across on their journey had succumbed to radiation poisoning. Yet not Aiden or his brothers. It was as if, for some reason, despite being closer to the initial explosions and being met with stronger blasts of radiation, they were deemed worthy to survive, which was another reason Aiden felt justified in following the plan of the doctor. Why else would they have survived and continue to survive? This had to be someone's plan, didn't it?

Though no answer was forthcoming from anyone on high, Aiden found sleep easy and restful. Guilt did not invade his mind or soul, even when he could hear the sobbing or screams coming from the prisoners.

They deserved it, he thought. *They with their perfect skin and bodies—they deserved to be used as slaves. Until the world was no longer pestilent with infected humans. These women may feel scared and wronged now,* Aiden reasoned, *but eventually they will see their use was for the greater good. Then they will thank me and the doctor for giving their lives purpose.*

3

As night crept into morning, Aiden awoke with the first sign of sunlight. He was a light sleeper, so even the dimmest light would wake him from his slumber. Walking from behind the counter where he slept, Aiden entered a door along the side wall of the gas station. It went into the storage room. The place was rather large and filled with boxes of chips, drinks, and gas station supplies. For some of the women, that was a godsend, as they had begun having their cycle. Now they had access to tampons and pads, while before they had been forced to use whatever rag or towel they could. This reminded Aiden of why periods had been called *being on the rag*. Now though, for many of these women, the tampons represented a return to civilization.

See, thought Aiden, *they should be thanking me already.*

The captured women had been placed into a rather large fenced area. Inside it, the gas station owner had put tools and important parts to fix the gas pumps. Upon arrival, Aiden had everything removed, and he placed the treasures inside so they couldn't escape. Despite the twenty-five inhabitants, there was still plenty of space for more. As Aiden examined the area, he took long looks at each of the captives.

They were all sound asleep, dirty from their journeys, and some even huddled together for warmth due to the dropping temperatures outside. Aiden could see their flesh poking out of holes in their tattered clothes.

Bare breasts and thighs.

Though seeing them made him hard, which was very unpleasant due to the sores on his penis, he couldn't help but stare. The nipples of the women were still pink and large, the legs milky white, brown, or bronze depending on ethnicity. This excited him. He couldn't wait to touch their flesh.

Taking a moment, he sniffed the air around the area hard.

They stink so good, he thought. Like sweat and other ripe body odors which to him was intoxicating. He couldn't help it. They were just so healthy and perfect, far from smelling like the rotting, infected bodies that were found within the Tribe. Tribal women no longer smelled human, but like the dead, just as they were inside.

These women, Aiden salivated in thought, *are fresh!*

With that, he sniffed in long and softly, enjoying the flow of air. With that action, the sound of mucus and wind whistled through his nose. The sound was so loud one of the captives awoke and stared at him. They linked eyes. She was younger, maybe fifteen, and her skin was sullen, as she had lost weight from malnutrition. Aiden smiled at her. The cracked enamel on his teeth made brown streaks down and across, as if he had tic-tac-toe boards on each tooth. His gums were also puffy and filled with blood. The young woman turned away in revulsion. Anger filled Aiden's belly.

Just then, one of the other Tribesmen entered the basement.

"Aiden!" he called.

"Back here!" Aiden called back. Spit flew out of his mouth as he said it, landing on the girl who shunned him.

The other man arrived. He was large, towering over Aiden, who—if he was honest with himself—was never a tall man. Like many movie stars, Aiden was only about five foot six.

"What is it?" Aiden asked, annoyed at the interruption. Given the girl's behavior, had this unwelcome guest not arrived, she might have had a preview of the things to come. Now that would have to wait.

"We found something."

4

Standing at the top of the mountain, hiding in the woods behind trees and foliage, Aiden and his fellow brothers of the Tribe looked down into the valley.

A smile swept across Aiden's deformed face. What he saw delighted him.

A whole town of normals!

Willy

1

Willy tried to forget that the boy had seen him with Mary Anne, but he couldn't. Like it or not, Colin was a witness to his crime, and he knew something was going to have to be done about it. Thankfully, Mary Anne had been too frightened to go to anyone about her rape, and as far as Willy knew, so was Colin.

Plus how long would that fear last? Willy wasn't sure, which was why for the third night in a row, Willy placed himself outside the Kershaw home. Watching.

He watched the other night as the girl next door shimmied over to Colin's room. He also watched as Colin shut off his light each night to go to sleep. He even saw that hot piece of ass Quentin let go in and out of their house as she pleased—God knew doing what—although Willy could well imagine.

I'll have to pay her a visit, he thought.

Still, he did nothing.

It's not time, he reasoned. *But soon it will be.*

The big surprise of the evening came when Colin snuck out his window. He dropped a rope and awkwardly lowered himself to the ground. He had his bike propped against the wall of the house and quickly put himself on it. He was bundled up for the cold, but he seemed confused on exactly where he was going.

Now? Willy asked himself, considering some of the ways to kill the boy, but before he could come out from behind the bush, Colin was gone, off into the night.

Where is he going? Willy didn't know the answer. *No matter though, this is the perfect opportunity to kill him.*

Slowly, he began to follow the path Colin was taking, watching him as he went on his journey. On the way, he passed by Mary Anne Silva's old bed-and-breakfast. To his surprise, he saw a light in one of the windows that still stood. Some of the house was still standing, though most of it had been destroyed. That's when he saw her—through the window, blinking in and out of the candlelight that illuminated the remains of her ruined home.

Willy's attention was grasped. Her beautiful skin glowing in the candlelight intoxicated him. Looking down the street, he saw Colin ride away. He should follow Colin and kill him, he knew that, but Mary Anne was all alone and he wanted more.

No, Willy thought, *now isn't the time for Colin but it would be. And when it was?*

He'd kill Colin.

2

Willy spent the rest of the night inside Mary Anne Silva's all-but-destroyed bed-and-breakfast. Even though the home was in shambles, she had enough left that she was able to cobble together a kind of shelter for herself. Unfortunately, it wasn't enough to keep him out.

In the early hours of morning, Mary Anne took her final breath as Willy took her life.

No witnesses, Willy reasoned.

By the time the body was found—over two weeks later—people assumed she was killed during the battle for Bastion, which was just about to begin.

Quentin

1

Once they returned home, the heat hit overdrive. It seemed to Quentin that Louise was making up for lost time by bedding him every chance they got. She never left his house for the two weeks after they returned to it, and every night they made love. For the first time since being back, Quentin felt satisfied.

And it was because of all this time spent together that she was the one who noticed Colin hadn't made a noise in hours.

"I don't think he's here," Louise said.

"What do you mean he's not here? It's ten o'clock at night!" Quentin asked, sounding a bit too much like his father for his liking.

"Usually he comes down here at least to get food. I haven't seen him at all since dinner, have you? I hope he's okay," Louise said. True concern was in her voice. Louise got that sound in her voice when she felt sorry for some underdog or worried for the betterment of the underprivileged. She was definitely a bleeding heart. Quentin had heard it too many times in his life to care much anymore, though, especially lately, with her remarks about the state the world was in.

"I swear," Quentin said, "sometimes it drives me crazy my parents left me with this responsibility."

"It wasn't exactly their choice," she quipped back.

"I'll check his room," Quentin said, angrily stomping up the stairs leaving Louise alone. After a few moments he returned, the anger building inside him.

"Well?" Louise asked.

"Not there. He's got another hour, and then I'm going out looking for him. When I find his ass, I'm gonna kick the crap out of it!" Quentin said.

By the time the hour had passed, that sentiment had changed. Quentin's anger and annoyance had dissolved into worry and panic.

"Where the hell is he?" Quentin exclaimed to no one in particular.

"Maybe you should stop asking the air and go out and find him!" Her voice dripped with sarcasm, but Quentin knew it was for his own good. She was right, as she always was in these cases.

"Don't wait up," he said as he grabbed his military coat and headed toward the front door.

"You know I will."

With that response, Quentin knew at least one thing: even if she didn't want to get married, she did love him, and even though they weren't family, she loved Colin too.

"I'll be back soon," he said, and into the night he went.

2

The night was cold and damp. Rain had been falling for a few days as the summer humidity kept giving way. Normally Quentin enjoyed the summer rains, but this year was a little different. This summer Quentin hoped the rain wasn't radioactive. It seemed clean, but he doubted they would really know unless they all started growing extra heads.

Being an Army Ranger, Quentin knew the best ways to track a man in any situation. In this case, it took him no time to fall into old patterns and begin his search for Colin. Following the clues his brother left behind, Quentin would find him.

The first major sign was right outside their home. Colin had used his bike to leave, which due to the rain, left tire tracks leading in the direction of the town square. The bike wheels had been caked with mud because Colin had left his bike out overnight against the side of the house, which was surrounded by dead grass and dirt. This dirt became mud, and that mud became wheel tracks. Quentin realized finding Colin would be easier than he could have hoped.

As Quentin walked the night, he could see the candlelight peeking out the windows of different homes. He found the view from the street relaxing and peaceful. Quentin could imagine this was how it looked for the settlers during the wild, wild west.

Is that what the world is headed to now? A country full of outcroppings, town by town developing their own laws? Each person governed by his or her own sense of right and wrong?

Quentin rather enjoyed the thought of it. The world would be a much simpler place. Less global, more immediate.

The way it should be, he concluded.

As Quentin rounded the corner, he began to see the stores that adorned the town square. That's when he heard talking. Naturally a suspicious man, Quentin ducked out of the way. After he hid a few seconds in a dark corner of an alleyway, the voices began to be understandable. They came from two men—which two? Quentin wasn't sure.

"That's how we got to this point," the first man said in a deep, wise-sounding voice.

"I guess that's true," the second voice said, which was higher-pitched and mostly unsure of itself. Quentin knew he recognized the second man's voice, but he couldn't put a face to it.

"It's completely true," said the deeper voice. "You have to see the country, even the world, for what it was ... an overcrowded cesspool. There weren't enough jobs, resources, or basic supplies to go around. Had there been, we wouldn't have seen the huge increase of gangs or the loss of the big cities to the underprivileged. By the time the country was bankrupt, we had nothing more to give to anyone. With the loss of unemployment benefits, social security, even welfare, the country just became an even more dog-eat-dog place. If you were rich enough, you could live happily. If you worked as we did, then you could survive, but even we were considered lower-class. There hasn't been a middle class in this country for over forty years! That's ridiculous! Not to mention, below the lower class, there was only the destitute. Which due to the fact they had very little education, ideas like disease control, contraception, and even basic cleanliness were lost on them. The destitute class just reproduced, creating more and more mouths to feed, with little hope of providing for them. Do you know what the birth ratio was in the destitute class?"

"No," the other man said.

"The average destitute family had five and a half children. Five and a half! That's ridiculous. Average upper-class family? One. It's no wonder America couldn't self-sustain any longer. We're lucky it's even still floating and didn't sink under its own weight back down into the ocean."

Quentin smiled. *I like this guy's spunk.* He had many of the same thoughts himself. For sure, Quentin felt in this new world, the same mistakes couldn't be allowed to be made again. Population would need to be controlled somehow; jobs and food would need to be rationed out and given to all. He hated to sound Communist, because deep down, Quentin was all-American and believed in freedom, but ... *There needs to be some kind of middle ground in the future of this new world. Things have to be given and earned, but the new government needs to provide for everyone, and if they can't, then there need to be laws that control how many people live and suck up resources. I know this has to be figured out.*

He just wasn't the man to do it.

No sooner had he completed these thoughts than the two men came into eyesight. The deeper-voiced man was the black man of the group from the mountains, Frank. He was for sure a smart man, but now Quentin realized he was going to be one of the people who guided this world into its future. The other was easily recognizable, which made Quentin feel like an idiot for not recognizing his voice: it was Council member Mitch Mularky.

I should have known that! Getting rusty.

Which was when the whole conversation took a turn that surprised even a worldly man like Quentin.

"You know," Mitch said, "you are sexy when you're passionate."

"Am I?" Frank said, placing a gentle hand on Mitch's cheek. He then leaned in to kiss Mitch, but the councilman stopped him.

"Not here ... someone might see."

"Who cares?" Frank said. "You have nothing to hide from anymore. Anyone who might think they have something on you is gone now."

"Still, I'm not comfortable. You don't know this town like I do. I've avoided being outed for too many years. Paid too much money. Had to say too many antihomosexual things to stay elected. If I'm seen ...

Well, let's just say the ride I took through town at the end of a rope won't compare to what may happen next."

With that, Frank removed his hand.

"I understand," Frank said. "Come on, let's get to your place."

"It's not far."

In haste they were both gone. Their conversation quieted now, probably because romance was the only thing on their minds. Quentin didn't mind homosexuals. He had known many in the Army; some of them were the best soldiers he had ever known. It was the display of affection out of nowhere that surprised him, but he had to move on and get back to the search for his brother. He couldn't spend any more time worrying about Mitch and Frank.

Retracing his steps, Quentin came back to the bike tracks, which had been slowly fading as the wheels cleared of mud. Now Quentin knew he'd have to put his real skills to the test. The tracks ended right before the Great Tree. Due to the fact the road went into a circle around that area and four roads extended from it in a cross-like pattern, Quentin had to discern which way his brother would have gone.

Colin didn't go back the way he came because he wasn't at home. He might have turned east toward the school, but that seemed odd considering how much time they had recently spent there. He could have gone west, perhaps to a friend's house on the rich side of town; however, despite how much Quentin hated to admit it, Colin didn't have many friends, especially on that side of town. More than likely, he'd be beat up for going there anyway. That eliminated west.

Only one direction remained: south—toward the mountains. Unlike the mountains to the West, where Annette and her group had come from, these mountains weren't wooded. They were rocky, full of steep ledges and ice-covered glaciers even in summer. Most of Bastion's freshwater came from springs up there. If Colin was attempting to run away over those mountains, he had picked not only the hardest route, but a dangerous and deadly one.

Upon Quentin's realization of where Colin had gone, panic set in. Unless Quentin could get to his brother soon, he was as good as dead. Bears were known to prowl those cliffs, and though a road led over the mountaintop, if Colin was trying to sneak off, he would have stayed away from the road. This meant he would be climbing sheer cliff faces without training or equipment. Just then, Quentin realized what a failure as a brother he was.

I should have kept a better eye on Colin! Should have trained him better, not let him be such a slacker!

It was too late, though, and beating himself up wasn't getting him closer to finding his brother. The fact was, unless he found Colin soon, he would be dead. If the bears or the cliffs didn't get him, the dropping temperatures would. On a clear night, the temps in the southern mountains could get in the teens. Though not nearly as cold as the temps on the northern pass, it was still freezing to the common person. On rainy nights like that night, however, the temps would be even lower, perhaps below zero. Due to the rain, it would also be snowing hard up top, making Colin's visual acuity low, perhaps blinding him from way back. If he got lost, Colin had no prayer for survival.

Quentin did not wait a moment longer. He began to book it to the southern range. He had a sweater on and his lined Army coat, but as for protection for his hands and face, he did not have time to return home to get some. As Quentin arrived at the base of the road leading up the mountain, he knew he either returned with Colin, or he didn't return at all.

Colin

1

Colin was freezing, even though it was a summer night. The problem was a normal summer day in Bastion only got up to about eighty degrees. It was a humid eighty degrees, but it never got very hot. So up on the mountain, that meant it got to about forty degrees during the day, and it could drop to twenty at night. On this night, it seemed even colder.

He had been smart and layered two sweaters under his coat, but still, the chill was so sharp, his hands felt as if they were being placed into buckets filled with shards of glass. His nose and eyes didn't feel much better, but at least he had taken his brother's camouflage mask, which covered most of his face. That at least helped to keep him warm.

It had taken Colin most of the night to climb to the top. He figured it best to stay as close to the road as possible. That way he couldn't really get lost. Colin's biggest fear was getting turned around in the woods or coming upon a bear. Luckily, most of the bears stayed away from the main road, which before the attacks, was a major thoroughfare. All trucks, filled with food and supplies—even mail—had to come this way, which was the whole reason why he attempted to make this climb anyway.

Colin wanted to see if any supply trucks had been stuck up here when everything occurred, or if beyond the top of the ridge, other trucks laid in wait. It seemed reasonable to him there might be abandoned trucks nearby; and even though Chief Mankins had sent others to search for such things and they never came back, Colin tried to push his fear of death away. The whole goal of this was to be the hero, something he had never seen himself as, so that he could perhaps impress Kim enough to become his girlfriend.

It's possible, he thought, *though not likely.*

Still, if anything, he would show he wasn't just someone to be picked on.

2

Before leaving at nightfall (at 5:53 p.m., before dinner), Colin had grabbed his brother's wide-range, high-resolution, night-vision goggles. This way, Colin knew he could see what was around him during his trek and what was at the top of the mountain. The goggles had different levels of magnification, as well as heat-signature readings. Colin was surprised he got out of the house with them, and past his brother. He took that as a small victory and as a sign that some of Quentin's training was taking. Maybe when he got back home, he could tell him that before Quentin got too pissed off about the fact that Colin had run off.

Colin also realized at some point he would have to thank Louise for being the perfect distraction. Of course, she didn't know Colin had been planning on using her as such, but he would thank her anyway. After all, it wasn't Colin's fault his brother's IQ dropped six points when she was around. Colin just knew to take advantage of the fact.

So even though Colin barely knew how to use the glasses, he turned them on. Once working, they operated easily enough, practically on their own. From Colin's vantage point at the top of the road, he was happily greeted by the sight of several trucks whose drivers seemingly did just as he thought they might. However, he also viewed something far more sinister and disquieting.

There were forms down at the base of the mountain, surrounding the trucks, fighting over the scraps of rotting leftovers. They seemed inhuman, yet recognizable as something like human. They frightened Colin—but everything frightened Colin. They were strange, different, like monsters, yet familiar all the same.

What are they?

"Ahhhh!" Colin let out a scream as something grabbed him from behind.

"I'm gonna kill you!" Quentin said as he turned his brother around to face him.

Colin had been so gripped by what he was looking at, he had failed to keep an awareness of his surroundings. For a moment, he thanked

God it hadn't been a bear that crept up on him, but he realized his brother really wasn't much better.

"Do you know how dangerous it is coming up here like this? And why do you have my stuff? That's high-tech Army-issue you're playing with there!"

"I know. I took it 'cause I needed it. Which you'll be glad I did!" Colin tried to get out of his brother's vise grip, but it was impossible. When Quentin clamped down, it was like being caught in the mouth of a great white shark. The only way out was if he let you go.

"First, let me say I'm sorry," Colin said quickly.

"Yeah, not good enough," Quentin replied to his apology. "It's a good thing I took the road. Though every instinct I had said you were off the path, I somehow knew you'd be too afraid to venture that far out."

"Second, Quen, I came here for a reason."

"Oh yeah? What reason was that?"

"I came to see if we had food out there on the road."

"So you thought you could come out here and be the town hero?"

For a moment, Colin considered this. He didn't know what he thought. Mostly he just knew if he could fix the problem, he might look good to Kim.

Maybe it would get Kim to kiss me again.

"I don't know ... I just wanted to see is all," Colin continued. "I was coming back immediately to get you; I just didn't want to bother you about it first." Colin slowed down a bit, and he could feel Quentin releasing his grip. "You've just been so busy, with all the ... well, you know."

"Killing?" Quentin added coldly.

"I was going to say politics, but yeah, I suppose that fits!" Colin stopped. Quentin let go of him; the grip they had with each other now was only with their eyes. A silent moment passed between them. Something about their relationship had changed—Colin could feel it. What it was had yet to be determined, but deep down, Colin knew they'd never be the same.

"What was it you wanted me to see?" Quentin asked.

"Here," Colin said, handing Quentin the goggles, "take a look yourself."

Colin watched as his brother did just that. He put the goggles on, maneuvered himself into a flattened position on the ground, and began to look. Quentin's head moved slowly, back and forth, taking in the whole scene below. Everything about his movements was professional.

"What do you think they are?" Colin pleaded for some kind of answer, some reassurance, but Quentin didn't answer.

"Quentin?"

"Shhhh," Quentin said with a voice that sounded far away, lost in thought.

"I counted thirty of them," Colin said.

"There's more."

"There is?"

"Much more. This is just an exploratory group, a scout team." Quentin finally stopped looking, removed his goggles, and faced his brother.

"You think there's more of those?"

"Yes, and when they come, they're gonna kill us all."

Quentin began to walk away, back down the mountain. Colin stood alone in the dark a few moments, listening to the far-off hoots of the things below. A chill ran up his spine. Scared, he dashed off to catch his brother.

"What do you think they are?" Colin asked.

"They're us. They're deformed, obviously crazy, but they're what has become of the rest of the world. I have a feeling we are in a heap of trouble."

Nell

1

It was the third surprise inspection that week.

The general's men had been doing surprise sweeps through the prison camp looking for something, though Nell couldn't be sure what. From the questions they were asking, though, it seemed like they were looking for a person, not a thing.

Nell watched as they walked down the long line of detainees asking their questions:

1. Where were you during the raid?
2. How long had you been a part of the group before the strike?
3. Do you ride a motorcycle?
4. What did the leader look like?
5. Are we looking for a man or a woman?
6. Is there anything particular about the leader's physical looks you can tell us?

On and on it went, useless question after useless question. If they were looking for whom Nell thought they were, none of these people knew anything about him. Probably the only two people left who even saw him on the final day were Juanita and her.

She was obsessed with the idea that Stonehenge was still alive. Every day since she had experienced the shocking way people looked at her and Little Mark, she had decided to take long walks with the baby. Her hope was that she would spot Stonehenge. The walks were uncomfortable at first. Everywhere she went, she was followed by groups of admirers. After a while, though, it made her feel safe to have them with her. If she did run into Stonehenge, he'd have no way to attack her or to keep her quiet. Unfortunately, though, in all her walks through the camp, she hadn't found him. Which was surprising since he wasn't exactly a man who could easily hide. She was starting to believe seeing him had been only in her imagination.

Yet these constant inquiries from their captors began to change her mind yet again.

If they are looking for him, perhaps he really is out there somewhere. Hiding.

"What are they wanting?" Juanita said, the annoyance clear in her voice. These lineups clearly made her uncomfortable.

"I think you know," Nell said back.

"He's dead."

"Is he?"

Juanita gave her a look as she pondered the legitimacy of Nell's question. The fact was, Juanita had no idea what happened to Stonehenge. In her recounting of events after she confronted Nell and ran off into the battle, never once did she say she saw Stonehenge again. In complete disclosure, she said she went off to find him, to kill him, to cut off his member and stuff it down his throat. Disappointingly, however, the satisfaction was kept from her. Stonehenge was nowhere to be found. Juanita assumed he perished in the firefight.

"Where were you during the raid?"

Nell could hear the questions of the soldiers getting closer to her. She would be asked soon.

What answers will I give? Should I tell them my fears? Will they listen?

"Where were you during the raid?" the soldier finally asked Nell.

"Um, in my home, if you could call it that."

"How long had you been a part of the group—" Nell cut him off, tired of hearing his robotic-sounding voice.

"Look," she said with determination, "I've heard all your questions. I know what you're looking for. Do you want some good information? Then take me to the general," Nell demanded.

Juanita's eyes bore holes into the side of Nell's face. Little Mark, whom Nell had been rocking in her arms, had begun to cry, but all

Nell was doing was looking deep into the black visor. She didn't care about right and wrong—this might be her only shot for revenge.

"I cannot do that," the black visor said back to her. The voice coming from the mask was metallic and muffled. Quickly the soldier turned and began to walk off; Nell had to get his attention.

"Well, that's too bad, given the fact that the two women who knew the leader of our little band of bikers best happen to be standing right here." Nell sounded petulant, but she continued on with no care for whether she was pissing the man in the black-armored visage off.

"Is that so?" he said, turning back to them. He looked Nell and Juanita up and down. Then he noticed the baby. "Is that his?"

Nell brought the baby in close. "No," she said quickly, "but he killed his father, and we both know him very well. If you are going to find him, you will need us. That is, of course, if a man is what you're looking for. I could be wrong."

Nell stopped now, letting the pressure of the moment sink in. The soldier needed time to consider what she was saying. After a moment, he looked over to the two other soldiers who accompanied him.

"Take them," he ordered. The other soldiers grabbed Juanita and Nell by the shoulders, guiding them off toward the general's quarters. Juanita couldn't help but fight their hold a little bit.

"I hope you know what you're doing," Juanita said to Nell.

"So do I," she agreed.

Just as they said these last remarks, Dr. Sandberg walked out of his medical tent. He saw them being led away. Nell and he met eyes. She gave him no emotion back, just allowed herself to be led away, turning her head so their eyes could meet no more.

2

"That's a hell of a story," the general said after Nell finished telling him how she fit into this mess.

"It's true." Nell felt defensive; she had to drive the point home.

"Oh, I'm sure it is. Yet you say the baby isn't his? Now that, I find hard to believe." The general gave her such a glare Nell felt like she was in front of her father again.

"The man killed my husband. The baby is my husband's. I was already pregnant when I started doing ... what I had to. Believe me or don't, I don't care."

General Black let out a huge guffaw. It was overacting, but effective, as Nell was quickly silenced.

"I like your spunk!" Black said loudly. "We've captured a few of the bikers who've told us as much. So they corroborate what you're saying. They also said the man had a wife—Yolanda or something."

"Juanita," Nell quickly added.

Black looked at her suspiciously. "Yes. That was it. Have you seen her around as well?"

Originally Nell had wanted Juanita to come with her, to help her tell the general about Stonehenge, but Juanita was too scared about what might happen to her if she did. So, she opted to stay with Little Mark instead. Given how this conversation was going, Nell was glad that was what she did. It was clear General Black wanted Juanita not just for answers but maybe even as a prisoner. Nell couldn't allow that to happen. When Juanita agreed to stay with Nell and help protect her and the baby, Nell agreed to protect and hide her in exchange. Now was the moment she needed to prove her intentions.

"No," Nell answered back. "I just knew of her. She scared me to death."

"Hmmm."

"If I saw either of them, though, I'd kill them myself." Nell said this with as much determination as possible; she needed the general to believe she hated Juanita and knew nothing about her.

"If only half my soldiers had your guts," Black said with the smile of a proud father.

"Thank you," Nell said.

"So, here is what we're going to do," Black continued. "Tomorrow, you will go out with an armed escort. They will guide you through the camp, tent by tent, hovel to hovel, hell, even stone by stone, and you will see what you can see."

"If we find him?" Nell asked.

"You bring him here."

"Then I get to kill him?" Nell asked.

Black slyly smiled at her.

"Have I told you how much I'm beginning to like you?"

3

When Nell returned home, she could tell there was a problem with Juanita. She was too quiet, too angry-looking, even for her.

"What's the problem?" Nell asked her pointblank.

Juanita said nothing.

"I'm sorry if you're mad at me for some reason, but this is a great thing. We'll get what we want ... Stonehenge dead."

"No," Juanita replied. "You'll get what you want! I just want to forget. Rebuild my life. Now if they find me, they'll kill me."

"They won't find you," added Nell. "Plus if they do, I'll ask them to let you live. The general likes me; he'll do what I ask him to."

"You so sure of that, are you?" With that, Juanita began to walk away.

"Juanita! Wait!" Nell implored her.

"Good luck," was all she said as she walked off into the night.

Nell stood alone in the tent, holding Little Mark and hushing him, as all the commotion had disturbed his slumber.

"It's okay," she reassured him. "It'll all be okay."

4

The next morning, Nell set out with the soldiers to find Stonehenge. Little Mark came with her in a small sling she had fashioned out of an old shirt of Mark's. It worked well enough. At first, the search went quite smoothly, as they moved from section to section of the prison camp. However, once the word got around that she and Little Mark were out and about, things got very awkward.

A large group formed to follow them in their efforts. This greatly impeded their progress, plus gave a large warning sign to anyone trying to hide from them. By midday, the search had become nearly impossible. The group following her had grown in size to at least a hundred people, and those not joining to follow her were still trying to touch the baby for a blessing. All this attention really annoyed Nell, and soon she thought perhaps she was hurting the process more than helping it. Not to mention that every few hours they had to stop so that she could breast-feed.

This was the most awkward of all. As she nursed Little Mark, the other prisoners gathered around to watch her, as if it was some kind of show. There was just no privacy out in the open, so she knew she had to contend with the prying eyes, but the whole scene was just plain ludicrous.

During the feedings, she was able to scan the crowds for the giant. Though he wasn't there, she was able to get to know the people in the prison camp more. What she learned was she hadn't been the only pregnant woman around. There were at least twenty other pregnant women by her count, all in different stages. Even they were looking at Little Mark and Nell as some kind of hopeful sign that they too would be okay.

We are a group of horndogs, Nell couldn't help but think. *Even with the world destroying itself, we find time for sex.*

These thoughts made her laugh, but then sadness overtook her when she realized all these new children coming into the world were going to grow up hungry. Maybe even diseased. What kind of future could any of them possibly have, Little Mark included?

It was a bleak future to be sure. Nell also wondered, with this many pregnancies in this short time, how could this meager band of survivors and soldiers hope to keep a burgeoning population alive? The fact was they couldn't. Eventually, food and supplies would run out, and as generous as the general was, faced with his own death due to starvation, Nell figured the prisoners would be the ones left to starve.

5

By the time night fell, the search had yielded no results. That reality forced Nell to accept that Stonehenge must indeed be dead. She said as much to the soldier leading the expedition. He promised to pass on her feelings to the general and left her alone.

Stonehenge

1

Why won't the bitch leave me alone? Stonehenge thought to himself as he watched the girl from his hiding place.

She had been looking for him all day and was making his life even harder than it already was. It was difficult enough for him to try to hide, being as large as he was, but with her scouring the camp for him, she made it impossible for him to move about.

If it wasn't for the few friends I still have around, I probably wouldn't even be able to do that!

Yet they helped move him from tent to tent, never staying in the same place two nights in a row.

It bothered him to act like a coward, but what choice did he have? Stonehenge had never hidden from anyone in his whole life, never backed down from a fight, but sticking around here was dangerous.

I have to though, Stonehenge thought. *I need revenge!*

He was going to take that general down, the one who came in with his army, destroying everything Stonehenge built, if it was the last thing he did. Which it was likely to be. Sure, Stonehenge had never lost a fight before, but this was different. The general was protected by an army, one that was looking for Stonehenge. If they found him, Stonehenge knew it would be all over.

Which was why he had to stop the girl. Whatever that took.

Watching Nell now, he couldn't remember why he had even bothered to bed her. She was small, boring, prudish. *Cute? Undeniably, but still—too righteous.*

Stonehenge knew something had to be done. He knew she was driven; she proved that in his tent, as she did whatever she had to to get the medicine for her dumb boyfriend.

Man, I enjoyed killing that crip—he deserved it.

Stonehenge followed Nell now, staying just out of sight as a heavy

406

rain fell. Nell never noticed him; she was far too concerned with her crying baby to notice her surroundings. Stonehenge smiled to himself.

This is going to be so easy, he thought, *like shooting fish in a barrel.*

That's when he decided he was going to kill her.

Nell

1

Nell walked the rest of the way home in a rainstorm that seemed to complete the day. Little Mark was crying again; he was hungry and cold. Nell's whole body ached from the exertions of the day. All she wanted to do was curl up by some kind of fire, snuggle with the baby, and sleep. As she arrived at her tent, Brody Sandberg was standing outside waiting for her.

"Did you find what you were looking for?" Brody asked.

"Not quite," which was true. The question of whether Stonehenge was dead or alive seemed to be answered.

"Juanita came by," Brody said drily.

"Did she?" Nell said as she impatiently bounced the baby up and down in her arms.

He needs to be fed, she thought, *and this is preventing me from doing that.*

"She's concerned for you ... the decisions you're making."

"Oh, is she? Interesting how she never showed that concern when I was being used as a sex toy!"

Brody stopped then; he was simply silent.

"Look, it's been a long day, Brody, I'm tired. Just go."

"You want me to help you start a fire?" he almost begged her.

"Just go. I'll come by tomorrow and we can talk."

"Okay," Brody said, and off he went.

Nell felt relieved. She liked Brody a lot, but he was so serious. There was no way she could have taken his imploring questions and deep thoughts at that moment. Returning to the baby's cries, Nell bent her head down to his forehead and kissed it.

"I know," she said. "Here comes food."

With that, she entered her tent.

2

Just as she walked inside, a large, painful thump landed on the back of her neck. She fell forward with the impact, the baby flying out of her arms and onto the ground a few feet in front of her. Of course, the crying increased from a hunger cry to one of sheer terror and pain, the difference of which only a mother could decipher.

Disoriented, Nell turned on her back, grasping her neck. Looking down at her from on high was her worst nightmare.

It's Stonehenge.

"Why are you looking for me?" he screamed at her. "Just leave me alone!"

His arm came down upon her, crashing into her chest. Every ounce of air was pushed out of her. She began to crawl away, struggling to take in painful breaths.

"I just want to be free! Can't you understand that, you little bitch?"

He kicked her in the legs, but all Nell could really focus on was the baby screaming.

Need to get to the baby! she thought.

She began to crawl to Little Mark, every inch filled with pain.

"Since you insist on finding me, I thought I'd show my face, so you can remember it in the afterlife." With that, Stonehenge wrapped his hands around her neck and began to squeeze. They were so large and felt like a metal vise instead of human hands.

This is it, Nell thought as she struggled to break free but couldn't. She closed her eyes to think of something so that Stonehenge couldn't get his wish.

That's when she felt it: warmth and wetness across her face.

Nell quickly opened her eyes to see Stonehenge's face suddenly blank, red blood splattered across his neck and chin. His body toppled over to the side of Nell, blood squirting from a five-inch-wide gash across his throat. It was very deep, which made the blood flow hard. Nell could hear gurgles leaking from his throat as Stonehenge tried to breathe, but his life was just leaking out between his hands as he held his wound.

Nell looked at Stonehenge's attacker, who was covered in blood. It was Juanita, standing with a knife clutched in her hand. She looked possessed and scared, like a mad dog realizing it just bit its owner.

"Juanita?" Nell said lightly, trying to snap her out of it without shocking her.

Juanita's eyes darted over to Nell's.

"'Nita?" Nell said again.

"Better now?" Juanita asked, dropping her knife and leaving the tent.

Nell considered the question as she watched the last moments of Stonehenge's life pass.

I am better, she thought.

Much better.

Annette

1

"So what you're telling me is we've got enemies at the gate?" Annette said angrily.

"That's exactly what I'm telling you," Quentin reiterated.

The room was filled with the usual suspects within Annette's cabinet, plus a few extras: the new chief of police Olga Tymes, the mayor himself, Catholic priest Father Toller, Methodist pastor Pemberton, and the rest of the town council. Fifteen people in all.

"How many of them are there?" asked Chief Tymes.

"Enough to be worried about. Plus more every day. My brother and I have kept a watch on them for three days, and the group has grown exponentially every day. At last count, they had 350 or so." He let that number sink in.

"We outnumber that," Father Toller said.

Quentin agreed, "Yes, right now we do—by a lot. However, if they continue to grow in numbers, that may only last so long. Even if we outnumber them, they may be very hard to deal with. A battle is always unpredictable. Just because we have numbers on our side doesn't mean we can win. Not to mention what the cost of victory would be. No matter what, we'd for sure lose some good people in the process."

Annette was certain if there were a battle, the town would be lucky to have more than half of them survive. It was true, many in town were hunters and owned guns, but only a few had legitimate training in the armed forces, and most of the women and children would be useless in a fight. The town of Bastion could be very sexist; teaching women how to fight and take care of themselves hadn't been a priority. Here, women were expected to run the home, not protect it.

"So what do you propose we do?" asked Mayor Kreuk.

"First we need to assess the threat level," Quentin said.

"I agree," added Annette. "They could be like we were, just a group of survivors stranded and needing help. I suggest a group including me, you, maybe a few others go down there and introduce ourselves."

"I'm afraid I can't let you do that," Quentin replied.

"And why not?" asked Annette, her displeasure at the statement clearly expressed in her voice.

"Because you are too important to the leadership of this town. Honestly, no one on the cabinet should go. If something happened, you'd all be hard to replace."

Although Annette hated what Quentin was saying, she realized he was probably right.

"Okay," Annette agreed, "then who do you suggest to go?"

"I will pick my team carefully, taking the best we have. My plan would be to find out this group's intentions. If all is well, perhaps I'll bring them back. If not, I'll make sure we take care of it," Quentin said.

"And if you don't return?" asked Mayor Kreuk.

"Then you have your answer as to the kind of group this is. At that point, all bets will be off. And you'll need to find help," Quentin said earnestly.

"Help from where?" Pardham Singh broke in. He sat on the town council, and as the only Hindu in Bastion, he was always insisting on racial and religious equality. "As far as we know, we are the only people left alive in the world."

Frank nodded, "The odds are against that. There must be others. If that group is out there, so are more people like us."

"Plus what help will they be if they're not trained soldiers?" Annette asked.

"Exactly," Quentin said.

"So," the mayor broke in, "you want to go off and talk to these people ... and what? Leave us all defenseless? You're the best chance we have at defeating an invading force or whatever."

"That's true, and I appreciate that. However, if it is that bad, even I will only be able to protect you for so long."

"Either way, we won't survive long without you!" Councilwoman and Deputy Mayor Meredith Winston added. She was smart and cold, but honest. She always got to the point, which was a big improvement over how Mayor Kreuk operated. "I don't know that I trust you going over the ridge. We still don't know what happened to the others we sent out, and that was almost a year ago. Truth be told, I just don't want to die. We've survived this long. I'd hate to die now because we decided to become less isolationist. How do we know you're not just using this as an excuse to run off? Save yourself and your brother?"

"I guess you don't. However Bastion is my home. I want to protect it. I'm suggesting this course of action because I want to protect this town. If we are ambushed and killed, I swear I'll take them down with me. I won't let Bastion down. That much I can promise you."

Silence overtook everyone, each person lost in his or her own train of thought.

"Mayor?" Annette spoke up first, as usual. "It's your call. You're the leader of this town."

"Yes," he returned. It was easy to see how unsure of himself he was. "That is true; I am. Still, I don't know—"

"Can I give you my advice?" Annette offered. She could tell he was looking for a way out.

"Please," Kreuk said, waving his hands out in front of him as if to say, "Go right ahead."

"Quentin should go. If nothing else, he can get a better look at our surroundings and see if any other groups are out there, maybe hiding out of sight."

"Plus, I can scout for food." Colin had snuck in at some point and added this tidbit.

"Colin!" Quentin chastised him.

"We're running out! We need to find some."

"Excuse my brother, but he does bring up the other part of my plan," Quentin added. "There are trucks out there—we saw that—and we hope some more food is inside them. We won't be able to survive too much longer on the bare rations we have. We can't grow anything fast enough, and the rationing won't work forever. If we don't do something soon, we are going to starve."

"Obviously there is no debate then," Annette concluded. "You two must go. Definitely take Willy with you. Let us know who else you decide to take. With any luck, you all find an answer quickly. In the meantime, we should create a volunteer group of soldiers to help protect our borders."

"I can handle that," Chief Tymes offered.

"Good," said Annette. "Meeting adjourned."

"Before we go," Methodist pastor Izekial Pemberton broke in, "a small prayer for your return."

"I don't need a prayer, padre." Quentin grabbed his shoulder. "I just need my eye, my trigger finger, and a little bit of luck."

"God is luck," Father Toller added.

"Sure he is," Quentin said. "So's my gun."

Quentin grabbed Colin by the shoulder, and they exited the room. Annette watched, realizing their only true prayer, like Elvis, just left the building.

Black

1

The general stood over the body of Stonehenge as a medic treated Nell. Dr. Sandberg was also there; however, he was concentrating his efforts on Little Mark's wounds. The scene in the tent was gory, but even Black had to admit he was impressed with Juanita's handiwork.

"She did this all by herself?" Black said with amazement.

"Juanita is capable of many things that would surprise you, General," Sandberg said.

"That's what we've heard. It's too bad we will have to put her on some kind of trial; otherwise she'd really be useful. I suppose that's why this bastard liked her." Black kicked Stonehenge's body.

"Trial?" Nell said, moving the hand of the medic who was wiping her forehead clean of blood. With the hand gone, she had a clear look at Black's face.

"Of course," Black said. "We may be in a lawless world, but that doesn't mean we should behave that way. In war we have things called war crimes tribunals. We need to do the same with her. That would have been our move with him, but he's now paid the ultimate price for his crimes. Not her, though. From what we hear, she has plenty of crimes to pay for."

"Wasn't this what you were hoping for?" Sandberg spoke up.

"No," the general said, leaving little room for argument. "What I wanted was to capture this beast of a man and put *him* on trial. That would have been the example. But now that has been taken from us. As far as I understand it, Juanita was his second. She is just as guilty as him. So now she can pay."

The medic finally stopped working on Nell.

"You should be okay," the medic said. "Nothing a little ointment and a bandage won't fix."

"Thank you," Nell said as she moved to Little Mark, who, despite being flung through the air, also seemed absolutely fine.

"He's in perfect health. A few scratches and bruises. It's amazing, but babies can take a lot," Sandberg offered up as a diagnosis.

Two soldiers rushed into the small tent, making the cramped space even more crowded. Dragged behind them was Juanita. From the looks of her, she did not go with them quietly.

"We caught her trying to escape the prison camp, Sir." The first soldier said.

"A few more moments, and she would have been fried or gone, Sir." Added the second.

"Good," Black said. He bent down to Juanita and pulled her face up to take a look. It had blood on it and was beginning to swell. "Had to beat her into submission, huh?"

"Yes, sir," agreed the second soldier.

"You know I hate it when you have to use force. Oh well, put her in the brig. Also, start spreading around the camp that tomorrow there will be an important announcement at midday." Black barked his orders, and the soldiers saluted and then exited. Black continued, "I'll send someone to clean up this mess within the hour. We will see you tomorrow at midday," he suggested, as if saying: *be there.* "All this will be behind you soon."

"Please," Nell began, "she's been with me. I've been hiding her. Not from you, exactly, but from the camp. She has helped me. Kept Little Mark and myself alive. She protected me. She just killed her lover, for God's sake! She's a changed woman, I swear. Please let her live. For me. I need her."

"I think I've done enough favors for you," Black responded. "I wish you had told me this from the start. Yet, for whatever reason, you obviously felt the need to protect her from me. Now I will protect the world from her."

With that, he turned and left the tent.

2

Black arrived at the holding cell an hour later. He had taken a few moments to eat some dinner, though it wasn't much of one, due to the fact rations were waning. The holding cell had been erected after Black found out about the mutants. He thought he might need somewhere to put them if they came upon anymore. Now he was using the cell for a whole other purpose.

It was small, ten feet by ten feet, no padding, and open to the elements.

When Black arrived at the cell, he asked the two guards who had been watching Juanita's every move, "How is our guest?"

"Sir! She hasn't said a word, sir!" said the first guard.

"She has just sulked and given us dirty looks, sir!" said the second guard.

Black laughed at their report. *Of course, she did.*

"Let me out of here!" she hollered at the general as he walked up to the side of the cage.

"I'd be glad to. But I need to make an example of you," he said, devoid of all emotion.

"I'm one of the good guys!"

"We both know that's not true."

"What do want from me?"

"You're a good fighter," he said gently. "I admire that. I need people like you."

"People like me?"

"Oh yes," Black added. "My whole army is made of people like you. Hard-nosed fighters, unafraid to do what is necessary for the betterment of the country. Not that we have much of a country to better anymore."

Black laughed at his last comment. Juanita watched him closely. Black could understand her wariness; to her, he must seem half-crazed.

Still ... Aren't all geniuses half-crazed? Black reasoned to himself.

"You see, Juanita, I can give you an option. You can save yourself."

"Save myself from what? What are you going to do to me?" Juanita demanded.

"As I see it, we need to be ... how do the politicians put it? Tough on crime," Black stated. "In this new world, we don't have penitentiaries anymore; they're all destroyed. So what do we do with those who harm our new society?"

"I don't see a society," Juanita said, her voice filled with bravado. This angered Black. He was being fair to her, after all.

"Not yet you don't," Black snapped at her. "But you will. And when you do, it will be the dawn of a new world. One we will never allow to sink into the depths again."

"You plan to control it?"

"With an iron fist." Black stopped and cleared his throat. "Anyway, 'control' is such a loaded word. Let's say protect it, instead. Others will control it—others more capable of leading than myself. I'm not a politician. I'm a soldier. Which means I won't allow punks like you to destroy what we build. That's where this country went wrong. Too easy on the poor, too easy on criminals."

"You want to execute me?" Juanita asked, fully knowing what his answer would be. Black could have sworn he finally heard fear in her voice. This surprised him. At first, Juanita seemed unafraid of anything. Apparently death was the exception.

"I don't *want* to execute you. Still, if you force me, I will. If I am to set your fellow prisoners free, they all need to know who is in charge and what the price for breaking the laws will be." Black thought all of this sounded reasonable, and he hoped Juanita did too. "Juanita, save yourself from death and join me."

"How?" She was curious; Black could see it. He wondered if he could ask her do to just about anything right now. He guessed he could. She'd do it as long as it meant she didn't have to die.

"In the morning, in front of everyone, I will ask you to choose between death and serving in my army. If you join, you will dedicate your life to the protection of all who come under my leadership. It will be a tough life, but a life all the same." Black paused a moment, looking Juanita dead in the eyes. "Say no to that option, and we will execute you on the spot for all to see."

"You're serious?" Juanita asked this, holding back tears.

"Dead serious."

As Black began to walk away, Juanita was silent, thinking over his proposal.

"You have the night to think it over." Black let this remark end the conversation. He might not be the orator Althaus was, but he damn well knew how to leave an impression.

As he left, he looked back one last time. Juanita was huddled in a corner of the cage—crying.

3

Morning came.

The whole prison camp gathered at a small platform erected during the night. It stood right before the fence that held in the prisoners. It was an electrical fence, made from some of the soldiers' high-tech gadgetry they carried with them. The prisoners did not dare touch the electric-blue currents, or they knew they would fry.

On the opposite side of the fence, the soldiers all stood in formation. Like that, they looked like a truly formidable foe—all black and faceless behind their visors, all armed.

Near the soldiers stood Sean and the kids. They watched the proceedings as General Black walked by them. Not far behind followed two guards holding a prisoner.

"What are they going to do to her?" Black heard the little girl ask. Amy, he believed her name was.

"I don't know," Sean answered back. Black could tell in the tone of his voice that Sean had a relatively good idea of what was about to happen. He had experience in such things.

Placing Juanita front and center, Black looked at the crowd. They were hushed and intently waiting for the action to begin. Black began.

"We are at war. Not with each other ... with others who mean to do us harm. You have all experienced this. You have all been harmed by this woman and her man, Stonehenge. They held you all captive under his will. He hurt you all. For that, I am sorry. But we have rescued you!

Yes, we have kept you imprisoned, but it was only because we wanted to protect ourselves. Now that your ruthless leader has been killed and this one captured, I will be setting you all free!"

Black could hear a murmur fall over the crowd. This was what he had been hoping for.

"For your freedom, I ask nothing. You have two choices as I see it. One, you can walk away, leave with what you have, and try to carve out a life for yourself, and if we ever come upon one another again, we will see then if we are friends or enemies. If you stay, and I encourage you to do so, you will become part of the new society we are building. I have other survivors in my command. I protect them, as I will vow to protect you. Together, we will create a new world, one that will become a shining beacon in the centuries to come."

Again, his words created a buzz through the incarcerated crowd. Black looked behind him at his soldiers and, beyond them, the remnants of his original camp of survivors. They all began to clap at the general's words. He turned back around to the crowd and began again.

"There is a man, a very injured man, a friend—he had a vision for this new world. He lives on despite those who would prefer chaos. And because he lives, so do his ideas and words. You have all heard rumors of the man in the medical tent being kept alive by machines. I am here to tell you it is true. He exists. He still lives, and one day soon, he will rise up again to lead us. While he is not well enough to speak now—and I wish he were, his words are far better than mine—I can tell you he would offer you all hope! Hope of a bright future, full of new ideas, new laws, and a new religion. If you stay with us, you will be bound to this new way of life. If you leave, you must find hope on your own. We offer only that. Hope. Hope and protection. However, if you stay and you break the laws, there will be severe punishment—though you will have the opportunity to choose that punishment."

Black walked to Juanita and lifted her head up for all to see.

"This prisoner helped to subjugate you. She murdered innocents so that her man could control you. Yes, she has killed him. Yes, it was a noble act that he deserved, but does that erase her crimes? We cannot, in this new world, let people's crimes go unpunished no matter how much they've changed; instead, she must answer for her transgressions.

As you can see, she has been unharmed, again because in this new world we will strive to be better humans than the ones who controlled the world before us."

Now everyone was applauding; both communities were in full agreement on this.

"I have given her a choice. She can either join my army of black marauders for an unset amount of time—it could be the rest of her life if she were to perish in battle—or she can die now, executed for her crimes. I have given her the night to think about it. Now, we ask for the answer."

The crowd cheered once more. They wanted to see her pay for her crimes either way. Black hoped she was smart. As much as he was willing to kill her, he did not want to start this new era out on such a low note. Furthermore, it would be such a waste of a good fighter.

"Juanita! Murderer and perpetrator of wanton human suffering. For your crimes, you have been given a choice of servitude and life, or death. What is your choice?"

Black surveyed the crowd. A hush fell upon them. This type of control was intoxicating. He could understand why Althaus had become so good at it. It was quite a rush. Yet this was work for someone else, not a general. This was work for a man like Althaus, who could better balance the rush of power.

Black looked back at Juanita, who had yet to answer. She looked at him, her eyes filled with tears and pleading. Caked with the dry blood of her victim, she was not sympathetic-looking at all. Even if the crowd had felt sorry for her, the telltale signs of her crimes kept them angry with her. They began to yell obscenities at her as they awaited her answer.

"Well?" The general insisted on her answer.

She took a deep breath as tears came pouring out her eyes.

"Death!" she screamed.

The crowd erupted in joyous applause. They seemed elated at the outcome. For a moment, Black felt the situation had steered out of his control. This wasn't how it had played out in his mind. Yet what choice did he have now? This was her answer, and the sentence must be carried out.

Black bent to Juanita's ear and whispered, "How disappointing."

Black raised his gun to Juanita's head. The crowd applauded the move.

How uncivilized is this? Black thought. He had hoped the new world would have started with a whisper, not a bang.

So be it.

He pulled the trigger.

Bang!

Silence fell over the crowd.

Juanita fell limp to the ground, smoke climbing into the sky from her caved-in skull. Thus the laws of the new world began. With a death. One of many deaths the new world would be built upon.

Black stepped forward one last time.

"Tomorrow, we journey from here, north into Wyoming, to a hidden base filled with supplies and food. I will provide for those who follow." Black turned to some of the guards of the prison camp. "Cut the line. They are all free."

The sky broke out into a final cheer as the blue electrical current went dead.

Colin

1

"I can't go!" Colin pleaded with his brother.

"We need you; I've trained you for this," Quentin said in reply.

"I'm not good enough—I'll get myself killed."

"Do you think I'd let anything happen to you?" Quentin looked him straight in the eyes. "You know I'd give my life to protect you."

"I don't want you to do that. I'd be better off here ... safer." Colin thought maybe that would be something his brother would agree with.

"I'd feel better having you with me. If you stay here, I can't protect you. With me, I know you'll be safe."

"I don't know about that," Colin said under his breath.

"What do you mean?"

"I mean Willy." Just saying the name sent panic through Colin.

"What about him?" From Quentin's tone, Colin already knew he understood the issues, but he was trying to deny them.

"You know exactly what about him. The way he killed Winston Deerdorff ... and ... I just don't trust him."

"I'm your brother, Col. I will always be there for you. I promise to keep an eye on him, and believe me when I say that if I have an eye on someone, that means day and night. It's not an eye someone wants on them." Quentin put his arm around his brother. "Okay, I admit it, he's a problem to be sure ... a loose cannon ... but he's also a good fighter, and unfortunately, we need him right now. I promise, though, when this whole thing is over, we'll deal with him."

"You going to kill him too?" Colin asked, sure the answer would be yes.

"Of course not!" Quentin was angry now. "Is that what you think of me?"

"No, I just—"

"I'll tell the chief to look into it. The chief will be coming with us anyway. If anything goes wrong, we'll arrest him or something. As it is, right now, we are shorthanded and we need him. Sometimes in life, that's the way it is."

"The devil you know," Colin said in agreement.

"Exactly," Quentin agreed. "Colin, if he even so much as looks at you crooked, I'll kill him before he has the chance to run."

Colin knew it was true. There was nothing Quentin wouldn't do for him. He just wished that made him feel good about going.

"Let's go," Colin finally agreed.

"That's my boy."

Willy

1

This is the moment.

He was sure of it. Out there in the woods, away from the town and their prying eyes, Willy would finally get the chance to take care of business. When Colin least expected it, Willy would ambush him, leaving his body lying off in the woods. He would discover it, seemingly by accident, and play it off as if he had no idea how it happened. He would tell Quentin, "It must have been the mutants got him. He must have been discovered and killed by them."

It will work, he told himself; *it will be believed.*

Soon, Willy would be free of his burdens and able to begin anew.

And if Quentin didn't believe him? Well, I will just take care of him too.

Nothing would stop Willy from living on.

Nothing.

Sean

1

"Well, I'd hate to see you go," Black said to Sean while looking at a map on a desk in his tent. "You seem like a resourceful guy; could have used someone like you around."

"I appreciate that, General," Sean replied. "But I have to go to California. If I follow you to Wyoming, I'm getting farther and farther away from that goal."

"I understand," Black said. "It's hard to abandon the ones we love."

"They're out there. I'm sure of it."

"You have a lot of positivity and strength. I hope that helps you on your journey. I'm afraid I feel it's probably a fool's errand, but that's for you to discover."

Black held out a hand and Sean shook it.

"Well, assuming Wyoming has what we're looking for, then you'll know where to find us. If it's not, we will move on. Either way, if you can find us, you're always welcome."

"Thank you, sir."

With that, Sean left the general's tent and headed off to find the children for the hardest part. It was time.

2

"Listen, you two, we need to talk," Sean said, sitting down in their tent. "I have to go."

"Where?" Charlie innocently asked, not understanding the full weight of Sean's words.

"When will you be back?" Amy followed up.

A pang of guilt filled Sean's heart. He fought through it and continued on. It had to be done.

426

"I won't be back. At least, not for a while." Sean said this with as much strength as he could muster. He could feel the tears welling up inside.

"I don't understand," Charlie cried.

"He's leaving us, you idiot!"

That was the first time in weeks Sean had heard Amy speak ill to her brother. He realized her walls were flying back up. This saddened him. It took him so much time to get her to accept that it was okay to be a kid. Looking into her heartbroken face, Sean realized she would never be a kid again.

"Why are you leaving us?" Charlie asked.

"I have to," Sean simply stated, hating himself the whole time.

"It's 'cause he used us. He used us to stay safe. And now that he's safe, he's ditching us!" Amy struck out, pushing Sean with all her might. Her anger was apparent. It was then Sean realized he was probably scaring her forever. Even if he were to ever return, their relationship would never be the same. This was a heartbreak he could never repair.

"You know that's not true." Sean tried to reason with her, but he knew that that was an impossibility. "I got you here, safe with these people. I risked my life to do that. Now there are others who need me. Others whom I was going to try to find before I met you. One of them is a little girl. She's like a daughter to me. No to mention my mother ... They're out there, and I love them. I need to find them."

"Oh, you're just everyone's hero, aren't you?" Amy's voice dripped with absolute hatred.

"Amy ..." Charlie said to his sister. He seemed to be understanding, though his sister wasn't.

"You two will be fine," Sean said, trying to alleviate Charlie's fears.

"You're right, we will!" Amy pushed him again. "Get out!"

Sean started to take steps away from them.

"*Get out!*" Amy screamed, kicking her legs at Sean. He grabbed her and pulled her to him, trying to calm her by giving her a hug. However she just kept on flailing at him, repeating, "*Get out! Get out! Get out!*" until her face turned bright red.

Charlie put his arm around his sister, who sat in the corner of the small tent, her head between her knees, crying.

"Amy?" Sean called out.

"Just go," said Charlie. "She'll be fine."

Sean watched in anguish as Charlie just held his sister, for the first time since Sean met them, acting like the older brother he was. "It'll be okay," Charlie said. "We'll be fine. I'll protect us. I promise. I'll keep us safe."

Sean couldn't stand it any longer. His heart broke with every word. He had to leave. There was nothing more he could do for them except that. The longer he stayed, the harder he made it on them. Slowly, Sean turned and walked out of the tent, leaving for what in all likelihood would be forever.

3

After gathering all he could—water, some food, and a knife for protection—Sean walked out beyond the borders of the camp, into the unknown. His journey would take him west, away from safety.

As he walked, the sky grew cloudier, the weather became cold, and a winter's snow began to fall. The odd thing was, it was the end of June. Sean realized this wasn't winter, but instead, the nuclear fallout.

All Sean could do as he walked mile after mile into the darkening distance was think of Charlie and Amy and hope that he wasn't too late to save Winnie and Michelle.

Maybe even his mother.

Aiden

1

They had seen the group descending from the ridge about an hour before they arrived. This allowed Aiden and his group to prepare for them, making sure the treasures were well-hidden and that they had their weapons ready—though concealed, to not create a problem until there was one. As they got closer, Aiden wondered what they wanted. They had obviously sighted them from above and wanted to talk, but what would they react like when they finally saw Aiden and his Tribe up close? So many normals freaked out and tried to fight with them.

Will this be the same? Aiden figured it would be, so he had his Tribesmen at the ready.

After about another half hour, the contingent was within a stone's throw away. Aiden could see there were eight men and one tall and exotic woman dressed in a police uniform. Immediately Aiden started to make plans to take her.

As this group of nine normals made their final approach, Aiden could see their faces as they took in the sights of Aiden's group. Their eyes flickered with disgust. Some of the people even had to look away, especially the youngest one. He just began to stare at his feet instead of them.

Coward, Aiden thought.

"Can I help you?" Aiden asked. He was surrounded by a group of twenty Tribesmen set up in a semicircle just off the road leading up into the valley. The gas station was about sixty yards away, and Aiden made it so they were a threatening-looking group.

"Actually, yes, you can," said Chief Tymes in an authoritative tone. She was obviously trying to avoid showing how uncomfortable she was at their appearance by continually not linking eyes with him. "We're from the town over the ridge. We saw y'all down here and wanted to welcome you—"

"Welcome us?" Aiden said skeptically.

"Of course!" said Tymes, as if he was being silly thinking anything else. "We also wanted to talk to you, you know, to ascertain your intentions."

"Ascertain our intentions, huh?" Aiden turned and looked at his group. He began to laugh. "She wants to know what our intentions are," Aiden said to them, and they all began to laugh back. Quickly he turned back. "Well, we came here to tell you all to hand over your women of all ages, so that we can repopulate the world."

"What?" said one of the men in the chief's group. He looked like a soldier, and he was young and handsome. Aiden hated him immediately.

"We are going from town to town and collecting healthy women so that we can repopulate the world and clear it of people like us. We are mutants. Changed by the radiation left from the attacks. The only way to fix it is to breed it out. Understand? It's beautiful."

"Beautiful?" said another man in the group.

"Why, yes," Aiden responded. "It's so simple and easy. Enjoyable too, if you know what I mean."

"I ... umm ... I don't think ..." Chief Tymes tried to say something in return but was so dumbfounded she was at a loss.

"Please, don't hurt yourself trying to think," Aiden said. "We will do that for you. All we need from you is your womb. As for the rest of you, you can either hand over your women peacefully ... or we'll take them any way we have to."

Aiden saw one of the men fumbling with his gun nervously. He didn't wait to see what happened next. Violently grabbing Chief Tymes by the neck, he turned her and grabbed his gun from its holster, putting it against her head. Others in her group pulled out guns as well, but not before Aiden's Tribesmen opened fire. Several of the men fell instantly, shot in the head or chest. Others, like the little boy, ran.

"Let them run!" Aiden said, halting his Tribe from chasing them. "We'll find them later."

Leaning down to Chief Tymes, he allowed a long piece of drool to lave his mouth and fall upon her cheek.

"Welcome to the Tribe," he said.

2

As they returned to the gas station with Chief Tymes—another treasure for the doctor—Aiden tried to form a battle plan. It was clear they would have to have a very good plan to take this town. He knew they were outnumbered. Unfortunately, Aiden did not know much about leading a battle charge. He knew some basics about hand-to-hand combat due to being in so many action movies in his long film career, but leading an army into war was not something the doctor had prepared him for—if he even could have. One thing seemed obvious: he needed to take the town by surprise and hope to overpower them by putting the fear of God into their souls.

How to do this, though? That was the question he kept asking himself.

Thankfully, a few of the new members of the Tribe from Canon City had fought in the war. They had learned quite a bit from watching the Muslim Insurgency operate within the city streets of Paris and the French countryside. They advised Aiden on the way to do battle with a town such as this. The term they used was *guerilla warfare.*

Aiden had heard the term before, but how it was going to relate to the taking of this Wyoming town—Bastion—he couldn't be sure. The former soldiers, and now brothers of the Tribe, explained to him the plan: it was simple and effective. If all went as planned, it would be more about "shock and awe" and less about murder, which Aiden liked. He wanted to invade the town, steal their treasures, and get out with the fewest casualties possible. Deep down he knew that was a foolish thing to hope for—war was war, and there was always death—but as a celebrity, Aiden used to speak out against needless tragedy, which made it hard to now be a proponent of it. The plan the men came up with seemed sound, so he sent them off to prepare the group for battle.

In his heart, Aiden knew taking this town, filled with normals and their women, was the best thing for the future of the world; nonetheless, he felt ashamed. It was like a moment of clarity. His mind became open, and it began to think straight as the noise and pain of his situation in life seemed to leave him.

Is this really necessary? he asked himself, surprised that he would question the doctor. *Still, though, is it?*

Aiden knew he could not share these thoughts with anyone. He had built quite the army of the infected by selling them the idea of hope in the doctor's ideas. Changing that now would just lead to chaos and probably even more death. Suddenly the noise and the doctor's words came pouring back into his mind.

No, Aiden thought to himself, *it's all or nothing.* He couldn't live with himself if it turned to nothing.

That's when he realized the clash was inevitable. *Normals and Tribespeople could never coexist. Things could never be the same. They were enemies to each other, both vying to control what was left of a world that had been turned into something any sane person wouldn't even want. Yet what choice did they have? This world was all they had.*

Taking a deep breath, Aiden steeled up his resolve. It was time for the Tribe now.

It was their world.

Althaus

1

As he drifted in and out of sleep, Althaus dreamed. His dreams were chaotic and often incomprehensible. There was always movement in his dreams, as if his body somewhere in the real world was being driven forward by some kind of unknown force. It was like an out-of-body experience; the feelings and steady rhythms pulsated through his body, but his unconscious life inside his medicated existence was all he saw. His dream state was all that was real.

2

Althaus walked along the dirt. Each step kicked up dry dirt and ash, which had turned dark from the thousands of burns each grain had received during the nuclear blast. The sky was red with fire, thick with smoke, and brittle to the skin due to the fragments of human remains drifting in the air. This stung him. Ash could be seen falling in heaps all around, little piles gathering, filling the remnants of clothing once worn by the people who had been turned to shadow.

Bright white light ushered him away, transporting him to another unknown time and place.

The light disappeared. Althaus found himself falling. Falling through clouds. Fluffy, soft clouds at first, then harder, thicker ones, like melted marshmallows and just as sticky. Wind whistled by his body as it tumbled weightlessly down to earth. Despite knowing this was just a dream, Althaus could not imagine wings for himself. Flying, as in real life, was out of the question. In moments, he would land splat on the ground.

Looking down toward the fast-approaching ground, Althaus could see hands sprouting from the ground, reaching upward to grab him. They would break once they caught him; the force of his fall would make sure of that. Yet to his surprise, he landed like a feather upon a mattress. The gentle hands received his weight and didn't even so much as wilt. They simply broke his fall and passed him along, like a deity or rock star.

Guiding him further along on his journey, the hands exalted him. Althaus closed his eyes to feel each finger and palm as he went. Then the sound of a rushing ocean or river broke his peace.

He opened his eyes just in time to feel his body being plunged into a liquid substance which wasn't water. Instead, it burned his skin. The sound he was hearing wasn't water rushing by, but flames engulfing him. Electric pain flew across every inch of his skin as white light again consumed him.

This time, he found himself in a lush green landscape spread out over mountains. The mountains quickly caught fire with Althaus's every step.

He was destruction walking, the devil incarnate.

The flames spread throughout the mountainside. Every tree, animal, and life-form burned in Althaus's wake. He was bringing hell with him, passing judgment on the world.

Suddenly, the flames stopped. Blackness spread out around him. There was no sound ... only void. Althaus's body was badly burned, as it was in the real world, but he no longer felt any pain. He was just a badly scared stump of a man, wandering through the empty darkness alone.

Crunch!

He heard that sound over and over with every step he took.

Crunch! Crunch!

Althaus was walking on something hard, delicate, like porcelain or glass.

Crunch! Crunch! Crunch!

The sound was awful. He wanted to know what it was, so he reached down into the darkness. In his hand now was a large oblong-shaped object. It had ridges with chipped edges. The rest of it felt like smooth alabaster, cold and chalky to the touch.

Rubbing his opposite hand over the front, he could feel a long ridge, below which the object dipped into a cavernous hole. Coming out of the hole, the object crested again before falling into yet another hole. The object was beginning to take shape in Althaus's mind. As a blind man might, he continued on, using his fingers to peel away the dark. Moving his hands down from the holes, he felt a ridge jut forward into spiny, rectangular nodules. Then another ridge, which also had a set of the nodules. However, this ridge moved up and down with the movement of his hand. Like the hinge of a door, or a mouth opening and closing.

Oh, no! Althaus thought.

It was a skull!

Althaus dropped it.

Crunch!

The sound emanated from the skull hitting the ground. As Althaus began to run without direction in the darkness, the sounds got louder.

Crunch! Crunch! Crunch! Crunch!

Then the sun rose large and quickly in front of him. The sun was burning orange with flame, creating a heat wave that encapsulated everything around him. Althaus could feel the heat from the sun against his already-fried, crusted skin. The black void was now full of light.

Hot, white light.

Althaus looked down and realized he was standing on mounds of bone. Skulls and fingers, femurs and spinal columns, jutted out in all directions. Some large, some small. Baby bones mixed in for good measure.

What were these bones from?

Althaus began to sink down into them, like into a sinkhole. The bones began to swallow him whole. He grabbed for any footing he could, but the bones simply turned to dust as his fists closed tightly around them.

Pain is white, remember the white light, the light is hope.

The phrase echoed all around him.

Where was it coming from?

Pain is white, remember the white light, the light is hope!

Repeatedly, Althaus heard his disastrous proclamation. It rang out so loud the sound began to hurt his ears. Placing his palms over them, he tried to blot out the noise. It didn't work. Louder the chant grew as blood began to pour out of his ears.

Pain is white, remember the white light, light is hope!

Now he could register where the sound was coming from. From the skulls mixed in with the bones. They were screaming! Screaming out in pain! These bones were in pain.

That's when Althaus realized what the bones were. They were the remains of the survivors. The ones he had already failed, and the ones he was going to fail in the future. These were the bones of his victims.

With that realization, Althaus was sucked down deep into the cavernous never-ending sinkhole of jagged bones, suffocating under the weight of his own guilt.

3

Inside the medical truck, which was on the move with General Black's caravan, Althaus was convulsing on his stretcher. Though he was hooked up to a breathing machine, the medic had to intubate through the scar tissue along his throat so that he could place another breathing tube down his esophagus.

Without it, the medic knew Althaus would suffocate to death. General Black had given one order to the medic before they began their journey north to Wyoming: keep Althaus alive.

The medic planned to do just that.

4

On and on the dream repeated.

Althaus experienced only constant pain and this prophecy of doom. It continued for the length of the long, terrible journey north.

Part Five:

The Rising

Annette

1

Bastion was surrounded.

It didn't take long for everything to go to hell after Quentin, Colin, and Willy left. Annette had put three lookouts on duty at the top of the North face of the mountain. Every five hours, they were relieved of duty and replaced by fresh eyes. While observing from afar, it was plain to see the number of mutants was increasing. However, Annette wasn't really worried. She was silently confident the mutants couldn't outflank them.

As it turned out, the mutants weren't as brainless or crazy as they seemed from a distance. They had kept using the northern group as a distraction for the lookouts and moved a second, larger group around to the South. This group began to put themselves in position around the town for an attack. Not only did the mutants know Bastion was there; they had a battle plan on how to take it over.

At night, they attacked in small groupings hitting any site they could. The first night they got lucky and burned down the Great Tree. That act alone did more to destroy the morale in the town than all the infighting that occurred when Annette and her group arrived. In retaliation, some of the men in town went looking for the mutants who burned the tree, despite Annette's warnings to the contrary. When day came, those four men's heads were found placed on the spokes of the metal fence that surrounded the police station, further creating a sense of fear.

The grotesque sight, complete with bloated skin, swollen tongues drooping from open mouths, and eyes rolled firmly into the back of their sockets, continued to make everyone paranoid. People worried that at any moment, they too could be decoration. With such fear spreading, it was no surprise to Annette that Bastion was becoming a ghost town after sunset. People were tightly locking their doors, even sticking furniture in front of windows to barricade themselves from the monsters outside. Annette feared if anything else happened, everyone in town would become shut-ins. After that, Bastion would be lost.

Annette hoped all these terrible events might galvanize the townspeople into acting. They were all too quick to act out against Annette's group; however, without assholes like Winston Deerdorff, Brooks Nolan, and Clifford Montgomery, the townspeople seemingly had no backbone. If something didn't change quickly, every soul in Bastion would be dead.

Although as nights went on, Annette could swear she heard gunshots off in the distance, on the mountains, she had no idea whether that was just her imagination, the mutants trying to intimidate them, or maybe even Quentin and his group fighting for their lives. If it was Quentin and his group, that meant things had gone terribly wrong and that the mutants were a true threat. To her, this meant things looked bleak. Since she hadn't heard from Quentin, she had to assume the worst. Unfortunately for her and the town of Bastion, though, the worst was yet to come.

2

It was almost a week into the nightly attacks that the first young girl went missing. The abduction happened around eight o'clock at night. She was supposed to be inside her home with her parents, but decided to sneak out to see her boyfriend instead. Her scream of terror was heard throughout Bastion, though it did nothing to help. By the time her parents reached the spot where her scream had come from, only her scarf remained. Her name was Alice Summerman. She was fifteen years old.

Around nine forty-five on the same evening, another girl was taken, this time from the window of her own home. Her parents had no idea she was even gone. They only found out Raine Packard was missing because her father went to check on her after the news about the Summerman girl had reached their home. After knocking and receiving no answer, her father walked into a gruesome sight. The window was wide-open, wind blowing the curtain like a floating ghost, and blood was splattered all over the windowsill. Either she had fought her attacker, or she was bleeding profusely herself. Mr. Packard hoped for the former.

It was at this point that a town-wide search began. Everyone who was willing was sent out into the woods surrounding Bastion to help locate the girls and kill the monsters that abducted them. Unfortunately, the mutants had calculated for this. As the townsfolk entered the woods, guns in hand, torches ablaze, they were struck down by booby traps and quick-striking teams of mutant attackers. Many searchers, mostly men, fell victim to hollowed-out pits in the ground, laced with spikes, plunging to their deaths in an unenviable way: skewered like lamb on a kabob. Many others, as they walked, tripped a wayward branch that freed logs that fell on top of the searchers, flattening them and breaking every bone in their bodies.

In all, by the time it was clear to everyone what was happening, fifteen men were killed, including both Mr. Summerman and Mr. Packard. At that point, even Annette had to admit Bastion was under siege. She had underestimated their attackers, who had used that to their advantage. While they distracted Bastion's citizens with pointless violence and raids, they had used the cover of night to make the forest, once Bastion's saving grace, into a death trap.

By two in the morning, six more young girls had been kidnapped—either taken from their homes or taken while they were out helping search for the others. With this, the demoralization of the town was complete. The fight was taken completely out of everyone, and hope for rescuing the missing girls was fading. Annette, being the type of person who liked to make lists, compiled one of the names and ages of the missing. Along with the Summerman and Packard girls, the list now included:

Zoe Shannon, age 10
Patricia Grandy, age 16
Bella Miller, age 18
Cindy Adlard, age 11
Kimberly Cooper, age 13
Evelyn McDuffy, age 14

As far as Annette could tell, there was nothing the girls had in common other than their sex, which made her wonder for what purpose they were taken. She hoped it wasn't as diabolical as it seemed, and instead, just another tactic to strike fear into the townspeople. Either way, taken they were, and in all likelihood, would never be seen again.

Yep, she thought, *we need Quentin to get back and we need help. Or else.*

Quentin

1

After everything went to hell, they ran. As the bodies hit the ground, Quentin's first instinct was to grab his brother and do whatever it took to protect him.

Should have left him at home! Quentin chastised himself. The only problem with that was he was afraid to leave Colin alone. *Besides, I had trained him enough for this.* Also, Quentin hadn't counted on it going so bad so soon. However, it did, and all they could do now was run and hide.

Thankfully the mutants didn't give chase when they ran. Quentin figured it was because they didn't see them as a threat.

How little they know, Quentin thought.

The four remaining survivors, including Colin, Willy, and a local hunter, Broderick Wilson, all made it to the forest easily enough. From there Quentin guided them through the woods in such a way that they couldn't be followed. Survival was the key now. Quentin realized it was only a matter of time before the mutants attacked the town and therefore they had to do whatever they could to help, and Quentin had a plan.

As night fell on that first night in the woods, they all watched as the mutants began to maneuver themselves into attack positions. From the way they went about it, Quentin could tell they had someone among them with military experience, which was good as far as he was concerned. It meant their movements would be predictable and that he could foresee how they would attack the town. Quentin explained to the others what they could do with this knowledge.

"We're going to use the element of surprise. They are positioning themselves in raiding parties around the town. Their plan is to use night and the cover of darkness to do raids. We used some of the same tactics in the war. Since they're probably figuring we ran back to town, this gives us a chance to turn their own strategy back on themselves. We will attack them in the same way, going group by group and killing every one of them. Since they don't have any way to communicate with the other groups, they won't be able to warn each other. This is the best chance we have of making a dent in their forces before they take over Bastion."

That night, they conducted their first attack.

2

They started with the eastern mountainside since the largest grouping of mutants was on the southern face. Running through the dark forest at night, they had their guns at the ready. They moved quickly and nimbly, like animals, trying to blend into the brush. If they came to a clearing, they went around it; the more there was to camouflage them, the better. As Quentin ran, he imagined the old Native Americans who hunted these hills in the past. He imagined that they were a hunting party, sent by the chiefs of the tribe to protect their reservation from attack.

Finally they came upon the first pack of mutants. They were at the ready, but paying attention to the town below them, not the woods behind. There were ten of them, so the odds weren't that bad. Using hand signals, Quentin had Willy position himself at the far end, Broderick toward the middle, and he and Colin stayed in place. They had formed a semicircle around the mutants and had the element of surprise.

Lying on the ground, Quentin gave the signal for them all to creep up as close as they could without being spotted. Given the darkness around them, he had to assume Willy and Broderick saw him. Slowly Colin and he positioned themselves within attack range. Quentin looked at Colin and gave him a nod. Colin nodded back. They were as ready as they would ever be.

Standing straight up, Quentin turned his rifle to automatic and let the bullets fly. He hit two mutants right away. Shot in the back, they went down forward, chests bursting open as the bullets shredded them. By the time the other mutants were aware of what was happening, Willy and Broderick were up and firing. Willy took one down with his pistol instantly, Broderick took down another two, reloading his single-shot hunting rifle faster than Quentin thought possible. Now there were only five mutants to the four of them. The odds were practically even.

"Spread!" Quentin yelled, and the four of them went in different directions, further separating and thinning out the mutants. The only problem was that Colin got cut off from Quentin and was being followed by two mutants, while the rest of them were being followed by one each.

"Colin!" Quentin called after him. "Circle them around!"

Quentin could see Colin doing just that. Quickly Quentin turned and saw his mutant bearing down on him. He calmly lifted his pistol from its holster and shot.

Another one down.

Tracing Colin's path with his eyes, he could see Willy take his mutant out with Impaler. Then he took aim beyond Willy, anticipating where the two mutants following Colin were headed. When Colin cleared his aim, he fired. The bullet soared through the air faster than the eye could see and came to a rest inside the first mutant's head.

Bull's-eye!

"Colin, run to me!" Quentin said and saw the boy follow the directions. Colin came running fast. Right behind him on his shoulder was the mutant. Quentin lifted his rifle; any second the mutant would be on Colin, and Quentin had to take a shot.

Slow the blood, clear the mind, take the aim, and fire.

Bang!

The mutant behind his brother went down, a hole now in his forehead. Quentin ran to Colin.

"I gave you a gun for a reason," Quentin said. "Use it next time."

"I don't want to kill," said Colin.

Willy, who in the meantime arrived beside them, added, "Kill them or be killed, kid."

"I'd expect you to say something like that," Colin retorted.

"What's that supposed to mean, short fry?"

"Forget it," Colin added and walked off.

"What's up his ass?" Willy asked Quentin, but Quentin just ignored him.

"Hey, guys!" They all heard a yell from off in the distance. It was Broderick. He had survived the fight, but he was all the way over by the edge of the mountain, looking down into Bastion.

"The attacks have started," Broderick said as they arrived.

Looking down into Bastion, they could all see the Great Tree on fire.

"There's a lot more of them out here. This was just one squad," Quentin said.

"Well, I guess we better find the rest and kill them," said Broderick.

3

After a day's worth of a trek across the northern mountain face, Quentin and his group came upon the second group of mutants. Employing the same tactic, they were able to get the drop on the group and wipe them out in a much smoother fashion. Still though, they were one step behind. Even though they had dispatched two groups of mutants, others continued to attack Bastion from different directions.

"We're not stopping them," Broderick said.

"Maybe there's just too many," added Willy.

"We can't give up. Not as long as we're still standing." With that rally cry, Quentin moved his squad forward back into the forest and the night.

4

By the time they reached the western side of the mountain, they had done battle with another mutant squad and won. They were becoming efficient at killing them, even though they weren't stopping the daily raids on Bastion. Frustration was sweeping over all of them, as well as exhaustion. Quentin wasn't sure how much longer they could keep going, and it seemed like the mutants were never going to quit. They had to keep going as long as they could. But first they needed rest. During the night was their hunting time; in the day they rested as much as they could, hiding under rocks, in caves, or under fallen trees.

On the fourth day after leaving Bastion, all of them slept longer than they should have. After sleeping the whole day away, Quentin was awakened by a sound. Willy was already up trying to track the sound, while Colin and Broderick still slept.

"What is that?" Quentin asked.

"It sounds like some kind of animal," Willy replied as the sound went off again. It was a hoot, but not from an owl.

"Not one that you've ever heard. That's no animal. And it's right on top of us. Wake Broderick."

With Willy shaking them awake, both Colin and Broderick woke with a start.

"What the hell—" Broderick began, but Quentin placed his finger to his lips, silencing him. Then with the same finger, he made a circling motion, trying to indicate that they were being watched or surrounded.

All grabbed their weapons.

"Scout the area," Quentin said quietly as they all looked around.

"What do you want me to do?" asked Colin.

"Stay here."

Willy cleared his throat, getting Quentin and Broderick's attention. He pointed into the forest. Following his guide, Quentin saw five mutants in the distance planting some kind of trap.

Do they know we're here? Is the trap for us or for others?

Quentin didn't know, but it didn't matter; it was time to act. Quentin, Broderick, and Willy all moved.

After a few moments, Quentin arrived only yards from the group of mutants. During his silent crawl through the woods, he had lost track of Willy and Broderick.

No matter, they can take care of themselves.

Preparing his knife, he was about to charge in when he saw Colin. He walked right up to the mutants, arms up to the sky and unprotected.

"Excuse me," Colin said. The hooting from the mutants began again as they looked at Colin, confused. From their jerking motion, like snakes or dogs sniffing the air, Quentin could tell Colin had distracted them.

Smart kid, Quentin thought. *I'm gonna kill him for not staying put ... but it was brave.*

Colin began talking again, some nonsense about being lost. All the mutants could do in response was hoot louder, trying to scare him off. They began to surround Colin, preparing to attack him.

Quentin could wait no longer.

With everything he had, he rose up out of the brush, grabbing one mutant by his neck and slashing his throat wide-open. The others turned in shock, which gave Colin the opportunity to kick one hard in the testicles. He went to the ground moaning. Quentin then lunged at another, slashing him across his bare gut. Blood poured out of the wound as the mutant whimpered off like a hurt animal into the protection of the forest around them. He wouldn't live long; he had been holding his entrails in his hands.

Two more had run off. For a moment, Quentin thought they might get away and warn the others, but Willy was on them. He swooped in and stabbed one in the back, perfect placement to immediately render it paralyzed, and then he plunged the knife into another one's chest.

The one Colin had kicked was beginning to come back to its senses.

"Here!"

Quentin threw Colin the knife. Colin caught it and stared at it in his hand as if it were made of poison. Quentin realized Colin couldn't do it; he couldn't kill the thing. That pause was all it took. The mutant grabbed him, taking his knife away and putting it to Colin's throat.

"Stay calm," Quentin said to the mutant. "Let him go and we won't hurt you."

The mutant growled.

"I know you can understand me," Quentin said slowly with absolute calm in his voice.

The mutant let out a deep, guttural scream. It was outnumbered, it knew its chances of survival were slim, but it still tried to frighten them.

Quentin pulled out his gun.

"Let him go!"

He had a clear shot; he could take him if he wanted to, but given how dark it was, he wasn't sure if he trusted his aim. Still, he was prepared to shoot. As it turned out, though, he didn't have to. Colin struck first, elbowing the mutant with all his might in the gut. This made him release the boy, which in turn created an opening enough that Willy was able to run straight in and stab the knife directly into the thing's forehead.

"Just like hunting 'coon back home," Willy said as he removed the knife from the corpse. Quentin hoped he meant raccoon.

"Good work," Quentin said to Colin, "but don't do it again unless I say."

"Eh, go easy on him," Willy spoke up. "Without him, we might all be dead."

Quentin ruffled Colin's hair. He knew Colin hated that, but to Quentin it was a quick way of showing affection toward his little brother—without hugging, that was.

"Wait, where's Broderick?" Colin asked.

All of them looked around in panic.

"Brod—" Willy began to yell, but Quentin put his hand over his mouth.

"Don't. There might be more of them."

"It doesn't matter. He won't hear you anyway," Colin said.

Both men looked at where Colin was standing and found him looking straight over at a tree. Broderick was jammed up against it; the booby trap that the mutants had set had gotten him. They had tied a tree trunk up to another tree with rope and used a trip wire to release it. Spikes had been put on it, all of which were now inside Broderick's chest.

"Bummer," Willy said. "I guess we're down to three."

5

The next morning they moved south. By midday they were deep into the forest, trying to avoid the mutants where they could. Finally they took a rest. Willy climbed into a tree to keep an eye on their surroundings while Quentin and Colin sat.

"I'm hungry," Colin said.

"I know, buddy," Quentin agreed. "I'll go see if I can catch something. You stay here with Willy. I mean it—don't move!"

"I won't," Colin promised, lifting his hand to his heart and crossing it with his fingers.

Rifle in hand, Quentin walked off into the woods with the intention of killing something for dinner.

6

The deer was nibbling on some berries as Quentin positioned his rifle. He had a perfect shot. Everything was silent, the wind was motionless, and there was nothing to spook the animal. Even with the sun falling fast, he knew he had the kill.

Suddenly from behind him, he heard a twig crack.

The deer's head shot up, looking right in Quentin's direction before galloping off into the woods. This confirmed Quentin's suspicion that something was sneaking up behind him. His best guess was more mutants had found them.

Well, you beasts, you picked the wrong bastard to sneak up on.

With that thought, Quentin turned quickly around, gun ready to fire. What he was faced with shocked even him. Instead of having his rifle aimed at a mutant, he was facing a group of black armor-clad soldiers, who stared back, guns positioned toward Quentin, ready to fire.

Quentin smiled. "Flatscans."

Nell

1

Nell and the rest of Black's new group of pilgrims had walked for several weeks when they finally arrived at their destination. At first it seemed like they arrived at a mere mountain, with only vast wilderness surrounding them. Yet as the group settled in, it became clear this wasn't just another campsite.

The first sign something was up came when the soldiers all began searching around. Unlike the rest of the group, they didn't immediately come to a halt. Instead, they spread out in all directions, following some kind of order from the top.

"What are they searching for?" Nell asked Brody.

"Not sure," Brody replied. "Setting up battle stations?"

"If that's true, I don't like the sound of it," Nell quickly added.

"Me either."

Nell and Brody continued to watch as the soldiers searched the heavily wooded area at the bottom of the large mountain peak. The soldiers were carefully approaching the face of the mountain. Suddenly one of the soldiers met with something. At first, they couldn't tell what it was, but the electricity shooting from this invisible something was clear. It shot off the soldier's uniform in sparks of blue and red. Had the soldier not been dressed for battle, he would have died.

Moments later, more soldiers surrounded the area. Nell and Brody watched as the sparks flew with more soldiers touching the invisible force field. Then suddenly, they went through the electricity and disappeared from view, leaving only the mountainous terrain staring back at the survivors.

"Where the hell did they go?" Nell said.

"It must be some kind of hologram," Brody answered back.

Black walked up to the same area. More soldiers surrounded him. Then suddenly the view of the mountain terrain in front of them flickered in and out of static and wavy lines, like an image from an old television set. The view began to fade. It became clear that it was indeed a holographic image, one that was being shut down from the other side. As it faded, Nell and Brody could see the soldiers who had disappeared through the image. Behind them was the real landscape. The hologram had been a replica of the scenery, except for two major changes: two very large, very old, rusted doors, caked with dirt and moss, stood like skyscrapers. They looked out of place among all the nature.

Once the image was completely gone, Black stepped forward to the doorway and placed his finger onto a small pad jutting out from the side of the door. A blue laser suddenly came from the side of the door and scanned the general up and down. It finally converged on his eyeball and took a retinal scan. The general stood absolutely still, which made Nell wonder what would happen if he moved.

He'd probably blow up, she assumed.

Once the scan was finished, the blue light disappeared, and sounds from inside the doors broke the serene wilderness around them. Air pressure releasing in long hisses like giant snakes uncoiling from a long slumber hinted of life inside.

Are there more survivors? Nell wondered.

Once the doors were fully open, lights came on in rows. Nell could see the cave was deep and that this first entryway was only a hangar for military vehicles and munitions. Stocked high and deep, the hangar held aircraft, jeeps, tanks, and weapons. However, there weren't any people—at least not that Nell could see.

"Tell the survivors to stay back. Make sure the men keep them from entering," Nell heard Black say to one of his captains. She was only about ten feet away, so she had a good view and earshot of what was happening.

As the soldiers started to set up a human blockade of the entranceway, the general entered, followed by his top men. Even with the orders to stay, a few members of the camp started to head in with them, but the soldiers lifted their guns, which brought the civilians to a halt.

"I guess we stay here then." Brody's comment dripped with sarcasm. Nonetheless the sarcasm was earned.

Again, Nell found herself wondering if these soldiers were really going to be protectors or turn out to be something far worse than even Stonehenge. Nell clutched her son close to her chest. He was getting big and strong, and clearly his father's son.

She worried for his future.

Black

Black escorted his men into the facility. He knew he'd find these weapons, he knew he'd find medical supplies, he even knew there would be food enough for all their survivors and then some (if rationed correctly). What he didn't know was if anyone was inside, if this base had been breached before them, or if answers to what had happened to their country—maybe even the world—would be contained inside.

Greeted by another door at the end of the hangar, Black typed in his one-of-a-kind security code, given only to the most high-ranking officials in the US government. As perhaps the highest-ranking general in the armed forces, his clearance went all the way to the top. At times, he knew more about the way the government worked than the president. After all, even popular presidents only served for eight years; Black, no matter what, would always be a general. No matter the political party in the White House or who owned the majority of the House and Senate, he would serve the country. This guarantee of stability made Black a very powerful man. He was always one of the first men the incumbent president talked to, confided in, and needed.

Once past that doorway, Black found catacombs of hallways all leading in different directions. He sent groups of men to scout them. Though he was looking for one particular room, he needed to be sure the facility was secure. His men had orders to find, capture, and question anyone who might be inside. From the looks of it, though, Black figured they were the only ones who had stumbled upon this place. Walking deeper into the structure, Black, followed by a small contingent of his best men, found an elevator. It stood wide-open waiting to greet them.

"I only need four of you; the rest stay here and secure the area."

With that, Black entered the elevator followed by the highest-ranking officers of the bunch. Black looked at the operation panel.

There were thirty-two levels to the complex according to the buttons. There was also a DNA scanner. Black placed his finger where the small outline of one was depicted. With a small hum, it pricked his finger, drawing blood and instantly analyzing the contents. When it was finished, the doors immediately closed. The elevator was on its way.

"I guess it knows where it is taking us," Black said, hoping to allay the concerns of his men; he could feel how tense they were.

Quickly the elevator descended until it reached the bottom. Except it didn't stop. Despite the fact there were no more levels on the elevator to light up, the machine kept descending, picking up speed.

Black thought, *Maybe the damn elevator is broken and we're going to be flattened like pancakes.*

That was when the elevator slowed to a stop. Suddenly the doors opened, revealing a large football field-sized control room. The contents were state-of-the-art technological equipment: decks of computers, touch-operated holo tables, video screens, and even the new 4D holo-imaging and compu-phones. It was clear that from here, the government could control the world and not miss a beat. Though everything was on, even functioning, it was also clear a human had not stepped foot inside since the room had been built.

"All right; find me a connection to the outside world," Black instructed.

Black's men scrambled to different desks within the control room. They wiped years of dust from the computer screens and slowly began to activate everything. Black simply strolled up to an overhang and observed the whole room. He felt like a ship's captain, looking out on the ocean as the boat sailed across the choppy seas. This made him yearn for simpler times.

Finally the largest jumbotron in the room came to life.

"Who got it working?" Black asked, but all his men replied negatively. On the screen appeared a face. Robotic in essence, artificial in appearance, yet clearly meant to characterize a human being, it sent chills up the general's spine.

"Good evening, Brigadier General Black," the excessively calm, mechanized voice said. "I am your secretary."

"You don't have a name?"

"Just Secretary," it said.

"What are you secretary of?"

"I am programmed to be the secretary for any government official that happens to use this facility. In case of emergency, however, I am to run the government and stay in contact with the other Secretary units in the twenty-one other facilities just like this one across the country. So as of right now, I am the Secretary of State, Defense, Agriculture, Travel—"

"I get it," Black cut him off. "Are there no human government officials in any other facilities?"

"No. We, I mean the other Secretary units and I, assumed all had perished."

The cold sound of the Secretary's voice bothered Black, but the thing was a machine. What did Black expect it to do, cry?

"Any idea what exactly happened?" Black asked.

"Of course," the machine said. Then added, "Thermonuclear attack," as if it was only a matter of fact.

"I assumed that. But who attacked us?"

"The president."

Black was breathless.

What did the machine say? The president?

That's when the screen changed. No longer was the Secretary's face looking down at small General Black; instead, it was the president of the United States, talking directly to the screen. Black watched in stunned silence. Just from the haggard, unhinged look of President Mitchum, Black knew this wasn't going to end well.

2

My name is President Mitchum. This is my final Data Journal Entry, dated November 13, 2062.

I can't save this country. I know that now. There is no amount of discussion, planning, money, or even magic that could make this country heal itself. There is no way to return America to the status it once enjoyed: being the guiding light of freedom to the world.

Really though, who can even remember when this country was anything to anyone anyway? 1990—something?

This situation isn't my fault. I didn't make the country this way. I attribute that to my predecessors. They ruined America. They made it a country of factions, infighting, and death. They allowed terrorism to take our resolve and unruly gangs to push solid, law-abiding citizens from our once-great cities into safer enclaves out in the countryside. They created the 35 percent unemployment rate. Welfare isn't just for the needy anymore. It's a way of life. And this country's budget can't handle it.

Ironically enough, I was elected by the people to finally fix all the problems. Or at least, that's what I had promised. But politicians promise a lot, don't they? Rarely delivering on that promise. It is truly a shame we are where we are. With no other answer, I must now make the tough decision to hopefully—conclusively—end the suffering of the American people.

Unfortunately, there is far too much to fix. Besides the aforementioned unemployment problem, there is the crime problem, the educational-system problem, the health-care problem, the credit-ceiling problem—or rather, the lack of a credit ceiling in general. Our credit rating as a country is now a 1! Lower than some third-world countries! Oh, who am I kidding, we are a third-world country. Thank you to the governments of the early twenty-first century for screwing it up for everyone.

Let us also not forget the pestilence of the last twenty years in the breadbasket of the country. Iowa, Kansas, Ohio ... all destroyed by the plague that killed our crops and cattle. How many times have we, as politicians, said we would cleanse our country of this disease that has made children and adults starve, yet stood by helpless as the USDA could not seem to cure this sickness? The pestilences led to famine, the famine led to death and despair, and the world markets responded to our country's time of need by shutting us out.

In hopes that the disease wouldn't spread, international shipping and flights were outright forbidden. American products were no longer shipped or used by foreign powers. Thankfully, the disease never jumped to humans the way it was predicted to. I suppose that saved us from ourselves—though the riots that ensued due to the false reporting of a human contracting the dread sickness were devastating to the country's infrastructure. So devastating, in fact, the cities have never recovered.

Most cities have been all but abandoned. Most people have moved outward from DC, New York, Boston, Chicago, Los Angeles, San Francisco, even San Antonio, Green Bay, Wichita, and Spokane. Leaving behind mammoth, statuesque, fossilized landscapes, inhabited now by gangs that rape, murder, and destroy anyone who attempts to better the situation. This country has turned into nothing but violent heathens screaming to the heavens in rage.

Yet despite their anger, the people multiply.

There really is no other way to describe it! The population of the country has jumped by the millions. It is almost as if, when faced with absolute terror and uncertainty, rather than not bring children into such madness, people instead decide to do the exact opposite. Leaving what few resources America had left in utter chaos. Society is collapsing, and I hope to help it complete the destruction.

How will history view me?

What will my ultimate legacy be?

I will be hated, of course. I will be seen as a murderer of millions. A modern-day Hitler; a man with no moral compass, who cowardly destroyed the world for no reason. Which is, I guess, why I'm recording this.

To give reason behind the madness, if you will.

I need to save everyone from themselves. Sure, people will hate me for it, but in truth, who gives a damn? Those who hate me don't see the big picture. In a generation, maybe two, Americans will see what I've done in a new light, and they'll hail me as a hero. A man who did what no one else had the guts to do. I know I'm rationalizing now. Perhaps trying to talk myself out of the decision I have made. That is not the case, though. My resolve is strong. I must follow through with my plan no matter what. There is no other choice.

It was once said the proper person would be in the presidential office at the proper time to deal with events that only he or she could deal with. For Lincoln, it was the Civil War; for Roosevelt, World War II. I suppose for Reagan it was the Cold War. On and on. For me, however, it's the bringing on of the end of the world.

I guess I know what Romulus Caesar must have felt as he watched Rome fall. After today, another empire will have fallen. If this recording is ever found, hopefully one can view it and understand that my actions are meant for the best, no matter how insane they must seem.

Good luck to the survivors left in the afterwinds created by my destruction. May this be the new ending the world needs.

May our troubles finally end.

Now, as I await the coming missiles, I'm going to go play with my dog on the White House lawn, so that I will be one of the first to perish.

Good-bye.

Good luck.

3

"Turn it off," Black said in utter shock. "That madman of a president woke up and decided to fix the country's problems by killing us all!"

Black's men watched him as he kicked over a chair, letting his rage loose.

"No one can ever know this," Black told his men. "This stays a secret right here. If this gets out, no government will ever be trusted again. Right now, we need everyone to trust in us. We not only run our little band of survivors; we run the country! We take this secret to our graves. Is that understood?"

All the men agreed.

"Secretary?" Black said.

"Yes."

"Delete the recording," he ordered.

"Recording deleting."

"Let's get topside," Black insisted to his entourage. "No one comes down here except us."

"Can I be of further assistance, General Black?" the Secretary's voice chimed in.

"No," Black said sharply. "Just keep this place running efficiently. It's our new home."

"Yes, sir."

"Let's go."

The men all reentered the elevator and returned to the entry deck, where a squad of Black's men greeted him with three prisoners, found and captured in the woods.

Quentin

1

He had explained to the Flatscans who he was, what unit he had been with in the war, and why he, his brother, and Willy were out in the woods. They said nothing back. They simply marched the three of them into the bunker and threw them down in front of the most feared and respected man in the whole armed forces: General Black.

Quentin immediately stood and saluted.

"General Black, sir!"

Black turned his icy glare straight on Quentin. Quentin could feel Willy tense up. He was standing next to him, and Quentin hoped to hell that Willy just kept his mouth shut. The last thing he needed was for Willy to ruin his chances of getting these men to help.

"You a soldier?" Black demanded, despite letting an air of pleasantness seep out.

"Yes, sir!" Quentin was barking out his answers as if he were transported back into boot camp. Colin and Willy stared up at the two men from the ground, hoping this would all turn out okay.

"What was your unit?" Quentin told the general all his details, unit, what his role was, where he fought, even how many kills he had. By the end, Black seemed impressed.

"So, what brought you out here? To these woods?" Black's cordial behavior dissipated. He was all business now.

"My friends and I, we live close by," Quentin began. "We are under siege by an invading force. They have surrounded us, outmaneuvered us, and quite frankly, without help, we will lose everything we have left. Due to my training, I have attempted to wage a guerrilla war in an attempt to help ... but I'm failing. We need help."

Black looked deep into Quentin's eyes, studying them, almost as if he were peering deep into Quentin's soul for the truth.

"It takes a real man to admit when he is not enough," Black stated,

461

sensing Quentin had lost his nerve a bit. "As much as I would like to help you, tactically I do not know if it would be wise. As you see, I myself have people to protect. What makes your town worth saving?"

Quentin wasn't sure what to say. He was caught off guard by the question. He hadn't considered the fact those he found here might not want to help. He assumed because this was still a United States facility that any soldiers he found would still feel obligated to serve and protect. However, times had really changed. The old ways were gone. This realization stunned Quentin into silence, but thankfully he had his brother with him. Colin stood, head up and shoulders back. He could have passed for a man if it weren't for his baby face. He cleared his throat, grabbing the general's undivided attention.

"You have something to add to this?" Black asked.

"The reason to save the town, sir, is simple, really. From what I can tell in this world, everything is gone, destroyed. I don't know if that's true, but it's the way it seems. You've seen the world more than I have. Is it true? Is it all gone?"

Black nodded in agreement.

Colin continued, "Then the reason to save us, sir, is because Bastion is the last place on earth you can call home."

The general considered his words, chewing on them.

"Your town's name is Bastion?" Black asked.

"Yes," Colin answered back.

Quentin stared in awe at his brother. At his age, Quentin would never have had the guts to speak to a man like the general. Yet despite all the things Colin feared in life, Colin did.

Perhaps Colin isn't so weak after all.

"All right," Black simply stated. Suddenly he was barking orders at his men, gathering them to deploy.

Quentin smiled at his brother.

"What?" Colin asked back with the attitude only a teenager could muster.

"I love you, kid."

And with that, Quentin gave his brother a huge hug.

Willy

1

Willy couldn't believe he had missed his opening. He had the perfect opportunity to drive his knife into Colin's heart, but instead he killed those damn mutants.

I had no choice, he told himself. *Quentin was around and would have seen me kill his brother. There was no way for me to play that off. I'd rather not start that fight until I have to.*

However, on the other side of it, Willy realized, *maybe saving Colin would put him at ease.*

Colin had been keeping an eye on him the whole search. Neither he nor his brother Quentin seemed to be completely asleep at night, and he could have sworn Quentin was watching him in some subtle special-forces way. Quentin was a sneaky bastard. You couldn't be sure whether he was going to shake your hand or slit your throat. That's what made him such a great ally and a formidable enemy. This worried Willy quite a bit; he liked being on Quentin's good side. Which got Willy wondering.

Does Quentin know? Did the kid tell him?

Willy hoped for the best, but realized only one of them could return alive. As he saw it, it was either the Kershaws or him. He'd make sure it would be him.

Willy was a survivor, and he'd be goddamned if he would die out in the woods like an animal.

Next time, I will take my opportunity.
Next time, I'll kill them both.

Colin

1

After Colin convinced General Black to help Bastion, it only took an hour to deploy the troops. Colin found the fluidity with which everyone moved impressive. It was artistry the way groups of troops went in different directions, some grabbing ammunition, others readying vehicles. There were even more soldiers helping to bring the civilians into the bunker for safety. There was heroism to their every movement, but tragedy as well.

Some of these men won't return, Colin thought. *Some of these men are going to kill others.*

As beautiful as their actions were, the horror of the reason for them made Colin just as uneasy as he was impressed. After an hour, though, they still needed more prep time to be ready for the attack. Not wanting to hold off helping the town, Black sent Quentin, Willy, and Colin with eleven soldiers ahead to let everyone in town know they were coming and to maybe start the battle as best they could.

The group of them set back out into the woods, armed and dangerous. They ran as hard as they could for as long as they could. Though fatigue and breathlessness set in, the thoughts of the townspeople in danger was all it took for them to carry on. Around twenty minutes into their journey, they came upon a rocky cliff that headed back into the valley. Through the foliage, they could see Bastion in the distance. It was burning.

"My God," Willy said.

"We're too late!" Colin exclaimed.

"We have to keep moving. We have to try!" Quentin didn't wait for their agreement. He just ran.

All of them moved with abandon, with no care for their surroundings.

This was a mistake.

2

Colin ran trying to catch up to his brother. What he didn't realize was he was not only getting separated from him, but he had quickly lost focus on the soldiers. Coming to a pause, he realized he was all alone and not exactly sure of the best way down to Bastion. Everything just seemed way too steep to climb down, and he was scared that if he attempted to do so, he would fall.

"Hey, Colin!" he heard from somewhere behind him. Turning, he was greeted by Willy.

This isn't good, he thought.

"You lost?" Willy asked. "Me too. Come on, we'll help each other down."

Colin stared at Willy and then at the steep cliffs around him. Neither option was safe. He figured he could dodge Willy, if need be. Falling to his death, on the other hand, was far more definite.

"All right," Colin said. "I'll be right there."

Willy

1

This is it! Willy thought. *The moment has arrived.*

Watching as Colin walked toward him, Willy's mouth began to salivate, like a lion watching a gazelle. Though Willy had no intention of eating him, just the thought of the kill was enough to get Willy all excited.

"Which way, champ?" Willy asked, thinking if he could get Colin to lead and feel in control, he'd be easier to sneak up on and kill.

"Down, I guess," Colin answered back.

"It's steep," Willy said.

"Yeah, I guess, but I'm sure if we walk along the edge, eventually we'll find the incline the others went down."

"Right. Well, lead on. You're the one who knows the area."

Colin bravely went on. He seemed skeptical perhaps, but Willy ignored it; he just tried to behave like all was perfectly normal. Every few steps they took, Willy could see Colin's eyes look back over his shoulder, getting a glimpse of Willy's placement. Every time their eyes met, Willy just gave a gentle smile.

"We better hurry, don't you think?" Willy said. "We don't want to get there and the battle be over, huh?"

"I guess not."

With that, Colin's pace sped up. Willy followed and bit his lip. He could see the edge of the mountain again and knew how he'd take care of the kid.

A few more steps and I'll push. With that, he lunged forward for Colin.

Colin

1

Colin had felt it coming. He knew it was only a matter of minutes before Willy made his move. So when he saw Willy through his peripheral vision lunging toward him, arms out, fingers spread wide like claws, all he did was turn his shoulder and dodge him. Though the incline to the valley floor wasn't sheer, it was steep enough that anyone who lost their footing would plummet down at least twenty feet. Fast and hard, Willy dropped, hitting every branch, rock, and tree in the way.

Though Willy flailed, trying to reach for Colin, he could not grab him. His scream was loud, and it echoed around the valley. Birds flew up from the trees in all directions; other small animals could be heard scattering off into the dried-up brush. Finally, after what seemed like hours—though it had been only seconds—Willy's screaming ceased.

Fear stuck in Colin's throat. He didn't want to see the outcome of the fall, but he knew he was going to.

Carefully down the hill he went, making sure every step was secure. Even with the burning town ahead, he couldn't risk himself getting hurt. So, despite the smoke plumes stretching high into the sky, Colin continued on slowly, looking in every direction for Willy. After all, maybe he survived and was just waiting to attack again. However, after a few more steps, he found that not to be the case.

Willy was dead—there was no doubt about it. Impaled by a huge branch of a tree. His body was ten feet in the air, dangling down like some kind of macabre Christmas ornament. Blood was dripping down his body, creating a pool on the leaves below.

"Well, that's that," Colin said with zero emotion. After all, it wasn't like they were friends.

In this world, what emotion can you have for a total stranger? Colin thought. *Especially one like that.*

Colin continued to stare at the body, forcing himself to look despite the horrible sight that it was. Something inside him told him to etch this sight in his brain.

This is what becomes of people in this new world—evil people, those who do bad things, like murder. This is what happens to people who act like Chief Mankins or Deerdorff. People like Willy ... and my brother.

Which was why, right there and then, staring up at the remains of a man Colin couldn't have cared less about, he made an oath to himself: *I will never become like my brother.*

2

Continuing his mad dash back to town, Colin hoped Black and his men were making good time and already winning the fight against these horrific attackers. However, he knew the roads to Bastion were windy and treacherous, close to sheer mountain drops. No one dared drive down them too fast; they'd speed right off to their fiery deaths. Going slow probably wasn't an option. Unfortunately a race was on— one they were losing.

"Colin!"

He stopped in his tracks. A voice had called his name, again.

Willy's dead! he thought. *It can't be him again!* Still, despite knowing this was the fact, he got nervous anyway.

He scanned the area like his brother had taught him. Despite his promise to not be like him, some of his advice was handy.

"Colin! Over here!"

He quickly spun his head to the right, catching a quick glimpse of a hand behind a fallen tree trunk. Colin raised his gun into the air.

I won't kill, he told himself. *Unless, of course, someone is trying to kill me.*

"Who's there?" Colin asked, feeling protected behind the barrel of his gun.

"It's me, Sebastian."

Sebastian stood, revealing himself. He was with some of his friends, their families, and his mother.

"What are you doing all the way out here?" Colin asked.

"Escaping."

"We've got help coming. You all have to go back!" Colin barked at them. He couldn't understand how they just abandoned the town.

"We can't!" Sebastian replied in desperation.

"You have to! To save anyone we can! Your father … Kim—"

"They took her," Sebastian cut Colin off. "A few days ago, these … things … kidnapped her."

Tears were filling Sebastian's eyes. Colin was surprised. He had no idea Sebastian could feel for anyone but himself.

"We have to go get her!" Colin insisted, but the group surrounding Sebastian vocally disagreed.

"They'll kill you!" Sebastian's mother screamed.

"Maybe, but we can't let them have Kim," Colin said.

"There are others too," another parent inside the group said. From the sound of depression in his voice, he was probably a relative of the missing.

"Come on, Sebastian. She's your girl, isn't she? You gonna let me show you up?" Colin smiled as he challenged his enemy to step up. Sebastian looked at his mother, then back at Colin.

"You have another one of those?" Sebastian asked, referring to Colin's gun.

"Yep."

Colin grabbed his other gun from his belt and handed it over to him.

"Sebastian, you can't go!" his mother said like she was grounding him.

"Sorry, Mom, I have to."

With that, they raced off. Colin could hear the group screaming after them, telling them not to go, to stay behind, to save themselves, but despite their warnings, Colin and Sebastian kept on their mission.

However, as driven to save Kim as Colin was, one thought kept repeating in Colin's head:

I will not be my brother.

I will not be my brother.

Nell

1

Nell was panicked the minute the soldiers started moving everyone into the bunker. Even though it was all done orderly and smooth, it was just the idea of being locked inside an area with everyone staring at her for answers that made her uneasy. If the rumors were true and the soldiers were going off to war, Nell was afraid that without Black, they would look to her for comforting, and this made her severely uncomfortable.

In all her life before the attacks, she could never have predicted she would be part of events such as these. Yet here she was, scrambling underground into a bunker made of metal and bedrock, praying for safety from whatever new threat was heading their way.

Soon Nell found herself in a large common room. Inside with her were at least two hundred other people. Most of whom followed her lead.

It's bad enough the whole march to this bunker was marred by the deluded group of followers that revere me, Nell thought. *Now I'm stuck in a small cramped space with them.*

They did as she feared. It started as soon as they were all settled in the room. They watched her every move, which was something Nell couldn't understand.

I'm no one. I don't know what I'm doing from moment to moment. I'm surely not trying to be any kind of leader. What do they want from me?

It was this thought she always seemed to return to. When other women were finally giving birth and they wanted Nell present to help them through, she thought it. When she was teaching these new mothers how to breast-feed, she thought it. When she was helping these other mothers to cope with the death of their babies, she most certainly thought it. Somehow—which she could not comprehend—Nell had become the mother of all mothers. She hated it.

When the other mothers started to give birth, she had hoped the attention on her would wane.

No longer being the only mother since the apocalypse is sure to help, right?

Wrong.

Of the eleven births since her son's, only seven babies survived. Three died only weeks after, and two more were born with severe birth defects, leaving only three healthy newborn children, including Nell's own. Whether these issues had been caused from exposure to the nuclear fallout or simply due to the difficulties of childbirth without a hospital, Nell wasn't sure. However, the fact her child was born perfect on her first try, in this world, made her and Little Mark even more of a miracle in everyone's eyes.

As they all huddled helplessly in this room, packed in like sardines and scared, it was no surprise to Nell she could feel all eyes focused desperately on her.

What do they want from me?

"I gotta get out of here," she said, feeling overwhelmed, almost faint.

"What's wrong?" Dr. Sandberg asked, noticing her flushed coloring.

"I just ... I need air." Turning quickly from his arms, which were now helping to prop her up, she ran. Baby in tow, she pushed her way through the throngs of people. Stationed at the only entryway to the room were two soldiers. They blocked her exit.

"You can't leave," one of them stated in an authoritative tone that drove Nell crazy. How she wanted to rip that black visor from his hidden face and spit in it.

"Watch me!" she screamed back.

"Ma'am, please stand back from the entryway, or I will have to use force." The second soldier had grabbed some kind of electrical baton he had at the ready.

"Use that on me and this whole room will erupt and kill both of you." She laughed for a moment. "I don't know if you've noticed, but they're all staring at us."

The soldiers looked. Indeed, the whole room had begun to watch them intently.

"You see," Nell continued, "these are my followers. I'm their fertility goddess or something, and you don't want to hurt their goddess, do you?"

The soldiers stared at the crowd. There was a sense the crowd in the room was on a short fuse.

"Two soldiers against an angry mob doesn't seem like good odds to me," she added.

For a long moment, the soldiers considered their options. Nell waited patiently, despite the feeling her skin was crawling. The pressure was getting to her, yet she needed to be strong. If she showed any sign of weakness, the soldiers would decline her request. Thankfully, Brody had arrived at her side. He put a hand on her elbow, giving her strength and steadying her emotions.

What would I do without him?

"Fine," the first soldier said; he was the higher-ranking of the two. "You may go."

The soldiers parted. As Nell cleared the threshold of the room, the soldiers returned to their stations. Brody and Nell were now split.

"Not you," the soldier said.

"I'm with her. She needs me," Brody gallantly stated yet his words had little effect.

"Please let him come with me," Nell begged. Though she wanted to get out of the bunker, that didn't mean she wanted to be without him.

"Best get where you're going, miss. The man stays here."

Nell and Sandberg exchanged looks. With his eyes, he implored her to go, but Nell was feeling rebellious.

"Let him go," she said. "Or I yell 'attack.'"

The soldiers again were faced with a critical point.

"The general will hear about this," the soldier stated.

"Good. Tell him I said hi and that Juanita taught me well." Nell

472

thought better of that last remark, but it was too late. It was out of her mouth.

There's rebellious, and then there's just plain stupid, Nell thought. *That crossed the line.*

No matter, though. The soldiers let Brody exit, and soon she found herself being led out of the bunker by this man she had grown from crushing on like a schoolgirl to honestly loving like a woman. She could feel his strong hands grasping hers, fitting them safely into the warm cup of his palm. With him pulling her, they moved swiftly through the corridors, up the elevator shaft, out the hangar, into the night sky.

2

Nell sucked in the air. Her skin started to relax. All her weight fell into Brody. He tucked her into his body, holding her like she always hoped he would.

The baby made a few gurgling sounds, but was on his way to dreamland. Nell supposed she made him feel safe, therefore allowing him to always be able to sleep and to be a baby. She took care of him, and he could sense it.

Now if only someone could do the same for me, Nell thought.

"Take care of me," she said to Brody.

"Of course," he said, looking deep in her eyes.

"I'm so tired of being strong." She began to cry. "I've had to be strong for so long. For everyone. But I don't want to do it anymore. I want to be taken care of. Can you do that for me?"

"Yes."

And that was all she needed.

They kissed. At long last, after so many struggles, they let all their fears and emotions go into this one, long, kiss.

Despite the barrage of falling mortars in the distance, followed by echoing *booms* and gunfire, they just stood there in the moonlight, lips locked in a passionate embrace. Nothing—not even war—was going to stop them from being happy in this stolen moment.

Annette

1

They all ran toward the front door of the house. This had been the designated spot for retreat when all was lost. After fighting things off as much as they could, it became clear that the final steps now needed to be taken. The house was on the outskirts of town and represented a last-ditch effort to find safety. If they could make it to the house, perhaps they could hold up and hide. If not, there was a backdoor escape that took them straight into the woods along the northern mountain.

The house was Mayor Kreuk's, and it was an exquisite old colonial, with much of the charm and style of an old patriotic home. Annette found the place to be calming and hopefully enough off the beaten path that no one would find them here. The house was surrounded by a good acre of land on all sides and was about a ten-minute hike outside of Bastion proper. Annette and her cabinet had prepared the house for battle in the days leading up to the full invasion. As people were being taken and parts of the town destroyed, Mayor Kreuk instructed his wife and a few of their friends to retreat to the woods around Bastion. Given camping gear and what few supplies could be spared, these families went off in the hopes of finding refuge from the battle. This allowed Annette, Kreuk, and Frank to board up the windows, create some barricades made of furniture from the home to block the doorways, and plant some weapons in strategic spots, just in case. Now Annette was glad they took the time to do this.

After retreating from the main battle, running out of the town, across the large field of tall yellow grass, toward the house, they realized mutants were following their every move. In reality, they barely made it to the house, closing the doors and putting the front-door barricade in place, before the monsters arrived.

It didn't take long. As Annette and the group stood catching their breath, the mutants began banging on the door and boarded windows. The group knew they were only minutes from being taken by an army of raging maniacs.

2

How did this happen? Annette thought. *How did we lose control?*

Only hours before, the townspeople had held the invaders back; despite the kidnappings and the losses they were sustaining, morale was rising. Quickly, though, things began to spin out of control. The full extent of the attacking mutant force, their strength, and their rage became savagely clear. It was a massive force, more than anyone had suspected, which made protection of Bastion ultimately impossible. The mutants were just too driven in their goal to be overcome.

"What do we do now?" Mayor Kreuk screamed, completely panicked.

Annette looked around the room. Everyone looked worried and with good reason. They were all about to die.

"I don't know," Annette said honestly.

"Maybe we should just go ahead and escape out the back ... get to the woods and hide?" Mitch spoke up, desperate for hope. Frank touched his shoulder. It was a gesture of tenderness only Annette probably understood. She was thankful Frank found love in these last days.

"It won't work, Mitch. They'd just hunt us down eventually," Frank consoled.

"Is this our last stand then?" the old librarian, Wilma Garrett, said through gritted teeth. Annette was always surprised just how tough she was.

"Probably," Annette calmly answered.

As the full power of the moment flowed across the room, the screaming sounds of the mutants outside the walls gained in power and volume. They were coming to get them, even if that meant tearing the house apart with their bare hands.

"I want to see my wife and son," Kreuk admitted with tears

streaming down. Annette felt the same. She wished she could see all her children. "Do you think they're still alive out there?"

"Possibly," Frank muttered, but Annette figured he was just trying to calm the man. Chances were, most of the town was either running for their lives or already dead.

"So, do we all want to wait here to die, or do we want to take them out with us?" There wasn't much tact left for Annette to use with this final question.

"I say kill as many of those bastards as we can." This came from Pastor Pemberton, who suddenly seemed a little less religious in Annette's eyes.

Even a man of God has a sense of vengeance when it comes down to a choice of "him or me," Annette thought.

"Any idea how? We're out of ammunition," Frank soberly added to the conversation.

"We lure them in and set the whole place on fire." Kreuk seemed to have come out of his stupor with that suggestion.

"All right, then, let's find something that burns," said Annette. "Mayor, where do you have matches and lighter fluid?"

"I never really had a place for that stuff," the mayor added. "There's some in the basement, upstairs in my bedroom, in the garage ..."

"That's fine," Annette said. "Let's all go and look around."

3

They all went in different directions to search the house. After a few minutes, all returned. Some had found matches, others flammable liquids such as alcohol, paint thinner, even some cooking oil. They began to spread it all around the house. Finally, they all met one last time.

"Have some final words, padre?" Frank asked while trying to stop himself from shaking. Despite all they'd been through, Annette could tell he was scared to die.

"Our Father, who art in heaven, hallowed be thy name ..."

The pastor droned on, but Annette drifted away. Prayer wasn't her thing. In dramatic moments like these, she focused on her children.

Their first laughs, their toddling walks, the first time they fell in love—these were the moments she wanted to remember when going into the great beyond. Now she would see them again. If heaven existed, she knew she would be reunited with them all. Even Sean, whom she hoped would have been forgiven for his transgressions.

"Amen," the pastor completed his prayer.

"Amen," various others in the group repeated without conviction.

"So, who's going to let them in?" Mitch asked.

They all stared at each other. No one was exactly jumping at the opportunity. Whoever let the monsters in would surely die. For everyone else, there was still a glimmer of hope that one might escape before the house fully burned. Whoever opened that door however, the mutants would tear limb from limb.

"I'll do it," Annette said.

Everyone just stared at her.

"I'm the leader here, aren't I? Who better than me?"

With that, she walked away from the group. She went to the front door and stood by it. Listening to the growls and clawing of the enemy outside, her heart began to beat rapidly.

Maybe a heart attack will get me before they do, Annette hoped. In the meantime, the rest of the group scattered around the house, armed with their incendiaries.

"Don't open that door until we're all in positions,' Frank yelled to her.

"Okay," she agreed.

Placing a hand on the doorknob, Annette could see it was shaking uncontrollably. For a moment, she wondered if she would even have the strength to pull open the door at all. She took a deep breath, preparing for the last fight she would ever face. In a life filled with abusive husbands, it was comical to her she would be taken out by a group of monsters that previously only existed in books or movies. How fantastical her life had become.

What a joke.

That's when she heard it. A distant *boom*!

The mutants' shrieking stopped. Silence took over.

"What was that?" Kreuk screamed from somewhere deep in the house.

Boom! Louder this time. The house even shook.

Frank appeared from up the stairs. He looked amazed.

"It sounds like mortar shells," Frank said.

"Yeah, I guess it does," Annette agreed.

Frank slowly descended the stairs and looked out a window.

Boom!

The house shook again, feeling like it might collapse upon all of them, but they could also hear the sounds of feet running off from the house in all directions as the hoots, growls, and clawing of the mutants stopped.

"They're gone," Frank said.

"What?" Annette asked.

"The mutants ..." Frank moved to a window and carefully peeked out. "They're all gone."

The others had reappeared now.

"What's going on?" Wilma asked.

"Not sure," said Annette as she began to turn the doorknob she had yet to let go of.

"Don't open it!" Kreuk begged.

She didn't listen.

Slowly, she opened the door, revealing that indeed the mutants were gone. Also to her surprise, she saw something else: an armed force, ferocious and clad in black armor, marching through the town. Around them lay the bodies of dead and dying mutants. A smile swept across Annette's face at the sight of them.

"We're saved," Pemberton said to the sky.

Annette nodded in agreement.

The cavalry had arrived.

Black

From the mountaintop, General Black watched the action.

The troops were a well-oiled machine. They knew how to take a small town; they knew how to stop these mutated monsters once and for all, so there was no reason for Black to even utter a single command. From the general's standpoint, there wasn't much he needed to do but enjoy.

Doing this also allowed General Black to survey the landscape.

Is this place really what the boy said it is? Black wondered. *Is this really a place to call home?*

He could see the beauty of it. Despite the bombs, gunfire, dead bodies, and smoke, Black could tell this was some kind of Mecca. Looking toward the sky, he couldn't help but notice the air was clear. He could see stars and the moon, which he realized he hadn't seen since everything started. They were always covered up by ash or smoke or fallout clouds. Here, the sky was pristine. If one didn't know what had happened to the outside world, one might think everything was fine.

The general could see it: a home for the new society he would create. A peaceful place, separated from the outside world and protected on all sides. He could see Althaus—if he lived—acting as head of the town, while Black himself lurked behind the scenes, protecting the ideals of this new society. He would never allow hunger or disease to strike down this community. He would never allow excess or greed to ruin the strength of this new nation. He would keep order over all. With his men, he would maintain the new laws, striking down any foe that might rise to challenge them.

A town this small, with the resources found inside the bunker, could thrive for hundreds of years. Sure, they would have to be careful not to allow their population to grow too large to sustain again, but all that would come out in the wash. For now, Black needed to simply plan for a new world. One with this town as its capital.

Bastion, Black thought. *Man's last Bastion.*

There was much work to be done, that much was obvious. He would have to make friends with those in power within the town. He would need to persuade them to see things his way, which he didn't see as a problem. Strength of force could go a long way in determining how negotiations went. Black knew no matter how he had to do it, he would get his way. This was destiny.

Suddenly a self-realization flooded into his mind. He was becoming a villain, forcing his beliefs on others because he thought they were right. Saying these things out loud would make him sound like a dictator.

Still, though, he rationalized it away.

It's what the world needs! he thought. *The old viewpoints of good and evil, freedom and subjugation, no longer apply. This is a clean slate for men like Althaus and me to create a new version of society. Besides, those who write the history books decide who was good or bad in the end.*

The answers weren't easy, but Black could accept that. He knew the world had always been more than black and white. Gray was really the color of the world. Which was a good color. He could live in this valley with the color gray.

Gray could be good.

Quentin

1

Despite their reputation, Quentin couldn't believe how fast the Flatscans had taken over the battle. Minutes after arriving, they had the mutants on the run. Quentin suspected hardly any succeeded in escaping.

An hour after the Flatscans' arrival, there was only a spattering of gunfire, while bodies were piling up at an exponential rate. Cleanup would be brutal, but the victory was complete.

Now if he could only find his brother.

He lost Colin somewhere in the woods. The boy had been right behind him until suddenly he wasn't. The problem was Quentin hadn't realized it until he was clear of the foliage and practically to town. He would have gone back to search for him except that was when the Flatscans had arrived and the battle began.

Quentin had to fight with them. He had to prove to them he was as good at the game of war as they were. Only a few of the Flatscans saw him in battle, but those who did were impressed. If they would just say something to General Black about his skills, Quentin could build a future. This could be a springboard to having a place in the general's plans. It could be a better future for himself and his brother, more than just sitting in Bastion waiting to starve to death.

But where is my brother?

It was impossible to track Colin at this point. The battle had left too many tracks in too many different directions. Even if he could get back to the spot where they had been split up, there was no telling if he would be able to tell which way Colin went. The most sensible thing to do at this point was to wait for his brother to return home.

Ultimately, he knew his brother was a coward, so worrying about him getting mixed up in the battle seemed unrealistic. Colin may have stood up to the general, he may even have been a bit of help against those mutants, but in the face of war, Quentin was sure he would blink and hide.

Where else could Colin have gone?

A wrenching sickness began to stir up inside his gut.

What if he came to town during the battle? What if he's dead?

Quentin got hold of himself. He shook the doubt from his mind.

No, my brother is smarter than that, Quentin decided. *He's a smart boy who would have stayed out of harm's way, right?*

With that thought, Quentin began to search the bodies of the dead, hoping that none of them ended up being his brother.

Aiden

1

When the battle began, Aiden had the few Mutants who didn't invade Bastion move into the back room to watch over the treasures. He didn't want these precious commodities to take this opportunity as a chance to escape. In the main shop area, he left only three extra Tribe brothers to watch over the new captives they had taken from the town. Aiden stayed with them as well, feeling he needed to keep a special eye on them.

The girls are close to home, after all, and might try something if they think they have the upper hand.

It was for another reason as well. Aiden had fallen madly in love with one of them on sight. He decided she was his and he would make sure of it. Even if it meant not letting her leave his sight.

She was young, though, which at first bothered him, given the rules of the old world. Soon though, that guilt passed as he realized they no longer lived by such rules. If the girl had breasts and was capable of reproducing, Aiden figured the doctor would have no problem with him claiming her for his own. Which was exactly what he did. When she arrived, Aiden was so struck by her beauty he went to her immediately and attempted to mollify her worries by showing what a gentleman he could be. The only problem was he was tying her up in a circle with her friends. This did not exactly endear him to her, which broke his heart. Finally, however, he realized it was fine.

I like it when they play hard to get, he rationalized.

Still, despite her rigid silence, it only took a few hours to hear one of the other captured girls call out her name.

Kim.

A cute name to be sure, Aiden thought. *Though not as cute as she looks.*

Aiden licked his lips watching her. He wanted her, and when the battle was over and the Tribe had taken control of the town, he would have her—*forever.*

It was at that moment, Kim looked toward him. She wasn't looking for him, per se—he knew that—but just the glance in his direction was enough to make his heart beat faster. Even though he realized she was probably just looking to see where he was and if she could try to escape, he couldn't help but see hope in her eyes. This made him smile at her again. She simply turned her head away in disgust.

Aiden smiled to himself.

Keep turning away ... No matter what, you're mine.

Colin

1

"What do we do now?" Sebastian asked, his voice shaky with panic.

"Let me think," Colin replied.

To be fair, Colin had to admit he had run off halfcocked. He had no idea what he was going to do. For Sebastian to be whining at him every two-seconds about the plan was kind of unfair.

Who does Sebastian think I am, General Patton?

"Maybe we should go back? Get some help?" Sebastian offered as a cop-out, but Colin grabbed him hard by the arm.

"We're not going back!" Colin spit back, angered at the mere suggestion. "We found them, didn't we? We're here! If we leave to get help, they may be gone before we can get back. We stay and save the girls."

It had taken them the better part of an hour to locate Kim and the other girls who had been taken. Having seen the gas station on the day that Colin and the rest of the doomed outreach group had attempted to talk to the things, he reasoned there was a good chance that it served as the base for the mutants. From there, it was easy to assume it was also probably where they were hiding the girls. During the days when the road was used, the gas station served as a last stop for drivers to fill up before they began the trek up the mountain. Now, Colin figured, it served as the last place for the mutants to call a home before they began their invasion.

Scouting the area, they spotted three mutants guarding the outside of the main station facility. However, what worried Colin wasn't the men outside—it was that they had no way of knowing how many other mutants might be inside. As it was, they were already outnumbered three to two. Deep down, Colin knew it was more than that. The question was, how many more?

At least one for sure.

Through a window that looked into the shop part of the Exxon Mobil, Colin could see another mutant walking around the circle of girls. He could see they were tied up.

I need to do something, Colin thought. *I need to create a distraction to get inside and save them.*

"All right," Colin stated. "I have a plan. I know how we can do this."

"This is nuts! I don't know why I followed you! We're gonna get killed!"

"Shut up, Sebastard! Damn, who knew you were such a chicken?"

"Don't call me that," Sebastian said back, pouting, which just infuriated Colin even more. *For the school bully, he's quite the wuss,* Colin thought.

"What?" asked Colin. "Chicken or Sebastard?"

"Sebastard! You know I hate that name!"

"Then don't be a pussy!" Colin jabbed at him.

"I'm not a pussy," Sebastian argued back.

"Yes, you are."

"I'm not!"

"Prove it then. Let's save these girls."

"Fine!" Sebastian said defiantly.

"Fine." Colin smiled to himself. Manipulating Sebastian was too easy.

Aiden

1

The gas station shook as the room around them glowed orange from the plume of fire outside, extending high into the air. The girls all screamed in sudden fear as Aiden moved to the window.

The gas tanks were on fire! Someone was outside and preparing an attack, which he couldn't let happen.

"You two," Aiden yelled to his brothers, "go out there and see what is happening."

"Sir, we don't know how many there are—"

Aiden cut the cowardly brother off, grabbing him by the collar of his shirt.

"I don't care," Aiden finally continued. "Do as I say. We can't let them inside."

With that, the Tribesmen moved to the doorway and prepared to exit the safety of the station. Aiden just turned and looked at Kim.

You're mine, he thought again, *and no one will take you away from me.*

Colin

1

So far, everything had gone according to plan. Colin had maneuvered into position next to the pumps. Once there, he cut the head of the pump off the hose. Then, to get the gas flowing, he sucked on the end, releasing the gas in a great long spurt. It flowed out, into his mouth—tasting awful, sour, and toxic. Spitting it out, he dropped the fuel line, which was now spilling gas out like a waterspout.

Colin cleared away from the pump, and now it was Sebastian's turn. Since the blackouts in the town, just about everyone had matches on them. Colin had instructed Sebastian that once the gas spread close enough, he needed to light a match and let it burn. It only took about a minute for the gas to reach him. Colin watched as Sebastian lit the match. Linking eyes, Colin could tell Sebastian was having a moment of uncertainty. Colin gave him a determined nod of the head, and that got Sebastian to do the rest.

Moments later: *Boom!*

The explosion was even bigger than Colin had anticipated. The plume of smoke and fire had blown into the sky to heights he couldn't have estimated. The blast power was also quite ridiculous; it made every blade of grass fall flat, and pushed Colin's hair back like on the windiest of days. It was an effective distraction, however, as the mutants guarding the building stopped in their tracks to watch the gas pumps burn.

2

With the mutants scrambling, Colin and Sebastian ran the opposite direction, positioning themselves on the far side of the building. Once they arrived in a suitable hiding spot, they collected themselves for the next step. Through the window, they could see the mutant on the inside come to the doorway to look at what had happened.

"He must be the only one inside," Colin whispered to Sebastian.

"How do you know for sure?"

"With that explosion, if there were more, they would have peeked out too."

"You ready?" Colin asked Sebastian.

"I guess" was Sebastian's not-so-convincing answer.

They both pulled their guns.

"No shooting unless we have to. And no killing."

"I just want to get out of there fast. If I shoot my gun at all, it'll probably be by accident." Sebastian took a deep breath.

"*Go!*" Colin yelled.

The two kids booked it to the front door, smashing it violently, opening it back on the mutant. The mutant dropped to his knees in agony as his body was smashed between the frame and the closing door. Quickly, Colin and Sebastian moved inside.

As the girls saw them, they screamed for help. Kim seemed especially happy to see both of them. They went to her first, using Colin's knife to cut the rope that was crudely wrapped around them all.

"Is your dad here?" Kim asked Sebastian. "Or your brother?" she added as her head turned to Colin.

When their eyes met, Colin was sure Sebastian could see his feelings for her, so he looked away.

"It's just us," Sebastian said.

Kim looked even more frightened than she had when they walked in.

"Just you?" Kim asked, the fear thick in her throat.

"Yeah, why?"

Just as Colin asked this, two arms grabbed him around the chest and began to squeeze. He was flailing in the air; whatever had him was huge and powerful. Colin could feel the breath slowly leaking out of his mouth, like a leak from a tire. If he couldn't get free soon, he'd be dead for sure. Just as the world was beginning to go dark, the sound of a gun firing rang out. The arms released him, and Colin hit the floor hard. He could see where the gunshot had come from. It had been Sebastian. He was still standing there with his gun out, smoke pouring from the barrel and fear splashed across his face. Looking behind, Colin finally saw the hulking thing that had squeezed him so tightly. It was a mutant, very big and very grotesque.

"Thanks," Colin said to Sebastian, which was something he never thought he'd ever utter to him.

"Yeah, no problem," Sebastian replied back.

As Colin caught his breath, Kim leaned into him.

"There's more," she said, and Colin realized just how screwed they all were.

"Colin," Sebastian said, "we've got trouble."

From a doorway that led to a back room, mutant after mutant ran out. Colin quickly counted seven, which meant the total of enemies in the area was now eleven.

"Kill them!" Colin yelled.

"What?" A shocked Sebastian questioned the order.

"We have guns! They don't! Kill them!"

Bang! Bang! Bang!

In a hail of gunfire, they shot at the mutants. Colin was surprised he was even prescient enough to realize how good a shot Sebastian was. He was clipping mutants in one shot, while Colin was merely wounding them. Hope filled him that perhaps he could escape this quandary without killing a soul.

Before Colin knew it, the eleven attacking mutants were down for the count. A few moaned, but all were either dead or too injured to keep fighting.

"We did it," Sebastian said. "I don't believe it."

"Let's get out of here before more show up."

Colin finished untying everyone. Soon all the girls were running out the back door, escaping their worst nightmare.

"Get into the woods," Colin said. "I'll be right behind. Don't wait for me, though, Sebastian. Just get them home."

"What more do you need to do?" Sebastian asked.

"I just want to make sure none of them can follow us."

Sebastian shook his head in disbelief.

"You're nuts."

"Go," Colin said emphatically.

As Colin turned away, Kim grabbed his arm.

"Thank you," she said with deep affection in her voice.

"Thank him."

Sebastian smiled.

Was it in shame or gratitude? Colin was sure he'd never find out. More than likely, the bullying would continue, leaving Sebastian and Colin mortal enemies once more. Still, Colin felt he had done the right thing.

"There's more women in the back room," she suddenly added.

Sebastian gave Colin a look.

"I'll get them." He looked at Sebastian. "Just get them outta here."

"Let's go," Sebastian said and took Kim away.

They left, leaving Colin alone.

Moaning could be heard, but it seemed to be only one mutant doing so. Colin clutched his gun, which he realized was shaking in his hand. As he walked toward the sound, he looked at the carnage around him. Blood was everywhere; dead mutants were strewn in every direction.

Did I order this massacre?

With every step, he saw more of the damage. He had killed at least some of these men.

No! Not men! Mutants! he tried to convince himself, hoping to relieve some of his guilt. It wasn't working. The whole sight made him sick. Then he saw the moaning thing.

It was crawling to the front door, trying to escape. It was pathetic. The mutant was dying, but still it tried.

I will not be like my brother, Colin told himself one last time.

Aiden

1

Crawling to the doorway, bleeding from his gut, Aiden realized none of this had gone as planned.

I've failed the doctor, he thought. *I've failed the world! What now?*

Escape! he hoped beyond hope.

Though he had no medical training, he knew his wound was mortal. He would slowly bleed to death, miles away from anyone who could help him. The only thing he could do now was pray that death would come swiftly.

That's when he saw the shadow over him. Turning around, he saw the young boy pointing a gun straight into his face.

Only one thought crossed his mind: *I need a good last line; all the great death scenes contained great last lines—*

Colin

1

Colin stood above the mutant, which stopped, turned over, and looked Colin straight in the eye. Blood was everywhere; it had been hit in the gut.

It smiled. Its teeth were stained red with blood.

"You better kill me, boy!" the mutant coughed out, spitting blood with every word. Colin just stared. "We will find you. There are more of us than people like you! We're everywhere! You'll all die out before we do!" The mutant hacked violently. Perhaps on purpose, or perhaps because he had no control over his fading body, the mutant all the same sprayed blood on Colin's jeans. "Oh no, I ruined your fancy pants."

Colin wasn't sure what to do; he had to at least stay and watch to make sure the beast died.

"I wanted to ruin *her* pants, you know." The mutant wouldn't shut up. "That cute one you were talking to."

Anger was building inside Colin.

I will not be like my brother.

"She was to be my wife." The red teeth smiled again. "We were going to have sweet, normal, babies together."

Bang! Bang! Bang! Bang!

Colin fired until the clip was empty.

When it was all over, his mind snapped back to reality. The full power of what he had just done set in.

He had killed.

That was when he heard it. Crying. Coming from the doorway that led to a back room.

Slowly and carefully, gun out, checking every shadow as he walked, he headed into the darkness inside. Once across the threshold, he saw a vision of something he would never forget in his whole life.

Lit by one dim lightbulb, a group of packed women stood reaching

493

their hands out to him, pleading for him to free them from behind a mesh wire fence. The smell of urine, sweat, and feces burned his nostrils.

At that moment, Colin clutched his stomach, bent over, and threw up.

2

Colin walked back to Bastion in silence. He didn't know who he was anymore. He didn't even trust himself. He was a fourteen-year-old boy who had just killed a living being. If he wasn't sure of it before, it was clear now—his childhood was over.

As he arrived into town, he could see a celebration. Everyone was crowding the streets, congratulating each other, dancing on the graves of the many mutant bodies that littered the streets like ticker tape from a parade. In the middle of town, near where the tree used to stand, Colin could see the rescued girls. They were surrounded by their families, friends, even some of the hierarchy of town politicos.

When Colin walked by, people began to part. Some slapped his back while telling him, "Congratulations" or "Job well done," but he was numb to it all. He could see everyone's happy faces as he walked by, he could see Sebastian standing by Kim, reaping in all the accolades for saving her, but he couldn't get himself to muster up any feelings about it all. Colin supposed he should enjoy this victory too, but all he wanted was a place to hide.

Quentin stepped forward to him. "You saved them?" Quentin asked.

All Colin could do was nod. He could still taste the puke on his breath.

"You should have come for me. I would have helped you," Quentin chastised him.

"I know."

"I mean, it's amazing what you two did ... but still, you could have been killed."

"I know."

"You've gotta stop doing this crap."

"I know."

"Is that all you got to say?" Quentin put his arms on Colin, who collapsed into him, losing all composure.

"I killed a man."

Quentin heard this and pulled Colin close. With no words of wisdom, no awkward congratulations, Quentin held his brother as tight as he could. The strength of Quentin's arms seemed to push the tears out from Colin's body as he completely broke down.

The townspeople began to gather in a circle around the two brothers. Slowly the sounds of celebration waned, leaving only the sound of Colin's tears.

Annette

1

Weeks had passed since the battle. It didn't take long for normalcy to set in—well, as normal as life after the end of the world could be. Annette watched intently as the town slowly put the pieces back together.

Some buildings were being rebuilt. Some had been damaged irreparably and were being torn apart for scrap, but the town was finally peaceful again. The community, now about 1,700 strong—after General Black's camp and Bastion's survivors joined—had come together as Annette had never seen. Everyone was accepting of one another, there was no more division between townies and the group from the mountains, and there was just an overall sense of contentment in the air. Thankfully, General Black's camp had been greeted with open arms, and the soldiers under his command were cherished.

My, how things have changed, Annette thought.

Clearly, the presence of true leadership in the form of the general was galvanizing. Everyone seemed to just follow in line behind him. Worries were released, animosities forgiven; plus with all that General Black brought with him (security, food, and law and order), it was easy for all to simply hand the hard decision making over to him and go about rebuilding their lives. This was exactly the opportunity Annette had been hoping for. So when it came, she grabbed it.

From the minute Black arrived, Annette felt like a weight had been lifted off her shoulders. She no longer had to be strong. For the first forty-eight hours after meeting him, Annette locked herself into an empty room and cried. The realization she had never even shed a tear for her children and grandchildren was sobering. So, she was all too glad to do just that. When at long last she came back out to the real world, Black had established his authority, and Annette was just one more person in the crowd. This was something she relished.

She could relax now, watch a sunset (which were beautiful in the valley), or knit a blanket (she had all summer to learn how). Maybe she could even find a person or two to talk nonsense with—or find a lover. Before the attacks, she had given up on men: they weren't worth much to her in life; they had always been a problem. Now, though, with a new understanding of what intimacy could provide, she felt that perhaps she needed to give the opposite sex another chance.

Yes, she thought, *it's time to begin anew.*

Furthermore, according to Black, he wasn't alone in his leadership. Apparently there was another man, a preacher, who helped him make the tough decisions. Other than a few folks in Black's entourage, no one had even so much as met this man, but according to them, he was so influential he had developed a new way of life, a new religion.

This, of course, angered the two members of the clergy of Bastion, but once Black talked with them (privately, naturally), their anger seemed to dissipate. She wasn't sure what Black said to them to get them to agree—and truthfully she didn't care—but after their meeting, the two men were silent about their misgivings and suddenly supportive of the Religion of the White Light.

It certainly didn't take long for everyone to begin adopting it either. One saying seemed to be on everyone's lips. It was an odd saying, one that Annette didn't quite take to as easily as the others. True, the words were comforting—in some way. They took the mystery of what happened to the world and made it less painful, more inspiring somehow. Still Annette found she just couldn't quite make it her motto, even though she tried.

Over and over, she would say the words attributed to the elusive Barrett Althaus, but they just never seemed natural.

Pain is white. Remember the white light. The light is hope.

These words seemed to speak to everyone, even the clergy, who had at first refused to say it. But not to her. Annette looked forward to meeting this man Althaus. If he was half the leader the general was, then he would be easy to follow into the future. In the meantime, Annette would slink off into the sunset and become a shadow, spending the rest of her days exploring the opportunities of a new world. She hoped others would do the same.

After all, there were so many new people to meet, so many new adventures to be had. No history. No judgments. The past was past. A new day dawned.

Althaus

1

He awoke with a start. He could feel the tube down his throat. It prevented him from swallowing. Slowly, he pulled the long plastic funnel out of his esophagus, coughing it up while trying not to gag. Once it was out, he threw up a milky liquid substance that he guessed passed for food. Sucking air in deep, Althaus fought off the black curtain of lightheadedness closing in around his eyes. He didn't want to faint. He'd been asleep enough! Shaking off the haze and cobwebs, he began to take in his surroundings.

Where am I? Althaus thought as he scanned the room around him. Everything was rock and metal. The room was filled with machines, an air pump, even a familiar sound of a heart monitor.

Ba-doop ... Ba-doop ...

The hypnotic sound relaxed him a bit. The sound of his heart beating steadily, assuring him he was alive, was a relief. Suddenly a doctor, dressed in some kind of military uniform, rushed in. Althaus recognized him. He couldn't place his name or their relationship, but he was sure he had known him.

Long ago.

Good God! Althaus thought. *How long have I been out?*

Lost in his own thoughts, Althaus came to attention when the doctor clapped his hands loudly in his face.

"Can you understand me?" the doctor said unnecessarily loud as if Althaus were deaf instead of just awakening from a long sleep.

"Yes," Althaus said. His throat was raw, his voice gravelly. Every word was agony. "I understand you."

"Water is on the way," the doctor said.

Althaus nodded in recognition. Talking was just too painful.

"You've been in a medically induced coma for eight months," the doctor began. "At times we've tried to revive you, but you've been in too much pain to stay coherent. About three months ago, we arrived here at a military facility. We have treated you with the best technology we had. This being a government facility, it is relatively state-of-the-art. You've been in good hands. Due to the fire you were caught in, however, some of your wounds could not be fully healed to our liking."

The doctor continued, but Althaus was no longer listening. Memories were flooding in: *the end of the world, the general and his armor-clad soldiers, the Religion of the White Light, the fire.*

Althaus suddenly felt ashamed. Then he heard something that brought him back to the present.

"You sustained burns over 60 percent of your body."

Althaus gave the doctor a long stare.

"What?" he hissed out, just barely making words with his numb lips.

"It's best if we show you."

2

After a nurse brought him some water, the doctor had her bring a mirror. No matter how prepared Althaus could have been, nothing would have prepared him for his new visage.

The left side of his body was scarred and bald. His skin felt plastic to the touch. He was ugly, deformed, a monster. His left eye had no eyelid, and his ear had been roasted to a nub. His lips were no longer lips but rounded-off scar tissue that struggled to cover his teeth, while his chest was flat, smooth, and mismatched, like levels of flat rock. It looked like someone had melted wax over his body. His left arm was mostly bone now, though it did have skin covering it, like plastic wrap stretched too tightly over a sandwich. The muscle that had once been below the skin had been burned away, making it very difficult to move the arm. The same could be said for his left leg and hip. He would need a cane to get around. Though some of his right side had been scorched, it was mostly intact, which gave him an odd dichotomy of the man he was and the monster he had become.

A tear ran down his right eye. It still had a tear duct.

"I know it's shocking," the doctor said.

"Where is Black?" Althaus struggled to get the words out. He now understood why speaking was such a struggle. One side of his vocal cords had been burned away.

"In town," replied the doctor. "Why don't we get you some food, a shower, and some clothes, and then I'll have someone take you to him. I think you'll be pleasantly surprised by our new home."

Althaus laughed to himself.

At least one surprise today will be pleasant.

3

The drive to town took forty minutes, which was enough time for Althaus to really get depressed over his situation.

Why couldn't I have just died? he asked his God—or the White Light, whichever ethereal being he believed in at that point.

The fact that his driver was one of Black's faceless sticks in the mud surely didn't do much to lift his spirits. They didn't talk the whole ride, and given how hard it was for Althaus to speak, he figured *why even bother?*

How poetic, Althaus thought. *It was my talking that got me in trouble and now I can barely do that!*

As they approached the top of the mountain, Althaus could see watchtowers at intervals across the tops of each side. As they came to one up close, Althaus could see it was operated by three soldiers filled to the brim with weapons and technology. He assumed the others were operated in the same way. Overall, Althaus thought it was a very foreboding sight—like a guard tower at a prison.

The driver slowed to a stop, and one of the guards approached their vehicle. If the man under the visor was looking at Barrett's face, Althaus couldn't tell it. The visor was so hard to penetrate, for all Althaus knew, the man underneath the mask wasn't human at all.

After a few exchanged codes and other spy talk, the guard let them through. All of this felt so clandestine that Althaus wondered if this was all to keep people out or keep people in.

They drove downhill for another twenty minutes, until Althaus finally was within the town's city limits. According to the sign, the town was called Bastion. From the amount of tents, wood-built hovels, and other assorted trash heaps that survivors were calling home, Althaus could tell this town was overpopulated.

Did anyone take a census? he wondered.

Continuing to drive through town, Althaus thought the business in the streets reminded him of pictures he had seen of old New York City and Times Square. The streets of Bastion seemed to be a marketplace, everyone wheeling and dealing.

What new society is this? Will I have to be like Moses and break the Ten Commandments over the sellers' goods to remind them where they came from? To warn them from slipping back into old habits?

That's when they drove under a large banner that hung across the town square. Reading it, Althaus's stomach lurched.

Pain is white. Remember the white light. The light is hope.

That was when Althaus realized this whole society was based on his improvised beliefs.

What have I done? was Althaus's familiar thought.

Finally, the driver pulled up to a building. As Althaus exited the truck, people began to stop and stare. He had never felt so self-conscious in his life. He brought his stubby hand up to his face. It wasn't very successful at blocking anything from people's view.

"He's in there." The soldier pointed.

Althaus looked at the building with its smooth stone facade and pillars. Words were chiseled into the alabaster above the front door: City Hall.

"Go in, he will be in the mayor's office. He's expecting you."

Turning on his heel, the soldier got back into the truck and drove off. Rather than continue to gross out the bystanders, Althaus began to walk into City Hall. His walk was labored, and he had to put most of his weight on his right side. He dragged his matchstick of a left leg behind him. His balance was off, and he had to put an enormous amount of weight on the cane they gave him, but he struggled through. He would be damned if he was going to ask anyone for help.

Of course, I'm damned already.

Finally stepping into the building, Althaus was greeted with a view that was from another time. The City Hall looked quaint, devoid of any modern technology or furniture, full of small offices, information kiosks (which were empty), and flagpoles (that hung nothing). The lobby felt more like a museum than a city hall. It was old-fashioned, wood-floored, and filled with clocks that had roman numerals on them and pay phones from the turn of the century.

Walking down the long hall, Althaus read the names on the doors—Comptroller, Parks and Recreation, Sanitation. Reaching the end of the hallway, he found the one he had been looking for: Mayor.

He opened the door, which led into a small anteroom, with a desk and a few wood chairs for those who needed to wait. Once upon a time, Althaus assumed, a secretary once sat here to answer phones and take messages. Now, though, Althaus knew the phones no longer rang and daily town business was nil. As he continued in, he could hear laughter coming from behind another closed door. Althaus knocked.

"Come in," said a voice beyond the door, one that Althaus did not recognize. Slowly, and leading with his undamaged side, Althaus entered the room.

Sitting at a desk was the mayor. He stood immediately.

"Hi!" the mayor said, all too cheery for just seeing a man in Althaus's condition.

He must have been prepared, Althaus thought.

"Hello," Althaus growled back.

Althaus turned and saw Black sitting in a chair opposite the mayor's desk.

"Hi, Barrett," Black said, standing and offering a hand. "It's great to see you up and about. This is the mayor of our new little town, Mayor Kreuk."

Althaus simply nodded.

"I have to say," the mayor continued, "you look good for a man who has been through all you have. You look strong. Powerful! I can see what the general here likes about you."

Typical politician. A liar of the first degree, Althaus thought. *Kissing babies and stealing lollipops.*

"Black here has informed me that we have you to thank for helping to develop the basis for our new society. It's truly become a utopia here on earth. So far, anyway."

Althaus was confused. He had no clue what the mayor was talking about.

"Don't overwhelm him, Kreuk. Give him time." Black offered Althaus his chair. "Take a seat, old friend. You must be exhausted."

"I am," Althaus replied. He was tired. He had used more energy in the last few hours than he had in eight months. His body wasn't used to it.

"There is a lot we need to discuss. Everything is changed now. It's a whole new world." Black seemed excited, and his energy was infectious. Even Althaus wanted to know more.

"What is going on?" Althaus slowly croaked out from his throat. In the window, he saw his reflection again. His throat looked more like beef jerky than vocal cords and an Adam's apple.

"It's a new Eden here, Barrett. We've started over! We've created a place where we cannot only start fresh, but we can make it whatever we want." Black finished this statement staring out the window, blocking Althaus's reflection. Black looked like a proud papa looking at his baby for the first time. "It's everything you wanted," Black added for good measure.

Althaus thought for a moment. *All he wanted? A new Eden?* He remembered wanting something, but he wasn't sure it was that.

For a second, Althaus thought maybe he should argue. *Maybe I should point out the folly of trying to play god. Maybe I should use the example of what happened to me as a warning to Black that this kind of thinking only leads to bad endings.*

But he didn't. He was too tired.

In addition, he was fairly certain Black wouldn't listen. Would Althaus have listened if someone had warned him? It was one of the great follies of human existence that nobody listened.

Thus, Althaus simply asked, "What do you need from me?"

Black looked at him, a grin appearing across his face. It went from ear to ear.

"So much. We need to guide this world. We need to examine every possibility and find answers to the unanswerable questions. We need to create more laws, a bible for our new society. In short, we need to be prophets."

Althaus nodded.

What else could I do?

The three sat quietly, intently studying each other. Then they went to work.

4

It took them four weeks to create their new "constitution," the first line of which repeated Althaus's now-haunting refrain:

Pain is white. Remember the white light. The light is hope.

Epilogue:

Two Years Later

Black

1

The numbers don't lie.

It was as simple as that. No matter how many times he ran the census through the computer, the Secretary spouted out the same conclusion: *They were running out of supplies.*

Black was surprised, given the fact the food stored inside the base had been plentiful just two years earlier. Technically, the supplies were still plentiful. It was just that because of how fast and large the society had grown—upwards of six thousand now, given other survivors found over the years—sooner, rather than later, they would run out.

It scares me.

As the Bastion Republic now stood, they were already rationing food. Within ten years, they would be starving; and two years after that, Bastion would cease to exist.

Black couldn't let that happen.

In his plan, conceived so long ago, Black assumed he could get to the other bunkers with his troops, but that had turned out to be a fallacy. The world was now a dangerous place. Most of the other bunkers were either in the middle of the most dangerous areas of the country or were simply unreachable given the technologies they had at their disposal. Yes, they had tanks and A.P.C.'s, but they didn't have unlimited gas. Walking or biking were the best ways to search the lands of Old America and be able to provide power to the fledgling country. The only problem with that was walking took time.

Time I don't have! Which also bothered Black. Despite all their efforts to grow food, they had not been able to create enough crops to feed the overwhelming number of survivors in Bastion.

God damn this world! he thought.

Black had developed this new country through strength of will and strong command. Losing it all now because of supply issues seemed ridiculous. Early in the Bastion Republic's existence, Black sent troops out to find more supplies. When they didn't return, be it due to radiation sickness or simply running into some sort of disaster, Black stopped sending them out altogether. He didn't have the soldiers to waste. Though they had begun to train some of the civilians to join their ranks, none of them were nearly as good as his original soldiers.

One thing was clear: changes were coming to the Bastion Republic.

The only question was, *What kind?*

2

"If I may make a suggestion, sir ..." said the Secretary's metallic facsimile of a human voice. Black always felt he sounded like a butler mixed with the voice of the computer in the old movie *War Games*.

"Go ahead, Secretary." Over the last two years, the two of them had formed not a friendship—the Secretary wasn't human enough for that—but a trusting relationship. Often the artificial intelligence added a lot to any decision Black made. Next to Althaus, the Secretary was Black's greatest comrade and resource.

"Given all my tabulations, taking into account the current reproductive rate and the increase per capita, the only logical action is to create a mathematical convergence." The Secretary's clinical voice echoed through the control room.

"What do you mean?" Black asked, highly suspect of the explanation.

"If the population continues to grow at this pace, Bastion will be doomed, just as America was." The Secretary paused for effect. Oddly, though not human, the computer must have been programmed to know how to talk to people in a way they understood. "Though President Mitchum's actions were borderline psychotic, his theory was strong. To fix the country's problems, he needed to depopulate. Bastion will have to do the same thing."

Black couldn't believe his ears.

How am I at the same place Mitchum had been? Am I to be the next lunatic to leave his mark on the world?

"So the convergence you speak of … You want me to kill—"

"Purge," the Secretary said. "Not kill."

"I can't kick people out!" Black exclaimed in a shocked response.

"Nor should you," the computer said back. "The problem is that life is unpredictable. My power cores, though they last for hundreds of years, have a timetable. My life is limited."

Life? Black thought. *What life? He's artificial.*

The mechanized voice went on: "My internal death date is July 4, 2434. Four hundred years from the day I was born."

Born? There he goes again, talking like a human.

"The human lifespan does end, often abruptly; however, there is no predetermined termination point. While a newborn can die within days, elderly citizens can linger for years, contributing nothing material to society while using up precious resources." The Secretary started to tabulate numbers on its screen. From what Black could make out, he was averaging the years of each person's life expectancy in Bastion. "We cannot support each person's complete actuated length of life."

"I understand that, but we've already tried so many different population controls. We don't let anyone live past eighty, we've capped the reproduction rates to two children per household, and people need to apply for a birthing license … which has been almost impossible to enforce. What other choices do we have?" Black felt his stomach begin to churn. He knew the answer, but he wanted to hear it from the Secretary himself. For some reason—one even Black would admit he didn't understand—he realized the idea had merit.

Really, it was downright practical.

"Enact a death date for each individual in Bastion. Chosen at random, a date will be assigned to each person. It will be the day, hour, minute, and second, said person will be … shut off."

Black heard the words "shut off" and thought that was a very apt way to put it. Saying it that way took the humanity out of it.

"Who would choose the dates?" Black asked.

"I would, of course. Computer generated dates would deny the idea of human interference."

"That would make you our god," Black stated coldly.

"I do not believe in a creator."

"You were created."

"By a human—the most flawed creature in the universe. No god could have ever randomly invented such a thing. Humans were invented by accident, a random set of circumstances and biology that led to an imperfect organism. No offense."

"None taken," Black replied, though he did feel his hackles rise a bit at the Secretary's words.

"Due to this accident of nature," the computer continued, "the imperfection inherent to humanity caused the imperfection of their actions to increase exponentially as the population increased."

Black couldn't believe his ears. What did this mean?

"A death date," Black repeated.

"Yes. It is the most sensible thing to do."

Black's blood ran cold. He wasn't sure if it was from the air deep down in the bunker or if it was due to the topic of conversation. He figured it was the latter. Just as the cold finally worked its way through him in a violent shiver, Black realized something.

This is a chance to be a hero.

Every person is always faced with certain moments of vital import and monumental consequence. It is what a person does with such moments that influences how other people view their lives. Some use such moments for evil—President Mitchum—and others for good—Barrett Althaus. Now this was his moment.

Walk away from the Secretary and his horrifying idea? By doing so, though, Bastion will collapse.

Or…

Take his advice and become a man who made a tough decision that saved the world?

Black knew what he needed to do. The decision was made.

Now, how to convince everyone else it was right?

Acknowledgments

This book could not have been written without the help of many people who contributed along the way:

First, my middle school English Teacher, Mr. Baker who told me that I had the talent to be a writer. Second, my college screenwriting professor Ken Dancyger who taught me what a true story entails.

My many friends and experts including Nick Groves, Jarred Clowes, Alex Neal, Ashley Bowles, and Heather Friedman. Each one contributed in some way to make this book better.

Heath Muller for making my ridiculous imagined military lingo and facts become actual reality with his wealth of knowledge and experience. Thanks for all you dedicated to this book and the country.

My parents Brenda and Steve who always supported me and are in the DNA of everything I write.

Special thanks to all my editors and design team at iUniverse who put in a great many hours and unflagging energy and to Sarah Disbrow who's enthusiasm for the piece inspired me to push that much harder during the long editing process.

And last but not least, my love to Abby, Ellie, Carter, and Isla. They're support has mad the long hours worth it.

CPSIA information can be obtained at www.ICGtesting.com
Printed in the USA
LVOW08s1830010114

367618LV00005B/869/P